She Pulled Him Down To Her.
There Was No Barrier

After all the time they had been kept apart, Francis reveled in the feeling of his skin, the calloused sword-hand, the surprising weight of his lean body. She could feel him swelling against her and she ran her fingers through his crisp, waving red hair and opened her lips to receive his kiss. Flame coursed through her veins as his mouth took hers.

She was fluid, molten, opening under his hands in whatever manner he desired. Her arms and legs fell open like the petals of a flower under the summer sun. . . .

HIGHLAND FLAME

A SIGNET BOOK
NEW AMERICAN LIBRARY

PUBLISHER'S NOTE

This novel is a work of fiction. Names, characters, places, and incidents either are the product of the author's imagination or are used fictitiously, and any resemblance to actual persons, living or dead, events, or locales is entirely coincidental.

SIGNET TRADEMARK REG. U.S. PAT. OFF. AND FOREIGN COUNTRIES
REGISTERED TRADEMARK—MARCA REGISTRADA
HECHO EN CHICAGO, U.S.A.

SIGNET, SIGNET CLASSIC, MENTOR, PLUME, MERIDIAN AND NAL BOOKS
are published by
New American Library,
1633 Broadway,
New York, New York 10019

First Printing, September, 1984

1 2 3 4 5 6 7 8 9

PRINTED IN THE UNITED STATES OF AMERICA

HIGHLAND FLAME

1

Edinburgh, 1597

The trial of Alasdair Cameron of Beauly for the abduction and rape of Lady Frances Cameron, his cousin's widow, opened in Edinburgh on a bitter March morning in the year of the king's peace 1597.

Despite the sleeting wind, a crowd of citizens gathered to watch the prisoner being brought down the Lawnmarket from the castle. They were disappointed in the slender red-headed figure in his sober suit of black velvet. He was pale from his months of imprisonment, and there was a halting quality to his gait that suggested he had been "questioned" by the king's executioner; but there was little in his reed-slim figure to suggest the roistering brawler of the stories. Could this really be the man who'd forced his way into Castle Beauly, threatened Lady Frances' brother with the gallows, and raped Lady Frances herself while his followers played the bagpipes to drown her shrieks of protest?

He did not look like the shaggy tribal brigand they'd been expecting, all strut and swagger. Only the firm line of his jaw and the dignified composure with which he sustained the stares of the crowd hinted at an underlying quality of strength.

"Sure, and I thought he'd be a wild Highlandman," commented an old wifie from the Nether Bow to her neighbor. "Where's his plaid and his tail?"

The neighbor cackled and jerked an elbow into Leezie's ribs. "Tail, is it? It's the bare legs of him you wanted to see, you lustful cow!"

"He doesna' look capable o' rape, whatever," the old woman said. "I'm sair disappointed." She stooped for a handful of half-frozen mud and tossed it in the general direction of the prisoner, but without enthusiasm.

The little procession of prisoner and guards marched on toward the grim hulk of the Tolbooth law courts, followed by such of the crowd as cared to elbow their way into the stinking main room and spend the better part of the day listening to the witnesses called against the prisoner.

Within the Tolbooth, the king's advocate, Sir Walter Kerr, was making his last plea to the lady who should have been his principal witness. He had forced his rheumatic knees up the stair to the long screened gallery that sheltered noble spectators in order to make this last attempt to get the lady to testify against her attacker.

In deference to the sensibilities of the victim, the gallery had been cleared of all spectators save Lady Frances herself, and her attendant. Sir Walter shifted uneasily from one foot to the other and waited for the lady to give him her attention.

The ladies had clearly just come in from outside, for Lady Frances' wraps were lying about her where she'd dropped them: the fur-lined cloak and gloves, the overboots muddy from the streets, the hood with particles of fine sleet still clinging to its fur edging.

Lady Frances sat on the hard, narrow bench that ran the length of the gallery. She clasped her hands before her, twisting and untwisting with a ferocity that seemed to have nothing to do with her otherwise still figure. The ill-fitting black dress she wore did little to disguise the fact that she was in an advanced stage of pregnancy.

"Lady Frances." The king's advocate coughed slightly to get her attention. "Lady Frances!"

She turned indifferent eyes upon him, and he was struck, as many men had been before him, by the quality of her beauty. A matter of the bones and spirit, it shone through even now, when her body was ungainly with pregnancy and her face thin and shadowed with worry and sleepless nights. Her black hair curled about her head, lustrous and vigorous, and the luminous dark eyes seemed too large for her face.

"L-Lady Frances," the advocate said for the third time, annoyed to find himself stammering like a schoolboy, "I c-came to inquire if you have changed your mind?"

The sparkle of hope that had started in her eyes died away. Her shoulders slumped and she turned imperceptibly away from him. "No," she said, gazing through the lattice at the hall beneath them. Her eyes were fixed with a look of horror on the black-suited figure of the prisoner. Weighed down by his chains though he was, standing before the judges who would presently pronounce sentence on him, he yet seemed to dominate the room. "No, I've not changed my mind. I will not testify."

The advocate withdrew, fighting the urge to stammer apologies. Dammit, he was on her side—she might at least be civil to him!

At length, the crowd outside, which had been growing ugly-spirited and tumultuous with the passage of time, was let in—or, at least, as many of them as could claw their way through the door and find places in the hall were admitted. Two guards with pikes held the unruly crowd behind an invisible line at the front of the room, while shouts of "Mind yer elbows, ye clarty sot!" and "My best cloak ripped clean away!" and " 'Ware cutpurses!" were heard throughout the hall. Nobles and gentles took seats in the padded chairs ranged around the sides of the hall, behind and on either side of the judges' table. They did not have so good a view of the proceedings as did the common people, but their dignity was upheld.

Chief among the noble spectators was the Earl of Glencairn. The king's advocate eyed him uneasily. This somber man, with his lean skull-like face crowned with close-cropped graying hair, was the moving force behind the trial. Sir Walter knew this man's money had paid for the witnesses' depositions, and Lady Frances was lodging in his house during the trial. It seemed a strange degree of zeal for the rights of a distant kinswoman.

Finally the Lord Justice Argyll took his seat and the prisoner was summoned. His wrists weighed down by chains, the red-headed figure, escorted every step by two guards, walked steadily forward and bowed to Argyll. The king's advocate frowned at the sight of the defendant. Sir Walter thought he was too pale, and there was blood trickling from the cut on one cheek where somebody had thrown a sharp stone at him. It would do the king's advocate's case no good if the lad were to faint during examination.

He caught himself up sharply on that. This was no boy, but a hardened mercenary soldier. Three years' service in Flanders; then returned to this country, contriving the death of his cousin, taking his cousin's castle, and abducting his cousin's wife. This was a cutthroat, murdering rapist, not a lad. It was hard to remember that he could be no more than twenty-five years of age, if that.

It was an ugly story that unfolded as Sir Walter read through the written depositions of the witnesses that he had prepared for the court. Although there were minor discrepancies in the testimony of the witnesses, they tallied to an amazing degree. All the Beauly servants interviewed agreed that Hugh Cameron, rightful lord of Beauly, had ridden out on the morning of June 8 to greet the prisoner, his cousin Alasdair, on his return from Flanders.

Hugh Cameron had never returned from that fateful ride. But Alasdair Cameron had appeared in the castle that night. Climbing by secret ways over the rocks, he had surprised the castle and taken it before the defenders were well awake. The one gentleman in the castle was Donald Murray, Lady Frances' brother. He had been hustled into one of the dungeons and chained to the wall to prevent his interfering with Alasdair Cameron's fiendish plan.

Alasdair had then awakened Lady Frances and brutally informed her of her widowhood and his plans to marry her himself. The lady had resisted—in fact she had fled through the castle, shrieking for help, but to no avail.

Here the stories diverged somewhat. One party alleged that Alasdair had locked himself and Lady Frances into her bedchamber, ordering his piper Sandy Ruadh Cameron to play the bagpipes to drown her screams. Another group would have it that Sandy Ruadh was the man who had held Lady Frances down and slit her stays with his dirk for his master's enjoyment. The piping, they said, happened later—the next day, when the village priest was sent for to perform a hasty and unblessed ceremony over the two—and its purpose was to drown out Lady Frances' refusal to marry her husband's murderer.

Whichever story you accepted, the witnesses painted a grisly picture that sent delighted shudders of horror through the crowd that listened.

They said that Alasdair Cameron had intended to remain at the castle indefinitely, amusing himself in drunken orgies with poor Lady Frances and taunting her brother Donald with the gallows being erected for him. Then he had received word that the Earl of Glencairn, Donald Murray's noble kinsman, was advancing with an army to retake the castle in the king's name.

Unable to defend Beauly against the army of retribution, and bowed down with guilt from his barbarous crimes, Alasdair Cameron had fled into the wild country of the Highlands, forcing Lady Frances to accompany him. The poor lady had eventually escaped and made her way back to her kinsmen, but bearing such evidence in her body of her forced sojourn as made her reluctant to show herself to the court today.

The lord chief justice frowned at this conclusion to Sir Walter's speech. "I didna' quite understand the lady's reasons."

Sir Walter gave up on polite circumlocutions. "She's pregnant." He swung round and pointed an arm straight at Alasdair Cameron. "With child by the man who forcibly abducted her—her husband's murderer! Shall he be allowed to profit by his crime?"

The lord justice gave a dry cough which neatly robbed Sir Walter's question of half its dramatic value. "He doesna' seem to be profiting by it at present," he observed.

Though the prisoner was still standing, he was chalk-white and the lines carved at the corners of his mouth showed the effort of will it cost him to remain upright. Sir Walter, worrying lest the prisoner gain sympathy by fainting, was taken by surprise when instead the man questioned him.

"I had expected to face the witnesses brought against me," he observed in a strong, pleasant voice that carried throughout the crowded room. "Will there be no one to speak for the truth of these stories, then?" He turned toward the Lord Justice Argyll. "I have heard that my lord of Glencairn acquired his lands by tricks of the pen. But I had thought better of Scottish justice than to see him buy a man's life by the same tricks."

It was a neat hit not only at Glencairn but also at the lord justice, head of the Campbell clan and infamous throughout Scotland for the same shady methods favored by Glencairn. A gasp went through the assembled audience, and Argyll scowled at the prisoner.

"It is not the Earl of Glencairn on trial here, but yourself. And you would be well advised to remain silent under such accusations as we have heard today." Then, just as Sir Walter was congratulating himself on the neat way Argyll had silenced the prisoner, he turned. "Natheless, a fair question. Have ye no witnesses, Sir Walter?"

Sir Walter choked and waved his hands at the stack of depositions, statements, letters, and documents which he and his clerks had just entered into evidence.

"I meant," the lord justice amplified, "present in this court? Is there no person here, apart from the defendant and Lady Frances herself, who actually witnessed the events of that night?"

Most of the witnesses, Sir Walter explained, were simple folk of the Highlands. They spoke no English and he had thought it would be more convenient for the court if their depositions were translated in Inverness, rather than having them traveling all the way to Edinburgh only to speak through an interpreter.

"Most considerate," observed the lord justice in dry tones that could have meant exactly the opposite.

Sir Walter passed a hand across his sweating brow and produced, with the air of a conjurer making his final flourish, one genuine and unquestionable witness: Lady Frances' aunt.

Grizel Cameron was a maiden lady of uncertain years and indomitable respectability. She had not witnessed the actual rape and declined to testify to it, but she could testify to having cleaned the bedchamber the following morning. She had found, among other items, the slit ribbons of a pair of stays.

A sigh of pleasurable horror rippled through the court at this confirmation.

This time it was Argyll who interrupted.

"Other items? Could you describe them, please?"

Coloring slightly, Miss Cameron reluctantly informed the court that she had found the broken shards of a chamber pot bestrewing the floor of the hall.

The prisoner made a show of wincing in memory and raised one chained hand to caress the side of his head.

"Clouted 'un wi' a jurden!" cried out one old woman of less discretion than Miss Cameron, and the crowd rocked with good-humored laughter. Sir Walter mopped his brow. Really, it was too much! How could a man conduct an examination before a crowd of the vulgar? He had that murdering bastard in the palm of his hand, and he kept wriggling out.

"Where's Lady Frances?" shouted an apprentice boy before the stir had died down. "Why don't she swear against 'im?"

The question ignited the crowd. "Lady Frances! Lady Frances!" they chanted in unison, rocking back and forth until the heavy benches came down on the floor with a satisfying thump between syllables.

Sir Walter felt the regular pounding chant like blows against his aching head. He envied the prisoner, who seemed to stand behind an invisible wall, shielded both from the malice of the court and from the rough humor of the crowd.

The Earl of Glencairn left his seat to consult with Sir Walter.

"My lord, the suit does not prosper," Sir Walter announced bluntly. "I fear we may lose our case if Lady Frances does not bear witness."

"La-dy Fran-ces! La-dy Fran-ces!" the crowd chanted through his words.

Glencairn cast an indifferent glance toward the latticed gallery. "Adjourn the trial."

"What?"

"You heard me," Glencairn snapped. "Ask for an adjournment. The crowd's unruly behavior gives you reason enough. I will reason with the lords justice tonight." His smile, cold and bright as the icicles outside, flickered up at the latticed gallery where Lady Frances sat. "Cameron's death is required—do you understand me, Kerr? Nothing less will do. Lady Frances' wrongs cry out for revenge." His mouth twisted in another ironic smile. "Keep to that line, Kerr, and let me reason with the justices."

Frances Cameron of Beauly could not make out Glencairn's low-voiced words from her place behind the lattice, but his smile and his confident nod to Sir Walter sent a shiver of fear through her. She passed both hands down her body, swollen and ungainly in the last stages of pregnancy. If Alasdair could see her now, would he still desire her?

She leaned her face against the lattice and peered at the red head of the prisoner. He had been standing in one position since early morning. If she was cramped and weary from sitting all these hours, how bitterly weary must he be! Her very bones ached.

"Alasdair," she whispered through the lattice. "Alasdair, my love . . ."

But he could not hear her as he had done so many times before.

When was the first time she'd called him to her? She could barely remember now. There had been so many times when he answered her needs. . . .

2

The Highlands, 1593

"Alasdair! Alasdair Cameron!"

Sixteen-year-old Frances Murray burst into the armory of Castle Beauly and skidded to a stop almost between the swords of the two men practicing there.

"Dammit, Frances!" The younger swordsman, a boy in his late teens or early twenties with the typical red hair and milky skin of the Camerons, halted his lunge inches short of her breast. "You spoiled my best stroke," he complained. "Could have got hurt, too."

He accepted the cloth tossed to him by his older partner and mopped his brow. "Will I try that feint and parry again, Duncan? I'm thinking it was near right that last time."

"My torture!" Frances stamped her foot and interposed herself between the two men before they could resume their practice session. "Will you be forever playing at the fighting, Alasdair Cameron, and yourself wanted in the great hall? Old Lachlan and his sons are at Gillivray for the rent rolls, and there will be murder that's in it for lack of a man to stop them!"

Alasdair sprang for the door before Frances could finish her speech, closely followed by Duncan. Dhu. "Lachlan? Why could you not be telling me at the first?" he tossed over his shoulder, and vanished in a blur of red hair and smoothly muscled shoulders.

Frances bit back a retort and ran after them across the courtyard, heedless of the way her plaid tumbled back to expose her face and the top of her threadbare dress. As she ran she prayed that nothing had happened in the few minutes she'd been away. When she left the hall, Lachlan Cameron had already been demanding that the old factor Gillivray hand over the list of tenants and their rents, saying that in Lord Gair's illness it was his place to take over the duties of the chieftain.

By the time she reached the door of the hall she had a stitch in her side. She leaned in the open doorway, panting and holding her side, and peered into the dimness within. Old Lachlan Cameron was still shaking his fist under the factor Gillivray's nose. Lachlan's frizz of white hair and full beard formed a shocking frame about his beaky Cameron face, now contorted with anger.

Frances' own nose wrinkled at the sight. She would no' have wanted Lachlan coming that close to her! He stank of his but-and-ben cottage where beasts shared the smoky rooms with humans. And his three sons, standing about him now and glowering under shaggy brows like wild beasts, were no better.

Alasdair strolled into the hall casually, showing no sign that he had been pelting across the courtyard just a moment before. "What! Trouble?" he exclaimed in astonished tones. Two strides brought him between Lachlan and the cousins, separating the old man from his strong, brutish sons. The young men put hands to their dirks, and one growled low in his throat.

Alasdair addressed himself to Lachlan, but without taking his eye off the cluster of young men. "Never say old Gillivray has been insolent to you! In the name of Lord Gair, I apologize, Lachlan. Gillivray knows that his only business here is to keep the accounts, and not to annoy highborn clansmen such as yourself with his posturings. Out of the hall, Gillivray!" he roared suddenly. "Out, I say! You trouble our guests!"

The trembling old factor scurried away while Alasdair addressed himself again to Lachlan Cameron. "My apologies again, Lachlan. Be sure that should the old fool trouble you again, he will be punished—as will anyone who disturbs the peace of Lord Gair's hall."

At the end of this speech he gestured around the large room. The Cameron cousins looked behind them and discovered that a raggle-taggle collection of servants and dependents, armed with everything from spits to pitchforks, had slipped into the hall while Alasdair had held their attention. Old Gillivray had vanished with his chest of papers held under one arm, and their father, Lachlan, stood between the naked wall and Alasdair's sword.

Lachlan submitted to his defeat with an ill grace. His beaky Cameron nose, the one feature discernible in the wild white mat of hair and beard, trembled with outrage. "Very well for this time," he growled, "but think well whom you offend, boy. Lord Gair cannot live much longer, and you would do ill to have the new chief for an enemy."

Alasdair sketched a bow. "Then it is well indeed," he replied, "that the next lawful chief is Lord Gair's son Hugh, who has always had a kindness for me."

"Hugh!" Lachlan snorted in disgust. "That daft gomeril? The Camerons will never take a lackwit for chief—no, nor a dandified Southron like yerself." He cast a disdainful glance at Alasdair's trews and laced jerkin, wrapped his own plaid about him, and stalked out of the hall. His three hairy sons in their saffron shirts and muddy plaids followed him.

Frances put a hand over her mouth to stifle her laughter at Lachlan's anticlimactic exit.

Duncan Dhu lowered his own sword and stepped back to stand beside Frances as the men left. He nudged Frances in great glee. "Did I no' tell you not to worry? The lad's a bonny fighter—wow, but he's even bonnier with the words! Tell me, is he as fast with the English?"

"Too fast for me, at any rate!" Frances admitted. Lord Gair had insisted that she learn enough English to cope with their occasional Sassenach visitors, but it seemed a clumsy, guttural tongue to her in comparison with the lilting Gaelic that was her childhood speech.

She was distracted from Duncan's next remark by the entry of her aunt Grizel. With her iron-gray braids wrapped around her head and her good cloth dress stiffly spread out over a starched farthingale, Grizel made her way down the winding corner staircase that led from Lord Gair's room as mincingly as if she were in the Scottish court, where she had served as a girl. She beckoned to Alasdair to follow her back up the stair. Frances frowned. What would Lord Gair be wanting with Alasdair? Was he worse? Ever since his illness that winter, they'd all lived in fear that the stroke that took the use of his legs would return and kill him entirely.

She waited in the courtyard, shivering in the thin spring sunshine, until Alasdair came out again to resume his sword practice. Then she jumped up and walked with him toward the armory.

"No, he's not worse," Alasdair assured her. "Gone soft in the head, maybe, is all. He was asking me to stay on here."

"And not go with Duncan? Oh, Alasdair!" Frances knew a leap of joy for herself, and sadness for Alasdair. For months past he had talked of nothing but his plan to go overseas and serve in the Scots Brigade in the Netherlands under their kinsman Colonel Murray. Two of the clansmen, Duncan Dhu and Sandy Ruadh, were willing to try their luck with him, and he reckoned that with a letter of introduction from Lord Gair, he would soon rise to an officer's position.

"No." Alasdair's mouth set in grim lines. "It is a matter of the clan, you see—Lachlan has the right of it. The clan will not be taking Hugh as chief. Not unless there's someone by his side, to be leading him the way he should go. Lord Gair has a notion I should be staying as the factor. Gillivray's near past it, you saw that." He stared across the courtyard at the pigeons wheeling above the dovecote, and the grim set of his face lightened. "So, Frances! There's one good part, whatever. Now we can be married at once, and not wait until I've made my fortune in the foreign wars." He hugged her round the waist until she squeaked, and swung her up in the air and halfway around. But his eyes were still grave.

"You might be asking a body first, Alasdair Cameron," she teased. "How d'you know I'll have you?"

Alasdair laughed, looking down at her fondly. "A fine thing if you'd be refusing me, and I taking the position of factor only to get you with it, Frances Murray."

Frances pulled a fold of the plaid across her face and looked slantwise at him across the tattered green-and-black stuff.

"Come now," Alasdair coaxed her. He slipped an arm under the plaid and hugged her to him. "You know fine you'd like nothing better than to have me, Frances. You told me yourself you liked me best of all the Camerons."

"That was three years ago," Frances cried, indignant that her childish confession should be used against her. "How do you know I will not have changed my mind? Maybe I do not like smooth-spoken fellows that dress like the Sassenach."

"Maybe you'd like one of Lachlan's hairy sons," Alasdair countered, "and go to live in a bothy and have your face wrinkled by the smoke of the peat fire? Don't be silly, Frances. I've already told Lord Gair I'll stay, and I want to have the priest call our banns this Sunday."

Now Frances was truly enraged by his patronizing tone. "And if he does call the banns, it's myself will be denying them," she cried, and ran blindly away from Alasdair, through the main gate and down the hill to the river.

Alasdair caught up with her before she was halfway down the hill. He scooped her over his shoulder, her legs kicking and petticoats flying, and started back up toward the castle with his prize.

"In the old days," he teased, "any man that was a man would no' wait for a lass to say yes. A real man would capture his bride, and throw her over his saddle, and ride away with her, whether she would or no. Stop that!" Frances had given up kicking in favor of tickling him.

"Bride-rape's no' in fashion!" she panted, and launched another assault on his ribs.

"Could be fun, though." Alasdair pinioned her wrists with one hand and dumped her unceremoniously on the ground with her back against a tree. "Hmm, nice legs on this one." His hand ran up under her petticoats while Frances squirmed and cursed him. Unperturbed, he continued to catalog her attractions. "A wee thing short of stature, but nicely shaped for all that. Pretty black curls, rosy lips, and—ouch! you vixen!—yes, definitely good teeth," he concluded, sucking the back of his hand where she had bitten into it. "Aye, this one will do." He knelt beside her and tickled her unmercifully with his free hand. "Now, mistress! Will I have the priest, or will ye take me without?"

Frances writhed and giggled. "Oh, stop, stop!"

she gasped. "All right, Alasdair, I'll marry ye. I always meant to, anyway."

They had not noticed Hugh's halting progress down the hill until his shadow fell upon them. Alasdair jerked upright, and Frances smoothed her skirt down over her legs.

"Frances, Alasdair." The piping, childish voice was incongruous coming from the body of a man near grown. Frances blushed and wriggled upright. There was something indecent in being caught by poor Hugh. A trail of spittle ran down his chin unheeded, as usual, and the sight of their play had roused an infrequently seen spark of curiosity in his blank blue eyes. "Will you play with me? I have a new mommet. Donald brought it from Inverness. I wish Donald hadn't come," he added as an afterthought. "He doesn't like me."

Donald! Frances jumped to her feet. Her half-brother had seldom bothered to visit Beauly since he had dumped her on the Camerons four years earlier, saying that she was half a Cameron and it was time the clan took a share in feeding and clothing her. He'd always had little fondness for Frances, the child of his father's old age by a Cameron wife, and little understanding of his father's aims to keep peace by joining his branch of the Murray clan with the Camerons.

Frances had always wondered if Donald could have had anything to do with the sudden illness that had overtaken her mother after her father, old

Iain Murray, died. Certainly he'd been quick enough to get rid of her after that, as though he feared she, his twelve-year-old half-sister, could somehow interfere with his plan to drink his way through his inheritance. Why was he visiting now, when the clan was so restless with the news of Lord Gair's illness?

Alasdair took his cousin Hugh's hand and smiled up at the ungainly bearlike figure. "Come with me, Hugh, and show me your mommet. You mustn't mind Donald. He wouldn't have brought you a new doll if he disliked you, would he?"

"Yes, he would," Hugh replied. "He called me the daftie. He said, 'The old man is dying, and the daftie's not fit to be chief.' "

"Dying!" Frances caught her breath.

"Don't fash yourself for a word, Frances," Alasdair reproved her. "I saw himself not half an hour since, remember? He was a long way from dying then."

But when they reached the castle, two pieces of news awaited them. One was that Lord Gair had taken a turn for the worse immediately after his talk with Alasdair. The other was that he had sent for Donald himself, some days previously.

Donald spent most of that day closeted with Lord Gair, emerging late in the afternoon with a pleased look on his fat face. That evening he sent for Frances. He had dined in his chamber and had lingered in his cups after the meal, and the room reeked of sour wine. His little eyes, almost buried in the rolls of fat on his cheeks, roved over Frances with a greedy pleasure that embarrassed her.

"What's this I hear of you and Alasdair?" he asked her brusquely. "The lackwit came in babbling that you two had talked of marriage." He gave her a sharp glance. "Not spoiled your maidenhead, has he?"

Frances stared at the dark fringe of beard ornamenting Donald's chin and refused to answer. But she could feel herself blushing.

"Good!" Donald answered his own question. "You can look higher than the factor of Beauly. *If*"—he sneered—"he ever achieves that exalted position."

"He might be higher," Frances retorted. "The clan might choose him for chief."

"Havers!" Donald leaned forward and stared at Frances. For a moment the family resemblance between them was visible: two stubborn chins, two pairs of snapping black eyes. "Alasdair's less right to the chiefship than yourself."

"Me?" Frances was stunned.

"Have ye never thought, girl?" Donald raised one hand and ticked off his points on fingers as fat and stubby as tiny hams. "First in blood is the daftie, Lord Gair's own son. But after that, you're his niece and the only other one in direct descent from the old chief, God rest his soul. Have you forgotten that your mother was sister to Lord Gair? Why d'you think I had you fostered here? You could not be chief yourself, but if anything happened to the idiot, you'd be heiress of Beauly, and the clan would take as chief the man you married. As for Alasdair, he's just another Cameron poor relation, for all he was fostered here at Beauly like yourself. His father was no more than cousin to Gair, though they grew up like brothers. That's no claim at all. Old Lachlan and his three sons would contest the chiefship with him—aye, and half the rest of the Camerons as well. It would go to the man the Earl of Glencairn favored. He's got King Jamie's ear on all that's done north of Stirling, and if there was to be a fight, Jamie would give the Cameron lands to the strongest man, just to keep the peace. He's tired of these wild Highlanders and their feuds."

Donald leaned forward again until the harsh stare of his small black eyes bored into Frances' face. "I intend to be that strongest man, Frances. And you're going to help me. Do you understand? So no more talk of Alasdair. If that cockerel gives me any trouble, I'll break him like a dry stick." He demonstrated his meaning on the bone of a greasy chicken wing left over from his supper.

Frances fled the room to the sound of Donald's drunken laughter. "Break him like a stick," he mumbled over and over. "Snap! Like that."

"Don't fash yourself," Alasdair told her when she related this conversation to him. "I don't know what Donald is planning, but there are more Camerons in the glen than there are Murrays. What can he do, he and his three or four men? Any trouble he starts, Duncan Dhu and I can finish."

Alasdair's confidence was all Frances had to cling to in the disheartening days that followed. Lord Gair was sinking fast now, barely able to raise his head from his pillow. It rained all the time, so that she could not have escaped outdoors even if she were not constantly watched. Donald seemed to like to have her in the hall, under his eye. He didn't care what she did as long as he was watching her.

As gray day succeeded gray day, Frances grew to hate the thick stone walls and dank corridors of Beauly. The castle was no longer her home, but a prison where every rustle of a tapestry or creak of a hinge might mean that someone was spying on her. She and Alasdair met only in corridors and spoke only in passing.

Three weeks after Donald's arrival, the recruiting officer for Colonel Murray came through the glen. He dined with them and left in the morning with five of the clansmen, among them Duncan Dhu and Sandy Ruadh. Frances listened to the talk as they marched away and learned that Donald had given all five men a present of gold to enlist. The recruiting officer, having no Gaelic, did not know this, and was mightily pleased to get such a fine turnout.

"Why, lass, Colonel Murray's my own kinsman!"

Donald told her when she asked about the present. "I wanted our men to make a good showing."

But all five men had been Camerons, and all of them friendly to Alasdair. None of Donald's Murray ghillies had gone, and none of the Lachlan Camerons. Frances counted heads and watched for an opportunity to talk to Alasdair. Donald had invented an errand for him up the glen, and he was not expected back until the day after the recruiting party left.

That morning Frances donned her clothes before dawn and was out of the castle before Donald stirred, resolved to spend the entire day on the path to the high meadows, if need be, to catch Alasdair on his way back.

She had not long to wait. The sun was still sending long streaks across the valley when he came trudging down the path from the shielings, leading his horse.

"Frances! How did you know?" He hugged her and lifted her up so that the tips of her toes barely brushed the grass. Frances felt his cheek, rough from three days without shaving, harsh against her own soft skin.

"Alasdair," she said softly. All at once his name seemed full of magic, a word that could free her from the dank castle and bring life to her like the sun coming over the hilltop. She kissed him on the chin and the tip of the nose and the eyebrows until, breathless with laughing, he put her down.

"Lord Gair?"

Frances shook her head. "Still holding on."

They walked slowly down the path, Frances within the circle of Alasdair's arm, while he explained his early return. His horse had cast a shoe and he had determined to come back early, rather than risk laming it.

Frances confided her fears that Donald was plotting something.

Alasdair laughed at her. "Seeing shadows! Think of something better—like giving me a proper kiss now that I'm back." He tethered his horse to a low branch where it could graze on the wild grass. "There, Bhiuiti, rest you, and I'll take my ain reward."

He turned to Frances with a crooked grin and put both his arms around her. She felt that half-drunken exhilaration that always seized her when Alasdair touched her, as though her blood were running as fast and furious as the turbulent mountain river. She twined her arms around his neck and returned his kisses, reveling in the warmth and the closeness of him and the supple, springing feel of his body.

When his hand cupped her breast she did not draw away, but put her own hand over his. Strange to feel his rough fingers under her palm, and the different sensations of his caresses through the coarse stuff of her gown. Where his hand moved against her breast there was a sharp sensation that thrilled and frightened her.

His fingers moved and teased her nipple erect, stroking through the rough fabric. She leaned against him, losing herself in this wash of new sensation, wanting nothing more than this. It was a wild, singing joy, like the hawks swooping through the sky.

"We've the day free," she whispered. "They'll no' be expecting you back before this evening."

She was to remember that bright jewel of a day often in the years to come. For a few hours she and Alasdair lived apart in a magic world of their own, as free of the storm clouds gathering at the castle as if they had wandered into a faery hill. Hand in hand, they walked down the glen until they came to a grassy circle close by the river. The castle was hidden from view by an outcropping of granite rock, the sun warmed the little dell, and a gnarled tree in the center of the grass offered shade and a backrest. Alasdair spread out the rough plaid he had carried for protection in the mountains and offered his hand to Frances.

She looked doubtfully at the tree. None of the crofters ever came near this spot. The smooth ring of grass around it was said to mark a dancing place of the Good Folk, the ones who could take you into their hills if they caught you there. But she didn't want Alasdair to think her superstitious. "The grass is a perfect ring," she said at last. He could make what he would of that.

Alasdair laughed. "And what if it is? You've been listening to too many old tales. The Good Folk are just a tale. And even if they weren't," he added, touching the short dirk at his side, "I'm wearing iron. You know they will not come where there is iron, or things made in a forge. Come now. D'you think I can't protect you?" He drew Frances down beside him on the improvised blanket and slipped an arm around her waist. The feel of his muscular body, warm and hard to the touch, banished her lingering fears. She remembered how he'd faced down Lachlan.

"I believe you could," she said slowly. "I believe you could protect me even from the Good Folk."

Alasdair's fingers were warm against her lips. "Hush!" His eyes were laughing. "Do not you know it is ill luck to speak their name, here in their very place? I'd best be stopping your mouth—for your own safety, you mind."

His mouth came down on hers and his body pressed against hers. When his hands gently caressed her breasts and then her long slim legs, Frances felt half-drunk, incapable of thought. Fear stirred in her at the urgency of his touch, then was stilled by the pleasure pouring through her veins. She willed herself not to think, not to fear. She tilted her head back and gazed at the pattern of sky and leaves through half-closed lashes. The warmth of the sun, the sweet-scented herbs and grass growing around them, and the other warmth radiating through her from Alasdair's caresses all joined together in her mind.

Suddenly Alasdair gave a half-strangled moan and broke away from the embrace. "That settles it. If Donald's against the marriage, we'll have to be handfasted. I can't kiss you and love you every day, Frances, and not have you in my bed. Do you understand? I'll get no bastard child on you, so handfasting it'll have to be."

Frances felt chilled and let down at his sudden withdrawal. What did Alasdair think she was, a toy that he could pick up and put down at his pleasure? She felt a fine, free anger coursing through her veins. "Do you not be so handy to tell me what must be, Alasdair Cameron. *You* canna' keep your hands off me? *You* have to have me in your bed? My grief! Will I be yours like your hawk or hound, then, and no voice of my own at all? I'll come to your bed when I'm willing, Alasdair, and not before."

Alasdair raised one crooked red eyebrow and laughed down at her with lordly self-assurance. "And d'you think I can't make you willing?"

Frances raised one hand to give his face a good slap, but Alasdair caught her wrist and pulled her back into his arms. His kisses this time set new fires alight in her body, until she moaned with delight and pressed close to him. He pushed the rough homespun skirt away from her legs and she shivered in pleasure at the feather-light caress of his fingertips along the inside of her thigh. She twined her own fingers through his springy red hair and pulled his head down against her breast. They were together now, the way she had always known they would be. Why was she not entirely contented? But wherever Alasdair touched her, this wild surge of wanting possessed her. She wanted him closer to her, holding him tighter.

"Oh, I do not know what I am wanting," she cried in exasperation.

Alasdair's laugh was muffled by the folds of her skirt, but Frances thought she detected a note of complacency in his answer. "Do you not? Then I shall have to show you."

His hands moved higher, brushing across the secret places where no one had ever touched her before. Frances felt warmth and wetness gathering between her thighs. She moaned and pushed herself against his hand. He raised his head from her breast and pulled her body firmly against his. Kissing the soft hollow of her neck and then her mouth, he parted her eager lips with his tongue and thrust inside even as his hand found its way to the center of her body.

Frances was helpless to resist, even had she wanted to, as his practiced fingers sought out those special little crevices that she had hardly known existed. There was a flooding sweetness that left her limbs limp, almost out of her control. The sensations he aroused in her mounted until they were almost unbearable. She became frightened and writhed against his touch, trying at once to escape and to prolong the sweet touch. But Alasdair would not free her from his maddening caresses, and the tensions mounted inside her until tremor after tremor of sweet release raced through her body.

They were both still for a long moment, as Frances' breathing quieted and Alasdair gently held and caressed her hand. Then, suddenly, Alasdair sat up and pulled her skirts down. "There! Now you know." His face was flushed, and his breath came heavily.

Frances sat up too. Something in Alasdair's voice chilled her. A moment ago he had been so loving, and now he seemed almost angry with her. "Alasdair?" she asked. "Did I do something wrong?"

Alasdair snapped a stick between his fingers and threw the pieces down into the rushing river. When he finally did look up at her, he was calmer.

"Nothing, Frances." His smile was a trifle strained. "But it's hard for me, d'you see? I want you, Frances. As a woman, in my bed, in my house. And I haven't got a house I can take you to. Not yet. And Donald will never let us marry. He's got other plans for you, fine plans."

"D'you know what they are?" Frances whispered.

Alasdair shook his head. "He's been hinting."

"But . . ." Frances clutched at the fragments of

her dream. "You're to be the factor for Hugh. Then we'll can marry. Lord Gair said so."

Alasdair shook his head again. "I doubt Lord Gair's word will carry much weight now. He's dying, Frances. Haven't you seen how he gets weaker every day? And Donald means to be master of Beauly. I don't know what his plan is, but he's something in mind."

He sighed and spun another stick through the air into the glistening river. "Maybe the best thing would be for me to go abroad after all. A few years' service in the Low Countries, and then . . ." His voice trailed off. What would be changed then?

Frances saw his face change as he pondered plans. Suddenly he seemed a thousand miles off already. Impulsively she threw her arms around him. "Do not be leaving me here, Alasdair. Stay here with us. You promised Lord Gair." She pressed her body against his and felt him rising against her. His arms gripped her and his kisses now were hot and demanding. "Stay," she whispered in his ear. "Stay with me." He was trembling with restrained passion and his body arched against hers. He would stay, she thought. He wouldn't leave her now.

He kissed her with the ferocity of a drowning man gasping for air. "You are air and water, food and drink to me," he whispered. "Frances, I can't let you go, and I can't stay here. Will you come with me to Edinburgh? We can be handfasted there, and if Donald doesn't find us before you have a child, he won't be able to stop the marriage."

Scots marriage law was simple enough to make this possible. All a couple had to do was declare before witnesses their intention to live together as man and wife. If there was a child of the marriage, it held good; if not, both parties were free to seek other partners. The gentry usually dressed it up with feasting and gifts, and Catholic families like the Camerons and Murrays called the priest, but none of these were necessary in law. Even the fact that Frances was but sixteen years old could not stop a handfast marriage.

Frances returned his kisses and pressed herself closer to him. It seemed too much to be true, that the long grace of his body, the gentle but strong hands, the crest of red hair, should all be for her.

It couldn't be true. "Donald will stop us. He'll find us in Edinburgh." She put up a hand to smooth his flame-red hair. It was like a fire in the summer sun, warm and smooth to her touch.

"Donald's not the clan chief," Alasdair said. He kissed her hungrily between words. "He's not even a Cameron. Once you're my wife, he won't have any rights over you."

The shadow of a horse and rider fell over them. Frances looked over Alasdair's shoulder and saw Donald, blocking the path on his big bay horse.

Three barefoot ghillies circled them, grinning, closing in on them.

"Brave words, my young cockerel." Donald sneered. He pointed with his whip at Alasdair and gestured to two of the ghillies. Frances saw with a sick feeling that they were Murray men, not Camerons.

"Get that dunghill cock out of my sight!" Donald ordered. He leaned from the saddle and caught Frances' arm. "And you, my fine lady, come back with me. Plotting behind my back!"

He hauled Frances up before him with a cruel jerk on her arm and held her so that she could not struggle without the arm being twisted even farther back behind her shoulder. He kicked the horse in the ribs and turned back up the hill. Each step brought a jolt of pain to her shoulder.

The last thing Frances saw was Alasdair's red head going down in the dust where he struggled with the ghillies.

3

Frances paced up and down the small stone-floored room. Three days now since Donald had hauled her through the keep and thrust her into this room; three days she'd watched the narrow bar of sunlight creep across the floor; three days since she'd had any company but that stupid Janet Beatty from the kitchens, who crept in twice a day to bring her a bowl of porridge and take away the necessary bucket. Two of Donald's men stood outside the door whenever Janet came, so Frances dared not even ask her any questions.

This small room, just off the great hall, had been a part of the original keep tower. Over the centuries the tower had sunk, or the level of the courtyard had risen, so that the room was half below ground level now. The one window was just too high for Frances to see anything but the sky unless she pulled herself up and stood on tiptoes. Then she looked up out across the bailey, her face at a level with the ankles of the passersby. But at least she could see all the way across the bailey, to the curtain wall and the thin blue sky above it.

The first day she'd hoisted herself up to the window for hours, hoping for a sign from Alasdair. Just once she'd seen his red head in the distance, walking the curtain wall in the company of the Murray ghillies. She'd not dared call out to him. But he was able to walk; and apparently he was free, not locked up like herself. She took some comfort in that. If Alasdair was free, he'd find a way to get her out. She had not doubted that for a minute.

On the second day her faith began to wane. There'd been shouts in the main hall, but she'd been unable to make out the words, even with her ear pressed to the door.

The whole of this long third day, Janet had not come to the door. The bucket in the corner was beginning to stink, and Frances hated the sticky feeling of her own unwashed body. It might be lucky, she thought with grim humor, that the odors were beginning to turn her stomach, for they'd brought her nothing to eat all day. But for all she had no appetite, she was growing faint and dizzy with hunger. She caught her mind wandering with strange fancies.

Twice she thought she heard Alasdair crossing the bailey, whistling his favorite tune. But when she'd pulled herself up to the window the first time there was no one in the courtyard but one of Donald's shock-headed grooms. And the second time she'd been too weak to keep her hold on the stones. She'd fallen back into the room and narrowly escaped striking her head on the stone wall.

While she lay against the wall, a coldness came over her that had nothing to do with the chill of the stone. It numbed her senses and carried her into a half-dreaming state where her visions seemed more real than the walls surrounding her. She thought she could see through the stone surrounding her, and there was Alasdair walking into the side of a hill. She screamed at him not to go into the faery mound, but in her dream her throat closed up and no words came, and the hill closed over him and she knew he was gone for seven years. Then it seemed it was herself that was in the mound, for she was walking down a long dark tunnel, and the other folk in it were not quite real to the touch—nothing real but herself, and something waiting for her at the end of the hall.

The sound of angry voices and the scurrying of feet in the great hall roused her from her stupor. The line of the sun had crept across the floor and halfway up the opposite wall. Frances shook her head to clear the cobwebs away. Dreaming! Or was it the Sight? She'd been troubled with these visions before; once when there was clan war on the hills, and she saw men coming to attack the castle hours before they really did; another time she'd had foreknowledge of a cattle raid. But those had been clear pictures. This was harder to understand, the meaning shrouded in dream symbols. Or was it? She shivered again, this time in fear. Was it something she could not bear to be seeing plain?

Her lethargy was gone, replaced by an impotent anger that fed on itself. How dare Donald keep her locked away like this! She paced up and down the narrow room. If only there was something to make a noise with. But the only implement in the room was the slop bucket, and her stomach revolted at the thought of spilling its contents out onto the floor so that she could hammer on the door with it.

After sundown Aunt Grizel came to let her out.

Frances glanced suspiciously up and down the corridor. There were none of Donald's men to be seen.

"How did you get away from them, Aunt?" she whispered. "Hurry now—we must be going from here before they come back." She caught at her aunt's hand and pulled her down the corridor.

"Hush now!" Aunt Grizel resisted the tug. "Get away? What havers is that? Your brother was overharsh with you, dear, and so I've told him, but you mustn't be thinking of playing such a child's trick as that. There's no need to run away, no need at all. Come along now. I've had Janet prepare a nice hot bath for you in my rooms."

Frances hesitated. Fighting her urge to run was the desire to be truly clean again. Besides, if Grizel could let her out, and wasn't afraid of Donald, things must be all right again. "Alasdair?"

"No need to worry about that one," Grizel said. She sounded angry. "He's done well enough for himself."

Frances put one hand to her aching head. Why was it so hard to think?

"Come along, dear," Grizel urged, seeing her indecision. "There's fresh oat cakes for you, and good mutton broth."

Frances felt sick and dizzy at the mere mention of food. She let Grizel guide her along the corridor to her own suite of apartments without protest.

Aunt Grizel's rooms seemed like a palace after Frances' three days in the stone chamber. Like all the rooms in the castle, they had stone walls many feet thick and flooring of heavy oak planks. But the floor was strewn with sweet-scented rushes, and the walls were hung with bright tapestries depicting hunting scenes. Best of all, a steaming tub of hot water, scented with dried flower petals and sweet herbs, stood in the middle of the main room.

Frances let Aunt Grizel and Janet peel the dirty homespun dress from her body and guide her into the tub. She sank into the warm water with a sigh of contentment and sat idly playing with the flower petals that floated on the surface. Behind her, she heard Aunt Grizel directing Janet to take the dress out and have it burned.

It's my only dress, she thought idly. Will I walk around naked, then? In her dreamy state the thought struck her as funny. She looked down at her body and marveled at the whiteness and smoothness of her skin where the sun had not roughened it.

She had seldom looked at herself like this. Bathing at Castle Beauly was usually an affair of plunging one's shivering body into the loch in summer or sponging off with a basin of cold water in winter. Often she had to break the ice in the basin first. The circumstances did not encourage leisurely, thorough appraisal of one's body.

Now, for the first time since she had grown into a woman, Frances looked at as much of herself as she was able to see. She trickled warm water from the sponge over her shoulders and watched the droplets run down between her breasts. High, firm breasts they were, and skin as white as Alasdair's. I'm nane so ill to look at, she thought. Alasdair had found her beautiful, and so she must be. Frances ran one hand lovingly over her body and fancied it was Alasdair. When they were married, would it be a sin for him to touch her so? She could never understand what the priest said about carnality.

"Aunt Grizel," she asked aloud, "is it a sin to let a man touch you?"

Janet Beatty squealed and giggled and hid her face in her apron. Aunt Grizel's skinny neck mottled red and her eyes refused to meet Frances'. "It's not a question for a good decent girl to be asking."

"I mean, after you're married?" Frances pursued.

Strangely, this seemed to embarrass Aunt Grizel more than before. "Och, you'll be knowing soon enough," she said. "Janet! Are Miss Frances' new clothes ready yet?"

Frances felt sorry to have embarrassed her aunt. Of course, Grizel had never married, so perhaps she felt it was not decent to be thinking of such things. She would have to explain about her and Alasdair.

Frances stood up in the tub and waited until Janet had wrapped a sheet around her. Then she put her arms around Aunt Grizel and gave her a kiss. "I'm sorry if I was rude, Aunt."

Grizel shooed her to a bench near the hearth. "Eat now. You'll not want to be getting your new clothes dirty."

Frances was surprised to find that her appetite had returned. She sopped up the mutton broth with pieces of bread while her eyes feasted on the fine new garments Janet was laying across the bed. There was a linen petticoat edged with cutwork and a boned corset, an underskirt of deep cherry-colored satin, and a black brocaded overskirt and bodice.

When she had finished eating, Aunt Grizel and Janet helped her into the new clothes. Frances sucked her breath in while they hooked the corset down one side. It was the first time she had worn such a thing, for her everyday garb of homespun dress and all-enveloping plaid were cut too loose to require it.

"I can hardly move," she complained to Aunt Grizel.

Her aunt nodded with satisfaction. "Time you were learning to act like a young lady. Hold still now!"

She fussed around with the skirts, looping back the brocaded overskirt so that the cherry-colored satin of the underskirt would show to best advantage. The low cut of the bodice seemed to bother her. The corset pushed Frances' breasts up and the black brocade emphasized their whiteness. Aunt Grizel clucked and sent Janet for an embroidered partlet of semitransparent white lawn to conceal the curves so temptingly displayed.

When they were done, Frances twisted and turned this way and that, trying to get an idea of how she looked. All she could see was a billowing expanse of black brocade, with gleams of red from the underskirt and from the knots of ribbons on her sleeves and bodice. The long, tight sleeves constricted her movements even more than the corset. She was afraid to raise her arms above her head for fear something would rip.

"They're awfu' fine clothes, Aunt Grizel," she said. "Fine enough for a wedding."

Perhaps they were going to let her marry Alasdair after all. Yes, that must be it. Donald would have been angry at first, but Aunt Grizel must have brought him round. Frances peered at her reflection in the bathwater and pinched her cheeks to make them red. Would not Alasdair be surprised to see her looking so much like a lady.

She whirled away from the tub and surprised Aunt Grizel blinking back tears. "What's wrong, Aunt?"

"You're too young," her aunt said. Her eyes were fixed on a point above Frances' head, as though she were arguing with some unseen listener. "I told them you were too young. But it was no use. . . . Listen, child. It's a wedding they told me to dress you for, that's true. Your wedding."

Frances hugged her aunt and felt a seam go in her sleeve. "Oh, Aunt Grizel, I knew it. Thank you for making them let me marry him."

"Let you?" Her aunt backed away and was staring at her as if she'd gone mad. "*Let* you? Saints above! I knew the child would agree," she muttered as if to that unseen observer, "for it's Lord

Gair's wish and the good of the clan, but I never thought . . . Frances, do you truly wish to marry Hugh?"

"Hugh!" It was Frances' turn to stare. "Have you gone gyte, Aunt Grizel? It's Alasdair I'm promised to."

Grizel suddenly looked grim. "Frances, that was a childish promise. You had no right to betroth yourself without your guardian's consent, and Alasdair won't hold you to it."

"Oh, yes he will," Frances retorted. The fine new clothes seemed like a prison, constricting her movements, even her breathing. She rushed to the door. "Where is Alasdair?"

Janet held her back. "Let me go," Frances cried. She felt all in a panic, as if everything around her were conspiring to hold her away from Alasdair.

She threw off Janet's restraining arm and flung the door open, only to find the way barred by Donald's massive figure.

Frances fell back, step by step, before his slow tread. Behind her, Grizel and Janet made no move.

Donald's face was flushed red with anger down to his beard. Frances stared at his midriff. She noticed that his doublet was stained with new greasy spots. He seized both her arms and forced her to stand before him. His fingers bit into her arms till they ached.

"I've had enough nonsense from you," he said. "So you're promised to the Cameron brat? Grow up! Young Alasdair thought to marry you and get Beauly. He enjoyed the illusion that Gair would disinherit his own son in your favor. When his mistake was made clear to him, he left to join the king's men in the Low Countries."

Frances reeled under the shock of his words. What was he saying? It could not be true. "I don't believe you. I don't believe you!" she screamed. She tried to wrench herself free, but his hands were too strong for her. She shook her head back and forth until the high-piled braids toppled about her face. "It can't be the truth."

Donald raised one hand and slapped her across the face. She saw the blow coming without comprehension. Her head snapped back so violently that she thought her neck would snap. There was a buzzing sound in her ears and her cheek burned.

"That's better," he said in the silence that followed. He pushed her down on the bench. "Now shut up and listen to me, you little fool. Your lover's gone."

"I don't believe you," Frances repeated, but more calmly. "Alasdair loves me. He would not be leaving me here." A new suspicion struck her and she started to jump up from the bench. Donald's hands on her shoulders pushed her back down.

"Where is he?" she demanded on a rising note of hysteria. "You've killed him, have you not? You and your servants."

Donald gave a laugh of genuine amusement.

"Kill him? Why should I bother? Oh, I had my men give him a good drubbing, I'll grant that. It was no less than he deserved for debauching you. That brought my fine young cockerel's pride down! But kill him? He was glad enough to leave, once Gair told him he'd no intention of passing over Hugh. It wasn't you he wanted, Frances. It was Beauly."

Frances put her icy hands to her cheeks. "I am not believing a word out of your mouth," she repeated desperately. But in spite of herself, she remembered Donald's earlier words: *You'd be heiress of Beauly, and the clan would take as chief the man you married*. And Alasdair had been insistent on marrying her only after Lord Gair became seriously ill. Had he been counting on Hugh's obvious unfitness to rule, and Lord Gair's fondness for her?

They had had so little time together since he returned from his law studies in Edinburgh. It had seemed like such a miracle when he suddenly saw her and loved her. She had adored him for so long. Was it Beauly he'd seen in her eyes?

Donald sat heavily on the bench beside her and put his arm around her. A nod from him, and Grizel and Janet scurried from the room, leaving them alone.

"Don't cry, Fan. You're not the first girl to be made a fool of by a good-looking rascal." He laughed again. "You don't really think I killed him, now, do you? You must have seen him yourself, these last three days. He's had the freedom of the castle. I had to keep you locked up until he was safely on the road to catch the Leith packet."

His fingers brought her chin up and forced her to look at him. "Come now, Fan. Cheer up. Let's be friends. I'm sorry I had to lock you up, but it was for your own good. I didn't want the plausible bastard getting to you with another of his stories—and I could hardly throw a Cameron out of Beauly, could I? I had to wait until he left of his own will." Another laugh. "It wasn't hard. I gave him a purse and the direction of a captain who sails for Flushing. He was in such a hurry to make the packet, he couldn't even wait to make his farewells to Gair. It seems he's friends in the Scots Brigade. He was eager to join them."

"Duncan and Sandy," Frances said slowly. That much was true. But what of the rest? Her head ached so, it was hard to think.

"I did see him once in the courtyard," she said, not aware that she was speaking aloud. "So I know you didna' kill him. And I heard him whistling this morning . . ."

Donald bit his lip to conceal a triumphant smile. He made a mental note to give a handsome reward to the red-headed groom who'd played Alasdair's part from a distance. A pity the fellow couldn't whistle! He'd had to pay another one to whistle the tune. But it had been worth it, if it served to convince his wild virago of a sister. Look at the silly girl now, drooping like a dead flower because she thought one man didn't love her! She'd be in the right mood now to understand the advantages of his plan.

"Well, sister," he said with a brisk air, "enough of that bastard. Don't give him another thought—he's not worth it. And you have a glorious future ahead of you. Mistress of Beauly! You're a lucky girl. And Hugh likes you."

So they were back where they had started. Frances felt a hot, sick feeling spewing up in her throat. Of course Hugh liked her. He would like anyone who was not unkind to him. But how could they talk in the same breath of her tall, clean-limbed Alasdair and poor shambling Hugh with his vacant eyes and perpetually snotty nose? Frances clasped her hands on the one solid fact left to her, her own will. "I'll not have him."

There was nothing else to say. Suddenly she felt very tired and incapable of arguing further. She wanted nothing so much as to run out of the castle, up into the wild free hills of the glen, to throw herself on the heather and sob herself into sleep. How could Alasdair have left her so casually, without a word? That was the one betrayal her tormented brain fixed upon. All those promises, all those kisses and caresses, and yet when the time came to go, he could not spare two minutes to pen a note of farewell.

Frances stared at the embroidered garden scene on the tapestry behind Donald's head. Perhaps, if she counted the stitches very carefully, she could prevent herself from thinking of anything else. She would not, she vowed to herself, she *would not* cry before fat smirking Donald.

Donald leaned toward her, and Frances drew back instinctively. "You see? You cannot do better than marry Hugh."

"Hugh?" Frances had actually forgotten Donald's plan. How could he talk about Hugh at a time like this? She swayed and leaned on the stone wall behind her for support. "Go away, Donald. I canna' think. Leave me alone."

"The inheritance—"

"Go away!" Frances screamed. "My grief! Can you not be thinking of aught but stones and gold?"

She picked up the nearest article, a bronze ewer, and hurled it against the far wall.

Grizel came running in as the echoes clanged and died away.

"It's all right, Grizel," Donald told her. "Fanny and I were just having a wee difference of opinion."

"No!" Grizel contradicted him. She was out of breath. "It's not all right." She turned to Frances, laying one hand on her bosom to control her agitated panting for breath. "Lord Gair is dying, Frances. He wants to see you."

The room was full of dark shadows that wavered menacingly back and forth on the walls and on the embroidered tapestries of the bed as the candles flickered. Frances went to pull a wooden shutter across the window, but Lord Gair stopped her with a wave of his hand. "Let me smell the heather," he said.

His voice was a threadlike sound, hardly more than a whisper, but it still carried the unmistakable tone of command. Frances left the shutters open and went back to sit on her stool beside the high tester bed. Lord Gair put out his waxen hand to smooth her hair, but he lacked the strength to complete the motion. His hand fell on her head and rested there as lightly as a flower. Frances felt it as an intolerable weight.

"You've been a good lass to me," Lord Gair whispered. "Glad I am that Donald sent you to me for fostering."

The tears streamed unchecked down Frances' face and splashed on the white lawn tucker Grizel had arranged with such care. She felt a constriction in her chest that had nothing to do with the confining clothes they had dressed her in.

"Frances . . ."

He was fighting for breath now, and the words came slowly, with many pauses.

"I had hoped . . . it would be many years . . . before I had to ask this of you."

A candle guttered in a pool of melted wax and then flared up wildly. A vagrant breeze from the window gathered the bed hangings into a billowing fold and presented the face of a hunter, about to strike down a deer, to the candlelight.

"Hugh . . . not fit . . ." The reedy whisper trailed off for a long minute.

"Is he dead?" Donald asked, starting forward.

An imperious gesture of one long bony finger stopped him. "Have the goodness," whispered Lord Gair with sudden strength, "to refrain from stripping my corpse until I am cold!" He surveyed Donald from hooded, deep-set eyes that still retained a little of their old sparkle. "You may leave us."

It was a royal command, coming from a man who had been chief in the days when the Cameron was a king in his own country. Donald stammered and backed out into the hall. At a sketched gesture from Lord Gair, Frances got up and shut the heavy door behind her brother. Then she returned to her seat beside the dying man.

"Frances." Again the urgency of the whisper reached out and called her. "Hugh . . . canna' hold . . . the clan. There'll be a bloody strife. The people . . . must see someone with strength. Donald thinks to take it, but he's a fool. The Earl of Glencairn will swallow us up. But there'd be . . . the fiery cross out . . . first."

Frances felt chilled to the bone even before his next words. Was this marriage what Lord Gair meant to ask her? Anything but that! she cried inaudibly.

"You're next . . . in the line . . . after Hugh. You two together . . . none could dispute . . ."

The night breezes that swirled about their heads seemed full of whispering voices, crying of long-ago battles. In the candle flames, now guttering and flaring with fantastic abandon, Frances fancied she could see huts and farms put to the torch.

The bed hangings billowed out again. This time the figure of the deer, trapped in the ring of its attackers, stood out in the fitful light.

Lord Gair beckoned her closer with one bony finger. She stooped over him to hear better.

"Donald thinks . . . to rule Hugh." A ghost of a chuckle. "And you. He'll not rule you, Frances. You're a true Cameron. Mistress of Beauly!"

The thin fingers closed over her wrist with astonishing force. "Mistress of Beauly," Gair repeated. "Will you do it, Frances? Will you take my boy, to keep the clan together?"

Disjointed images flashed through Frances' mind. Old tales of murder and rapine mingled with the picture of Alasdair saying: *I've agreed to stay and be Hugh's factor. Because he needs my help, and because then we can be married.* But then Alasdair had run away, so what were all his words worth?

She would not be a traitor like Adasdair.

Mistress of Beauly.

To hold the clan together.

After that, the arrival of the tubby little village priest, red-cheeked and perspiring from his desperate toiling up the hill, was almost an anticlimax.

He bustled into Lord Gair's room, followed by a weeping Grizel, and was laying out his holy oils when Lord Gair stopped him with an imperious wave of his hand. "I've better work for you . . . tonight . . . priest," he told him.

After that events moved so fast that Frances felt as if she was being borne along on the crest of a great sweeping wave. Grizel and Janet combed out her long braids until they fell down her back in a great rippling swath of black satin, to show that she came virgin to her marriage. Servants wore sent to rouse Hugh and dress him, while candles were lighted in thc castle chapel.

No one thought to order torches for the long passageway that Frances must traverse between Gair's room and the chapel. She picked her steps carefully across rough stones half-sunken with the passage of the years, her eyes fixed on the candles at the chapel door. Grizel and Janet accompanied her halfway down the long hall, fluttering about her to straighten her dress, and offering bits of advice so inappropriate as to be grimly humorous. Finally Frances told them to stay where they were.

"If I must do this," she snapped, "I'll do it in my own time. Aunt, Hugh will not care if my ribbons are awry. And, Janet, ye're a bigger fool than I took ye for, if you think the marriage bed has aught to do with this mummery."

They let her go forward alone then. The priest awaited her at the door of the chapel, and Hugh was inside with one of his men who had helped him to dress and guided him there. His bewildered eyes were those of a child.

"Frances, what are they going to do to me?" he burst out as soon as he saw his cousin. "Why are you crying, Frances? What's wrong?" He was very near panic at the strange events of the night. For all his grown body, Frances thought, he was nothing more than a child that wanted comfort.

And so she found it quite easy, after all, to take Hugh's hand in hers, and even to smile at him. "Hush now, Hugh," she said gently. "Nothing is wrong. Do what the nice man tells you, and after you shall have a sweet, and see your father."

Throughout the brief ceremony she was aware of Donald, standing in the back of the chapel as a self-appointed witness. His eyes burned through the back of her brocaded dress.

The priest clapped his book shut on the last words. "Most irregular . . . most irregular," he complained. "But Lord Gair's wishes . . ." Of course he would not dare to cross the head of the clan. But now that he had carried out Gair's orders, he scurried back to the dying man's bedside.

Now Frances and her aunt and the priest gathered around the Cameron's bedstead. Grizel wanted Hugh there too, but when he whimpered in fright, Frances told him to go into the hall and wait there.

Lord Gair had fallen into a fitful sleep that lasted some hours. Near dawn he awakened and glanced around the room. His eye fell on Frances. "Is it done?" he whispered.

Frances raised her hand so that the light glittered on the great emerald in the Cameron ring.

Lord Gair gave a jerky nod. "Sons of the hounds . . . come and get meat," he whispered, and his head fell back on the pillow.

It was the ancient Cameron war cry.

The priest hurried forward, mumbling something about the sin of dying with such heathenish words on one's lips, and calling on Lord Gair to repent. Frances ceded her place by the bed to him.

"You canna' trouble him now," she said with the calm of utter exhaustion, emotional and physical. "He is dead."

She walked to the narrow window, and leaning her arms against the sill, looked out to the east, where the sky was lightening. Somewhere farther east still, the same sun would be rising on the sailing of the Leith packet.

In the parcel of wild, Gaelic-speaking Highlanders on board the Leith packet for Flushing, many thinking their end had come with the first throes of seasickness, no one had time to spare for a red-headed boy whose illness was caused more by the great matted wound on his forehead than by the pitching and tossing of the boat. They were two days out before Duncan Dhu even discovered that his clansman was on board the same boat.

Thereafter he and the other Camerons nursed Alasdair through the two stormy days that remained before they reached Flushing.

Disembarkation, like everything else, was delayed by the inability of most of the new recruits to understand any tongue but Gaelic. To add to the confusion, most of this lot were inland crofters and cattle lifters who had no notion of a boat whatever and could hardly be persuaded to sit down in the skiffs appointed to ferry them to shore.

The recruiting officer ran from one end of the packet to the other, shouting orders in English, which was useless, and occasionally striking a man with the flat of his sword, which the Highlanders took as open incitement of mutiny.

Presently he noticed that there was slightly less confusion at one end of the boat than at the other, and found that a pale red-haired lad with a half-healed wound in the head was capably directing groups of men down the rope ladders and into the boats. The recruiting officer very sensibly sat down on a coil of rope and had a dram, and let the new recruit do his work for him.

"Man, if ye can handle them that way on the battlefield, there's a commission in it for ye," he said when the last party had gone down. "What might your name be?"

When told, it struck a park of memory in the recruiting officer's mind. "Alasdair Cameron. I've a letter about ye." He fumbled in his breast pocket. "Ah, yes! Ye're not to be allowed free until we report to the colonel." It fair went to his heart to call the guard and have irons placed on this man. He didna' look much like the desperate murderer described in the letter. But it would no' do to be angering a kinsman of the colonel's.

4

The Highlands, 1596

Frances paused before the polished steel mirror hanging on her door for the automatic check on her appearance, as she had done every morning of the three long years since she became Hugh's wife and lady of Beauly. There was still no proper looking-glass in Castle Beauly, but then, as Aunt Grizel never tired of reminding her, a decent wife hardly needed such aids to vanity. All that was necessary was to see that her small starched ruff was clean and that her hair was neatly tucked under the linen coif worn by all married women. As usual, a few black curls peeped from under the edge of the snowy coif. Frances tucked them back with a practiced hand.

Usually the momentary glance in the mirror would not have halted her progress down to the hall. Had she not enough to do, with overseeing the work in the dairy, the weaving and the supplies brought in from the farms, keeping Hugh out of mischief, and seeing that the estate accounts were brought up-to-date? She could scarcely remember the days when a careless girl clad in a single ragged homespun garment had stolen every opportunity to escape the confines of the castle and run free over the hills. Three years of responsibility for the lives and fortunes of the Cameron tenants had changed that willful girl into a quiet, pale, competent matron with a perpetual worried frown between her brows. Her cheeks were thinner now, and Frances knew instinctively that if she had possessed a looking-glass, it would have reflected none of the bright color and sparkling glances that Alasdair had used to tease her over, calling her his little spitfire.

Alasdair. . . . Strange how the thought of him still had the power to hurt her. Not a word had they heard from him since the night he made his escape from Beauly to join the Scots Brigade abroad, leaving her to shoulder the responsibilities of a dying chief and his half-wit son.

Frances' lips thinned to a hard unpleasant line and she turned away from the polished steel, not pleased with the wavering picture reflected back to her. What did it matter that Alasdair would scarcely see much to please him if he came back now? He cared naught for her and never had, or he'd not have left her in such a strait. For three years she'd found peace, and even a measure of satisfaction, in keeping the lands and castle that old Lord Gair had left to her to safeguard for Hugh. But now . . .

Now it was summer again, and one of those rare bright days that she had been used to spend out on the hills with Alasdair. She looked in the mirror and saw herself growing pinched and proper before her time. Neither maid, nor wife, nor widow, she thought. I've been wedded without being bedded. Devil take me if I'll be buried without having lived! And on a rebellious impulse, she snatched up her worn tartan cloak and ran down the stairs to the hall, calling to the stable hand, Peadir, to saddle her horse.

Grizel was sitting in the hall as usual, stitching away at her everlasting tapestry in the thin light from one of the high windows. Frances knew a stab of pity as she looked at her aunt. She had grown thin and old at Beauly, giving her life first to her brother Gair and then to raising Frances and Hugh.

"I will be going out to the peat cutting," she told her aunt. "They should be almost through. A pleasant ride it is, and the sun shining for once. Will you come with me?"

Grizel gave a patient smile and pressed one

hand to her side in a habitual gesture. "No, dear, you know my bones ache too much after this cold spring."

"All the more reason to be getting out in the sun when we have it," Frances persisted, though she did not really want to be tied down to the plodding pace of her aunt's fat gelding.

"No, I must finish this chair cover." Grizel swiveled her tapestry frame so that Frances could see the intricate design of birds and flowers, picked out with stitches too small to tell apart, that covered three-quarters of the canvas. "But do you take Hugh with you? He would be the better of an outing."

"No." Frances bent to kiss her aunt's withered cheek. "Today I'll not play nursemaid. Let Hugh ride out with one of the grooms, if you think he needs the air."

She felt heartless for refusing, when she knew what pleasure Hugh took in her company. But his aimless chatter and the need to guide him daily were among the things that weighed on her so heavily that she felt as though a great weight were pressing on the back of her neck. This ride to the peat cutting would be no holiday if she had to lead Hugh's horse beside hers.

Grizel sighed but ventured no further remonstrance as Frances ran eagerly out into the pale sunlight. It was easy to forget that the child was only nineteen, Grizel thought. Had she and Gair placed too great a burden on her, expecting her to grow up overnight and shoulder all the worries of the clan? But what else could they have done?

It's not right, Grizel concluded. She should have a child at the breast and one hanging to her skirts by now, instead of riding about the lands like a man and doing the work of the steward. That would keep her from . . . Even to herself, she dared not finish the thought.

God forbid the rumors should be true! Why would Alasdair come back to disturb their peace, after so long abroad without a word? And what would Frances do? If she'd been a proper married wife, she would have her children to keep her busy and out of temptation. But as she was neither maid nor wife . . . Grizel gave a sharp sigh and bent over her needlework again. Perhaps she had failed in her duty, encouraging Frances and Hugh to live together as chastely as brother and sister. But it was doubtful whether Hugh was even capable of giving her a child.

Frances would have told her that he was not. One of the blessings of her difficult position was that Hugh was as slow to develop physically as he was mentally. He looked on Frances as a specially beloved nurse, followed her about her work in the castle, showed her the pretty flowers and rounded stones he found, and had never questioned the arrangement that gave them separate rooms in their private wing of the castle.

For all Frances' complaint that she was neither maid, nor wife, nor widow, she was thankful that Hugh had never attempted to claim his rights. She had learned to tolerate him as a sort of perpetual child; the thought of him as a lover made her almost physically ill.

No, it was not Hugh she wanted on this fine brisk day with the birds crying overhead and all the branches breaking into new leaves and the meadows green with the spring rains. But what, then? What could quiet the feverish stirring of her blood?

Frances drove her spurs into the mare's side and urged her on at a reckless pace. All she needed, she told herself, was the blood-stirring excitement of a good gallop. No wonder she was restless, spending her days in the castle with no more exercise than the daily round from dairy to kitchens to stillroom, nothing more to read than last winter's accounts. She was bored, that was all the trouble. When next they sent the wagons down to Inverness to sell their grain and malt, she would go with them, and spend some of the price of the grain on some new books to read through the next winter. And she would go riding every day, or perhaps every other day. . . .

"Jesu." Frances spoke aloud, and the mare, sensing her changed mood, slowed to a walk. Is *that* all there is to be for me? To ride around these hills in the summer, and be grateful for a new volume of verses to read in the winter?

All at once the small indulgences she'd promised herself seemed utterly barren. She could see herself dwindling into a copy of her Aunt Grizel, withering away with a book of verses in her hand instead of a tapestry needle.

I might as well be a prisoner all my life, like poor Queen Mary that had her head cut off by the English. The execution of Mary, Queen of Scots, had been a horror story of Frances' childhood. Only lately had she begun to consider that the queen's years of imprisonment might have been a worse fate than the final beheading.

But there was nothing else she could do, Frances concluded soberly. She could not renounce her crown. And I—I cannot stop being what I am. *Whatever that is,* a mocking voice in her head jeered. She was no wife, nor the true chief of the clan, for a woman could not be the chief. And yet she was bound down by the restrictions of both positions. What was left for her? To take a lover? That would be to betray all trusts at once—even if there had been any man in the valley but Hugh and the crofters.

Frances kicked her horse and trotted around the mountain to the green bogs where the peat cutters worked. By the time she reached the first of the scattered groups of crofters, she had damped down her fleeting moment of resentment and was back in the role they expected of her: lady of Beauly, and head of the clan for her weak-witted husband.

The heavy work of cutting the peats had been finished sometime past, and the men were back on their own holdings digging and preparing the land while the stacked peats dried in the sun. Two weeks earlier the individual blocks of peat had been stacked in the pattern called *cas bhic*—"little feet"—three peats leaning against each other like a tent, with a fourth set on top to make the roof. Now the women were piling these half-dry stacks into larger heaps so that the weight of the stack could squeeze the last remaining water out of the peats. If the good weather held to the end of the week, the peats would be dry and all the crofters would be out with sledges to carry the stacks home to each household.

That was Frances' excuse for riding up, to see how the work was going. It was the custom for Castle Beauly to supply draft animals to help drag the heavy sledges back, in return for a share of the peats cut by each man to keep the castle's own fires burning. Frances had heard of rich Lowland holdings where the trees grew so thick that the lairds burned real wood all year round, but she had difficulty in imagining such wastefulness. On her heather-covered hills, the few trees that could survive the sleeting winters and brief summers were jealously guarded. Wood was for roof beams and the handles of spades, not for burning. And how could one get properly warm, save at a fire rich with the smoky tang of the dried peats, each one releasing its store of compressed sunshine in the crackling flames of the hearth?

Frances had always loved the holiday atmosphere of the peat-stacking. In truth there was no need for her to ride up here to oversee the work herself. The people knew what to do better than she did, and they would have sent word to the castle when the draft horses were needed. But it was a treat for her to be out here in the sunshine, where the women were scrambling over the peat mosses with their skirts kilted to the knee, laughing and calling to each other. For many of them the two or three days of the stacking were the first relief they'd had all year from the monotonous chores of the byre and the smoke-blackened hearth. Moving the peats from one stack to another was light work to women accustomed to bringing their water from a spring at the foot of the mountain and to carrying loads of fodder to the cattle during the deep snows.

Frances smiled and greeted a few of the women by name, but she was in no mood for conversation that day. She was content merely to sit on her horse and look over the scene of bustling activity. The women's bare arms and legs gleamed white in the sunshine, and their faded plaids made splashes of color that blended softly in with the dun shades of heather and moss. Some of them were singing as they worked, but most took advantage of this rare gathering to shout gossip and jokes to each other in high screeching voices that sounded from a distance like the cries of birds on the mountainside.

How could I ever want more than this? Frances thought. It's lucky I am that I did not have to marry outside the glen. With that thought she could almost be contented in her marriage to Hugh, seeing it had kept her in the glen that was so dear to her.

Almost.

"It's yourself that's in it, Leddy Frances?" It was Morag, the wife of Tammas Oig, who had marched for the Low Countries with Colonel Murray and the others. "My youngest is down with the fever again, same as last month. Will you be looking in on your way back?"

Frances promised to ride by that evening with one of Grizel's herb brews to bring down the child's fever. Another woman pushed forward to ask that her man's day service to the estate be forgiven this week due to illness, and another wanted Frances to see the new, clear red she had dyed her wool by mixing the bark of lady's-bedstraw with the usual brew of crotal lichen.

"Ah, but it's easy work, blending dyestuffs," teased Seonaidh, the daughter of Euan of the high hill croft, when Ealasaidh brought out her skein of wool to show.

She put a hand to the small of her back and straightened with exaggerated effort. "Ealasaidh is thinking to be a fine lady like Leddy Frances, with no more to do than sit on a cushion all day and embroider—not like us poor souls down in the muck!" The laughter in her voice made a teasing challenge of the statement to which Frances responded instantly, looping the mare's reins and jumping lightly down to face Seonaidh on the level.

"So you think castle folk are not up to a day's work! I'll soon sort that notion, Seonaidh! How many *cas bhic* can you stack before the sun goes behind the Devil's Hoof?" She pointed to a local landmark, a craggy rock that reared from the side of the hill and shadowed the peat bog for two-thirds of every day.

Seonaidh and Frances squared off at the beginnings of two new rows, and the other women laughed and clapped their hands as the contest began.

In truth, it was harder work than Frances had remembered, and she recognized with regret that she'd grown soft in the years since she'd run free over the moors. Strands of hair curled loose about her temples and stuck to her damp face, and she soon discarded her overskirt and tight bodice to work in her kirtle like the other women. But it was fun for all that, bending, lifting, and tossing, with the good clean smell of peat and heather in her nostrils and the fresh breeze off the mountain to cool her. For half an hour she lost herself in physical work, pushing herself to her limits to beat the other woman.

And it was thus that Donald found her—muddy, laughing, with her hair blowing loose and her skirts tucked up like any crofter's woman.

The sudden silence among the women first warned Frances that something was amiss. She tossed the last peat on a high stack and straightened, unconsciously putting her hand to her back in the gesture Seonaidh had used to tease her.

Donald was looking down at her from the back of the heavy-boned stallion that he required to carry his weight. He had ridden his horse right in among the rows of peat stacks, knocking over several *cas bhic* in passing and breaking the fragile, half-dried turfs. The women had retreated, leaving Frances and her half-brother alone among the stacks.

"So." His voice was heavy with scorn. "Is this how the lady of Beauly amuses herself? But you always had peasant tastes, hadn't you, dear sister?" His eyes roved over the curves displayed by her sweat-dampened kirtle in a way that made Frances wish she had her plaid to clutch about her like the other women.

She returned his look with a long, dispassionate stare before which his eyes finally dropped. She had learned that trick of managing Donald, with much else, in the years she had been left alone to manage Beauly. At first he'd thought to stay at the castle and rule from behind her petticoats, but it had not taken Frances long to get his measure.

Donald was bored with what he termed the rustic savagery of the Highlands. A generous allowance from the estate—more generous than it could rightly afford—and he was happy enough to dice and drink away his days in Edinburgh. He returned no more than twice or thrice a year, usually to demand more money. At first Frances had given in; later she had tried to argue and show him the account books that proved they could give him no more without starving the peasants, and finally she had learned to wait out his demands with the silent stare that proved most effective. "Ask more," she had told him flatly, on his last visit, "and you'll get naught. There's a limit to what it's worth to me to keep you away from here."

At the time he'd seemed to accept her ultimatum. His allowance was paid quarterly through an Edinburgh banker with an office in Inverness, and he'd not troubled them at Beauly for nigh on a twelvemonth. Now Frances wondered if he'd come to call her bluff. Was there really a limit to what she was prepared to pay? She was hardly sure. And so she fell back on silence again, staring at him and appraising the effects of his last year of dissipation while she waited for him to speak.

The years had not been kind to Donald. At the time of Lord Gair's death he had been just sliding over the edge that divided a sturdy man from a gross middle-aged one. Now his eyes were bleared from nights of drinking and his hands shook slightly on the reins.

Not for the first time, it occurred to Frances how ridiculous it was that the estate should be bled white by the threats of this travesty of a man. When she had first told him to leave, he had threatened to come back with all the Murray men and make common cause with Lachlan Cameron against Frances and Hugh. At the time, paying him a small allowance to stay in Edinburgh had seemed the best bargain she could make. But over the years Lachlan had aged and his sons had gone south to seek their fortune. It would be harder for Donald to make trouble now.

Perhaps Donald did not realize how his hold on her had weakened even as his demands grew. He rode here, in the midst of her people, as if he could still enforce the threats he had made years earlier.

Let him threaten to stay! she thought. Accidents are easy to arrange.

A cold wing of fear brushed her mind. Merciful Mother of God, what had she been thinking of? Not murder? No, she hastily promised herself and the Blessed Virgin. Only a little accident, enough to frighten him away.

But the unvoiced thought remained in her mind as she faced him, and with it, the knowledge of how much she herself had changed in the past three years. The young girl who had been Frances

Murray would never even have thought how easy it was for a man unfamiliar with the hills to meet with a fatal accident. Lady Frances Cameron of Beauly had had to learn to think like a man.

At last Donald broke the silence. "Delighted as always to see me, little sister? If you can put aside your rustic amusements for a while, you'd best return to Beauly with me. We have matters of import to discuss." He wheeled his horse and cantered away without waiting for a reply, taking her compliance for granted.

For a moment Frances thought of defying him, staying out here for the day as she'd planned. But it was a pointless gesture. She'd have to return to the castle and face him eventually, and better to get it over with now. But first, there were the women to reassure. Too often, they'd seen Donald's visits as the precursors of some demand that fell as heavily on them as on the castle folk.

Frances drew the back of one hand across her sweaty face and glanced down the rows of finished peat stacks. Seonaidh's was longer than hers by a good two stacks. She grinned and held out her hand. "It's in the right of it you were, Seonaidh. You will be laughing at me for my easy living and my soft hands! But we never settled what the prize was to be. What do you say to a barrel of good Beauly ale for the next *ceilidh*? You can send your father down tonight to claim your winnings."

Her confident tone had the desired effect. The

women began to gather around her again, laughing and congratulating her on a good contest. But to her surprise, Euan's daughter dropped her eyes and would not take the proffered hand.

" 'Twasn't a fair contest," she muttered. "I was tiring. If you'd been let finish, Lady Frances, you might ha' drawn ahead of me yet."

Frances smiled. This was Seonaidh's way of showing sympathy for the unexpected descent of her brother. "But I didna' finish. Come up for the ale tonight. And now, who'll help me mount?" As a girl she'd been able to scramble unaided onto the bare back of her shaggy Highland pony, but Lady Frances with her tall English mare, her sidesaddle, and her skirts had had to give up many such small freedoms.

On her slow ride back to the castle Frances had time to mull over the mystery of Donald's sudden appearance, but without coming to any conclusion. It must be more money he wanted—it was always money. But would she pay? Not this time, she vowed. The simple, monotonous life would soon bore him, and if that were not enough, they would have to see what "accident" could be contrived.

Frances' new resolution was shaken almost immediately, when she came into the hall blinking against the sudden change of light. The shadow of a man scuttled away from her and crouched over the wooden bench in a far corner. As her eyes adjusted, she could make out Hugh's tall, loose-limbed frame and shock of fair hair. On the other side of the hall, Grizel was sitting with her hands raised in an attitude of helplessness.

Frances crossed the hall with swift strides and bent over the shaking form of her legal husband.

"Why, Hugh, what's this coil? Has someone been teasing you?" Belatedly she noticed that his hands were empty. "Where's thy mommet?"

"Donald took it," Hugh blubbered. He rubbed one hand across his tear-swollen face and left a trail of snot behind. "Donald says I must learn to be a man now and I must not play with mommets anymore. He said I should play with you instead. But I told him, I told him you rode out and didn't wait for me!" His voice rose in an aggrieved howl of protest. "He said I should make you be my wife, and then you'd not leave me alone anymore. What does he mean, Fan? Aren't you my wife?"

Frances conquered a shudder of revulsion at the words that he repeated without understanding.

"Frances . . ." Grizel had risen at last, and tiptoed near enough to hear their conversation. Now she laid one pleading hand on Frances' arm. "He's only a child, Frances. He doesn't know what he says—he is only repeating words Donald put into his mouth."

Frances forced a crooked smile. "D'you think I do not know that, Aunt? It was only . . ."

The sentence died unspoken as Hugh tugged at her skirts for attention. How to voice the frustration she had felt this morning, riding out and working at the peats to exorcise it, only to come back to this smoky hall and the reminder that she was tied for life to an overgrown child? It wasna' Hugh's fault. She forced back the words and found those that would calm him.

"Yes, Hugh. I am already your wife. There is nothing different that you must be doing. And Donald will be giving back your mommet as soon as I have speech with him."

But that was a promise she was not able to keep.

"I threw it in the fire," Donald told her.

"You did what!" Frances paced furiously up and down the length of the room, her full skirts swirling behind her at every turn. "How dare you come riding in here and . . . and . . ."

"Take over the governance of Hugh," Donald supplied the words for her. He leaned back in his chair and smiled at Frances. "I've been talking with a friend in Edinburgh. An advocate in the service of Glencairn."

Frances halted where she stood. Glencairn! The earl had always been eager to join the Cameron estates of Beauly to his own holdings. He was becoming as great a power in the land, men said, as Campbell of Argyll, and by the same means: one small sept after another was being swallowed up in his vast holdings, some by tricks of inheritance, some by the chiefs being attainted or mysteriously dead in battle. Since Lord Gair's death, she had known that if there were an open struggle for the chiefship of this branch of the Camerons, Glencairn would take advantage of the disorder for his own ends.

"Aye, Glencairn." Donald smiled maliciously as the blood drained from Frances' face, leaving her as white as her snowy starched coif and ruff. "I thought you might remember that name. My friend advises me that where the chief of a clan is incompetent to rule, as in the case of a minor child or"—he smiled again—"a madman, it is within law for the crown to appoint a guardian to look after his rights."

"Hugh's no' daft," Frances countered. "Just slow. And I can take care of him."

Donald's smile broadened. "A woman guardian? Don't make me laugh. And ye might find Hugh's sanity hard to demonstrate before a court of inquiry, were they to see such a scene as he made in the hall when I took his mommet from him."

"You did that a-purpose!" Frances accused. "Hugh's aye been well enow when Grizel and I have the ruling of him."

"Of course he has, my dear," Donald agreed. "I only hope you can prove that to the satisfaction of the court of inquiry that Glencairn will appoint. How well will Hugh show, d'you think, after the unsettling experience of being dragged to Inverness and kept chained on straw with the other lackwits until his case comes before the judge advocate?"

Frances stood with her hands pressed to her cheeks, trying frantically to find a way out of this new trap. What she could not see was how Donald benefited. "If Glencairn takes Beauly, where's your allowance?"

"I might . . . come to an accommodation with his grace."

"It is running in my mind that you will have done so already." The pattern was becoming clear to Frances now. "He bribes you to say that Hugh is daft, and the two of you are in it together, to argue that a woman's no fit guardian, with not even an heir to come after her. You think Glencairn will be more generous with you than I've been? You're a fool, Donald. I've bled this estate dry to keep you in Edinburgh. Glencairn'll no' be so soft."

"He may not," Donald agreed. "I'd as soon come to an accommodation with you, my dear. But I've pressing debts. Glencairn would pay them for me. If you could see your way to doing the same . . ."

He let the implied promise hang in the air.

"How much?"

He named a sum that was more than twice his yearly allowance.

"I havena' the gold, Donald. Wait till harvest-time." It was a vain half-promise. No harvests would bring in enough to satisfy this demand. The only alternative was to sell off some of the land. And what would become of the tenants then?

"If I wait," Donald said, "I wait here. 'Twould suit me well enough—especially now."

Frances began to wonder if there was a strain of madness in her family. "Why now?"

Donald cursed his slip of the tongue. Obviously Frances had not heard the rumors of Alasdair's return. Well, if the guards sent with him by Glencairn did their job aright, she'd not hear until it was too late. But until then, best not to unsettle her. He gave an unconvincing laugh. "Why, only that I daren't go back to Edinburgh with my creditors on my tail." He placed one pudgy hand on each arm of his chair and pushed himself upward. "Think it over, my dear. I'll just go down to the hall and have another little chat with Hugh while you do. Do you know, Fanny . . ." he paused, favoring her with a smile the very mirror of her own, "somehow, I have faith you'll find the money."

5

Frances spent the rest of the day going over the accounts and rents of the last three years. Since Gillivray's death she had taken over this task herself; doing accounts was at least less boring than the rest of her household duties, and this way she saved the cost of hiring a lettered man from Inverness. She had come almost to enjoy setting her wits against the problem of balancing the rents in malt and meal and the outlay in cash and clothes. But tonight, trying to find a way that she could squeeze more money out of the estate to meet Donald's latest demand, she felt only a weary frustration.

The thing was not possible. Even in a good

year, the income of Castle Beauly was mostly in tenants' rents, paid in kind: so many sacks of malt and meal; a share in the herds of black cattle that grazed on the hillsides; wool, meat, and tallow from the small brown hairy sheep that grazed around every hut.

A few sacks of wool, and most of the animals, could be sold in Inverness, and from the twice-yearly trips to market there came the silver that paid Donald's allowance and bought a few small necessities for the estate. The rest of the rents in kind were turned into cloth to cover the folk of the castle and glen, ale for them to drink, and food stores to get them all through the bitter months of winter.

Even now, Frances found herself remitting rents in a bad year, and sending round to the crofters' huts the food they had paid as rent the year before. If she raised the rents, people would starve. And the things that brought silver money for Donald—the wool and meat from the herds—could not be increased. Could she make twenty sheep live where there was not pasture for ten, or turn one starving milch-cow, its bones showing after a long winter, into a healthy beast with a calf beside it?

Long after dark, Frances pushed the long rolls of accounts aside and snuffed out the one stinking tallow candle that was all she allowed herself in the evenings. "The thing is just not possible," she repeated. Yawning, she stretched on her wooden stool and rubbed both fists into her eyes like a sleepy child. But sleep was far from her mind. The hours with the rent rolls had served only to reinforce what she already knew, and to distract her from the new threats hinted at by Donald.

Would he really connive to turn over the lordship of Beauly to Glencairn? Such a threat set at naught her first plan of letting Donald sit at Beauly until the boredom of rural life, or a few "accidents," convinced him he would be happier in the city. She would have to play for time, convince him he stood to gain more from a prospering estate under her guidance than from any promises Glencairn might make. But how?

Frances took the unanswered question up to bed with her. She needed no candle to find the way; every inch of the castle was familiar to her. She gained her own room without disturbing anyone. After Lord Gair's death she had refused to take his chamber; there would always be ghosts there for her. Instead she had had rooms cleaned and furnished for her and Hugh in the newer wing of the castle that was built like a manor house, with latticed windows and paneled walls. Having their own suite of rooms cast an appearance of normality over the marriage, though it was common knowledge that they slept separately.

Frances' chamber was simply furnished with a large bed hung with curtains of plain serge, a press for clothes, and a basin and ewer set on a table against the wall. Frances kept her few treasured books locked in the clothes press, where Hugh would not be tempted to take them out and play with them if he came into her room.

Tonight she was too tired to unlock the clothes press and lay her clothes neatly away. A personal maidservant was another of the luxuries she had dispensed with in the unending struggle to keep the estate solvent and Donald satisfied; the girl who looked after Aunt Grizel also laundered and pressed Frances' linen, and she took care of her personal necessities herself. This evening she did not even trouble to light a candle, but laid her outer clothes across the press to be put away in the morning and sponged herself off at the basin in the dark. The cold water raised goose pimples on her flesh and she was thankful to climb into the bed and sink into the comfort of the feather mattress.

"Frances?"

The sleepy murmur from the other side of the bed wakened her at once. A flash of fear coursed through her body and stiffened her muscles; then she relaxed as she recognized Hugh's voice. Poor child, he must have been lonely and scared this evening, after all Donald's teasing! He would have crawled into her bed for comfort.

"Frances." The voice was more assured now, and the muscular arm that encircled her was not a child's. "Donald told me to wait for you here. He told me what to do. Do you want me to show you?"

Frances pushed unavailingly at Hugh's arm and froze in revulsion at the feel of his body pressed against hers. "I know what married people do now," the whisper continued in the darkness. "Donald showed me. We've been doing it all wrong, Frances."

A hand scrabbled between her thighs, and Hugh planted a sticky wet kiss on her neck. Frances twisted away from him and jabbed her elbow into his ribs. Letting out a cry of surprise, Hugh let go of her. Frances rolled to the side of the bed and wrapped the holland sheet about her.

"Hugh, that's wrong. You must not be sleeping in my bed. Indeed, you must not!"

For a moment she could not tell whether her sharp words had penetrated his fuddled brain. A shifting of weight on the bed warned her that he was moving closer, and she scrambled backward off the bed with undignified haste.

"No . . . no, wait, Hugh!" With shaking hands she lit a candle.

The first sight of Hugh's tear-streaked face reassured her.

"Are you angry, Frances? I didn't mean to hurt you. Donald said you'd like me better if we did it."

Frances found herself stroking Hugh's tousled hair to comfort him. "It's all right, Hughie lad," she murmured. "Donald is not understanding our ways. I like ye fine now, Hugh. Only you must not be coming into my bed again."

"Mustn't come into your bed," Hugh repeated like an obedient child. He sniffled and crawled out of the tangle of holland sheets.

Frances swallowed and looked away hastily at the sight of his powerful naked body. His mind might never have got beyond childhood, but she and Aunt Grizel had been wrong to keep treating him as a helpless child. The poor confused mind was housed in the body of a mature man.

"Jesu, only look at you, Hugh. You'll catch cold. Here, wrap this around you." She gave him one of the warm woolen plaids from the bed and he obediently clutched it around his body like a cloak. "Now, go on back to your own bed. Hurry, now."

The familiar tones, half-scolding, half-indulgent, reassured Hugh, and he shuffled down the corridor to his own room without protest. Frances saw him safely into bed before she took the candle and returned to her own room.

For the first time she regretted that her door had no bolt on it. Since the three days she'd spent imprisoned in that tiny room before Lord Gair's death, she had had an unreasoning horror of enclosed places and being locked in. Many nights her door stood open to the cold draft, just to reassure her that in this much, at least, she was still free. But now she pushed the heavy door shut and dragged the clothes press to stand before it.

She did not think Hugh would trouble her again that night, but she had a horror of again enduring his fumbling embraces in the dark. It was some time before she could even bring herself to blow out the candle, and then she lay long awake in the darkness, startling at the slightest noise. Finally she wrapped herself in the heaviest plaid and finished the night lying on the floor. The soft, enveloping feather bed had become hateful to her.

In the morning she was relieved to find that Donald had ridden out without leaving word of where he was going. For a few minutes she entertained the wild hope that he had given up on his attempt to extort more money from her and had simply returned to Edinburgh. But in that case, he would turn to Glencairn.

She was almost relieved when she saw two of his men lounging in the castle courtyard, picking their teeth and casting dice for the odd bits of their harness. But where were the others? The stable hand Peadir had complained yesterday of having to house five men of Donald's and their horses. Why would he take his men out riding with him?

When Frances asked Grizel, her aunt gave a start and dropped her tray of embroidery silks.

"Wheesht, child, how should I be knowing what

your brother does? Do you think he would confide in me?"

Frances nodded and helped her aunt pick up the scattered silks without considering that it was an oddly evasive answer for Grizel, who was usually plainspoken to a fault.

She was too nervous to go out herself that morning. Instead she spent the morning in the weaving room, sorting skeins of dyed and undyed wool and combing out the rolags of wool for tartans with long wooden combs until her wrists ached with the unaccustomed effort. She was too agitated to settle to the fiddling work of setting up the great loom with the complex sett of a tartan plaid, and she had never been skilled at the spinning.

By midday her hands were soft with the lanolin from the wool and her arms ached up to the elbows with the work of combing the rolags for spinning. The sound of hurrying feet in the hall was an excuse to leave the monotonous work for a few minutes.

Grizel was standing in the hall wringing her hands and crying, while Peadir stood before her, stammering excuses with muck from the stables still clinging to his bare legs.

"Aunt! What's the matter?" Frances came hurrying down the stairs, and both faces turned to her as if expecting an instant solution.

"Hughie's gone!" her aunt blurted out. "Puir

innocent lad. Was I not telling you to take him out with you yesterday, Frances? Now see what happens if you are leaving him alone. He will have taken his horse out all by himself, while this lazy loon was sleeping in the stables!"

Frances had to suppress a desire to laugh at her aunt's description of Hugh. "Puir innocent lad" indeed! She'd not have thought so if she could have seen him last night. Nor could Frances understand why Grizel was so upset.

"Hugh will be clever enough with the horses," she soothed her aunt. "Of course it was naughty of him to go out without anyone else, but it's certain I am that he'll be safe home soon as he is getting hungry—aye, and mightily proud of his adventure." She was not entirely sure that Hugh had the wit to find his way back to the castle from the glens, but every horse in the stables knew its way home.

"Aye, he'll be fine," agreed Peadir. "Dinna' they say that the daft ones always falls soft?"

This was no comfort to Grizel, who fell into renewed sobbing. "You don't understand! You don't understand!" she repeated, and then, "It's all my fault."

"Well, no, Aunt," Frances snapped, "I do not understand, nor can I until you tell me what is in it to fash ye so."

"He will have gone to meet Alasdair," Grizel whispered.

"To meet . . ." Frances froze, and then there

was a queer leap of something like hope in her breast.

How often, in the bleak nights of her first year of the mock marriage, had she dreamed that Alasdair was somehow come back to tell her it was all a mistake, to take her away with him? It had been a long, hard lesson she had learned, but finally she had schooled herself to the realities of life, as the long winter nights stretched on and no word came from Alasdair. He had never really cared for her, had run away at the first sign of trouble, and there would be no knight on a white horse to rescue her from her hard and lonely life. Only after acknowledging that to herself had she been able to find a measure of contentment in the life of the glen. It was cruel, cruel of Grizel to stir those useless hopes up again!

But Grizel was shaking her gray head. The wrinkles that ran from her nose to either corner of her thin mouth seemed to have deepened into great grooves in the last hours. "There's talk that he is back," she told Frances. "He was seen in Edinburgh three weeks ago."

"Three weeks!" Frances bit back a hysterical laugh. "Why so afeard now? If he was content to roister in the stews this long, he may well rot there." Her boned corsets felt tight, as if she could hardly breathe.

Why should it hurt so much, to know he'd been as close as Edinburgh, yet still could not trouble himself to come north to see her once? "I hope he does rot there," she added, and then a new thought struck her.

"Is that why Donald's here?" *Especially now,* he'd said, and then couldn't explain himself. Could this threat from Glencairn have anything to do with Alasdair's return?

"We thought it best not to tell you," Grizel admitted.

"Body of . . ." Frances bit back an oath. "Aunt, I'm not a child anymore, to be cosseted and protected. This castle and the folk of the glen are under my hand. I must be knowing what is happening here. And it sticks in my mind that there will be more you've not told. Why should Hugh ride out to meet Alasdair? Will he be coming here?"

Grizel nodded. Her white, bony hands twisted unavailingly at a small edge of trimming that had come unstitched from her skirt. "Donald left men to watch. This morning they said he'd been seen. Hugh must have overheard them and crept out after Donald left."

Frances frowned. "So? 'Tis but natural he should wish to see his cousin. Hugh aye worshiped Alasdair when he was here. But Donald . . ." She halted as a new and horrifying thought struck her. "Aunt, *why did Donald ride out to meet Alasdair*?" She bent over her weeping aunt as if she would shake her by the thin, bowed shoulders.

"Is it that he is meaning to kill him?" Without waiting for an answer, Frances turned sharply to pace up and down the hall. Her long skirts rustled on the stones as she walked. The constriction of the corsets was become well-nigh unbearable; there were black spots before her eyes. "Oh, brave! An ambush, is it? To kill an unarmed and unsuspecting man? Why does he hate Alasdair so? And you—you're but concerned lest Hugh be caught up in the fighting."

Grizel raised her head to face her niece's wrath. "I raised him from a wee lad," she said. "You and Alasdair, you were already half-grown when you came here for fostering. You never needed me. But Hugh would have died without my care. His mother dead, and Lord Gair wouldna' look at the puir thing with the big head on him. Wouldna' even have him put out to nurse, till I came home from court and insisted on it. Aye—Hughie was all mine. Even when he fair worshiped the pair of ye, you and Alasdair, he was mine first. Didn't I watch him all these years, to see he never wetted himself in the burn or fell when he tried to play your rough games? Didn't I see to it, when Gair died, that he had you to safeguard his inheritance? Donald would never ha' thought of it by himself. I've taken care of Hughie all these years, and now he's like to be killed between Donald and Alasdair. The puir innocent! The puir lad!" And she buried her face in her hands and burst into noisy weeping.

"Donald means to kill him." Frances was still taking the thought in. Grizel's hysterical behavior was all the confirmation she needed. "But . . . why?" And what was all this babble about how Grizel had seen to it that Hugh's inheritance was kept safe? She couldn't take it all in now, not with her aunt collapsing into hysterics. She turned to Peadir.

"You must send men out by the south road at once . . ." But Peadir was no longer there. Frances raised her voice to call after him, then realized it would do no good. Donald had been gone for hours. It would take hours more to gather up the crofters from their scattered farms, explain the urgency to them, and send them after him.

"What can I do?" she cried out aloud. "Blessed Mother, what can I do?"

Grizel stopped her weeping to look up. She was suddenly quiet, and a smile hovered about her lips. "You can wait, child, and pray. Like me. 'Tis a dreich employ, but it is all a woman can ever do. Time you were learning it."

6

Alasdair Cameron, late of Colonel Murray's brigade in the Low Countries, was not consciously expecting an ambush as he rode along the narrow boggy track that led to his home glen and Castle Beauly. But he had seen three years' hard campaigning in a land where few of the inhabitants could be considered friendly. As he rode with his two men, he kept his eye on features of the landscape that might provide shelter for an enemy—a stunted tree, a thicker-than-usual growth of heather, a turf hut, or an outcropping of rocks that leaned above the trail. It was almost out of habit.

With two-thirds of his mind he was enjoying the fresh clean scent of the heather and the line of the hills above the horizon. A braw country, after these years of a flat landscape broken only by occasional dikes and the more recent three weeks in Edinburgh's crowded and malodorous wynds. Alasdair inhaled deeply of the sweet air and let the free part of his mind wander to thoughts of home, and Frances.

The other one-third of his mind never ceased being a soldier.

For these reasons, and others, he reined in his horse some hundred yards short of the gorge where the river Beauly plunged downward between steep cliffs sparsely covered with tufts of heather and tough, pale grass. He motioned Duncan Dhu and Sandy Ruadh to come close beside him.

In the instant before they reached him, there was a flash of motion in the gorge before them.

With the unthinking reflexes of a trained soldier, Duncan whistled soundlessly between his teeth and half-raised his hackbut, ready to fire as soon as the rider drew clear of the bushes that concealed him. There was a brief glimpse of a bare head between two clumps of high bushes, and he took aim at the point where the path emerged from the gorge.

Then three things happened at once. Alasdair knocked Duncan's hackbut up, so that the shot whistled harmlessly overhead; the rider called out a cheery greeting, the words slightly slurred; and a body of armed men erupted from the other side of the path, where Alasdair's sharp eye had caught the glint of sunlight on mail somewhat earlier.

After that first warning, Alasdair had no time to look to his men. The first and heaviest of the men in mail galloped straight at him, cutting down the solitary unarmed rider with the first swing of a viciously curved steel half-moon that then came straight at Alasdair's neck. Alasdair spurred his horse forward, ducked under the first swing, came up inside the rider's guard, and drove his short dirk into the unprotected slit between headpiece and body armor. The impetus of the charge carried both riders away from each other. When Alasdair wheeled to return to the melee, there were two men lying on the ground. One rider spurred away across the moors to their left, and the remaining one was locked in hand-to-hand combat with Duncan Dhu. Sandy, temporarily blinded by a slashing cut across his forehead that poured blood down into his eyes, was fumbling for his hackbut.

Three years in Flanders do not leave much respect for the old knightly rules of single combat. Alasdair snatched the hackbut from Sandy's saddle bow and fired into the back of the third assailant at two yards' range. The man's mail coat exploded in a shower of metal and bloody flesh and he fell from his horse, dangling by one stirrup. The terrified animal threw up its head and would have dashed away, dragging the dying man, had not

Duncan halted it by a savage jerk on its trailing reins.

For a moment the scene was stilled, with no sound but the heavy breathing of the three men who'd survived the murderous attack. Then Sandy Ruadh broke out in a stream of curses as he struggled to wipe the blood from his eyes so that he could see.

Duncan was the first to collect his wits. "That third loon will ha' gone for help," he said, pointing over the moors. "Will we go after him, then?"

Alasdair, already dismounting, shook his head. "Not yet."

He knelt in the dust between the two men who had fallen at the beginning of the fight. One, the mailed man who had attacked him, lay still clutching the splintered shaft of his half-moon.

The other, the one who had fallen first, lay bareheaded in the dust, with blood and air bubbling from an open wound in his chest. At Alasdair's touch, Hugh opened his eyes and a weak smile moved his lips. "Coming . . . to meet you." He struggled for breath, and an ominous bubbling sound interrupted his words. "Heard Donald telling . . . You're not angry?"

Alasdair's face had darkened at the mention of Donald. Now he forced a smile to his own lips, and reached out to smooth Hugh's tangled straw-colored hair away from his face. "No, Hughie lad. How could I be angry with you?"

Behind him, Duncan Dhu shuffled his feet and cleared his throat. "The lad's done for, Alasdair. Will we wait here for them to come back and trap us, then?"

"I stay," Alasdair snapped over his shoulder. "You and Sandy do as you wish."

But when he turned back to Hugh, the time for waiting was over. Hugh's pale eyes had glazed over and he was staring up at the sky with the same puzzled look he had worn in life. The blood that had been spreading among the heather roots was already congealing into a dark puddle.

Alasdair closed his cousin's eyes and crossed his hands over his breast. There was no time to do more. He stood up. "I'll come back and see ye have a proper burial, Hugh," he promised. He swallowed convulsively. "It's the last thing I can do for him."

He turned on Duncan and Sandy with a bellow of rage. "And ye, ye slack-lipped gomerils, what were ye thinking of to let the boy ride into an ambush, and him the chief of the Camerons? Was not your first duty to him? Did ye no' see the mail glinting through the trees? Three years I've brought ye through the mud and stinking blood in Flanders, and for what? To come back and lead the Cameron to his death? Ye should have been guarding him! I could take care of myself!"

Duncan and Sandy endured the tirade in silence, understanding that it was only the expression of the grief Alasdair could not let himself voice in any tenderer way. Hugh had been cut down in the first seconds of the surprise attack; there had been no possibility of protecting him.

They took the upland route, a long detour over rocky hills and through passes where they had to dismount and lead the horses single file, while wild nesting birds screamed about their heads. Alasdair led them in a wide half-circle around the straight road to Beauly, first up across the hills until men accustomed to the straight level plains of Flanders were sobbing for breath and the muscles of their thighs trembled uncontrollably at every step; then down through stinking black bogs where the ground quivered underfoot and a single misstep could send a man down into the sucking black morass for good.

"An' I thought I knew the glens," whispered Sandy to Duncan at a brief halt where they let the horses drink from a black pool in the bog.

"He's run the hills since he was a boy," Duncan whispered back. "Some things you dinna' forget. The simpleton, now. Hughie fair worshiped him when they were bairns. That's what lays so hard on Alasdair now."

"But he'll bid fair to be the next chief, now," Duncan whispered back. "Donald did him a favor, getting Hugh into that ambush. Has he no' thought of that?"

"That too," said Duncan heavily. "That's what makes it so bad."

Alasdair strode back from the pool where he'd been dashing water over his face, and Duncan and Sandy fell silent like a pair of schoolboys.

"Stop gossiping like old women," he said, vaulting into the saddle, and motioned for them to follow him. "We've some way more to go before dark."

His face was still white and set, and the droplets of cold water that clung to his red hair and trickled down his forehead blended in with the mist that settled in upon them as night fell. They moved at a funereal pace through the white blankness, scarcely seeing each other's forms at a distance of a few feet. The dampness clung to their faces and clothes and condensed into droplets of water. The swirling whiteness seemed to swallow up all sound, even the clop of the horses' feet, so that they might have been moving through one of the enchanted lands of the Sidhe where all sound died.

Night fell and the white mist turned to blackness around them, but the rise of the ground under their feet signaled a return to higher ground where they might see clear when the moon rose. At the top of a ridge Alasdair signaled a halt. They fed the horses and themselves out of the hard flat bannocks in their saddlebags, and Duncan opened a flat leatherbound flask of spirits that put new heart into all of them.

"We'll wait here for moonrise," Alasdair told them. "Then around by the course of the Beauly."

He sketched out his plan, and Duncan nodded agreement. It was a daring throw of the dice, but it might work, if they could get into position this one night, before Donald would be expecting them.

Before night fell over Beauly, Donald had returned from his expedition. Only one of the three men who had gone with him came back. He refused to discuss what had happened to the other two, and claimed to have seen nothing of Hugh. His one concern seemed to be that the castle should be shuttered and locked as if they were expecting an immediate attack.

"You'll not shut the main gate." Unexpectedly it was Grizel, not Frances, who opposed him. "Not until Hugh comes back."

She stood in the path of the gate, arms crossed in a defiant attitude. The men whose shoulders were poised against the weight of the gate—two Camerons and a Murray—exchanged doubtful glances.

Donald moved to Grizel's side and put one arm around her skinny shoulders. "Aunt, forgive me. I didna' want to tell ye this—not yet."

She looked into his set face for some measure of hope, but found none.

"Hugh is dead. Killed by that murdering bastard Alasdair, as the lad rode out to welcome him home. My man saw it, but came too late to save him."

Grizel's screams brought Frances running from the stillroom. She found her aunt laying in the dust, Donald kneeling beside her with a helpless and yet satisfied look on his face.

"Help me get her inside, you useless lumps," she snapped at the men. Two of them dropped the work of preparation and started forward to help Frances.

With some effort she got her aunt quieted, indoors, and in her bed, but without gathering more than a garbled sense that something terrible had happened. When Grizel was quiet, with Janet to bathe her temples with lavender water and give her small sips of wine and water, Frances confronted Donald.

He repeated the story he'd given Grizel, but with some embellishments.

"He means to return and take the castle and lands from you. I did not want to tell you before, for fear of alarming you, but now you see . . ." He spread his hands. "You're a widow now, Frances."

"I am not believing it." Behind her mask of indifference, Frances' brain was working at top speed. Hugh dead—and she free! She did not know whether to weep or rejoice first. She'd prayed for freedom, but without visualizing the price. But one thing was clear to her. "Alasdair would never have killed Hugh."

"Frances, I'm sorry." Donald enclosed her hand in his two meaty paws. "My man here saw the body."

"And did not bring him back for proper burial?" Frances jerked her hand free.

"Alas, he dared not. Alasdair's men would have killed him too, as they did the other witnesses. He barely got away at the risk of his life."

The account of the brief and bloody fight had been convincingly detailed. In the account Frances heard, Alasdair had attacked Hugh first, then gone for Donald's men, who were coming to his aid but arrived too late. She could visualize the details of the brief and bloody scene—three of Donald's men confronting an unspecified number of hard-bitten veterans of the Flanders campaign, over Hugh's body bleeding in the dust. Sickened, she leaned against the wall for support.

"I'll not believe it," she repeated dully.

Alasdair had been ten times more patient and protective of Hugh than she ever had. The memory of a thousand small moments rose up like bile in her throat—all the times she'd brushed Hugh aside, omitted a kind word or smile when she knew they meant so much to him, left him alone in the darkness of his mind while she bustled about being the keeper of Beauly. The times when she'd been too busy to admire the brightly colored stones, the curiously twisted sticks, the bird's eggs and butterflies he brought her.

All those little things now added up to so much more than the terrifying moments of last night. She was ashamed to acknowledge her own sense of relief that she would not have to fear another night like that. Tears slid down her face and collected in the folds of her starched ruff. Half-blinded, she could not see the considering smile on Donald's face as he watched her.

"As I recall," he reminded her, "you were loath to believe it when Alasdair abandoned you three years ago. Grow up, Frances. He's a self-centered killer who cares for nothing but Beauly, and you're a widow now. Thank God you have a brother here to protect you."

And he left her there weeping against the wall, while he strode off to supervise the preparations for defense.

By moonlight the walls of Beauly looked calm and peaceful. No sign was visible of the frenzied preparations against siege which Donald had made in the closing hours of the day. Truth to tell, there had not been much he could do, beyond closing and barring the main gate and setting guards at the outer wall. There was not time to bring in additional provisions, and Frances had flatly refused to call in the crofters from their fields to work at shoring up the crumbling inner wall and blocking the low windows of the manor wing.

Donald had grumbled that he should command the clan as her guardian, but he had not been willing to bring it to a test of authority. There had been sullen looks enough when he told the peasants coming up from the peat cutting that Beauly would spare no beasts to drag the peat sledges until this danger was past, yet refused them and their families sanctuary in the castle.

"I'll hear it from Lady Frances hersel'," grumbled Euan, the spokeman for the little group.

Donald twitched his fingers behind his back, and his three remaining men stepped forward, one raising a wound crossbow.

"You'll take orders from me in future," Donald said.

The bare-legged men had retreated, muttering to each other and scraping their coarse goathide shoes on the stones of the bailey, but they had not directly challenged his authority. Donald felt well enough pleased with his achievements for the first day. Getting Hugh killed had been no part of his plan, but it had been a lucky accident—the more so, as he could pin it on Alasdair. Now, if he could but keep the castle locked up safe until Alasdair saw there was no welcome for him here . . .

Within the week, he promised himself, he'd be master of Beauly in all but name. His first impulse of defending the castle against siege had been but a moment of panic, as though he'd been fool enough to believe his own tale of Alasdair marching with a small army to take by force what he could not inherit by right. What sort of siege could be mounted by three homeless soldiers returning from the wars? Let alone, Frances might have let him in and been swayed by his smooth talk. That was the worst danger he had to face, and he'd adroitly circumvented that by getting in first with his story. Let Alasdair see his case was hopeless here, and he'd go back to Edinburgh to drink himself sodden and enlist again.

As for Frances, she was but a woman. When the shock of her loss was over, she'd be glad enough to let him rule matters as he should have been doing all along. Then he could put the choice to her again: either maintain him in the state proper to the lord of Beauly or hand over all to their kinsman of Glencairn. His case was even stronger now that Hugh was dead; the king would never hear of the glen being held by a woman without some kinsman to guide her. Yes, a lucky accident.

Donald picked his teeth and the bones of a roasted fowl alternately, thinking over his good fortune until the wine he'd imbibed so freely over dinner overcame him and he sank into an uneasy sleep.

By midnight, when the full moon shone high over the castle, Frances was the only one left awake. The guards had responded to Donald's sense of relaxation by falling asleep over their pikes, Grizel was snoring off the effects of some herbal nostrum brought by Janet from the stillroom, and the handful of servants were sleeping around the embers of the kitchen fire. Only Frances was left to pace restlessly up and down the stairs of the keep.

The changes of the day had been too many for her to assimilate until now, when at last she was alone. Hugh dead . . . Alasdair near . . . and Donald proclaiming himself lord of Beauly! Frances clutched her forehead as though it would split in two. How much truth was there in Donald? How much of his story could she trust?

That Hugh was dead she believed, whether by accident or at his hands. He'd not have moved so quickly to make capital of her widowhood if he had any fear of Hugh returning. But Alasdair? Mighty convenient for Donald, she thought cynically, if another claimant appeared to take the blame for Hugh's death, then disappeared into the mists of the Highland night. Otherwise, folk might question the "accident" that left Donald so conveniently in a position of power.

They'd heard no word of Alasdair since he went to the wars. For all they knew, he might have been killed in the fighting in Flanders. Perhaps Donald did know that, and was but using his name to cover up the murder.

A stab of pain shot through Frances at the thought, followed by guilt that she felt so little grief for Hugh and so much at the mere thought that Alasdair might be dead. She murmured a contrite prayer and vowed that in the morning she would take a party out to search for his body and bring it back for proper burial.

Frances' musings had carried her from the keep

to the newer manor wing of the castle. This wing was not so well fortified as the tower, since the inner wall could not encircle it completely. The wall stopped at the cliffs on the north side, and for several hundred yards the castle's only defenses were those jagged cliffs that fell straight to the rushing waters of the river Beauly where it poured through the narrow gorge.

Even the windows on the side facing the cliffs were too large for proper defense, filled with a latticework of small glass panes, as if to mark the builders' arrogant confidence that none could breach the natural defenses created by the river gorge and the cliffs. More than once, when they were children, Alasdair and Frances had used those same windows to take unauthorized leave from their tasks, climbing down the steep cliffs like spiders clinging to a wall, and jumping from stone to stone across the river rapids until they reached the freedom of the hills.

We were mad, Frances thought with a reminiscent shudder. If Aunt Grizel had ever guessed their escape route, she would have fainted twice—once for the danger they ran, and once for fear Hugh might be tempted to follow them. Frances pushed open one of the leaded casements and leaned out to survey the sheer drop of the cliffs, white now in the moonlight, and the thin black strand of the river below.

The stark light picked out in relief the crevices

of the cleft they'd used to climb up and down, a thin broken line that disappeared into the inky blackness of the gorge. Frances stared at it, trying to retrace their path, until her eyes failed and the path seemed to be moving before her.

She rubbed her eyes and stared again. No, it was no illusion. There were new shadows that did not belong on the face of the cliff. Shadows that moved in and out of the crevices she remembered, tracing hand- and footholds with agonizing patience. They had come nearly to the top of the cliff now, or she'd not have been able to make them out. And it was still impossible to identify the shadowy figures. The moonlight bleached all colors out to a ghostly landscape. Even a head blazing with red hair like a fire would look cold and pale in this light. But Frances had no doubts.

She left the casement swinging wide open and retreated into a dark corner of the room. She had not long to wait. The intruders found the open window, and she saw the shadow of the first man cast long across the floor.

One after another they jumped in, landing lightly on stocking feet. Three men. A burly figure that might have been Duncan Dhu; a stocky younger man who could have been Sandy Ruadh grown up; and last, the slim figure that haunted her dreams.

Alasdair did not scramble across the sill like his friends, but vaulted it with one hand, landing on the floor as lightly as a dancer. Frances caught her breath, remembering how he'd delig trick as a boy. She had tried and trie him, but had not the strength in arms a -ders that he'd built up in hours of tedious [illegible]aining at swordplay and at the archery butts.

She heard him giving low-voiced instructions to the other two men; then they moved off and he stood for a while alone in the center of the room, gazing up at the high carved beams as if lost in some memory.

Some instinct warned him before she moved. He sprang toward the corner, one hand on the dirk at his waist.

"Alasdair." Frances came out of the shadow before he could challenge her.

He gave a low, exultant laugh and caught her round the waist with both hands, swinging her up in the air and down again to rest in his arms. "Frances! Now I know my luck's in." His lips just grazed hers—a hasty, unsatisfactory kiss—and he set her down again. "Donald?"

"In the tower keep. Asleep over his wine."

"How many men?"

"Only the three, I think. But you—"

"Duncan's gone to open the gate," he told her. "There are more outside. Euan and a few others were not so happy to hear Donald styling himself lord of Beauly."

Frances caught her breath. "He dared that? Mother of God! It's myself will have the head of him."

Alasdair laughed and caught her wrist. "Not so fast, my little spitfire. I've plans for Donald myself. Just show me where he sleeps. I'd like fine to have him safe before the sounds of the fighting waken him." He paused and looked down at her, his eyes deep pits of shadow in a face that might have been carved of marble. "Frances . . . ye know about Hugh?"

Speechless, she nodded.

"It was an accident, Frances. Donald's men set upon us, and he was in the middle."

"Donald said . . . you meant to kill him."

"You didna' believe him." It was a statement, not a question. Alasdair bent, brushed his lips across the wrist he still held, then tugged at her lightly. "Come on, now, show me where this 'lord of Beauly' sleeps tonight."

And, as always, Frances was swept along in the wake of his energy, all her questions unanswered and all her longings unsatisfied.

7

But for an unlucky accident, the castle might have been taken without a blow struck in anger. Donald, snoring over the remains of his roast and wine, was bound before he was well awake, with a strip torn from his own sleeve stuffed in his mouth lest he should call and alert his men. There were three guards left, and the two sleeping in the hall were taken as easily as Donald had been, by Duncan, Sandy, and a group of crofters led by Euan. They hustled the prisoners into a locked stone-walled pantry for safekeeping before the victims had time to lay hands on their arms.

But the third man had been the one who fled the ambush and reported it to Donald. He was no

Murray man, but a servant of Glencairn's placed in Donald's entourage to report on him to the earl. He had not made the mistake Donald had, of underrating Alasdair and putting his trust in the castle's walls. Between a fat, stupid lordling behind stone walls, and the lean tough man who'd killed his two mates in the river gorge, he knew which he'd back for a fight.

And so he'd been intermittently wakeful through the first part of the night. It was sheer bad luck that Frances' light step, as she passed through the hall on her way to the manor wing, had chanced to disturb his troubled slumbers; worse luck that he was neither sleeping with his mates nor watching the gate when Duncan and Sandy stole through to open Beauly to the crofters. Instead he had stumbled into a corner of the outer bailey to relieve himself of some of the ale he'd downed on his return to the castle. He watched from the shadows while the gate was opened and the crofters stole in, and then made his way to the stables, where he quietly saddled a fresh horse. He might have escaped the castle unobserved had he not chanced to step on Peadir's outflung hand as he led the horse out of the stables.

Peadir woke with a yell that died away into a gurgle as the soldier's dirk found his throat. He flung himself into the saddle and kicked the horse into a gallop, heading straight for the open gate. But the damage was done, the castle alerted. Shouts from within and torches springing to life spread from the hall to the rest of the tower keep as the soldier bent low over his horse's neck and galloped for freedom.

In the darkness of the keep, no one knew who was friend or foe. There were some sweaty, cursing moments and some blows struck amiss in the darkness before enough torches were lit to count men and establish that Donald had, in fact, no more supporters than the two men captured in the hall. In fact, the keep was well-nigh empty. Every man who could be spared had been out working the fields, taking advantage of the brief dry season to prepare the land for the summer's planting. If Donald had only his two servants and the one man who'd escaped, Frances and Alasdair had only Duncan, Sandy, the five crofters who'd come with Euan, and the castle servants. These last, not being on one side more than another, had mostly disappeared into whatever discreet hiding places they could find. Grizel had locked herself in her room, and her maidservant Janet was hiding in a linen press.

Alasdair ordered Donald brought down from his sleeping chamber in the upper levels of the keep to the great hall, where torches were lit. He should stand hostage until the castle was searched and they knew whether any more of his men were there. When Duncan reported that the castle was clear, Frances and Alasdair stood staring at each other over Donald's bound body until Alasdair gave an uneasy laugh and sheathed his sword. "That will be the lot, then, mistress? A pity one of them got away."

Frances nodded without speaking. After the long waiting and wondering of the day, this brief violent reunion had left her entirely unsure of herself. At first she'd been eager to aid anyone who would help her against Donald and his plans. Now she stared at this lean, tanned man in his steel helmet and padded leather coat, and wondered whether she had not delivered herself into the hands of someone worse than Donald—more competent, more ruthless.

She hardly felt as though she could recognize Alasdair's boyish visage in this grim soldier's face with the scarred temple. Who was he—this man who'd run away three years ago, and now returned as a conqueror? And now that he had so quickly disposed of Donald and taken the castle, what were his plans for her? A sudden draft blew through the hall, making the torches fixed on the walls shake, and Frances gave an involuntary shiver. But she kept on watching Alasdair, waiting for a clue to his plans.

Alasdair's eyes dropped first. He turned to Duncan, who stood with his sword in one hand, waiting for the order to slit Donald's throat. "Take this"—he pointed contemptuously at Donald, pale and straining against his gag—"out of our way.

There's a wee room on the ground floor of the old keep that has a good thick door and bars on the windows. It'll do to hold him for the night. No, don't kill him. I've my own plans." His smile was unpleasant.

He watched, still smiling in that grimly withdrawn manner, while Duncan and Sandy hoisted Donald up and carried him down the steep steps to the bottom floor of the keep. When they were gone, he turned to Frances. His smile changed, lightened, and a devil's flame danced in his eyes. The reflection of the torches, Frances told herself. But her throat tightened.

"Frances." He pushed his steel helm back with one hand and dropped it on the rushes behind him. It bounced on the stone with a series of hollow clangs that echoed through the stone-walled rooms of the keep. "I've waited long for this."

His hands were hard, callused, a soldier's hands. The roughness of his skin, the gentleness of his touch as he slid his hands up her bare arms under the wide sleeves, made her shiver. Fear or desire? She could no longer separate the two.

He drew her to him, and the velvet of her gown met the old patched leather of his coat, but their straining bodies were still separated. He bent her head back and her lips parted for him. It was a conqueror's kiss, plundering, invading her mouth.

Frances shivered, torn between fear and desire. The uncertain boy who'd loved her beside the

Beauly was gone forever, replaced by this hard man who took what he wanted. Who wanted her. Who could make her knees go weak with his kiss. . . .

She put her hands to his shoulders and felt the hard swell of muscle under his coat. His hands slid under her chemise until they were topped by the hard edge of her whalebone stays.

"What the devil . . . ?" He disentangled himself from the embrace and swore in a tongue unknown to her. Frances laughed at this first check to his confidence, and found her own restored. "You must not have loved many fine ladies in Flanders," she teased. "Have ye no' heard of stays?"

"I've heard of ladies with the decency to take them off when their lovers came calling." His hands were fumbling with the back of her gown. "Devil take these clasps! Darling mine, I'm delighted to be caught in the net of your long black curls but I fear I'm all unhandy as a lady's maid. What happened to the ragged Highland girl I used to know?"

The reminiscence was like a shock of cold water to Frances. What had happened, indeed, that she should fall like a ripe plum into his hands as soon as he deigned to remember her? She slipped from his grasp and stepped back a pace.

"Many things have happened that you know nothing of, Alasdair," she answered. "Perhaps we should talk about them before we go further."

Alasdair came after her with arms outstretched, but she deftly sidestepped and evaded him. "No! Body of God, you left me without a word, and now you think to have me like one of your tavern sluts? I tell you, Alasdair, there will be either more or less between us than that." And with an aching heart she thought that the truth would have to be less, much less. She could not bind herself to a man so faithless. She could not cut the cord that bound him to her heart.

"Oh, Alasdair!" she cried in real pain. "Why could you no' have stayed by me when Lord Gair died? I'd never have deserted you so! Now it is too late. We canna' be going back to what we were."

Alasdair's hands dropped to his sides and he stared at her with an expression of stunned disbelief.

"Yes," he said after a long silence. "Yes. You're right."

Frances' heart sank. Had she still, childishly, been hoping he could explain his desertion of her?

"We have to talk. But . . . not here." He laughed and flung up one hand in the gesture of a swordsman calling for a respite, and in the gay lift of his head Frances thought she saw something of the boy she had known. "Surely this castle, poor though it's become, can boast two chairs and a private room?"

Frances nodded. "The manor wing?" She felt more sure of herself, acting as hostess. She picked up her long, full skirts and led the way out of the hall. Alasdair followed her with a torch.

Settled in the room Lord Gair had optimistically called a library, with its deep carved wooden benches and two precious books chained to a table, she felt unsure of herself once again. Alasdair had lit a branch of tallow candles, wrinkling his nose at the smell.

"Sorry I am they're not fine wax for your lordship," Frances snapped, humiliated by what she took to be a slight on her housekeeping. "Beauly's not one of your rich Southron domains. Perhaps you've forgotten that?"

"No, but it used to be able to support the chief of the clan in relative comfort."

Alasdair ignored the bench on the other side of the table and perched himself on the table near her, booted feet swinging. Against her will Frances was aware of the lean, hard thighs and the powerful arms that supported him in his casual pose.

"What's happened, Fan? Could you not keep up the estate after old Gillivray passed on? When I heard you'd taken Hugh after all, I cursed you for a mercenary bitch. But from the looks of it, you got little good from the marriage."

Even in the little light cast by the tallow candles, the signs of neglect and poverty were plain to see. Even Frances' much-mended dress of black velvet had grown rusty with age. Seeing the room and herself through Alasdair's eyes, Frances felt shamed. He must think little of Beauly after the rich foreign places he'd known. And what, she wondered, did he think about her?

Alasdair put one hand on her shoulder and gently forced her to turn toward him, to face the light. He spoke as if nothing more than idle curiosity impelled him, but his face was taut and there were deep lines graven at the corners of his mouth. "What made you do it, Fan? Could you not be waiting for me? Or was Beauly too much temptation?"

Frances could hardly believe the words she heard. She felt as though she must choke if she sat there any longer under his hand. She struck his hand aside with a violent gesture of repudiation, jumped up, and stood facing him.

"Wait for you! Wait for what? You told me we should be handfasted, and then you hadna' the courage to face Gair yoursel', but ran away to the army. What a boy's trick! Wait for you, you who couldna' keep faith even for three days? You who never troubled yourself to inquire after me all these years? What should I have waited for—for you to ride back in here in your own fair time, booted and spurred like the great conqueror, and announce that now you're ready to take your lordly pleasure?"

The bile of anger rose in her throat. Let him pay now for her empty, wasted years. "You call me mercenary. I am thinking that is the name for a soldier like yourself, who fights for the siller of foreigners rather than to stay and fight for his ain people. What were you thinking that I would do? There was Lord Gair dying, and yourself run away. With no *man* to lean on, he turned to me to keep faith. D'you think old Lachlan and his pack of wolfhound sons would ha' sat quietly by and seen Hugh inherit? Gair begged me to marry his son and hold the clan together. On his deathbed he begged me, and I . . . I kept faith. But you would not be understanding such a thing, I'm thinking."

Abruptly she stopped. What was the good of telling him about the nights she'd waited and prayed that somehow he would come back to her, the lonely nights when her body ached for a man, the bleak days when she knew herself tied for life to a child in a man's body? Let him think, if he would, that she'd not grieved for him long. Pride was all she had left, and that was little enough.

"I kept Beauly," she said, more quietly. "The people would accept Hugh as Lord Gair's son and the rightful heir, so long as they knew they could come to me. As to where the money's gone—to Donald, mostly. Are you thinking I have had an easy life of it here? A good allowance I pay to keep him in the South, where he made no trouble for us. Whenever he came here, it took weeks to get Hugh quieted again. And I couldna' raise the rents. We've had hard years here. The people would have starved, or been out to lift cattle from the Murray country, and that would ha' given Glencairn the excuse he wanted to take over, claiming I couldna' hold my clan. But I managed!"

She lifted her head and flung the words at him proudly, defiantly. "I kept Donald, Glencairn, and Lachlan all from starting clan war over the land. I've been chief of the clan where Hugh could not do it. And now you and Donald ha' killed him between you, and there'll be war and burnings in the glen, and all I promised Lord Gair to keep us from."

She slumped back in her chair and leaned over the table, feeling the weariness of defeat. The time was past when she could have responded to Alasdair as a woman, she thought. She'd spent too long in planning and contriving for the clan. Even his betrayal of her was little compared to the disaster that was about to overtake the Camerons of Beauly.

"Frances." His voice was gentle, belying the harsh lines carved in his face by years of war. "Frances, who told you I'd . . . run away?"

"Does it matter?" If only he would go now, and let her sleep. It seemed years since she'd slept untroubled.

She could have laughed at the irony, if there'd been laughter left in her. So many nights she'd lain awake and aching for the memory of Alasdair. Last night she'd lain awake in fear of her lawful husband's touch. And tonight? She would sleep alone again. The only difference was that now she had a place in society. Now she was a widow.

Alasdair would not leave her alone. "I did not leave you, Frances. Look at me!"

The note of command in his voice roused her. She looked up and saw him touching the ragged scar that ran from one eyebrow across his forehead, to vanish under the thick red hair. "Did you think I got this in battle? One of Donald's men knocked me on the head and put me on the Leith packet full of men for Flanders."

He laughed harshly. "I thought myself a man who could protect you, and I was only a kid-napped boy. I didna' come to my senses till we were days out. When we landed, the captain of the troop had a letter about me, from Donald to his kinsman Colonel Murray. I was kept in irons till we were in the camp, another two days' march. Then Colonel Murray showed me the rest of the letter. It said you'd wedded Hugh of your own free will, the day after Donald caught us. The priest had signed to attest to it."

"Lies. They lied to you as they did to me." Frances felt sick with revelation. She swayed and caught at the table for support. A carved head on the arm of the wooden bench seemed to wink at her in the flickering candlelight. "They kept me locked up for three days, then said you'd gone. I'd seen you—so I thought—in the courtyard. Walking about freely. And heard you whistling. Then . . . Lord Gair was dying. I was telling you how it was with me, then."

Alasdair nodded. "The devil's own tangle. I thought . . . Forgive me, Frances. You know what I thought. I was a proud young fool. I knew how you loved Beauly. Though I couldna' blame you for doing what you could to stay in the glen. I was a landless man with no better prospect than to be Hugh's factor. It seemed you'd made a logical choice."

"Logical." This time Frances could not restrain her laughter. "Oh, Alasdair, Alasdair!"

She flung her arms about his waist where he sat on the corner of the table, buried her face in his leather coat, and laughed into the shabby patched material. "You were too long at the law in Edinburgh, at that! When was a Cameron ever logical?" She raised her head and looked up at him again, her eyes wet with tears of laughter. "But what brought you back, after so long?"

"I came for you. What else? I wearied for you sore, Frances. I couldna' put you from my mind."

They were the words she'd wanted to hear. Why could she not take them at face value?

"And you were looking first in the stews of Leith and Edinburgh?" She could not help the sarcasm.

Alasdair leaned back against the table, supporting his weight with both arms. A trick of the light made him look older, deepened the lines in his face. "I lost my courage. If you'd chosen Hugh of your own will, what was I to do about it? And what place would there be for me here? I, too, promised Lord Gair I'd protect Hugh. I couldna' take you away from him and Beauly. I'd naught to offer you—why should you go with a landless man who lives by his sword, who couldna' even wed you? So . . ." A harsh laugh, revealing much of what he'd gone through in those weeks in Edinburgh. "I drank. Mother of God, how I drank! Duncan and me found every low . . . You don't want to hear about that."

"Yes, I do," Frances corrected him.

Alasdair studied her, and the corners of his mouth lifted in an unwilling smile, while one red eyebrow twitched up to match them. "Mayhap you do. No sense of shame or decency, Grizel always said! But I am not proposing to tell you. All that matters is: Donald drinks too, and he canna' hold it. I heard somewhat of his plans, and rode north to warn you. But he was before me . . . and, as you say, poor Hughie got caught between us. One of Donald's men killed him, first blow out of the ambush. It might ha' been planned, might not. I canna' say; I was busy there for a few minutes."

He stopped, stood erect, and spread his hands as if waiting for a judgment. "There's how it was. Can you forgive me, Frances? You're free now, but God be my witness, I never meant it to come this way."

His very reluctance to accuse Donald of planned murder convinced Frances as nothing else could. She moved forward into his waiting arms and felt them close around her, holding her against his heart in a clasp not to be broken. "I believe you, Alasdair. As you said—it's been the devil's own tangle."

She raised one hand to his neck and felt the pulse of life beating strongly under the warm skin. Her fingers brushed over the triangle exposed by his open shirt and she felt him tremble with desire. His arms tightened convulsively around her and she knew a wild exultant singing in her blood, a dizzy feeling that she'd thought never to know again.

"Tomorrow's for mourning, Alasdair," she whispered, no longer caring if he thought her forward. "Tonight is for us."

Alasdair hugged her to him exultantly. "Tomorrow's for the priest," he corrected her. "I mean to wed ye, Frances. But I canna' wait for that."

Somehow, she knew not how, they made their way up the stairs of the manor wing in the dark, whispering and giggling like children. The room she'd made into her bedchamber was dark, all but a sliver of moonlight that came in at the window.

Alasdair unhooked her gown and let it slide to the floor, but the tightly laced stays defeated him again. "How the devil do you women abide these things?" He held her away from him by the slim waist and teased, "Perhaps I'll leave them on. Perhaps I'll content myself with admiring the picture you make in your shift, your long black hair down and your skin so white in the moon."

His control broke; he pulled her into his lap and buried his face and hands in her black curls. "A man could drown in this sea. . . ." His hands were hot and urgent, seeking under her shift and above the edges of her stays, finding the tender flesh wherever it was free. In spite of herself, Frances knew a moment of fear. Just so had Hugh fumbled at her last night. . . .

Sensitive to her slightest hint of withdrawal, Alasdair stopped at once and freed her. "Frances? Is aught wrong?"

She shook her head but could not refrain from glancing at the great tester bed where Hugh had surprised her the previous night, as if to reassure herself that he was not lying there again.

"The bed you shared with Hugh." Alasdair made to rise from his chair, but Frances pressed him down again.

"No, Alasdair." Her cheeks flamed, but it must be said. "Hugh . . . never shared my bed. We lived as brother and sister." She gave an unsteady laugh. "I think he never knew aught else, till Donald put notions into his head. . . . But I would not have done that, Alasdair. Not for the clan—not for anything."

By the relieved look on Alasdair's face, she knew she had been right to tell him what he would have discovered anyway in a few minutes. Had he been torturing himself, all these lonely years, with the vision of her bedded down with half-witted, dribbling Hugh for the pleasure of enjoying his lands and title? No wonder he'd cursed her in his mind.

"So, Frances." He gathered her in his arms again, but this time his touch was gentler. "So this is your wedding night? Did I frighten you? I promise to go slowly, sweetheart. I'll not hurt you. Do you want to wait for the priest?"

"No." Frances slipped from his lap and stood before him, proud in her bare shoulders and legs, conscious of the rosy tips of her breasts that were pushed up by the stays and barely covered by her long black curls. "I am wanting you, Alasdair. No priest can change what's between us. And I am not afraid." To prove her point, she reached forward and began undoing the laces of his shirt.

Alasdair groaned in pleasure at the gentle, tantalizing touch of her fingers. She began to make a game of it, undoing each crossing ever so slowly, leaning forward to give him a good view of her full white breasts. When he reached for her, a gentle pressure of her fingertips warned him that he was to stay in the chair until she was finished. He strained his head forward, but his lips could barely brush the white curves so temptingly exposed to his gaze.

Even that mere breath of a touch excited Frances almost past bearing. She felt her nipples stiffen in response and a warm excitement sprang up between her thighs. But the more she prolonged the game, the more intoxicating it became. She let her fingers play across his bared chest with each lace that she untied, reveling in the rapid rise and fall of his breath and the pounding pulse in his throat. Soon, soon she would cool the fever in her blood. Soon she would know what she had only dreamed about in her involuntary, half-shamed night visions. But this was no dream.

"Body of God, sweeting." Alasdair twisted in the chair as her soft fingers stroked lower and lower. "I promised to go slowly, not to let you torture me to death!"

Frances laughed softly, exultant in her new power. The singing in her blood was very demanding now. She turned and presented him with the taut laces of her stays.

"I'm a lucky man." Alasdair's hands roved over the soft curves of her hips before he started to work on the laces. His fingers spread and gripped her there with a foretaste of the urgency that was to come. "Tonight I get one dream fulfilled, and tomorrow another."

At Frances' startled jerk, he grinned. "No, sweeting, I didna' mean another woman. Only that tomorrow I'll hold Beauly twice over—by my own right of inheritance, and by right of marriage to you."

Frances felt as if cold water had been dashed over her. She pushed his roving hands away and turned to face him. "Is that what you will be marrying me for? A way to get Beauly?"

"Why, no need," Alasdair said. He reached for her again. "What a tiny waist you have, sweetheart. I can almost put my hands around it. Don't they feed you here? . . . But I'm the next in line to inherit Beauly, nearest in blood to Gair."

"After me," Frances corrected sharply.

Alasdair laughed. "Well, yes, but they'd never take a woman as chief, any more than they'd have accepted Hugh alone."

It was an unfortunate comparison. Frances slapped his hands away and retreated to the edge of the bed, paces away from him. "So you think I'm of no more account than a lackwit? I wonder you trouble to marry me, then."

"Frances—Fan—you know I was not meaning it that way." Alasdair advanced toward her, his hands outspread for an embrace—or for a trap? Frances thought sharply. "I only meant, you and I together, we'll keep Beauly as it was meant to be."

Frances could feel the sour disappointment within her making the lines of her face long and ugly. "You'll forgive me for wondering. Is it me you want, or only Beauly? You talk as if you were making a business partnership." So long ago, Donald had said Alasdair only wanted her for Beauly; so long she'd believed it. Donald was a liar. She knew that. But she wanted to hear it from Alasdair. Could he not spare the love words to set her mind at rest?

"Many wives would be grateful to be considered partner in their husbands' lives," Alasdair snapped. "Would you prefer I claimed Beauly without reference to you? Should I tell you to go and tend the kitchen and the stillroom, and leave the clan to me? Come to bed, sweeting. You're tired and overwrought. You'll see things my way in the morning."

Frances' precarious thread of patience snapped. "You mean ye'll ha' made sure of me and my lands by morning! By God, Alasdair, you shall have neither Beauly nor me."

She tried to dodge past his outstretched hands, but he was too close. His fingers closed on her bare shoulders and he pushed her back on the bed, against the drawn hangings. The weight of their bodies ripped the tapestry hangings loose from one end of the bed.

"Have ye no' learned to curb that temper yet?" Alasdair said between his teeth.

Frances struggled against his bruising grip. The bed hangings were taut under her. She felt her bottom sliding down the tapestries and over the edge of the bed, let her knees go limp and landed in a heap at Alasdair's feet. Before he could grab her again she had dived under his arm and was making for the door. He clutched after her and she felt a backward jerk as his hand closed on the hem of her shift. There was a rending sound and he staggered backward onto the wreckage of the bed, holding a handful of linen. Frances hurled the water ewer at him and ran for dear life.

8

"Vixen!"

Before the crash of the ewer, he had moved. His pursuing feet were heavy behind her. Frances skidded perilously around a corner and down wooden steps smooth with age, skipping every other one. She ran lightly on her bare feet through the manor wing, toward the great hall and tower keep, and heard him cursing behind her.

He was too close for her to risk pausing to bar the heavy door between the hall and the manor wing. She ran on into the hall and dodged behind the long trestle table that careless servants had left standing overnight.

The flickering torches had all gone out by now.

Alasdair paused for a moment in the darkness, then picked out the white gleam of her shift and bare shoulders in the shadows. He came straight at her, heaving up the trestle board with one hand and tossing it aside. There was a clatter fit to wake the dead as pewter tankards and serving dishes, knives and trenchers, and one sleepy dog fell onto the stone floor of the hall.

Frances caught a tankard and hurled it at him. It was still half-full of ale; the splash of liquid caught him in the eyes and blinded him for a moment. She ran for the kitchen, but he was before her. She doubled, slipped on the rushes where grease from a spilled dish had soaked into them, and was up again with a shooting pain in her ankle. No way to run but up, into the tower keep. Three stories up along the spiral stair and no way down again. But her ancestors had defended it well. She could do the same, with wit and luck and whatever came to her hand.

Moth-eaten tapestries lined the staircase wall. She tore one down and threw it over his head as he started up after her. His curses were muffled for a moment.

Her side was aching when she reached the head of the stairs. Below, Alasdair was still cutting his way free of the dusty tapestry. Grizel and Janet, still locked in Grizel's chamber high in the keep, were crying out in alarm while prudently not coming out to investigate. And Duncan and Sandy, watching from a floor above, leaned on the walls and laughed themselves silly.

"I hate you!" Frances shouted down the stairs. She limped into the weaving room that occupied most of this floor and looked for something to kill Alasdair with. The great loom was still set up with a half-woven plaid on it and the spreader stick in place—a smooth limb as thick as her arm and as wide as a plaid, with spikes stuck slanting in each end to grip the woven length of cloth and keep it from drawing in. She pulled it free of the plaid and heard delicate warp threads rip. But it made a satisfactory club to swing at Alasdair as he stumbled in, still half-blinded by the dust from the hangings.

He ducked under the vicious swing of the spiked club, laughing, and made a grab for her arm. But he was laughing too hard to hold on. Frances twisted free and threw herself at the small stair that twisted upward from the corner of the weaving room. It led into the room Donald had taken for his own, on the floor where Duncan and Sandy were watching.

They had decided to take the fight as part of the evening's entertainment. Comfortably settled on a carved chest, Duncan called out suggestions to Alasdair but made no attempt to stop Frances as she limped past him. Sandy was helpless with laughter. Somewhere behind a barred door, Grizel was still screaming.

Alasdair erupted through the narrow stair door and kicked the chamber pot Frances had pushed into place before she ran on. Donald had used the jurden extensively during the evening. A flood of foul liquid and broken pottery shards filled the room. Alasdair ducked back down into the stairwell and avoided the worst of it, but the trap delayed him long enough for Frances to reach an empty room beyond Grizel's.

His boot slid into the crack between door and wall before she could swing the heavy door completely shut. She stamped on it with her bare feet and only hurt herself. She leaned her whole weight against the door and felt herself being pushed slowly, inexorably back by the pressure of Alasdair's arm on the other side.

Just in time to avoid being crushed against the wall, she let go and stepped back. Alasdair came tumbling in, taken by surprise at the sudden release in pressure. She snatched for the dirk at his waist and his hand came down hard in a chopping motion against her wrist.

Frances backed farther into the room and waited. She could scarcely breathe for the stabbing pain of the stitch in her side. The room was dim with a flicker of torchlight from the hall. Alasdair closed the door behind him and even that faint light vanished. Only his heavy breathing gave her the clue that he was moving closer.

"I hate you," she repeated. "It's not me you are

wanting, it is Beauly. You're as bad as the rest of them. I would rather die a widow than be taking you for my man!"

Put into words, her defiance sounded childish and not even very real. It was like protesting against the inevitable coming of night. Alasdair reaching for her now was as inevitable in its way. When his hands found her bare shoulders and moved slowly down her back, she offered no resistance.

"Will you die a virgin too?" he murmured. "Or did I not understand what you told me of Hugh? Frances, we belong together. Don't fight it."

His chest still rose and fell in a ragged, uneven rhythm, but there was no trace of uneven breathing in his light, quick speech. His hands were warm against her back, and his lips very cool on her forehead, her cheeks, her mouth. She was enveloped in the spicy smell of old leather and the indefinable scent of a man close to her, something quite different from women with their soft skin and rose-petal lotions. In the darkness of the room there was nothing but Alasdair holding her close. She moved against his hands and felt desire stirring in her.

"It's you I am wanting, Frances. Not for Beauly, not for the clan. You were always mine. Now I'm going to make you mine before God and man, so that no one will ever separate us again. Do you understand?"

Wordless, Frances laid her lips against the skin of his cheek, where it was rough with the beard starting. He gave a low, exultant laugh, stooped and picked her up with one arm under her knees and the other supporting her shoulders. Two steps, and they were at the bed. No tapestries hanging in this room, and the straw-filled tick was rough against her skin. This room had not been used in a long time. Disjointed thoughts and images filled Frances' mind. What did it matter about the rooms? What mattered was Alasdair bending over her, the weight of his body that she would feel on hers.

When he straightened she gave a moan of protest and clutched at his leather jacket.

"A moment, sweetheart." Then he was at the door, calling for lights. Someone—Duncan Dhu? —handed in a tallow candle, and the door was shut again. Then he was bending over her, the candle stuck in a niche in the wall, his face grave and intent but for the one obstinate eyebrow with its upward quirk.

"It is lovely indeed you are," he said softly. "More beautiful even than you were in my dreams, these long weary nights that I lay alone in Flanders."

His hands and lips softly caressed every exposed inch of her bare flesh, the white throat and shoulders and breasts thrust proudly forward by the whalebone stays. He lifted her petticoats and laid them back to expose her legs, white as the thrice-bleached linen of her shift up to the triangle of dark hair at the top. His hands trailed along the soft skin of her thighs until she moaned and pressed upward against his touch, all shame and fear gone.

When he brushed across the triangle of dark hair and lightly touched the swelling parts within, she cried out and pulled him down to her. Their lips met and she felt the weight of his body on hers as she'd so often dreamed it, memories of that day by the riverbank mixing with desires she knew only in dreams. But it wasn't enough. What more was there? She moaned again at her own ignorance.

Alasdair pushed himself up and stripped off his leather coat and the half-open linen shirt below. His hand dropped to his belt; she saw the flash of a blade and her eyes widened in fear.

"Here's an end to these damned stays," he said. Two quick strokes down either side, and the laces were dangling free. Frances raised her body slightly to help him as he pulled the cumbersome garment away from her. It went into the growing heap on the floor, followed seconds later by his dirk and heavy leather belt. Now there was nothing between them but her shift. His hands went to the gathered neck with its linen openwork. He pulled, there was a ripping sound, and she was bared to his eyes and hands.

Now when her hands went about his neck and she pulled him down to her, there was no barrier. She reveled in the feeling of his skin, the callused sword hand, the roughness of hair on his thighs and chest, the surprising weight of his lean body. She could feel him swelling against her belly and she shivered involuntarily. But Alasdair's hands were firm and gentle and his voice was soothing in her ears as he murmured endearments in the tongue of their childhood.

Frances ran her fingers through his crisp waving red hair and opened her lips to receive his kiss. Flame coursed through her veins as his mouth took hers. She moaned as his lips moved lower down, teasing her freed breasts into response, circling the nipples with his tongue until they were erect and throbbing, sensitive to the slightest touch. At the same time one knee pressed between her thighs, and his hard, hair-roughened leg against the sensitive inner skin of her thighs roused her to new desires. She was fluid, molten, opening under his hands in whatever manner he desired. Her arms and legs fell open like the petals of a flower under the summer sun.

When he poised himself above her, then thrust deeply, there was an instant of pain that caused her to stiffen and cry out in surprise. But soon that was lost in the wonder of feeling him deep within her, filling an aching emptiness she had not known existed. A spark of sensation kindled at the center of her being that made what had gone before seem like the fumblings of children. She clasped him tightly with arms and legs and pressed herself against him, while with every motion of his body the spark became hotter and more demanding. She was just on the edge of finding out something that was more than she'd ever known or guessed, something that made all her previous life like a dream before the real world begins. Then he shuddered and collapsed against her, holding her so tightly she thought her ribs would break, and she cried out in frustration.

Alasdair's weight was heavy on her and she could taste the salty sweat on his bare skin. His clasp tightened about her, then relaxed. He lifted himself on one elbow and looked down at her with that familiar half-smile and quirk of an eyebrow. His breathing was light but ragged. Frances clasped her hands about his hips and held him close to her when he would have withdrawn.

"Too soon for you, sweeting?" With one hand he stroked the clusters of dark curls away from her forehead. "I didna' want to hurt you your first time."

Frances shook her head. "You didna' hurt me. Not for long, anyway," she amended with irrepressible honesty. But there was something else she wanted to ask, and didn't have words for. "Is . . . is it always like that?"

"No. I'll not be having to hurt you again."

"It's not that was in my mind." The momentary pain seemed a small price to pay for the treasures she'd glimpsed but lost again. She struggled for the words to express herself. "I mean . . . like a wave getting higher, and never quite breaking over?"

Alasdair chuckled, and his light eyes gleamed steel-gray in the uncertain light. "So! Most girls will not be feeling so at all, and it their first time. I thought 'twould take a while to lead you into the gardens of delight. But if you're ready so soon . . . No, Fan. There's more. Tomorrow I'll show you."

"Now." She put his hand on her breast and heard his breathing quicken, felt him rising against her again.

Alasdair laughed. "You said that when I put you up to ride my pony for the first time—remember?"

"You said it was sore I'd be in the morn. And I was. But I learned to ride!"

"Yes. You'll be sore tomorrow, too. But with such a willing learner, how can a man resist?" With a lightning-quick motion he rolled over onto his back, taking her with him so that she straddled his narrow hips and looked down into his eyes where the candle flame danced.

"But it canna' be done like—"

He stopped her mouth with a kiss. "Yes it can, if you'll just . . ." His hands guided her and she sank onto his erect shaft. This time there was no pain, only a deep sense of being touched and known in places that were lonely for it. Then the gentle pressure of his hands on her hips guided her, rocking back and forth until the spark blazed up within her and her body took over, moving to a rhythm old as the glens themselves. The pulsing demand within her grew and she moved over him, teasing him with lips, teeth, fingers, and the trailing edges of her long black curls, until he cried out and gripped her thighs, forcing her to stillness.

"I canna' bear it," she moaned. "Let me go!"

"In good time." And he held her while the shivers ran through her body, keeping her on the edge of that high wave that never crested over. Then his hands moved again, bringing her down against him, and the waves broke and she collapsed against him and he held her while the ecstasy rippled and shivered through her body.

"And it's not always like *that*, either," he warned her when at last she lay still against him. And then he thought again. "But with you . . . I don't know, Fan. We were made for each other, you and I. You know it now. Are you surprised I went near out of my head when I thought of you sharing this with someone else?"

"I could not have," she whispered. "Not with anybody but you, Alasdair."

"See you remember that." His face fell into the lines of the soldier's mask. "You're mine now, Frances of Beauly. It's the seal of my flesh upon you now. You could entangle a thousand men in your long black hair. Best remember that you belong to nobody but me."

The proprietorial tone in his voice stirred Frances to rebellion. "Belong? Like your sword and helm? Or like your horse maybe?"

"Well, you're not made for war, my dear. But mine. Now and always. Is that not what you were wanting?"

Perhaps it had been. But that had been with a different Alasdair. A younger man, not this lean hard fighting man who talked of her as if she were a piece of property.

Then his hands moved over her again, and she forgot all else in the reawakening wonder of their bodies' joining. This time, neither of them was driven by that fierce need. It was a slow sweet joining that melted imperceptibly into a shower of tender touches and kisses, many little droplets falling upon the sand instead of the great curling wave that crested and broke and carried her away with it. And from this coupling she drifted into sleep, her head pillowed on Alasdair's shoulder, feeling at rest and at home with him on this musty straw tick as she'd never felt on her feather bed in her lonely room.

With the first light of morning Alasdair was up and inspecting the state of the castle as though he'd never been away. He'd not been about for ten minutes when a cry from the stables brought both him and Frances hastening to find Peadir's dead body, lying sightless in the straw with a glaze of blood over the gaping wound in his throat. Alasdair thrust his arm out to keep Frances from seeing, but she pushed past him and knelt in the straw to say the last prayers over Peadir's body.

"God have mercy, he died unshriven," she murmured, trying to close the eyes that stared unblinking up at the stable roof.

"Men do," said Alasdair, "in time of war." His mouth had hardened to a thin line. He lifted Frances to her feet and brushed the wisps of straw from her gown. He forbore to remind her that Hugh had gone the same way. Then he turned to Duncan, who'd come to the stables with them. "Three men, you said? And the other two are safe in the storeroom? We'll see what they have to say of this one who escaped."

But he would not let Frances join him. "Peadir was my man," she protested. "His death is on my head."

"The man who killed him is many miles distant," Alasdair told her, "and this is soldiers' business now. Do you go and attend your aunt." A flicker of a smile lightened his countenance. "Belike she'll be ready to come out of her chamber by now, or do you think she means to stay walled up forever under a vow of silence, like the holy women of ancient times?"

Frances could not restrain her own smile at the image. "Silence is one vow Grizel will never take."

But she felt like a child being sent off while the grownups did their work. Alasdair was everywhere at once, sending Euan with two other men to recover Hugh's body, setting the remaining crofters to building something in the courtyard—promising them that they'd be compensated for the time lost—and then taking Duncan Dhu with him to interrogate Donald's two Murray men.

Frances had little enough persuading to do with her aunt; Grizel popped out of her room as soon as she heard Frances' light step on the stairs.

"Has he gone? Is he gone yet?" Grizel demanded, clutching at Frances like a fearful child. She looked in her niece's face as if expecting to see her changed forever by the night's events. "My poor child, did he ravish you? Ah, my heart bled for you, but what could Janet and I do, two weak women against so many? Widowed and ravished all in a night—'tis ruined you surely are now, for what decent man will take his leavings? Oh, oh . . ." And she fell into noisy weeping.

Frances removed Grizel's fingers from her sleeve with a feeling of distaste. She was beginning to suspect that her aunt's copious fits of weeping were a disguise for something else. "Calm yourself, Aunt," she said. "Alasdair did not force me, nor do I consider myself ruined. We're to be wed the day."

"And Hugh not cold in his grave!" As Frances had suspected, indignation cut short Grizel's hysterical outburst. She could hardly restrain herself from inquiring whether Grizel would prefer to see her and Alasdair living in sin. Was it more important to pretend a mourning she could not feel for Hugh than to regularize her new union?

But there was no time to tease Grizel now. She had a more important question to ask.

"Aunt. D'you mind the night I was wed to Hugh?"

Grizel's lined face crumpled and easy tears filled her eyes again. Frances caught her by the shoulder, digging her fingers into the flesh. "Do not you start greeting and wailing again! I have to know something. You told me Alasdair had run away to join the army. Where were you hearing that? Who was telling such black lies on him?"

Grizel nodded slowly and her eyes dropped before Frances' clear gaze. "It seemed for the best," she whispered. "You'd never have wed Hugh if you'd known the truth."

"Body of God!" Frances was startled into letting go of her aunt and breaking into a most unladylike expletive. "The lie was yours."

At most she'd thought to force from Grizel some evidence that Donald had spread the story of Alasdair's defection, that her aunt had been fooled like her. Now she remembered what Grizel had said when she heard of Hugh's death—taking the credit for the marriage between Frances and Hugh, as just one more thing she'd done to protect her nurseling.

"The lie was yours," she breathed again. "Tell me, was it you arranged to have Alasdair kidnapped?

No, you would have been wanting Donald's help. The two of you would be in it together, then. How much of a reward was he promising you?"

Sickened, she turned from her trembling aunt and picked up her skirts for the stairs. The only place she wanted to be now was by Alasdair's side.

"It wasna' like that!" The despairing shriek drew her unwilling attention to Grizel, now leaning on the arm of her maid Janet and seemingly near collapse. The lined face quivered horribly and she lifted one bony finger like a witch about to call down a curse, "My only reward was to do my duty and see Hugh safe. I did the best for all of us. If you weren't blinded by the lusts of the flesh, you'd see it too. He's bewitched you! I pray God to forgive you, you vain, foolish girl."

Frances regarded her aunt with a long, chilling look. "And I," she said at last, "pray God that someday *I* may find it in my heart to forgive *you*."

She turned and swept down the stairs to the hall, her black skirts trailing behind her with a rustle like ghosts whispering on the wind.

9

The sight of Alasdair striding about the inner bailey, bareheaded and bare-armed in his old leather jerkin, restored Frances' equilibrium. She was able to forget the three years wasted, and even to find some measure of forgiveness for her aunt. After all, they were together now, and today was her real wedding day. Poor Grizel had never known love. How could she hate her? She'd been cheated out of life, giving all to the needs of the clan. She had only expected Frances to make the same sterile choice, perhaps not knowing there was anything better.

And if Alasdair had set so many things in motion without asking her—what of that? As he'd said, from now on they would rule Beauly as one. And she'd no fault to find with any of his arrangements.

Excepting one.

"Donald's well lodged," she said. "Could you no' find a more interesting place to keep him in? One of the old dungeons? There's one has a permanent drip-drop of water down the walls, where you and I were playing when we were bairns. 'Twould be doing him a favor to acquaint him wi' the sight of water again. There'll no' be so many fine French wines in his future."

If she could not hate Grizel, she felt no such compunction toward her half-brother. It was easy to persuade herself that the entire plan to kidnap Alasdair and trick her into marrying Hugh had been his, Grizel only following where he led. And Hugh's death, too, could be laid at his door. Oh, she found it easy to hate Donald.

Alasdair only laughed and slung one careless arm around her shoulders. "My little spitfire! Nay, Donald will be doing well enough where he is. That room has a window looking onto the bailey."

"I remember." In spite of the warm sun, Frances shivered.

"I want him to see out."

Instead of explaining further, Alasdair took Frances' hand and guided her around the corner of the tower, to where the sounds of hammering and sawing had been going on. Frances gave a gasp of surprise at the sight of the crude structure being so hastily assembled from the timbers that had been laid aside for repairs to the outbuildings.

"A gallows!" Her fingers bit into Alasdair's arm. "You mean to hang him?"

Alasdair's lips hardened into the thin line she had come to dread. "As lord of Beauly, I have rights of justice against those who trouble the peace of the clan."

His voice was pitched slightly higher than usual, and Frances realized with shock that their words must be clearly audible through the barred grating of Donald's window. The rooms in this level of the keep were slightly below ground level, and the window was only a foot above the stones of the courtyard. Sandy Ruadh sat beside it, whittling on a stick and talking in a low tone to the prisoner.

"Alasdair, no! You'll not be killing him out of hand, and him not shriven of his sins, whatever?"

"The priest's sent for."

Before Frances could speak again, Alasdair had towed her back around the corner. "Thanks, sweeting. You played your part well. Your shock must have been very convincing."

"I played no part!" Frances blazed. "Or do you think we are all mommets to dance to your piping? What is it you are planning, Alasdair?"

"All in good time."

And not another word could she get out of the infuriating man, until the priest arrived from the village an hour later.

* * *

Donald Murray had passed an unhappy night and an excruciating morning. Not physically—Duncan and Sandy had been rough with him, but not beyond the bounds of reason, and the room where he was locked had a pallet, a jug of water, and a bucket. But he was in great distress of mind. Through the night he'd been unable to sleep, wondering how much Alasdair knew of his dealings three years ago and now, and what he would do about it.

This morning it had seemed that his worst fears were to be confirmed. From the barred window he had an excellent view of the gallows being constructed. And, lest he should harbor any doubts about its purpose, Sandy Ruadh kindly sat outside the window and reassured him that he was to have the honor of being sent to hell on his own specially ordered gallows.

"And lucky at that, man," Sandy commented between thoughtful strokes of his dirk on the crude wooden figure he was shaping. "The Cameron—"

"Don't call him that!" Donald's fury and frustration finally exploded. "He's no more the Cameron than I am."

Sandy ceased whittling and looked at him for a long moment. "No? And who is, then?"

Some shreds of Donald's former assurance returned to him. "A sept left without a chief is either absorbed into the parent clan, or, that being impractical in this case with the Cameron clan being mostly on the east coast and separated from us by other groups, a tutor or guardian may be appointed to protect the king's peace."

Sandy spat on the ground just outside Donald's window and resumed his whittling. "And where might such a guardian be found? The Lady Frances' brother, mayhap?"

"Mayhap," assented Donald. He beckoned Sandy to come closer. "What d'you say? See me safe out of here, and you'll not be the poorer for it when the king appoints me here. There's money to be squeezed out of Beauly—I should know." And he rubbed his thumb and forefinger together with a suggestive motion.

"Aye," Sandy agreed, with a twinkle in his eye that should have warned Donald, "a poor man could come to great wealth that way, I've no doubt. There's just one or two wee things troubles me about the arrangement."

"You have my word on it," Donald burst in, all excitement now that he thought he could suborn one of Alasdair's men. "Nay, better! I'll sign a paper."

"Mphm." Sandy's dirk carved shavings off the wood figure in long, precise strokes that left a little pile of white wood curls at his feet. "It's no' your word I'm doubting precisely. But how long, think you, might a poor man be left in peace with his great wealth, once Alasdair heard of his betrayal?"

"We can deal with Alasdair," Donald asserted. "He trusts you. You can get close to him. One blow with that"—he pointed at Sandy's dirk—"and we've no more to fear from him."

"Mphm." Sandy paused again to complete a clean stroke along the wood. "And Glencairn? Nae doubt you'll have come to some arrangement with him, some legal matter too complicated for a poor crofter like meself to trouble over."

"Yes, yes, precisely." Donald could hardly contain his eagerness. "You're in it, then? You'll let me out?"

"Well, now." A long, agonizing silence followed while Sandy twirled the rough wood carving on the point of his dirk. "I'll tell you what I think . . ." He let his voice trail off while he focused narrowed eyes on the spinning wooden figure.

"What?" Donald prompted when the silence grew unbearably long.

Sandy brought his dirk down in a stabbing motion on the mossy crack between two flagstones. The carved figure, impaled, split apart with a sharp crack, and the handle of the dirk quivered where it stood upright.

"I think you're main lucky to be getting a quick death this day!" He flung his head back and guffawed at the sight of Donald deflated like a burst pig's bladder.

"Seriously, man!" Sandy lowered his voice once again. "The Cameron's got an awfu' way with him, where he suspects treachery. And one like you, as sold him to the Colonel three years syne so you could wed his woman to the daftie chief—I tell you, it's surprised indeed I was to find he means no worse than hanging. I thought surely he'd want to practice some of the fine ways we learned of the Flemish soldiers on you. Did I ever tell you of the time we took a poor body Fleming trying to sneak into the camp and spy on us? Took ten minutes to make him talk. Alasdair was right disappointed. He likes to see them writhe a bit first, you see. What he did wi' this loon . . ."

And Sandy was off, spinning a long and magnificently ingenious story about the tortures which he claimed Alasdair liked to inflict on prisoners, especially those who gave him trouble or resisted him. A horrid fascination kept Donald at the window to hear all the grisly details fomented by Sandy's imagination, and he believed all of them completely.

By the time Alasdair pushed the priest into Donald's cell with orders to hear his confession, the prisoner had lost his breakfast oatcake into the necessary bucket and the weakness of his knees had forced him to collapse trembling on the straw pallet. He no longer doubted that Alasdair meant to hang him out of hand.

"Make a bonny tale of your sins," Alasdair advised him with a grin. "Not too long, mind! I'd like fine to hear the full story, but I'm a wee thing pressed for time. If ye spin it out too long, the priest'll no' have time to shrive you." Alasdair settled himself against one wall while Donald fell on his knees before the priest.

"Oh, Father, you'll not stand by and see murder done?"

But his pleas were useless. The village priest had been too long at the beck and call of the family in Beauly Castle to dare question anything they might order. He was not likely to risk his neck now by setting his will in opposition to that of this lean, frightening man who might as easily have decided to hang him for his part in Frances' marriage to Hugh.

He did venture a stammering protest at Alasdair's evident intent to stay while Donald made his confession. Alasdair merely shrugged. "As you will. I'd as soon see him die unshriven like my cousin whom he killed. It's the mercy of his lady sister pleading for his soul that brings you here at all. But it's true I'm pressed for time. Be as convenient to hang him now as after."

"No!" Donald scrabbled across the floor on his knees and flung his arms about Alasdair's boots. He was in a paroxysm of terror. "Not so soon. I want to confess—I must confess!"

"Then I stay," Alasdair said. He raised his voice slightly. "Holla, Duncan! Bring in the writing stand."

A grinning Duncan lugged in the tall, slanted writing stand at which old Gillivray had been used to do his accounts, along with a bundle of ill-assorted parchment pieces, a much-sharpened quill pen, and a bottle of watery ink.

"Make a fair copy as he speaks," Alasdair bid the priest. " 'Twould be a pity to have so many black deeds lost to the grave. I'm minded to have a ballad made of it that children can sing in the streets of Edinburgh."

But this request was too much for the priest, frightened though he was. "I'm here to shrive a man," he told Alasdair, "not to make a travesty of the confessional. If you want a record, make it yourself."

Alasdair grinned. "An excellent idea, Father. I'm told I write a fair clerkly hand, and I'll not be tempted to leave out anything, as you might do."

There was, in truth, little in Donald's halting confession to make a good ballad. Apart from arranging to have Alasdair kidnapped for the foreign army, he had little to tell but a sordid history of backstairs fornications, drunken parties that usually ended in the wreck of someone's tavern, and a certain amount of inept cheating at cards. He drew to a close with the account of how he'd settled with Glencairn to take the lordship of Beauly out of Frances' hands by having her husband declared insane.

"A bonny tale," Alasdair declared when Donald's

halting voice stopped. Alasdair's voice interrupted the priest before he could pronounce absolution. One hand rhythmically slapped the hilt of his sword in a light, warning gesture. "But there's one small thing ye forgot to include."

Donald wrung his hands. "Nothing—nothing. Dinna torture me."

"No? I'll have to help your memory." Alasdair took up the pen again. "I'll just write"—his pen scratched busily over the paper—"how Donald Murray acknowledges that he has no right or title to the lordship of Beauly. That he repents him of the grievous sin done in trying to usurp the rightful place of the head of the clan, and that he now acknowledges Alasdair Cameron as chief of clan, Cameron of Beauly, together with his heirs by his wife, Frances Murray."

A moment more with the pen, and Alasdair shook fine sand over the paper to dry his writing.

"Your hand on it," Alasdair ordered the shrinking Donald, holding out the pen to him. "Write it fair, now. I'll not have you claiming later that it is a forgery."

"Claiming . . . later?" Donald stammered. "Ye'll not hang me, then?"

"If ye sign," said Alasdair, "I'll no' need to."

"No court in the land will witness a signature obtained under threats," put in the priest.

Alasdair rounded on him. "The gallows is still

standing, priest. When I want your opinion, I'll ask for it."

Donald put a shaking hand to the paper and signed it. Alasdair sprinkled sand over the wet sheet to dry the ink, read over the final statement twice or thrice, and finally folded it and slipped it into an inner pocket of his jerkin with a nod of satisfaction.

"Now, priest. I hear you're a fine hand at the nuptial Mass."

The priest quivered in his rope-soled sandals, thinking Alasdair now meant to seek revenge for his part in Frances' marriage to Hugh. " 'Twas Lord Gair ordered it, and none of my doing," he quavered. "Ye'd not have me defy the rightful lord of the castle?"

Alasdair's right eyebrow went up in the quirk which signified high good humor. "Why, no, so long as you remember that the rightful lord is now myself. There's another wedding toward. Come with me to the chapel."

Frances, ordered upstairs when the priest arrived, had been too angry at her exclusion from Alasdair's plans to do the least thing toward decking herself for her wedding. Her attempts to leave the manor wing and peep into the bailey to find out what was going on had been foiled by a grinning Euan.

"Himself says it's no' work for a leddy," he announced with satisfaction.

"I'll be remembering this next time you are

wanting to borrow the draft oxen to finish the plowing, Euan," Frances threatened, but her only reply was another grin.

"Aye, but if I cross himself, I doubt I'll live to finish the plowing."

Frances gave up and retreated to her bedchamber with what dignity she had left. So this was what Alasdair called ruling in partnership! Already he had usurped her authority with the folk of the glen and castle. She sighed and faced the bitter truth. Her years of tireless work in the glen meant less than nothing, next to the chance of a fighting man to lead them.

Even though their branch of the clan was a small and weak one, even though she had tried to turn the crofters from their time-honored pursuits of lifting cattle from the Murray lands to more peaceful occupations of plowing and tilling their own fields, they were still ready to follow the man with his sword lifted for war. Alasdair's lightning-quick strike on the castle had taken their fancy, and his announcement that he meant to marry her had been all that was needed to legitimize his claim.

Frances rose and paced about the room, her full skirts swishing over the floor at every step. Jesu! Was this, as Grizel had warned her, all there was in a woman's life—to wait and weep? A dreich employ, indeed. Sooner she would have been out fighting like the men.

By the time Alasdair appeared at her door, flushed with success, she was so angry that she scarcely noticed the folded sheets he carried like a gage of victory.

"All's in order," he informed her. "The priest is waiting to put church blessing on our union, and what I have here will give us King Jamie's blessing too, for what that's worth."

Frances tapped her foot. "You take my blessing for granted. What if I'll not have you?"

Alasdair put his hands over her slim waist. "A wee late for that," he informed her, still smiling. "I made you mine last night. Or do you want another reminder? I'd be glad to oblige, sweet, but we mustna' keep the priest waiting." He kissed her with careless confidence, then put her away from him. "Do ye no' want to see the fruit of my morning's labors?"

Curiosity impelled Frances to bend over the crackling sheets of parchment that he spread out.

" 'I, Donald Murray, in the fortieth year of my life, do make this general confession—' "

"That's no' Donald's hand," she pointed out.

"No, but it's his confession. Under fear of death, and not a sin forgotten! Aye, it's a fine tale, but maybe not so fit for a lady to read. And I've his hand on the tail end of it." Alasdair turned to the last page and pointed out Donald's signature, the sloping letters looking shaky and ill-formed under the lines in Alasdair's firm black writing.

Frances focused on the few lines above the signature and caught her breath. " 'Acknowledge the right of Alasdair Cameron of Beauly . . . his heirs by the Lady Frances . . .' "

She looked up at Alasdair with accusation blazing in her eyes. "So, *now* ye'll wed wi' me. I see why you wanted to wait. Fine timing! Last night ye made sure of me in your bed, and this morning you made sure of Beauly. Was it not worth having the priest till you got Donald's name on this bargain? And what's the worth of a deid man's name to ye?"

"Donald's not dead," Alasdair told her. "My part of the bargain was to let him go free."

Suddenly Frances felt an involuntary shiver and was caught by the strange feeling that someone had walked over her grave. The coldness grew, then enveloped her like a cloud. Alasdair was still speaking, but she could not hear what he said. The walls of the castle became thin as smoke before her eyes. It seemed to her that she could look through the stone and over the glen of Beauly to see flames leaping from thatch, to smell smoke, and to hear the keening of women driven from their homes.

As quickly as the unasked vision had come, it left her. She passed one hand across her brow and looked around the room, surreptitiously putting one hand behind her to feel the stone wall and assure herself of its solidity.

Alasdair still stood before her, but now he was quiet and looked at her curiously.

"It's an unlucky thing," she murmured, "to build a gallows, and it not to bear fruit. Oh, Alasdair, take it down. The thing will have blood if ye leave it standing."

Even as she spoke, she knew her plea was useless. The Sight never came upon her except in times of great trouble. Nothing as simple as dismantling a wooden contraption would avert the ill that hung over the glen. Last time her marriage to Hugh had been the price of keeping peace. What sacrifice would be demanded of her this time?

Alasdair saw her blank, inward-looking expression and took her in his arms, kissing her roughly, bringing her back to this world by the force of his will. He remembered other times when Frances looked into herself like that. Whether it was the true Sight or no, he would have no fresh shadow cast over their wedding day.

"Frances, Fan, look at me!" he demanded with rough urgency. His kisses blazed a trail of fire over her cold cheeks and lips until she responded, returning his kisses with a fierceness that equaled his own. He felt the shudders of desire running through her body, igniting his own senses.

It was woefully hard to step back and free her when every nerve in his body clamored for immediate fulfillment. How much easier, Alasdair thought, to pick her up and carry her over to the great tester bed where they'd never yet lain together. But she had resented his haste last night—though, by God, she'd not resented it at the time!

No, Alasdair reminded himself, this time all things should be done decently and in order. He meant to get sons on her to found a new line of Cameron chiefs. No one should snigger that they'd anticipated the wedding. And the sooner they were wed, the less chance there was that Lachlan Cameron, or Glencairn, or anybody else would try to seize the newly widowed lady of Beauly as a counter in the game of power.

"The priest is waiting," he reminded her when her eyes opened to him at last. He picked up the parchments spread out on the table and tucked them back into his jerkin with a proprietary gesture.

Frances' eyes followed the movements of his hands. He seemed to take more care for those damned papers than for her! Her anger, stilled momentarily by the unwelcome visions of the Sight, blazed high again.

"And he may go on waiting for all I care!" she said, her eyes flashing at him. "You've been aye careful to arrange all to your liking, Alasdair. A body would think you were heir to Beauly, not I. I'll have no more of being sent upstairs like a bairn while you and the other *men* thrash things out to your satisfaction."

"And I'll not bend my neck to petticoat rule!" Alasdair blazed back. He grasped Frances' wrists and pulled her away from the window, forcing her to face him. "We'll work together where it's right and fitting we should do so, but there are places my wife does not go. When we stand before the priest, I'll take an oath to protect you, Fan. And that means that you don't meddle in things I tell you to stay out of. Would you have wanted to watch me break your brother's will? What if it took more than words and threats? Would you have heated the irons for me yourself? God's blood! Next you'll be demanding to ride into battle beside me."

"Better that than staying at home to weep and pray." Frances tried to free herself, but the bruising grip on her wrists was as unbreakable as an iron band and Alasdair's arm across her body held her fast. Alasdair laughed and kissed her behind the ear. She hated herself for the involuntary shiver that coursed through her body at the brush of his lips.

"You'd stay lady of Beauly for a sennight," he told her. "As soon as the word of Hugh's death gets out, the jackals will be gathering. You need a man to protect you, and I'm the one you'll have."

He relaxed his grip and freed her mouth, laughing down at her. "Unless, of course, you don't want me. Well, mistress? Go on. Say you don't want me. You don't love me. My touch is repugnant to you."

Frances slipped one arm around his neck and

drew his lips down to meet hers in a prolonged kiss that sent small fires running the length of her body. "I love you, Alasdair," she said softly. "Only I don't want to be treated like a bairn."

He stopped her words with another kiss. "Hush, now. Will you be quarreling all the way to the altar, and shame us both? Let's get married now. We can fight later . . . if you still want to." And his impudent hands, traveling over her body with a will of their own, suggested they might find pleasanter amusements afterward. Frances felt her knees shaking. When he released her at last, she kept fast hold of his hand as they went to the chapel.

"Sandy!" Alasdair shouted as he emerged from the manor wing, propelling Frances before him with an arm clasped tightly about her waist. "D'you mind how you used to play the pipes before a battle? We'll have some music to this wedding."

And so Frances found herself once again standing in the tiny chapel while the frightened priest gabbled the words of the nuptial Mass over her. But this time Alasdair was beside her. It was a new beginning, as if the years apart could be wiped out and all things made new again.

At the conclusion of the ceremony Alasdair thrust a gold piece into the priest's hand and pushed him out into the courtyard. "Good, Father whatever-your-name-is, you've earned your fee today. Now, get along home, there's no more . . ."

He stopped and both eyebrows shot up at the sight of the sad little group huddled uncertainly in the bailey. Sandy's pipes had drowned out the noise of their arrival.

A cloaked figure lay recumbent on an improvised stretcher. Grizel knelt over the figure, wailing and wringing her hands, while the two men he'd sent out earlier for Hugh's body shuffled uncertainly behind her.

"There he is!" Grizel's voice rose to a keening shriek and she pointed one bony finger straight at Alasdair. "There's the murderer, taking the widow while his hands still reek of my Hughie's blood!"

"It seems I was mistaken, Father," said Alasdair. "We've one more task for you here." He turned to Frances. "What ails your aunt?"

"I think the shock has turned her brain," Frances whispered back. She moved forward and attempted to raise Grizel to her feet. "Come, Aunt. You should rest."

"Not while the murderer goes free!"

Frances tugged urgently at her aunt's arm. "Aunt, you're mistaken. Alasdair didna' kill Hugh—'twas one of Donald's men, and an accident. Let me help you inside, do."

"I'm no' mad," Grizel announced. "Whoever struck the blow, it's Alasdair's fault. If he hadna' come back, my Hughie would be alive today." She pointed her hands at Alasdair again. "Come forward if ye dare," she cried shrilly, "and see if my bonny lad's wounds do not bleed afresh!" With the strength of madness she broke free from Frances' grip long enough to tear the cloak from the dusty corpse.

"Oh, for God's sake." Alasdair stamped past the group and into the great hall, his patience in shreds. "Father, say what words are fitting, and these two will bury the lad. And somebody get that madwoman inside."

But the two men he'd sent out followed Alasdair into the hall, instead of awaiting the priest's bidding. "There's something ye should know," the older of them said. "When we were on the road back . . ."

As he went on, Alasdair propped one foot on a bench, and leaning forward, listened with such intentness that he seemed scarcely to be breathing.

10

Once Alasdair was out of sight, Grizel calmed down and consented to be led inside, away from the grisly scene in the courtyard. Frances shepherded her into the manor wing, where she would not have to face Alasdair again, and gave her over into the charge of her woman Janet.

"And see you that she doesna' come down again," she instructed the frightened woman. "Not until Hugh is safely buried, God rest his soul." Automatically she crossed herself. As much of a memorial as Hugh was likely to have, Frances thought as she hurried from her weeping aunt back to the courtyard.

His face and the upper half of his body were still

uncovered, and the deep gash in his neck showed clear, all filled with clotted black blood. The men who'd brought him home were nowhere to be seen. Frances averted her eyes and twitched the plaid up to cover the wounds, but stopped for a moment before covering his unmarked face. In the repose of death his countenance had gained a dignity and maturity it had never shown in life. The slack lips were closed now, and in the molding of his mouth and chin she could trace the lineaments of what Lord Gair must have been before old age and illness brought him down. Someone's hands had closed his eyes and smoothed the tow-colored hair that had always been so wild, uncombed, and full of small twigs and leaves.

"You might have been a proper man, Hughie lad," Frances murmured. She felt tears prickling behind her eyes, and hastily drew the plaid over the calm, dead face.

Before she could straighten, the cold dizziness came at her again, and she fell forward on her knees beside Hugh's bier. There seemed to be flames crackling along the curtain wall now, and she could hear shouts and the heavy footsteps of armed men running. A scream from the byres, where the soldiers had trapped some woman. Smoke pouring from the castle windows.

And through it all she knew that no one had moved, there was no fire; she was kneeling on the hard uneven stones beside Hugh's bier, and there was a light mist sprinkling her face, and no one else in the bailey at all.

Her head was whirling and she remembered, incongruously, that she had eaten nothing since the previous day. There was a weakness like water in her bones, and her hands gripped each other so tightly that the finger ends were white.

Now it was the glen she was seeing, spread out before her as if she could soar through the air like an eagle: green turf and the purpling heather, twisted stunted trees growing among rocks and the silver thread of the river Beauly running through it. But where were the people? She soared over the valley for an eternity before she realized that the smoldering clumps of ashes dotted here and there were the remains of the crofters' huts.

It was summer in the bailey where her body was kneeling beside Hugh, but here where she was overlooking the glen through other eyes, she could feel the bite of winter in the air, and a hint of snow on the bitter east wind. Now she flew up into the mountain pass, where the cliffs were steep and honeycombed with caves. Mere shallow niches in the rock most of them, but she saw women and children huddled in them for what shelter they could find, and the children's eyes big in their heads with hunger.

Who dares do this to my people?

A wave of anger brought her back to the castle. And there she saw a troop of men in plate armor guarding the bailey, and the gates locked against the people who were starving in the cold outside. The anger rose in her like smoke, shimmering and distorting the vision, and when she saw clearly, it was summer again, and no one in the bailey at all but one black-haired girl who knelt beside a heap of blankets on the stones.

Then Frances knew blackness, and a falling sensation, and suddenly she was seeing out of her own eyes again. She had fallen forward across Hugh's body under the plaid, and the musty smell of the damp wool was choking her nostrils. She shook her head and struggled to sit upright. A hand on her shoulder guided her back.

"Control your grief," Alasdair advised.

Frances used his arm to haul herself up. She was beyond pride, though his eyes were cold and clear as the east wind in her vision.

"A thought unseemly, wife, to mourn the old husband on the day you wed wi' the new," Alasdair gibed. Dimly Frances could sense the hurt pride behind his words. But it didn't matter now.

"It's not Hugh," she managed through a throat so constricted that it seemed she could scarcely breathe except in sips. She clutched at Alasdair's sleeve to keep her balance. "Not . . . I am seeing . . . It is the great trouble that will come on the glen, Alasdair. We must leave here. Quickly! Before the soldiers come."

As she articulated the words, the constriction

left her throat, and she breathed in great gulps of the sweet fresh air. Yes, that was it. Now she knew, it was all right. It was always better once she knew what had to be done.

Alasdair folded his arms and frowned at her. "Now, how did you hear that?"

"Hear?"

"I've just had the report myself. That man of Donald's who got away—he was no Murray man, but a spy of Glencairn's. He rode to warn the earl, and Glencairn's men are marching on Beauly now. They've been seen over the mountain and will be here before nightfall. We've scarce time to close the gates, let alone to drive the herds in." Alasdair was looking past her now, his lips moving silently as he enumerated to himself the tasks that must occupy the next few hours if they were to make any defense at all.

"We canna' keep the castle," Frances said. Her fingers fastened about his arm until he winced. "Alasdair, listen. Half the people of the glen will be already up on the shielings. Will you be driving the herds in from the high grazing places? Glencairn's men will be on you before they are half brought down. They will fire the cottages. The people who canna' get to the castle will die. Split on pikes or homeless and starving, what does it matter?"

"When did the men of Beauly ever refuse to follow their chief?" Alasdair demanded.

"Never," Frances flung back at him. "But I am the lady of Beauly, and I am saying that they shall not be called out."

For a long moment they stared at each other, standing over the plaid-shrouded body in the courtyard. This time it was Alasdair who first looked away.

"Alasdair, it is that I know," Frances said in an undertone. In the moment of victory she felt the need to justify herself. "I have seen what will come to the glen if we do not go away from here. We canna' hold it, and I will not see you and all the rest die on a point of honor."

Alasdair gave a short, brittle laugh. "No . . . you'll likely ha' the right of it. If I've learned one thing these past years in Flanders, it was not to make a stand where the fight is hopeless. These gallant last stands make fine songs, but they never won any wars. But I'd like fine to know how you kenned that Glencairn was coming," he murmured as he turned away and gave orders to have the horses saddled.

Within the hour Alasdair and Frances, accompanied only by Duncan Dhu and Sandy Ruadh, were riding from Beauly, leaving Donald to welcome Glencairn's army as he saw fit.

They carried nothing but what they could sling from their saddles. Alasdair, Sandy, and Duncan had hastily loaded up some packs of provisions from the castle stores, and Frances had made a bundle of her best cloak and the few brooches and chains that had not yet gone to feed Donald's demands for money. The ring of the Camerons, with its great flawed emerald, she twisted inward on her finger so that it looked like a plain gold band, not to tempt those they might meet with on the roads.

Grizel refused to come with them. Somewhat uneasily, Frances had left her in the care of Janet.

"Glencairn'll not harm her," Alasdair reassured her. "He's no cause. 'Twill give him some flavor of respectability, to have one of the family still dwelling there. She'll not challenge his right to the lands, whatever." He gave his short laugh again. "Lord, I'd like fine to see his greeting to Donald! How long, d'you think, before he has your brother turned out of the castle and living in Edinburgh again, and on less allowance than you were making him? Donald's no' canny, to trust Glencairn."

Frances laughed too, at the thought. And so they rode out of Beauly laughing, though the fine mist was falling and she knew not where they should go, or when she'd see the home of her childhood again. She was with Alasdair, and all else could be settled as it would.

"We ride for Eilean Duin," Alasdair told her when they stopped to rest the horses. They were some miles from Beauly and sheltered in a curve of the hillside from which they could watch all approaches without being seen.

Frances crunched a dry oatcake between her strong white teeth and swallowed, coughing, from the flask that Duncan Dhu held out to her. In the worn homespun dress she'd put on for riding, with a plaid over her head to keep the mist away, she felt young and free again.

The mention of Eilean Duin, the isolated island at the head of Loch Duin, increased her sense of an escape into an adventure. Alasdair's father had had nothing to leave him but this scrap of barren land high in the hills, and though Alasdair had ridden to see it several times while he lived at Beauly, Frances had never been able to tease him into taking her along. It was too long and hard a ride for a girl, he had said, and besides, Grizel would never give her permission.

"It will be a hard ride," Alasdair said now, and Frances laughed at the way he'd echoed her thoughts.

"That is what you were always saying," she reminded him. "But now you must take me, and I will be showing you whether I can keep up." She scrambled to her feet and shook the sprigs of heather out of her clinging skirt.

By the time they had covered half the distance, her bravado had changed into a gritty determination not to give up. In these last years she'd had but little leisure for riding or walking, and the unused muscles in her thighs shrieked in protest at the continued effort necessary to hold her on her horse's back. Worse than the constant effort of staying upright was the necessity to guide the horse through rocky scree and treacherous bogs where Sandy went on foot before them to determine the path.

Alasdair was determined to avoid all habitations on this flight, and time and again Frances dismounted and held her horse behind the shelter of a few bushes while they waited tensely for men to pass. As they rode farther into the hills, such encounters grew rare, but the faint paths they had been following disappeared altogether and she had nothing to guide her but Duncan's horse ahead of her. Alasdair rode last, continually looking over his shoulder to guess if they were being pursued, and only pride kept Frances upright in the saddle so that he should not see her slumping with fatigue.

When next they paused she was afraid to dismount for fear she would not be able to force her numbed limbs to obey her. She urged the mare close to the rock face where they were resting and leaned against the cliff, mechanically chewing and swallowing the remains of the oatcake while Sandy fed the mare some oats out of his cupped hands. She was beginning to hate Sandy and Duncan, who dropped out of their saddles at a word from Alasdair and ran forward, crouching in the darkness, to spy out the land ahead. They had done this not once but a dozen times, while she was only held in the saddle because her legs were too stiff to let her fall off. She hated Alasdair, too, who pressed them onward without a word of sympathy for her.

"Tired?" Alasdair asked at that precise moment. "I was thinking it would likely be too much for you."

After that, of course, there was nothing for it but to go on.

The sky was lightening from velvet blue to shot-silk gray when the mists lifted and she caught her first glimpse of Eilean Duin.

The rocky island was nestled between cliffs, guarded on both sides by fast-rushing waters. From the height of the ridge they looked down on the steep rock face, plunging sheer into the water, that guarded the island where the river eddied around it. Above the rocks there was a green place bounded by close-set thorns and briers. A few massive stones lay with their mossy sides tilted together, like the ruins of a giant's toy house. For the space of three breaths the rising sun struck through a cleft in the hills behind them and touched it all, stones, briers, and rushing water, with gold; then the mists came down again and Frances was shivering in the cool gray air of first light.

She could see no path by which to reach the island, but Alasdair knew the way. She followed where he led, the exhausted horses delicately picking their way along a rocky path that meandered in and out along the line of the ridge, and presently they were down beside the water's edge. They turned away from the river then, until it seemed to be lost behind them, and came out of the forest at a clear place where a bend of the river ran wide and shallow. On the other side the island rose up in a gentle, welcoming slope before them.

Frances was too tired to protest whan Alasdair took her reins.

"It's the only ford," he said, "and no kind of a ford at all in the rains. It is safe you will be here, Frances. You can rest now."

There was as much pride in his voice as if he were welcoming her to a fine manor house with broad acres surrounding it.

"But I would rather be here," Frances said in her exhaustion, and realized from the expression on Alasdair's face that whatever she had said made no sense to him. It was all perfectly clear to her, as crystalline as the dawn that was lifting the mist from around him, but somehow it was too much trouble to explain.

After they splashed through the shallow waters of the ford, there was green turf where the horse put its head down and began grazing. When she slid from the saddle her numbed legs would not support her and Alasdair lifted her in his arms without a word. That was the last thing she remembered, the hard strength of his arms holding her, and the plaid falling away as he carried her onto his island.

In later years Frances was to remember that summer as one of unclouded sunny skies and unbroken peace. Surely it must have been cold and wet sometimes? But in her memory there was only an unbroken string of sunny days. Little news reached them from the outside world. There was a village a few miles away, scarcely more than a cluster of black houses huddled in the shelter of the mountain, and on his infrequent trips to purchase fresh eggs and an occasional scrawny chicken from the crofters, Sandy brought back such scraps of information as they had. Thus they heard that Glencairn had occupied Beauly and, as Alasdair predicted, had lost no time in turning Donald off to live as his pensioner in Edinburgh. The people of the glen were sullen but offered no outright resistance to the new rule.

That much was a relief to Frances. But Alasdair colored and swore vilely in Flemish at the next scraps of gossip that Sandy brought back from the village.

"It is a rape they are calling it," Sandy recounted. "That black devil Glencairn has put it about that he is much concerned for the welfare of his dear kinswoman the Lady Frances, her having been abducted by Alasdair Cameron and his band of villains."

Frances laughed and rolled over on her back. She had been lying on her stomach beside the swift-rushing river, chewing a stem of grass and trying unsuccessfully to tickle a trout before her fingers were numbed in the cold water. "Much obliged to my dear kinsman!" She giggled and extended one sun-browned hand to Alasdair, pulling him down to sit beside her. "Truth, and ye are an unsavory group!" Her mocking gaze roamed over the three men, taking account of their tattered clothing and unkempt hair. "Should I be feared for my life, then?"

"You might that, wife," said Alasdair, "if you burn the oatcakes again."

And the tense moment passed in laughter.

But later Frances wondered about the story, and sought out Alasdair in private.

"How can Glencairn call it a rape," she asked, "when we had the priest to wed us? Doesn't he know that?"

Alasdair was polishing his steel helmet with an old leather scrap. He turned it in the sun, and the reflections dazzled her eyes.

"Glencairn may call it what he pleases," he replied after a while. "The kirk is Protestant, and the estates. Jamie's had trouble with the high Catholic lords of the Highlands, these ten years or more. Until we have a child, our marriage stands in law just as long as the great lords please, no more." He gave Frances a curious sidewise glance.

"Glencairn may have it in mind to take you for himself. 'Twould strengthen his claim to the land."

"Donald told me he was an old man," Frances protested.

Alasdair bent one of his hard looks upon her, his eyes as bright and glittering as the steel helmet that he was polishing. "He's not sixty yet, and he's buried two wives. He might like fine to get a bonny black-eyed lass who could bring him another castle and bear him sons." He paused and shook his head. "Sandy will have to stay away from the village from now on. I've no fancy to dangle at a rope's end in Edinburgh so that Glencairn can have my woman."

Later, when he saw that Frances was troubled by his words, he laughed and kissed her and told her not to worry over his fancies. "I've been a soldier too long. Look you, I see trouble behind every bush. We'll just stay clear of the village for a while. Glencairn's gold could be a sore temptation to some poor soul. You'll not mind getting by on oatcakes and fish and berries?"

Frances pulled his head down to meet her lips in a long, lingering kiss that said all she dared not put into words. But Alasdair broke off the kiss before she was ready, and left her standing with a puzzled frown on her face.

In the days that followed, he seemed imperceptibly to withdraw from her. And he was forever apologizing for the difficulties of their primitive life on the island. She wished she could find the words to convince him that this was all she'd ever wanted and more than she'd dared dream, this long secluded idyll with Alasdair beside her. After the last three years of constant worry and strain, she was reclaiming day by day the youth she had put aside when Lord Gair put the welfare of his people into her hands. Alasdair's presence, by turns light and serious, laughing and loving, was the additional joy that she'd never envisioned even in her dreams.

Sandy and Duncan kept their distance, hunting and fishing, and let the lovers enjoy their summer undisturbed. Sometimes they would spend the day like two children, wandering in the thickets of the lower end of the island to gather berries, arguing about who could pick the fastest and whether it was worthwhile stopping by the deep pool where an old trout eluded their best efforts to capture him. On other days Alasdair became Frances' tutor, opening up a new world to her with his stories of Edinburgh and the Low Countries, repeating the scraps of poetry and tales he'd brought back in his head and drawing plans of battle with a crooked stick in the sand. It was a strange sort of education she got from him that summer, learning techniques of siege and sortie mixed in with the law he'd learned in Edinburgh and the poems in the Lowland tongue. As friend and tutor, she could wish for no better companion than Alasdair. There was just the one shadow over their summer.

Since the day he had heard of Glencairn's rape accusation, Alasdair had not made love to her again.

Once or twice she lay close to him at night. She could tell from his quickened breathing and the tension in his limbs that he desired her. But when she put out a tentative hand to touch him, he put her away gently.

On a clear bright morning when she was kneeling by the river cleaning fish for their morning meal, he came and knelt beside her on the broad stone that jutted out into the river.

"It's hard work for your hands," he said.

"No worse than I've done at Beauly," Frances replied. She rinsed the fish in river water and laid them on an improvised basket of plaited grass. Alasdair caught her wrists and held her hands out in the merciless sun, exposing the scraped knuckles and broken nails. "I could do the work for you," he said. Then, after a moment, he added, "But you would still be a fugitive. On my account. And what about winter? . . . Frances, I am thinking that maybe you should go back to Beauly. Glencairn would do you no harm."

Frances stood up and covered the fish in the basket with a layer of green leaves. "He might make me pretend to be his wife," she answered. "Do you call that no harm?"

Alasdair stood too, and walked away with long strides.

"Do you not mind?" she called after him. But there was no answer.

That was the day when Frances knew it was impossible to go on this way, pretending there was nothing wrong between them. If Alasdair had truly tired of her and wanted her to go back to Beauly, she vowed to herself, she would go.

But he would have to prove it to her first.

After the fish had been fried and eaten, she asked him to go exploring with her again. They would need to get well away from Duncan and Sandy in the camp, or she'd never have courage to play the scene she had in mind.

They spent an hour clambering over the rocks, mounting higher and higher into the rocky fastnesses, when Frances vowed she could hear the sound of water.

"Of course you can," Alasdair laughed at her. "Doesn't the island itself divide the river, and it like a ship dividing the ocean? It's the river on either side you hear."

"No." Frances was sure now, after some minutes of listening. "Can't you hear? It's a different sound."

She took the lead, pushing branches aside and scrambling up over the rocks with as little regard for her skin and dress as she had had when they were children. After a sweaty climb over fallen tree limbs, her insistence was rewarded.

Frances caught her breath and stopped suddenly as the waterfall came into view. Alasdair came up behind her so quickly that he bumped into her. The stream that fed the waterfall seemed to come from nowhere, bursting out of the solid rock and falling in an unbroken sheet of water down to a clear pool bordered by a narrow grassy verge. Before he could move away, she slipped her arm around his waist and nestled close to him as they gazed at the vision. He tensed and tried to move away from her. She let him slip free, but kept hold of his hand. This was the perfect setting for the test she had planned.

"It's a fine sight, is it not?" she said.

Alasdair pulled his hand away from her and leaned against a tree, arms folded. "It is that," he agreed.

"Rare, too," Frances went on with assumed innocence. "A waterfall on an island must be near as uncommon a thing as a man who never makes love to his wife."

She stood in front of him, so close that her breasts rising and falling under the loose-fitting homespun dress almost touched him. Alasdair's eyes were drawn there almost against his will. He clenched his jaw and looked out over the waterfall instead.

Frances moved a little closer, tempting, touching him. She ran light fingers down his arm and felt the muscles tense under her hand.

"If you are not wanting me anymore, Alasdair, you will have to tell me so." She shut her eyes and prayed, waiting for his answer.

His hands fell on her shoulders, gripping her lightly, with restrained passion. And holding her body apart from his.

"You know that is not it."

"Then what is it?" she almost shouted into his face.

"You should not be here," he shouted back. "This is men's business. You should be somewhere safe, where I can protect you. Not running and hiding like a fugitive in the wilds."

His hands dropped from her shoulders and his voice dropped too. "What sort of man am I, to take a wife when all I can offer her is this island, and the soldiers from Glencairn searching to kill us both?"

Frances raised herself on tiptoes to kiss him. "The man I want. The only man I love. The man I married. Is that not enough?"

Alasdair's arms went about her slowly, and he held her close to him without speaking. "I do not deserve you," he said.

Frances laughed. Everything was going to be all right now. "No? Remember that next time you will scold me for burning the oatcakes." She reached up to his head and drew him down to her. "But, oh, my love," she whispered, "do not speak again of sending me away from you. There is no life for me where you are not."

Then their lips met in a kiss that blazed between them as bright as brushfire on the hills, burning out all that went before and replacing it with the passion that ignited their bodies.

Alasdair was the first to return to the present. Tenderly he lifted Frances in his arms, carried her down a short, rocky slope to the grassy verge of the pool, and laid her gently on the ground. He knelt beside her and kissed her again as he drew the rough gown from her shoulders, exposing her full white breasts, her nipples already taut with desire. She shivered as the smooth white skin of her breasts and stomach was exposed to the cool mountain air. Still she clung to him.

"Do not leave me," she begged. "Do not ever be leaving me."

"Hush, love."

In a moment, Alasdair was rid of his tartan trews and leather jerkin. He bent his head to her breast and caught the nipple between his teeth. She gasped as tongue, lips, and teeth teased her aroused senses. She arched her body toward him, longing for his touch, and his hand lightly stroked her thighs until she cried out with desire for him. Alasdair laughed deep in his throat and moved closer to her, only to tease the other nipple into a state of arousal. She felt his manhood hard against her leg. Now his hand stroked higher and higher between her thighs until it found the moist proof of her desire.

She put her arms around him and tried to pull him on top of her, but his merciless hand held her down and stroked her knowingly until she reached the height of her passion and cried out in helpless pleasure. Quickly, before the pleasure had left her body, Alasdair drew her to him and entered her. The pulsing of his body inside her brought her to new peaks, waves breaking inside her over and over until she felt completely drained of her strength. The world went black and she felt her limbs relaxing on the grass in utter satiation.

When she roused herself again, the sun had hardly moved across the sky, but Alasdair was standing by the edge of the pool, watching her with a gaze at once tender and mocking.

"Time you were coming back to me," he teased, "and I at such pains to pleasure you."

Frances drew a corner of her plaid over her body and looked slantwise through the fringed edge. "There will be no end to your generosity," she teased back, "or . . ." She mimed dismay at the sight of his limp manhood. "Och, spent a'ready! 'Tis no sort of a rapist you are at all, my love, and so I'll be sure to tell Glencairn."

"Wheesht now! Watch the rude tongue on you," Alasdair advised. He moved closer with the light, quick step that meant menace. "Was no one telling you that I am the very worst kind of villain? Ah . . ."

Frances had tried to get her feet under her to get away from him, but he was too quick for her. He knelt, gripping her wrists with one hand, as he continued. "I always drown my victims after I take them—particularly if they laugh at me!" With the last words he gave a mighty heave and tossed her into the pool.

Frances began squealing even before she was in the water. Her flailing arms, grasping for purchase, knocked against Alasdair's legs. Her fingers closed around one ankle even as she tumbled backward into the pool.

There were two mighty splashes in quick succession. Frances gasped as the first shock of the icy water hit her, then sputtered out the mouthful of cold mountain water she'd taken in surprise. Luckily the pool was shallow. Her feet were already on the rocky bottom. She waded to shore a few steps ahead of Alasdair.

He gave her a stinging slap on the bare bottom as she was climbing out of the pool.

"You're no gentleman," Frances retorted, "to take advantage of a lady in a vulnerable moment like yon." She wrapped herself in her plaid and retreated, planting herself safely away from the cold waters. She giggled as Alasdair climbed out in his turn, making a great show of shivering.

"A fortunate thing the water was shallow," he

said with great solemnity. "And I'll no' need dinner the day, having swallowed a small trout or two as I went under. But it's awfu' cold in there. I doubt you'll have to take me under your plaid, lady."

"Mm," Frances sighed a little later. "A wonderful restorative thing, cold water. Will I be giving you a cold bath every morning, then?"

Alasdair laughed and tweaked one of her curls before his hand strayed back to pleasanter places. "Insatiable woman! If I'd been knowing what a wildcat I brought along with me . . ."

"Well," said Frances demurely, "since you won't let us go into the village, I must be doing something for amusement."

Then the plaid slipped off, and she was not demure any longer.

11

In the end it was Frances herself who was the first to violate Alasdair's ban on going to the village.

Throughout July and the first part of August she had been perfectly happy to be isolated with Alasdair on Eilean Duin. But as the summer drew to a close, she began to wish for the company of another woman with whom she could discuss certain symptoms that had begun to trouble her.

Grizel had been far too prudish to teach her anything, and Frances had never heeded much to the talk of the married women of the glen with their endless nattering of births, deaths, and illness. Such tales had meant little to the healthy young girl who carried a man's burden in caring for the land and its people. But now she began to wish that she had listened more carefully when Mairi and Janet put their heads together and began to reckon on their fingers, while casting sidelong glances at one of the young girls of the glen and muttering that such a one was surely no longer entitled to wear the maiden snood.

"A girdle to bind your waist?" she'd heard Janet screech once at a girl who'd been caught trying to smuggle a scrap of cloth out of the weaving room. "It's your hair you should have bound up, you wanton, and long ago! Look at her," she appealed to Grizel. "Four months gone if she's a day, and has the impudenee to . . ."

They'd caught sight of Frances, then thirteen, and their voices had dropped to whispers. Now Frances wished she could recall more of that long-ago scene. The girl had been thick in the waist, but might not that have been due to the folds of cloth she'd tried to smuggle out under her gown?

That night, when she was undressing in the hut, Frances surreptitiously tried to measure her slim waist with the girdle she'd just taken off. But the sun-bleached creases in the cloth fell into the same pattern they'd always held. No, she was getting no fatter there. But when Alasdair came up behind her and put his arms around her, cupping her breasts in his hands, she gave an involuntary cry and jerked back from his touch. Her breasts were so sensitive that the light caress was painful rather than pleasurable.

"What, shy of me?" He laughed, thinking it a game. But Frances retreated to the pile of heather that was their bed and sat down heavily, drawing the plaid about her shoulders. Her head was spinning and for a moment she could not answer him.

"It will be nothing," she said when her head cleared and she was aware of him standing and watching her with the wary look of a soldier who fears an ambush ahead of him. Of course, he thought she had been troubled with the Sight again. And didn't that always portend some disaster?

Frances forced herself to smile, to answer him. "Truly, Alasdair, 'tis not the Sight. It is only that I was dizzy for a moment."

Alasdair's face cleared and he gave a satisfied nod. "You should have told me it was your time, Fan. You know I would not trouble you. I'll lie outside tonight, with Duncan and Sandy." He turned and left the hut, while Frances stared after him, shaking her head. Her time? Lord knows, that was not her trouble—nor had it been these two months. It was that had started her thinking.

Then, without warning, there was sour bile in her throat and she ran out to spew up her supper outside the hut. Luckily, Alasdair had wandered and did not notice her.

In the morning Alasdair looked in while she still lay abed, to inform her that he was going hunting with Sandy and Duncan. If she had not been feeling so ill, Frances would have laughed at the mixture of deference and fear that had replaced his usual lordly attitude. Had he been in soldiers' camps so long, surrounded only by men, that he thought there was something magical and dangerous about a woman in the flowers?

But that wasn't her trouble; so much, at least, she knew. As soon as she could drag herself out of bed, she washed her face and arms in the cold water of the river and dressed herself as decently as she might. Barefoot in the faded homespun dress, with her old plaid pulled over her head, she looked like any peasant girl. It should be safe enough to go to the village in this garb. She wouldn't stand out as a stranger, not like Alasdair and Sandy with their soldiers' looks.

The track on the other side of the river was easy enough to follow, once she'd gotten through the band of trees that grew right down to the water's edge. The sun dried the droplets of water clinging to her bare legs and the hem of her dress, and as she walked over the springy turf, she felt so good that she was tempted to dismiss her illness of the night before as a passing thing. Why not go back to the island, and not risk Alasdair's anger when he found out she'd been to the village?

But she encountered the narrow footpath that led to the wisewoman's hut while she was still debating. The position of the hut apart from the rest of the village, the scraps of red thread and herbs tied to the bushes that lined the path, were clues enough to Frances. Here would be some old woman, called a witch by her neighbors, who lived apart and made a living by selling small charms to keep the cow's milk from drying up and such like. Such a one would be safer to visit than any other crofter, for to protect her small income she would have learned not to gossip about those who came to her for help or information.

The turf-walled hut was even lower than the cottages around Beauly, but the air was sweet with the smell of bunches of dried herbs that hung from the low ceiling. They brushed Frances' forehead as she passed under, and left dry, sweet-smelling leaves crackling in her hair.

"Lucky, lucky," crooned her hostess, stroking the tangled curls back from Frances' brow. "So sick this early, it must be a fine boy you carry that makes you so ill, my little lady. Lucky you are to come to old Moidhri. I'll see you stay strong for your lying-in. Not for many months yet." She cast a sharp glance at Frances' young, firm body under the ragged dress.

And so, as simply as that, Frances' nascent suspicions were settled. Moidhri was calculating the months to the birth before Frances had voiced her question. Then the old woman disappeared into the smoky back of the hut, only to reappear with a nauseous, bitter green mixture which she insisted

Frances swallow. She took the nasty mess in one gulp and found herself, to her surprise, feeling better afterward.

"Boil a cup of these herbs every day," Moidhri instructed her, "at least till the sickness passes. And walk." She kneaded Frances' legs with her gnarled old hands. "Ah, good. 'Tis young and strong you are. Dinna' be taking to your bed yet. You fine ladies are aye easy with yourselves and it goes aye the worse with you in the end."

"I don't know what you mean," Frances muttered, remembering her assumed role. "I be no lady." She left quickly, before Moidhri could question her further.

It was sheer bad luck that Frances' return from the village was observed by a boy who had nothing better to do than to follow her through the heather, pretending he was a grown clan warrior following the track of a cattle raid, and who was young enough to babble to his father about the black-haired foreign lady whom he had followed down to the river's edge where there was the ford to the haunted island. The father remembered what the foreign soldiers had said—gold for the man who discovered the lady of Beauly.

Two days later, at dawn, Glencairn's soldiers crossed the ford.

If Alasdair had been a simple Highlander, given

to cattle raiding in the summer and storytelling in the winter, they might have surprised the camp and captured all. But years of soldiering in the Low Countries had left him with the irrational habit of setting a guard each night, even in this peaceful backwater where there was no need for it at all. Sandy Ruadh's cry of alarm, and the clash of steel on mail, wakened Alasdair and Duncan while Glencairn's second man was still balancing from rock to rock in the river.

Alasdair slept with his sword beside him. He was up and out of the hut before Frances had rubbed the sleep out of her eyes. She heard the shouts and the clashing of swords and for a confused moment thought herself in a dream. Then the flames crackled at the door of the hut and she knew that this time it was no dream.

The back of the hut was a slender construction of branches daubed with mud. She broke through the wall and crawled out with her plaid wrapped over her nose and mouth to keep the smoke from smothering her. Hard hands caught her before she was through the rough hole and drew her the rest of the way. There was a chuckle from her captor.

"Here's the one, lads. Be off now! It's no part of our bargain tae get ourselves killed by the red-heidit madman."

The enveloping plaid stifled Frances' shout for

help. She writhed in her captor's arms, got her mouth free, and raised one despairing cry.

"*Alasdair—*"

A hand covered her mouth and she was swung up onto a horse, steadied on the saddlebow like a sack of meal. "Let's awa', lads," the man who held her shouted to his companions. "Kind of the little lady to come so swift to us—no need to wait about now!"

They splashed across the ford. Three men, but six horses. Frances craned her neck and realized that they had cut loose the horses in the camp and were driving them before them. Without a mount, Alasdair would have no hope of following them before they were lost in the winding paths of the mountains. She twisted and kicked out in the hope of throwing herself off the horse, but a hand twined in her girdle kept her prisoner.

"Ah, don't make it difficult," her captor chided her. "After you were so kind to show us the way, and all."

On the other side of the ford, Alasdair heard the careless words and dropped his sword.

"Yes, 'twas your lady here showed us the path to the ford," called back one of the other men. "Think she's growing tired of the country life?"

Their laughter drowned out any response Alasdair might have made. As they kicked their horses into a trot, Frances, jolted almost to insensibility, realized two things at once.

It was her foolish trip to consult old Moidhri that had betrayed them.

And Alasdair had given up the attempt to follow her. He was still standing on the island side of the river, watching like a statue while Glencairn's men carried her away.

12

For an hour or more after leaving Eilean Duin, Glencairn's men rode at top speed over the winding, precipitous trails. At the first halt Frances was pulled roughly upright to sit before her captor on his horse, her wrists tied in front of her with a leather strip that was firmly attached to the saddle girth. Before long her arms ached with the constant strain of the one position, and the jolting ride made her head swim. She could not identify the territory they covered or hazard any guess as to where she was being taken.

The sickness of the previous day returned in full force, and soon she had to concentrate all her faculties on the twin tasks of sitting upright and not spewing out her guts in front of the men who had taken her. Through the waves of illness, some scraps of their conversation came through to her and reassured her. She had not been taken in a private raid as part of some clan struggle, but on the direct orders of Glencairn, who had been searching for her all summer. Alasdair was to have been taken too, but the men had not been prepared for his prompt resistance and thought it the better part of valor to escape the fighting while they still had their prize, the lady of Beauly.

Glencairn! Through the jolting and the nausea, Frances tried to concentrate her mind and remember what Alasdair had said. He had some notion that Glencairn wanted to wed her himself, and some other talk about their own Catholic wedding not being recognized by the kirk in Edinburgh. But that was all havers. She was Alasdair's lawful wedded wife, and quickening with his child. No one could set all that aside.

From what the men said, Frances guessed that their orders had been not to harm her in any way, but only to bring her safe to Glencairn. So great was her relief at discovering she was not to be raped or killed in some private act of clan vengeance, she could not imagine what Glencairn could possibly do to hurt her and Alasdair. At worst he would keep her prisoner for a time.

The sun was just rising when they slackened their pace. Frances guessed that they had been riding for a little over an hour. At the moment, they were going east, into the sun, but the paths they followed had twisted and turned so often that she had no idea whether that had been their general direction.

Then they came around a curve that showed the whole barren hillside and the valley below, and Frances slumped over the horse's neck, sick with despair. The hill was alive with soldiers. North or south, east or west—what did it matter what way they had ridden, or how far and fast? Even were Alasdair minded to follow after her—and that seemed unlikly, for after those words at the camp, he must think she'd betrayed him—they would never get free of the close to fifty men she saw about her, rising from the heather with their steel helms glinting red in the rising sun.

There was no attempt at concealment, no stalking from bush to bush as true Highlanders would have done. They were simply rising from the ground where they had slept and going about their business. Some were just rubbing their eyes and staring about them in the light of the rising sun; others, half-naked, were splashing and swearing in the cold mountain stream that ran down into the valley; most were already armed and dressed. Frances noted in particular one tall, spare man with silver-splashed hair, mounted on a fine horse that she'd have been glad to see in the stables at Beauly.

As they drew nearer, riding past knots of men,

she saw that most wore some scrap of a distinctive red-and-green tartan twisted around their helms or thrown over their body armor.

"Why do they all wear the same pattern?" she asked.

The man who held her before him chuckled. "A notion o' the earl's," he explained. "He'll have all his men wear the same plaid—that way we'll be knowing one another in battle." He twisted his head and spat into the path. "Fool notions these gentle-folk get. If a man's such a fool as not to know his ain side, will he stop to count the colors in a plaid?"

"Perhaps it is really to serve the earl's pride," Frances suggested. "He will be showing how many men he has in his service. I have heard that the Earl of Glencairn is a powerful and greedy man who cares for nothing but to amass the lands of those less fortunate. This seems to me just one more way of showing off his wealth."

The tall silver-haired man who was so well-mounted had ridden up to Frances and her captor during this exchange. Frances saw that his dour countenance was enlivened by laugh lines around his eyes and that he sat as erect in the saddle as any of the younger fighting men around them. Like the other men he was dressed simply, in a leather jack and plain trews. An aging mercenary captain, Frances guessed, recruited into Glencairn's service when the life on campaign abroad grew too hard for him.

"You mistake the matter, Lady Frances," the new arrival said, lifting his hat and bowing courteously over the arched neck of his horse. "The earl is indeed proud, and justly so, of his efforts to bring peace to the Highlands. But among civilized folk, a man's wealth is no longer counted in the tail of barefoot ghillies he has running behind him. These"—his gesture encompassed the men spread out around them on the barren hillside—"represent the least part of Glencairn's power."

"Peace!" Frances gave a bitter laugh. "Is that what you call it, when a man robs the lands of his neighbors and kinfolk? Aye, even in Beauly we've heard of the methods of the great Earl of Glencairn. When a Highlander lifts his neighbors' cattle, it's called thieving and you southerners will hang the poor man if you can catch him. But when a clever Sassenach takes the lands of his neighbors with lawyers' tricks, you call him a great man and bow and scrape to him. Well, you may tell your fine earl that it will be a long day before Frances Murray of Beauly will be thanking him humbly for the great favor of stealing her home and lands. We have our own name for that in the Highlands, and so the earl will find it, if he dares show his face north of Stirling."

The stranger seemed not in the least put out by her fiery speech, but only chuckled to himself as if very satisfied by something or other. "Oh, he dares," he said, as if to himself. "He dares, indeed. 'Twould be worth the journey, indeed, to meet with a lady as brave and beautiful as Frances Murray."

Frances looked down at her mud-splashed skirt. With her hands bound to the saddle horn before her, she could not even push back the tangled curls from her face or wipe the stains of mud and water away.

"I am thinking there will be no need to mock me, sir," she said, more quietly. "Or will this be the fine Sassenach manners we are hearing so much about?"

"Look about you," the stranger advised. "These are Highland men, though they serve one you despise. And Glencairn himself is a Highlander, albeit a civilized one, and will be pleased to dine with you at his castle of Beauly."

Frances sat straighter in the saddle. "Long will be the day before I will be dining with Glencairn in *my* castle of Beauly," she declared in ringing tones. "And so you may be telling your master, should you see him before I do."

Another dry chuckle greeted these words of defiance. "My master? You mistake, lady. I doubt my master would be overinterested in your plans. I serve King James, and his only interest in the matter is to see another pocket of rebellious Highlanders brought under control by a good and faithful servant such as the Earl of Glencairn."

"And so you will be helping the earl," Frances concluded. "Have you no battles of your own to fight, then?"

"Indeed I have," he responded. "I think I may have a very great battle before me. I look forward to it."

And raising one hand in salute, he rode away.

Half the men on the hillside joined Frances and the man she rode with, forming a formidable armed escort for the remainder of the journey. They turned south, and riding at a slower pace along the cattle drovers' tracks, made a three-day journey of the trip that Frances and Alasdair had covered in less than twenty-four hours' hard riding north.

At night they stopped and demanded shelter in crofters' huts. The peasants were willing enough to give whatever hospitality was in their power when they saw the gold coins that the leader casually tossed out, and Frances was impressed against her will by this display of wealth. Truly the Earl of Glencairn must be a powerful and wealthy man! So much gold was hardly seen from year's end to year's end at Beauly as his man threw away on these poor hills.

And, insensibly, she began to think a little better of this mysterious earl. Few soldiers, riding armed through these hills, would have bothered to pay for their lodging. They would simply have taken what they wanted and counted on their rapid passage to take them out of the reach of clan vengeance.

Wherever they passed, the peasants would be

frantically driving their stock up into the hills and hiding their few possessions. But the sight of gold changed their attitude at once. On the first night, the crofter that Glencairn's men caught trembled with fear and pleaded that he had nothing, nothing at all that might serve the noble gentlemen. But the man brightened amazingly when the captain of the troop tossed a gold coin at him. Raising his hands to his mouth, he bit it with decaying black teeth and gave a horrible grin at the sight of the bright metal.

"Gold! For such a piece as that, hersel' could have the old cow and the wife her nainsel', let alone a night's lodging."

The same feeling was expressed at their second stop. Although Frances was racked by anxiety for Alasdair and fear for what lay ahead of her, she could not complain of her treatment on the journey. They rode by easy stages, stopping to rest whenever she complained of tiredness, and in the evenings she had the best of what poor hospitality the crofters could offer: fresh-cut heather for a bed, a hen killed and popped into the caldron for soup, a swallow of burning uisque-baugh from the captain's flask to revive her when she was too tired and sick to eat.

That had been mostly on the first day, that she succumbed to exhaustion and self-pity. The change was too great for her to take in all at once—one minute leading an idyllic life on the island with

Alasdair, the next snatched up and taken prisoner by Glencairn. And the worst of it was that Alasdair had seemingly believed that she betrayed him.

Over and over Frances tried to convince herself that Alasdair was merely doing the sensible thing when he stopped, that he and Duncan and Sandy would be coming after her as soon as they could get new horses. And over and over she heard the soldier's damning words, thanking her for showing them the way to the camp. What a cruel jest!

She went round and round the same track so many times that, wrapped in her own thoughts, she hardly noticed or cared where they were taking her. And at night, lying in the rude shelter of the crofter's hut, a new thought came to torment her.

"I never had a chance to tell him about the baby," she whispered to herself.

That was a black night. Lying in the darkness, wrapped in the plaid that one of the soldiers had given her, she wept into the springy heather that was her bed, wept silently until her aching eyes imagined red stars and circles in the blackness of the hut. Thinking of Alasdair, she might just be able to bear. But thinking of his ignorance of their child was more than her heart could tolerate.

And in the morning, because there was nothing else to do, she rose up and went on with the soldiers. A calm fatalism had settled over her that somehow made holding up easier. She would go where she was taken and do what she must to keep herself and the child alive; everything else was beyond her. Thinking of Alasdair was entirely beyond her now. If she was to survive at all, she must put him out of her mind and concentrate her wits on whatever new challenges lay before her.

Late in the afternoon of the third day Frances saw the towers of Beauly rising before her. Even though she was returning as Glencairn's prisoner, she felt a pulse of joy at the familiar sight. Here, at least, she would be on her own ground, while Glencairn would be a "foreigner," disliked and distrusted by the people of the glen. Here, surrounded by her own people, she could find *some* way to outwit him. She began to feel alive again.

Only the thought of Alasdair was too painful; her mind skittered around it and seized on any distraction. And Beauly was a good distraction.

Her comfort in the familiar walls of Beauly, glowing in the afternoon light with their grayish-gold native stone, diminished as they rode in and the heavy outer gate clanged shut behind her. Among all the men in the outer bailey, she searched in vain for a familiar face. And when she dismounted, her guards very respectfully prevented her from going into the manor wing. Instead, it seemed, she was to be lodged in the tower keep.

"It is damp in the tower," Frances protested. "I could become ill. My lord of Glencairn will not be pleased to hear that you mistreat his prisoner." If she could persuade them to lodge her in the manor wing, she might escape the castle by the same route Alasdair had used to enter it.

"Orders of Glencairn and Beauly," the captain of the troop responded laconically.

Frances stiffened in outrage. So he dared to add the name of her ancestral lands to his own!

The anger carried her, stiff-backed, up the stairs of the tower keep to the narrow barred room, where she suffered the ministrations of a hatchet-faced Lowland woman in place of Janet Beatty. The woman had no Gaelic, and Frances even began to wonder if she spoke English, for her only response to Frances' questions was the often-repeated, "My lord of Glencairn will speak with you when he is ready."

At least she did not call him "Glencairn and Beauly," thought Frances when at last the woman had withdrawn, leaving her to her own reflections behind a locked door.

Too tired even to pace up and down the room, she sank down on a low stool and gazed at her entwined hands. It seemed her life was always coming round to this point—locked in a room, waiting the commands of some man. Perhaps it was true what Grizel had told her, that all a woman could do in life was to wait and pray. Perhaps she should stop trying to manage affairs that were beyond her, and settle to her proper lot in life.

Wouldn't it be enough to spin and weave and care for the babe that was to come, and let the men decide the fate of the land? They always won in the end anyway. Even Alasdair, for all his talk of sharing Beauly with her, never consulted her on any decisions. And she was so tired! One might as well give in. Glencairn was not so bad after all; he had seen that she had hot water to wash in and clean clothes after her journey, and it must have been he who ordered that they travel slowly and spend gold like water to give her what little comfort could be procured on the rough ride through the Highlands.

Frances derived an insensible comfort from the luxuries that surrounded her. To feel her skin clean and soft again, her hair shining and combed back smoothly from her face, to hear the rustle of her stiff skirts, all these small things reassured her and made her feel that a man who could give such orders for her comfort could not be the monster she had imagined him.

She was still seated on the low stool, indulging in this uncharacteristically softened mood, when the door opened and the man she had talked with on the hillside entered.

Then he had been dressed like the rest of the soldiers, in a steel-plated leather jack and a strip of Glencairn tartan around his helmet, with nothing but the tall black horse to signal his quality.

Now he was dressed like a gentleman. His stiffly starched white ruff was higher than Frances' own, and there was a band of silver ribbon decorated with pearls around the brim of his black velvet hat. His padded doublet, also of black velvet, was slashed to reveal white satin sleeves embroidered in a silver trelliswork that matched the white and silver of Frances' gown. The rich costume stood in sharp contrast to his spare frame and the severe lines of his gaunt face.

Without speaking, he bowed before her and extended his arm. Frances rose at the gesture and placed the tips of her fingers on his sleeve.

"Is it you are to be escorting me to my lord Glencairn?" she asked.

"I am. He bids me inquire if the service has been appropriate to your degree."

Frances inclined her head in answer, while a feeling of unreality came between her and the courteous, attentive features of her interlocutor. Only three days ago she had been seized, shrieking, from the arms of her husband, by the orders of the same man who now, it seemed sent this high-ranking gentleman to be her escort.

"The Earl of Glencairn is well served," she murmured, perceiving that some verbal answer was necessary. Her eyes frankly appraised the man beside her, from the pearls in his hat to the silver-and-diamond buckles in his shoes. "I am surprised, sir, to find you doing his bidding like any lackey. Did you not tell me that you owned no master but King James?"

Her escort gave the dry chuckle with which he

had greeted so many of her remarks. "I have heard it said that the Earl of Glencairn is such a man as any gentleman may be proud to serve."

"But you yourself—what will be your opinion of him, sir?" Frances pressed on. They were halfway down the tower stairs by now.

The gentleman in black and silver coughed as if to cover up some slight confusion. "Why, as to that, my lady, I share your own opinion."

"Mine?" Frances halted in the great hall, one hand pressed to her bosom in amazement. "I have never met the man."

The hall was empty of all but a few servitors, none of them known to her.

"On the occasion of our previous meeting you described him as a powerful and greedy man. Both those adjectives are appropriate. It remains only to add that he is invariably successful in attaining his objectives."

"I make no doubt of it," Frances answered while they traversed the courtyard and entered the manor wing of the castle, "if his objects are always so unworthy of such a powerful man. It will be easy for him to be taking the lands of defenseless women."

They had reached the door of a small salon on the ground floor of the manor wing. Frances' escort paused and gave her a quizzical look before handing her into the room. "I had not thought of you as defenseless, Lady Frances. Nor as . . .

defeated. His lordship will be disappointed to find you so cast down. It is an ally the Earl of Glencairn seeks, not a prisoner."

His words echoed the fears that Alasdair had voiced. Frances would not consider the possibility that Glencairn might want herself as well as her lands. "I think you cannot know so much as you pretend of the earl's desires," Frances snapped, and stepped into the salon.

Inside, a small table was laid with an assortment of cold meats and pastries. A bottle of wine stood already opened, and two high-backed wooden chairs were drawn up to the table. But apart from these furnishings, the room was empty.

At the sound of the door closing behind her, Frances whirled and faced the man who had escorted her from her room. His thin, almost fleshless face was creased in what she had come to recognize as a smile.

"Pray be seated, my dear," he requested. "I find the raw air of this barbarous Highland place improves my appetite." He drew out one of the chairs for Frances, and seated himself on the other without waiting to see her reaction.

Frances gasped in surprise. "You . . . you are Glencairn?"

"It took you long enough to guess it."

And a fine fool she had made of herself, seeking to question this man about himself. "You tricked me!"

"No. You tricked yourself, my dear. But do not allow it to distress you. As I have just told you, you have said nothing of my character with which I do not agree. I am indeed proud, unscrupulous, and ambitious. And in you, Lady Frances, I have found the perfect match for my talents."

At his words, accompanied by that dry, fleshless smile, Frances felt another wave of nausea overtake her. She stumbled to the chair he had offered her and sank down, her head in her hands.

It was some moments before the full impact of his words struck her. "Are you so eager for my poor lands, then?" she murmured. "But you have Beauly already. What do you gain by keeping me here?"

"Our marriage," Glencairn instructed her, "will bring a measure of legitimacy to my occupation of Beauly. As you yourself have said, I prefer to gain my estates by the lawyers' pen rather than by the sword. Then, there is your charming self into the bargain, a young and lovely wife to bear the sons of my old age."

He carved a slice from the spiced breast of chicken on the table and held it out to her. "May I offer you some of this chicken? It is accounted one of my cook's greatest accomplishments."

Frances ignored the proffered food and raised her head to look him straight in the eyes. The mocking, thin-lipped smile stirred new fear in her. "I . . . think you mistake the matter, sir. I am the wedded wife of Alasdair Cameron."

"Come, come, my dear," Glencairn chided her gently. "This tale of a hasty marriage was well enough in its time, but with me as your protector you have no need of such stories to cloak your shame. Soon you will be my wife and the unfortunate experience you have undergone at the hands of this young ruffian will be forgotten."

His eyes traveled over her figure, noting the full breasts and the pallor around her mouth and eyes. He held out a platter with some slices of fresh wheaten bread and the pieces of chicken breast. "Eat, now. You will need more food to nourish the child you carry under your girdle."

Frances' head snapped up. "How did you know? I have only been knowing myself these two days."

"Ah . . . so it is true. I did not know, but suspected. You had the look of an increasing woman. Tell me, does young Cameron know yet? No? All the better. I shall think how best to use the information. A pity, of course, that our wedding will have to be deferred until you are the lighter of your child. I have no mind to give my name to a base-born brat. We will send it out to nurse. No doubt you will be happy enough to be rid of the unfortunate reminder of your abduction and rape."

Frances gripped her hands together under the table digging her nails into the flesh to combat the weakness she felt. "You are mistaken on several counts. There will be no marriage, for I am already wed. There was no rape. I went with Alasdair willingly. He is my lawful husband and the father of my child."

Glencairn shook his head and poured a thin stream of red wine into Frances' cup. "A sad case. I have heard that breeding women suffer from such delusions. I hope your terrible experience may not have turned your brain permanently, my dear. Well, there is time for you to accustom yourself to your new situation. I doubt you'll be delivered of the child before March. And by that time there should be no question of a marriage."

He tilted the cup and held it to her lips. "Drink. . . . That's better. I must leave Beauly tomorrow, and I should not like to hear of your starving yourself while I am gone. After all"—his eyes flicked over her tight-laced waist and flat stomach under the satin gown—"we must think of the child, must we not?"

Frances felt at the end of her strength, unable to make any reply to Glencairn. She took up a piece of the bread and nibbled on it. The odor of the fresh-baked bread had tempted her nostrils until she could resist no longer, and the wine Glencairn had made her swallow was making her feel light-headed and hungry. Indeed the fresh bread was good.

Suddenly she realized how very hungry she was. She devoured several slices of the spiced chicken and all the rest of the bread, and then reached for a dish of comfits. There were miniature castles and soldiers of pastry, filled with honey and garnished with marchpane—such delicacies as had never before been seen on the table at Beauly. Frances demolished two of the sweet pastries and leaned back with a sigh of repletion.

"Good, good." Glencairn had contented himself with a piece of cheese and a sip of claret, but it seemed to please him to see Frances eat. "While I am gone, you must command my cook to prepare whatever delicacies commend themselves to a woman in your condition. I must confess that my experience with breeding women is slight. My first two wives were, unfortunately, barren."

Frances looked at the hooded eyes and the cruel twist of his mouth, and shivered. She could not help but wonder what fate had befallen those women who failed to meet Glencairn's needs.

"Do not trouble yourself." Glencairn spoke as though he read her thoughts. "It is clear that you will prove most satisfactory in every respect . . . as soon as you get over your delusion that being raped by a Cameron by-blow constitutes a marriage."

Frances roused herself to respond to this taunt. "Alasdair is no by-blow . . . and it is a true marriage. You cannot wed with me when I have a husband already."

Glencairn dabbed at his dry lips with the linen napkin and regarded her with something of pity in his expression. "Do not trouble yourself over that small matter. Did you not understand? In a matter of a very few days, the legality of whatever form of marriage you were forced to go through will cease to be of import."

When Frances clearly did not understand his words, he continued. "Since my incompetent men did not complete the task I gave them, I am going to oversee it myself. I am leaving Beauly in the morning, Lady Frances, to hunt down the man who dared to insult you and to avenge the honor of my kinswoman, in the true swashbuckling Highland style."

He paused again, and then said in a voice without expression, "Before I return, my dear, this so-called husband of yours will be dead."

13

In the weeks that followed, Frances was kept close in the castle, while Glencairn returned to the North to hunt down Alasdair. He did not pursue the hunt very long himself; sooner than she liked, he was back at the castle, having left his soldiers to look for Alasdair while he concentrated on her.

It was not that he was unpleasant to her. In a queer way she even enjoyed their daily battles of wits. But there was something in his slow measuring glances and secret smiles that frightened her. They seemed to say that he knew her better than she did herself, that he had no need to force her because it was only a matter of time before she forgot Alasdair and found herself in his bed.

Then, too, there was the practical matter that she had little freedom of movement while Glencairn was at the castle to oversee her days. She was allowed to leave her room, but still confined to the castle and the inner bailey. She had chafed at being thus kept caged, but her complaints fell on deaf ears.

"There is air in the bailey," Glencairn told her, adding in a disgusted aside, "fresh enough, at all events, forby it's somewhat wet—and as much sunshine as is to be had anywhere in this land. When I've dealt with Cameron, my dear, I shall take you to France. I have a small manor in the Languedoc, where the sun shines and the grapes ripen. You will like that."

Frances spread her wide skirts and curtsied. "I thank you, sir, but I prefer to remain in Scotland while my husband is here." And she withdrew before Glencairn could respond with another of his gibes at Alasdair.

She retired to the weaving room, where great webs were spread for the winter weaving, and good wool going to waste because the women were afraid to come up to the castle and work with Glencairn's soldiers everywhere. There was some relief in bending her mind to the tedious work, though she still could not keep from thinking about Alasdair and the men pursuing him in the cold hills of the North.

The battle of her thoughts went on long hour

after long hour: The sett is ten red, two yellow, ten red. Then four bands of green with red between them. If there is sleet in the hills, the rocks will be icy; take care that you do not slip and fall when climbing over them. Now the threading of the warp. Reach out and hook a thread, draw it through on the first harness. Reach out for the next thread. My right arm aches from the work. You trust the crofters to give you food and shelter, but Glencairn's gold is a sore temptation for a poor man; take care that you tell no one where you are going next. Reach out and hook a thread . . .

For the first few days she worked alone, with no company but her fears for Alasdair. Grizel kept to her room these days, humming a tuneless song and stitching away at a shapeless black piece of embroidery. Frances had made a few duty visits in her first days in the castle, then gave up entirely. Her aunt's grasp on reality seemed to have snapped under the pressure of recent events. She lived in her memories, and cried whenever Frances mentioned anything that had happened since Hugh's death, and refused absolutely to join her in the weaving room.

As the days passed, the women of the glen began returning to use the big looms, which made a stronger and finer cloth than they could weave at home. From their guarded hints, Frances got her first oblique news of Alasdair.

News passed in the hills by informal routes, from

deerstalkers to tinkers, from women gathering dye plants to fishwives tramping inland to sell their catch. So it happened that Frances was soon better informed than Glencairn about the progress of his quarry.

More than once, hearing Glencairn wonder aloud about the hunt that he had abandoned in the hills, she had to cover her mouth to hide a secret smile. The tales of how Alasdair had decoyed his enemies out into the loch in a leaking boat, or had led them in a day-long chase over the hills, only to end at their own camp, made good hearing and were rapidly spread over the Highlands.

Frances had no doubt that she could even get a message to Alasdair through this informal network, should she so desire. But what was there to say? "I am being held prisoner at Beauly; pray, put your head in the lion's cage to rescue me." She laughed when she was alone, and there was the bitterness of the east wind shrieking around the castle turrets in her laughter. If she could not do better than that—she, Frances Cameron, who had carried the burden of all the lives in Beauly glen for so long—if she could do no better than that, she would send no message at all.

But even with the relief of hearing occasional oblique news of Alasdair, the long days of confinement passed slowly. Often and again she complained to Glencairn that she had not been brought up like his fine Southron ladies to sit before the fire and stitch at her tapestry. But she got no chance to leave the castle walls until the chill October day when Glencairn received his own news of the hunt for Alasdair, in a letter from the captain he had left in charge.

Glencairn's men followed Alasdair as best they might, but they had not the benefit of such skilled guides as Duncan Dhu and Sandy Ruadh. Hailing mostly from the gentler hills of Perth and Moray, they were discouraged first by the terrain, next by an unseasonable thundershower which soaked them for thirty-six hours and dampened the priming of their guns, and finally by an ambush in which Alasdair and Sandy, firing from hiding, sent them stampeding for shelter into the mouth of a narrow ravine. Once they were well into the ravine, a minor kind of bloody avalanche of rocks kept them from exiting, and broke Tam o' Willie's elbow for him. Duncan Dhu spent an enjoyable ten minutes rolling down large rocks on them before decamping to rejoin Alasdair higher in the hills.

The written report from Glencairn's captain was a less-than-polite summation of his feelings on the matter. He laid heavy stress on the "unfordable rivers, narrow glens, and prodigious rocky high mountains and woods" before reminding his lordship that the journey had "broken and bruised many of bothe officers and souldiers their leggs and arms and many of them have taken feavers at their return, besides the loss of firelocks broken with the falls." Should these natural difficulties not serve to explain his failure, he added that it had been almost impossible to come up with the murderer Cameron and his accomplices, both because of Cameron's great cunning, which caused him to keep himself at a distance from them, and also because of the favor the Highlanders bore Cameron, giving him constant intelligence of their motions.

The captain had then scrawled his signature, but in a postscript had added, "As it hath proven near impossible to surprize the murderer, I think it best to ly and quarter in the place which he must frequent for supplies, and so I will waite for him in this town of Invergarrie while waiting yr Ldships further orders."

"The damned lazy, useless gomeril!" Glencairn tossed the blotched and ill-spelled letter across the polished oak table of the library at Beauly. No one else was present to witness this rare display of emotion.

After some moments of silence, he stretched forth his hand and took up the letter again. This time he read it more carefully, and as he read, his thin lips curved upward in a smile. "So, my redheaded bird is overclever for the hunters. Then we shall try if he will come to the net." And, calling his servants, he gave certain orders which surprised them.

Frances, too, was surprised when at last, on a cold October night, Glencairn acceded to her request for some measure of freedom.

"You are looking pale," he told her that evening over their dinner, before she had even raised her complaint again. "I do not wish to endanger your health. I have decided that you may ride out each morning. Suitably escorted, of course." And his eyes slid to the corner of the room, where the captain's letter lay on top of a pile of his usual correspondence.

Frances bent her head over the table to conceal the excitement bubbling up in her at his words. The first step was won. She could get out of the castle! In her imagination she was already free and with Alasdair. She made an excuse to leave Glencairn's presence as soon as possible. Alone in her room, she paced the floor till dawn, unable to sleep for the new hope that was growing in her. If only she could get free of Glencairn and meet Alasdair once more, surely she could explain that she had never intended to lead the soldiers to Eilean Duin. And Alasdair would believe her. He had to believe her. There was the child that they had made. Frances pressed one hand to her stomach in a habitual gesture of reassurance.

The first step was to test the limits of her new freedom. The degree of liberty she was allowed seemed to vary from day to day, depending partially on which of Glencairn's men were freed of other duties to ride with her. Some kept careful watch on how far afield they rode and for how long, using Glencairn's concern for her health as the pretext for ordering her to turn back. Others let her roam more or less at will.

One whom Frances marked down as worth further attention, Rabbie o' Peats Mill, even let her go on out of his sight on the hill croft while he stopped to chat with Euan's pretty daughter Seonaidh.

Frances used the brief moments of privacy to have a talk of her own with Euan. She slipped a pearl brooch from the collar of her riding habit and gave it to him with instructions to send it on to Alasdair by whatever secret route the peasants were using to pass messages.

"I do not want to know how the message goes," she emphasized. "Glencairn . . ."

She could not quite put into words her fear. She no longer thought that Glencairn would do anything so barbarous as torturing her for information about Alasdair. Rather it was her own weakness she feared. She could not respond to Glencairn as a man, but in the long bleak days of her imprisonment she was coming more and more to look forward to their daily verbal fencing over dinner. She did not know what she might let slip in an unguarded moment. Better if she knew as little as possible.

"If Alasdair . . . still wants me . . ." For a moment she could not go on. The fear that was worse than the imprisonment, that he would refuse even to see her again, stopped her tongue. With an effort she recovered herself. "You ken the old cave beyond the north side of the glen? Tell him I will wait there. Three days from now, if I can get away."

Euan nodded and stowed the brooch in a fold of his plaid.

Glencairn seemed to be in especially good humor that night, and went out of his way to inform Frances that she would have to suffer the shiftless Rabbie as her only escort for the next few days. The rest of his men, he said, would be busy on some exercises he had planned for them.

"What sort of exercises?" Frances asked.

Glencairn chuckled. "Oh . . . tracking exercises. Hunting practice, you might say."

"They would do well to take lessons from the local people," Frances said. "Your men of Perth and Moray will never equal a true Highlandman for following the spoor of the red stag."

"No? But there are many sorts of game to be found in the hills. I do not despair of yet achieving some mild success."

"Whatever will be amusing you," said Frances politely. She could not resist a small jab. "You will be bored here in these dull days. Sad I am that I can be offering you no better entertainment in my castle of Beauly. Perhaps you would prefer to rejoin the court in Edinburgh."

Glencairn smiled and seemed to be looking at

something far away. "Perhaps I shall, soon. May I offer you some of this ragout of mutton? I think you will agree that my cook has done wonders in transforming plain Scots fare into a dish fit for the court. But I believe I may well equal his achievement." His eyes flickered over Frances' new dress of emerald-green velvet looped back with small silver chains, a gift from him that she wore in the evenings at his express request.

Frances was well pleased with the scraps of information gleaned from this conversation. The opportunity for her escape could not have worked out better if Glencairn had planned it that way.

The third day after her talk with Euan dawned bright and clear. Frances dressed for her morning ride with a mounting sense of excitement. This close to freedom, she would not even allow herself to think that she might fail, or that Alasdair might choose not to meet her. She promised herself that before night fell she would be in his arms again.

Glencairn, as was his custom, strolled over to the stables to bid Frances farewell as she set out. He raised one eyebrow at her substitution of a simple gray homespun for the gay riding habit in Glencairn red and green which he had given her. But he accepted without question her explanation that the finer dress had been soiled from constant wear and that she had given it to one of the women in the weaving room to cleanse and mend.

It was a fine bright day after weeks of mist. The

autumn sky was pale and clear, with a snap in the air that meant that winter was not far away. Frances' horse broke into a brisk trot moments after they left the castle gate. She noted with satisfaction that even now, when the child within her grew to proportions that thickened her body and affected her balance, she could easily outride the gangling Rabbie. But after a few hundred yards she reined in her horse and proceeded at a sedate walk which offered him plenty of chance to catch up with her. It was no part of her plan to make him suspicious by seeming to try to outrace him at the start of the day.

She visited two nearer farms, dawdling over the milk offered her at one place and the ale at the second, before sighing that she was weary and thought she might turn back for the day.

"A pity to waste the first fine day, missus," Rabbie suggested. "Euan's croft is just over the hill. If ye could ride so far, ye might rest for a while and see did ye feel up to going on."

Frances smiled a secret smile of triumph and allowed Rabbie to persuade her into the visit.

Once they were at the farm, it was easy enough. Seonaidh came running from the dairy, all smiles as though she had been thinking of nothing but Rabbie's last visit. Rabbie took a horn of ale from her hands and only gave a preoccupied nod when Frances told him she was going over the hill to see how Euan had got on with building his stone fence around the far field.

And it was as easy as that. In the tumbledown brush hut in the outfield, Frances found the supplies Euan had laid ready: a warm cloak, a leather sack of bannocks still warm from the hearthstone, and a flat stone flask of ale.

She slung the pack from her saddle horn and just touched the horse's flanks with her spurs. With any luck at all, she would be well away before the besotted Rabbie noticed her long absence, and safe in the hills before he gave up his search for her and sounded the alarm. And even then, it would take Glencairn some hours, maybe days, to recall his men and send them out to search for her.

The ride through the sharp cool air brought color to her cheeks and a song to her lips. Free at last, after these weeks of being watched wherever she went, shut up in the castle and subjected daily to Glencairn's smooth assumption that he would eventually possess her! Frances was humming under her breath, and once or twice raised her voice in song before she remembered the need for secrecy.

The path to the cave was narrow and steep, shaded on both sides by tall-growing bushes. For the last quarter-mile she had to toil uphill on foot, leading her horse. The exhilaration of escape gave way to fatigue and a growing light-headedness. Ruefully she acknowledged that though the sickness of the first weeks was over, she did not have the strength to push herself as she had done on the wild ride to Eilean Duin.

"You take the strength from me," she murmured, laying one hand over her loosely tied girdle. "Never mind. Alasdair will protect both of us. Glencairn will not have you now—nor me."

The bushes growing before the mouth of the cave provided a natural concealment. Frances had to break one branch to get the horse inside, but she was able to push it back after they were in the cave so that no disturbance should be evident to a casual glance. And in any case, she thought, who would search for her here, so close to Castle Beauly? They would think her riding north to Eilean Duin.

It was dark and chill inside the cave. The branches and leaves across the entrance made a mosaic pattern, like a finely wrought iron grille against the bright cool sky. Frances spread out the heavy frieze cloak to sit on and leaned back against the cave walls.

When she awoke, the pattern traced by leaves against the sky had faded to black on dull gray. She was stiff and cramped from sleeping in an unnatural position, and it took her a moment to remember where she was. But when the memory came back to her, it was accompanied by a flash of triumph. Close on nightfall, and still they had not found her! She was safe for sure, for the cave was so close to Beauly, Glencairn could have had her back in two hours, had he known where to look.

The soft rustling at the cave's mouth, the sound that she realized now had awakened her, was repeated. Her heart leapt in fear. The branches were pushed aside and a dark figure, stooping, was outlined across the sky.

"Frances?"

"Alasdair!"

In the first moments of reunion they had nothing to say. Frances clung to Alasdair with all her might, feeling with joy the sinewy outlines of his lean body, luxuriating in the fierce grip of his arms that held her as though they would never let her go.

It was Alasdair who drew away first, with a sharp motion, when Frances' horse whickered softly in the darkness. Then he laughed at himself.

"Forgive me—I've grown nervous these past few months. It's no' just precisely a peaceful life, keeping one step ahead of Glencairn's men."

Frances thought of what his life must have been, hunted through the hills, never sleeping in one bed two nights, never relaxing his vigilance. She offered the only thing she had. "Are ye hungry? I've ale and fresh bannocks . . ." She broke off and gave a rueful laugh as she felt for the packet. "Well, they were fresh. I've been sleeping on them."

Alasdair fell upon the offered food and crammed handfuls of the broken cakes into his mouth.

"We don't lack for food in the hills," he apologized after clearing his throat with a swallow of ale, "but fresh bread's a fair treat. Most days we daren't light a fire." His arm went around her and he hugged her to his side. "That's not what I've missed the most, though. Maybe you can guess?"

His fingers were busy with the knot of her girdle as he spoke. Suddenly his hands stilled and he drew a sharp breath. Then his right hand flattened, palm against her swollen belly, while his left felt upward in the darkness.

"You did not tell me."

"There's been scant opportunity for conversation," Frances pointed out.

Alasdair laughed under his breath and kissed her. "We'll make up for it now."

He laughed again and lifted her up off the ground, pressing his face against her swollen stomach. "Fan, Fan! You're to give me a son."

He lowered her gently back to the floor and kissed her mouth and her tangled curls. "And I have you back. Do you know what it's been, these last months without you? Just . . . nothing. My life is nothing without you, Fan."

"I know what it's been," Frances said. The nights she'd spent aching for him beside her. The nights when she'd wondered if he even wanted her still. The question could not be repressed any longer. "Alasdair, why did you not come after us when the soldiers were taking me away?"

Alasdair's arm tightened protectively about her.

"They drove our horses away. Remember? What was the good to chase barefoot through the heather?"

"Oh." Frances gave a long sigh of relief, and for the first time she felt secure in their reunion. "I was thinking you maybe heard what that man was saying. About my leading them there. I thought you maybe blamed me. There was no chance to tell you how it was. I—"

Alasdair stopped her mouth with a kiss. "You do not need to be explaining anything to me. I knew 'twas a black lie."

But Alasdair was only speaking part of the truth. Yes, he'd known it was a lie, but only later, when he came to think about it. At the time, the shock of the words had stopped him cold. Only for a moment, but that moment had given Glencairn's soldiers time to make sure they could not be followed. A thousand times Alasdair had blamed himself for that instant of doubt, and now he was resolved that Frances should never know he had lacked faith in her, however briefly.

He ran his hand over her growing breasts and the curve of her stomach again, exulting in his fatherhood. "This settles matters, Fan. You canna' live like a fugitive in the hills, as I've been doing. I've only stayed in Scotland these last two months because of you, anyway. Now I've got you back, we'll awa' to Flanders. I've still some friends with the Brigade there, who'll give me my captain's post again." He kissed her lingeringly, letting his fingers toy with the curls that fell down about her neck and ears until she shivered with pleasure. " 'Twill be a rough life compared with being lady of Beauly."

"It's what we always planned, you and I." Frances spoke more firmly than she felt, to cover up her involuntary start of sorrow at the thought of leaving Beauly for good. "Remember? We were to be handfast, and you were to go to the Low Countries to make your fortune. Why should I mind, when things have turned out just as we always planned?"

"Good," said Alasdair, somewhat absently. "That's settled, then."

He had the bodice of her gown unlaced now, and his hands caressed her full breasts until the nipples rose in taut peaks of desire. Frances caught her breath and pressed forward against the palms that teased her into pleasure. In the back of her mind there was a tiny seed of irritation that Alasdair should take her agreement with his plan so much for granted. But what he was doing now with his fingers and lips left her no breath to voice that feeling. Instead she moaned with ever-mounting pleasure and desire.

Suddenly, just before he had the gown off her altogether, Alasdair stopped. "Frances?"

"I didna' mean I wanted conversation *now*," she informed him, and replaced his searching hand where it had been. But then she paused and asked, "This won't harm the child?"

Alasdair chuckled. " 'Twould take more than that to dislodge a Cameron from his rightful place! We'll not harm him."

"I've wearied sore for you," Frances whispered as his hands roved over the body, feeling how the familiar curves had ripened and softened in the last months. Frances shivered in the dampness of the cave and he pulled her close to him, trying to surround her with the warmth that burned in his body. But the growing swell of her midsection frustrated their attempts to be close. Another involuntary shiver ran through her body and Alasdair sat up suddenly.

"Ach, this will never be doing," he said. "I'll not have you catching cold for my ain selfish pleasure. There's a better way." And he turned her gently on her side facing away from him, curled up close to her, and pulled the edge of the frieze cloak up over their nested bodies.

He clasped her to him firmly, warming her body at last, but his hands would not stay still. He cupped her breasts, teasing her swollen nipples while he covered her neck and shoulders with a rain of small fiery kisses that sent shivers of desire through her. She moaned in sweet agony as the desire mounted inside her. Then she felt him growing hard between her thighs. A hand strayed in the darkness, down from her breast, across the full curve of her stomach and through the tangle of dark curls, to the moistness between her legs.

"Oh, how I am wanting you, Frances," he breathed in her ear. "You are art and part of me—d'ye ken that?"

Her lips were hungry for the touch of him. She twisted her head around and their lips met in a passionate kiss that lasted until the strain of the position forced her to break off, all unsatisfied. Then he was moving, softly, demandingly, and she felt him enter her, filling her body with pleasure that began to quench the agonizing fire he had lit in her. Gently he probed, and she moved to admit him into the deepest part of her being. Slowly, deliberately, he stroked her until her passions rose uncontrollably and she cried out, as he simultaneously quenched and relit the fires within her with his movements and the pressure of his hand against her. Over and over he brought her to that summit of pleasure, until finally he gave a deep, almost stricken sigh and joined her in one long moment of ecstasy.

14

Afterward, there was time to spare for conversation.

As she lay in Alasdair's arms, both their bodies covered by the rough frieze cloak Euan had supplied, Frances told him the story of her escape. She thought he would be as pleased as she was to hear how easily things had worked out for her. Instead, he shook his head when he heard the story.

"Too easy," he said. "I don't like it."

The silence and the darkness pressed down between them, suddenly forming a heavy barrier. Frances waited, knowing fear from the tone of his voice before she knew what to be afraid of.

His next words chilled her even more. "Were ye followed here?"

"Why, no . . ." Frances started to say, even as she remembered the slight sounds, the rustling of leaves, the echo of hoofbeats that she had laid down to her own imagination and excitement. She swallowed painfully, her throat suddenly gone dry. Had she led Alasdair into a trap? "That is . . . I don't know."

This time the silence was so long that she had ample time to consider and regret her own folly. How could she not have seen the trap! After all these weeks of being penned close, what else could Glencairn's sudden laxity have meant?

She had been forced to dine with the man night after night, she had heard him speak of the political intrigues of the South, his majesty's fight to put down the Catholic earls, the strange and shifting ways of his own coming to power. She, of all others, should have known the twisted subtlety of Glencairn's mind, should have been on her guard against just such a trick as this.

"Don't blame yourself, sweeting," Alasdair said, as though he had read her mind. "Didn't I rush into the net myself like a bird coming to the hand of the fowler, and me wi' not a thought in my mind but to see you again?"

He laughed, and Frances heard in his voice the edge of that same bitterness that had tinged her laugh of late. "And maybe I'd have come anyway.

What profit in being hunted like a dog up one side of the Highlands and down the other, if I may not have so much as one night with my sweet wife? Else, I'd as well have gone to Flanders these six weeks syne."

He caressed the swell of her belly with the palm of his hand. "And, but for tonight, I'd not have known of the child. Our child. That was worth a little risk. Make a strong son for me, Frances, my love."

Frances turned her face aside so that he should not see her tears. "Go now," she whispered. "Go quickly. Perhaps there's time to escape them yet. Oh, Alasdair, please go, before they take you."

A strong hand turned her face toward him again and wiped away her tears. "Not yet," he told her. "Look, 'tis still half-light outside. They will be waiting for dark to take me . .. and I'll be waiting for dark to slip away, the way they won't be seeing me at all on the hillside. D'you think twenty stumbling Perthshire men can take a Highlandman on his own land? Don't cry, now, sweet, don't cry at all, for we've an hour before nightfall, and I mean to make merry with my sweet wife for that hour." And he kissed away the fresh tears that sprang up under her lids.

But there was little merriment in them as they lay in each other's arms for that hour, watching the deep gray of the evening sky darken to the velvet black of night. In the hour between dark and moonrise Alasdair would try to slip out of the cave unobserved. Until then, there was nothing they could do but wait, and pray that Glencairn's soldiers would not be ready to take him before then.

"They may not have seen me enter the cave," Alasdair comforted her. "You'll understand, I was not overeager to advertise my presence." He gave a soft laugh. "I'd like that. If they're still waiting to see me come, 'twill be a sour look on their faces when they see the backside of me! Never fear, Fan. Duncan is waiting just over the hill with our horses. It's but to slip away as I've come, and then a fast ride through the heather."

But they both knew the danger was grave. Alasdair had put on his trews and leather jack again, and while he held Frances with one hand, the other was on the hilt of his sword.

"A fine thing," he joked again, trying to make her laugh, "to be making love to my wife for the last time, and us with a naked sword between us."

"You must ride for Leith," Frances said, perhaps for the third time. "From there you can take ship for the Low Countries, perhaps from some Flemish captain who'll not recognize the red head of you."

"I know my way," Alasdair said. "You needn't keep telling me. Though I'm not so sure I should take it, and leave you here."

"You know I'm safe now," Frances argued.

"Glencairn treats me well. There's no more reason for you to stay."

It was only too obvious to both of them that Frances could never stand the punishing pace of the ride that Alasdair would have to make, through bogs and over hills, once again avoiding all civilized places. Nor would he consider exposing her to the risk of his escape from the cave. He insisted over and over again that there was no danger to him at all, it was but to play hare to the hounds of some heavy-footed Lowland soldiers. But Frances, he said firmly, must stay in the cave.

"I'll be back," he promised. "For you and the child. No, by God, before that! I'll have you from Glencairn's keeping by the next boat that sails. I've a few friends yet in Edinburgh."

"No," Frances cried out, so wildly that Alasdair put his hand over her mouth to hush her. "No, promise me you'll not show your face in the city. If you have friends, Glencairn has servants and gold. Promise me," she said, shaking off his restraining hand, "promise you'll make straight for Leith and safety. Or, by God, I'm coming with you." She paused and looked away. "Then we'd die together."

"Hush now, hush." Alasdair rocked her back and forth in his arms like a child being cradled to sleep. "Nobody's going to die, and I'd tie you up and leave you here before I'd let you risk your life and my son's for a fancy like yon . . . All right, all right. Straight to Leith. I'll away to the Low Countries, and when I'm established there I'll send Duncan and Sandy to get you away from Glencairn. I swear it. On the life of our son that's to be. Will that content you, wild woman?"

For a few minutes more Frances clung to the shelter of his arms, caressing and kissing him as though it was the last she would ever know of him. Then it was she who drew away.

"The sky is dark," she said. Her throat ached with the sobs she would not voice. "You must go now. Go quickly, and . . . and God keep you."

She stood in the rear of the cave, beside her horse, and heard the branches rustle once in the darkness. Then the shadows inside the cave were empty, and she listened with aching heart and straining ears for the shouts and gunfire that would mean he was seen and pursued. But no sound came; not even the scrape of a foot on the sloping, treacherous hillside, to let her know he'd got safely away.

It seemed an age that she listened there, in the enveloping darkness. When she thought that surely he must have got clean away, she counted to a hundred, and said over all the poems they'd learned together that summer, when he was so bent on improving her English. Now, because they reminded her of Alasdair, the scraps of poetry were sweeter to her than the strains of the Gaelic bards on which she'd been reared.

When she had done with all the words she knew by heart, she reckoned that surely he must be gone far over the hills and safe. Then, and only then, she sat down on the frieze cloak, put her face in her hands, and cried silently for the warm days of summer that were gone, and the cold winter of Glencairn's icy self-confidence that she must face again.

They found her just before dawn, chilled and stiff, sleeping in a huddled bundle under the frieze cloak. The men who brought her back to the castle were polite and gentle, and listened without much interest to her story of losing her way in the hills.

They took her to the great hall of Beauly, where, unwashed, cold, her hair tangled, she faced Glencairn, who was immaculate in his suit of opulent black velvet with the starched ruff. He sat before the fire; she stood, and repeated her tale. It seemed to her that he was not even listening as he drank down his breakfast ale and warmed his feet on the hearth.

"And the cloak?" he said when she came to the end of her explanation.

Frances took too long to answer. Could she claim it had been left lying in Euan's house, and she stole it? But why would she have stolen a cloak, if all she meant was to ride on a little way and allow Rabbie and Seonaidh some privacy, and then come back? Perhaps she could claim to have found it in the cave? Ridiculous; nobody in these parts was so rich as to abandon a perfectly good warm cloak in that manner.

"Never mind," Glencairn said, and drained the last drops of his ale and set the richly ornamented silver tankard he had brought from his southern house. "If you don't wish to tell us what you have been up to, the girl will."

Frances started in surprise as two men half-dragged, half-carried Euan's Seonaidh into the hall. The girl hung limp from their hands and there was a swollen, darkening bruise along one cheek. But her eyes were open and bright with intelligence.

"Do not fear, my lady," she whispered in Gaelic when she saw Frances. "I have told them nothing."

Glencairn watched Frances' face and gave his dry smile of satisfaction at her look of consternation.

"She has not been seriously hurt—yet," he told Frances. "Nor need she be, if you confess to your plot and tell us your lover's plans. Otherwise, it will be necessary to put her to the question."

"Let her go," Frances said in a dull, toneless voice she hardly recognized as her own. "She knows nothing. All she did was to obey my orders. The people round here are used to obeying me, you know."

"It is time," Glencairn purred, "that they learned another master. Nor do I believe that she knows nothing. Your people are too stubborn and stiff-necked to act without understanding the matter.

But I will not question this small matter, if you are truthful with me from now on."

At a gesture from Glencairn the two men holding Seonaidh retired to the far wall, and he fired questions at Frances so quickly that she was hard-pressed to answer him. How had she paid Seonaidh for her trouble? What supplies had she been given, beyond the cloak? Any weapons? How did she know of the cave?

All that was easy enough, and lulled Frances into a sense of security, so that she was unprepared when the real question was slyly introduced.

"And what did young Cameron say, when he came to you?"

Just in time Frances realized the true import of the question. If she admitted having been with Alasdair, they would know he could not be far away now. How could she best safeguard him? Saints preserve them both, there was no time to think, and Glencairn's eyes boring into her like the points of two pikes.

"He never came," she said, and allowed a touch of petulance to creep into her voice. "I waited all night, and cold I was, but he never came."

"Oh?" To her relief, Glencairn seemed to accept the story. "Strange, that so devoted a leman should not have an equally devoted lover."

Here, at least, was ground on which she could fight him. "The terms, my lord Glencairn, are 'wife' and 'husband.' I have been no man's leman, nor shall I be."

"And you are not stirred to doubt by your lover's defection?"

"Perhaps he had not my message," Frances said, "or, being better versed than I in the treachery of such men as you, sensed the trap."

Glencairn leaned forward, a smile of triumph on his face. "Ah, so there was a message! And who sent it? Your innocent peasant maid here?"

At a gesture from him, one of the men-at-arms thrust Seonaidh forward and twisted her arm up behind her back so that she fell on her knees between Frances and Glencairn, her face contorted with pain.

"Of course there was a message," Frances cried. "Let her go! Do you think I'm such a fool as to run away from you with no plan? If Alasdair had come for me, we'd have been far away from you by now."

She stuck to that story through the painful scene that followed. She repeated her answers like a litany: No, Alasdair had not come to the cave. No, she had no idea where he was now, and neither did Seonaidh. Word was passed through the Highlands in circuitous ways that no one person could follow.

"You know nothing of Cameron's plans?" Glencairn repeated.

Frances gave him back a stony stare. "Nothing. Except that they apparently do not include me." Please God he would believe her. Her stomach was a tight knot of fear.

Glencairn leaned back in his high carved chair, twisting the great ruby ring on his finger. "I wonder . . ."

He signed to the man holding Seonaidh. With a grin, the fellow twisted her arm up higher, almost between her shoulder blades. The girl shrieked in anguish.

"Let her go," Frances said, dry-mouthed. "You are not thinking. I thought you had more wit, Glencairn." She clasped her arms tight against the roiling of fear in her belly.

The shriek ceased and Seonaidh fell forward, limp as a doll, on the stones of the floor. Her long reddish-brown hair, unbound, spilled out around her head.

"Elucidate." Glencairn twisted the ring around his finger again.

Frances had to look away from Seonaidh before she could make the gay, heart-free speech she had planned. It hurt too much. That might have been Alasdair in the hands of Glencairn's torturers. Might still be, if she could not convince them to cease looking.

"Did you not set your men to follow me? Were they not watching all around the hill? If Alasdair had come, how could they not have seen him? No man could slip in and out of a cave, through a guard of twenty men, and not one of them see him." *Except Alasdair, her fine fighting, loving, hunting Alasdair, who knew these hills like the back of his hand.*

The second soldier, the one who had taken no part in torturing Seonaidh, stepped forward. "The lady speaks truth, my lord," he said in a voice made hoarse by fear at speaking out of turn. "Me an' my mate was freezin' behind a whinny-bush all last night, and the thorns stickin' holes in me arse every time I so much as shifted with the cramp in me legs. Nothing stirred on the hill, my lord, from the time she went into the cave."

"Perhaps he was already there," Glencairn suggested. He glanced at Seonaidh, still prostrate on the floor. "Hot irons skillfully applied have been known to wring truth from the most stubborn lips." But it was Frances he watched, as if gauging the effect of his threat.

She felt her stomach twist and turn over again. But it was not time to plead yet—not yet. Instead she gave a loud, ringing laugh and stepped between Glencairn and the prostrate girl. If he tortured Seonaidh further, she might not be able to hold out. She must distract them.

"Perhaps he is still there," she cried. "Did your men not search the cave, Glencairn? Perhaps he has turned himself into a stone. Perhaps he has flown away like a bird of the air." She gathered her dusty skirt in one hand and made Glencairn a disdainful curtsy. "You waste my time and yours with these fancies, my lord. Accept that your plan has failed, as did mine, and let us cry quits. It little suits your dignity to torture this child out of spleen at your own failure."

Without waiting for permission, she turned and stalked out of the hall. She snapped a curt command at the two soldiers over her shoulder. "Take up the girl and bring her to the solar. I will tend to her myself."

As the procession left the hall, Frances heard a sound behind her that stirred the small hairs on the back of her neck and sent a shiver of apprehension down her spine.

Glencairn was laughing, very softly, almost to himself. But she felt certain he had meant her to hear.

That evening she learned what he was laughing at.

She had spent the day in the room assigned to her in the tower keep, twisting a piece of embroidery in her hands and following in her mind every step of Alasdair's progress through the treacherous Lowlands to the water of Leith. How long would it take him to get there? She had never traveled south and could not estimate such a journey.

She looked up, startled, when the door swung open to reveal Glencairn. Expressionless as ever, he entered without waiting for permission and crossed the small room to stand beside her chair. The candles had not yet been lit, and in the fading light of the autumn day his face looked cold and hard as the stones of the castle.

Frances stabbed the needle into her embroidery

to cover up her involuntary shiver of fear. Why had he come unannounced to her room like this?

"We leave for Edinburgh in the morning," he said after the silence had stretched out long enough for her imaginings to fill it with a thousand fears. "Prepare yourself. You will be allowed no servants."

And that, apparently, was all. He turned and left the room as silently as he had come. Only, with one hand already on the door post, he turned back to regard Frances' immobile figure for a moment longer. His lip curled in distaste as his eyes traced the swelling of her body.

"You will understand," he added, "that after yesterday, I can no longer offer you the freedom you have been used to. I am very certain there is more to the story than you are telling me, my dear. You force me to treat you as a conspirator with Cameron, rather than as his willing victim."

This time he did leave, and the door slammed shut behind him with a heavy, final sound, leaving Frances to wonder just what he meant by that last statement. Did he mean to torture her for information about Alasdair?

A clammy sweat of fear broke out under her arms and she shivered with a cold that had nothing to do with the approaching chill of winter. There had been a time, earlier today, when they had threatened Seonaidh with the hot irons. But that had never come to pass. Perhaps Glencairn repented his mercy.

She had no chance to ask him what he meant that night. Instead of the usual summons to dine with him in the manor wing, one of the men-at-arms brought to her room a tray of the coarse fare served in the kitchens.

Frances sat with the wooden bowl of kale and oatmeal on her lap and picked at the food with little appetite. Well, if this was what Glencairn meant by treating her like a prisoner, she thought with a flash of humor, she could bear it well enough. She was not yet grown so soft as to require French wines for her dinner and French sauces for her meat, like these Southron lairds.

"Better Glencairn's harshness than his friendship," she murmured, remembering how at first he'd tried to woo her with caressing words.

But in the cold light of morning some of her courage failed her, as Glencairn's meaning became clear.

"What are these?" she demanded, incredulous, as a man-at-arms came toward her in the great hall with chains looped over his arms. She shrank back against the rough, damp stones of the wall and turned to her Aunt Grizel, who had made one of her rare exits from her chamber to see Glencairn and Frances off to Edinburgh. "Grizel, you'll not let them chain me!"

Grizel hummed in a high tuneless voice and plucked at the threads of her sewing work. "We all have our bonds to bear, child. Mine were of love.

Pray that yours be no heavier." And she looked down again at her everlasting work, the tapestry all in black that she was sewing, she said, to be Hugh's grave cloth.

Glencairn too was wearing black, but sumptuous and opulent black picked out with silver lace and bordered with pearls. There was no appeal from the judgment she saw in his eyes.

"A prisoner," he said, "cannot expect to be treated as a guest."

The village smith, Peadir's brother, was waiting in the bailey with his tools. At first he had refused the work, and three of Glencairn's men had tied him to his own forge and flogged him.

When they met the smith in the bailey, Glencairn addressed Frances. "Make this man understand that if he does not do the work I order, my soldiers will. They are not skilled and may hurt you. It will be better for you if he affixes the fetters."

Frances spoke to the man in Gaelic, explaining as Glencairn had ordered. She could not think clearly in her fear—she knew only that the smith's brother Peadir had been killed by Glencairn's man in June. No more of that family should die for her sake. But there was a cold horror in her as she laid her wrists across the anvil for the fixing of the manacles.

Tears dripped into the smith's shaggy beard as he did the work, and she spoke to him reassuringly, soothingly, telling him that indeed she did not blame him, promising him that, although this earl and his men had the power now, it would not always be so.

"No, lady. You will come back? And the Cameron?"

"We will come back," Frances promised him.

Glencairn cut them off, striding over to Frances and examining her chains. "Are they fixed fast? Good. Help her to mount."

A scant eighteen inches of chain joined the manacles, and another chain led from those to a belt about her waist. Glencairn had the key. She could move her hands, if she cared to fight the dragging weight of the chains. But she could not mount a horse unaided, and there could be no thought of escaping, so encumbered. She supposed, dully, that this was what Glencairn had in mind.

As they rode out, she realized it all seemed quite unreal to her. She did not feel at all like Frances Cameron, lady of Beauly, riding out of her castle for perhaps the last time, and herself in chains, the way the common folk who had gathered outside would be telling the story down the generations of their children.

15

The ride to Edinburgh was hard, and Glencairn set a punishing pace. There were none of the small courtesies she'd been offered when his men brought her back from Eilean Duin. Then she'd been newly a captive, and not knowing what was in front of her; now it seemed to Frances that she had grown old in captivity.

And this time she knew exactly what lay before her. Glencairn had been at pains to tell her as they rode along the first morning. And in some ways, the rough treatment that she had had since made the knowledge easier to bear, for it dulled her mind somewhat.

"We have dallied long enough in this matter,"

Glencairn said. "I thought to woo you by soft words and fair promises, but as you are stubborn in your unrighteousness, so shall the arm of the Lord punish you."

His manner of speech was strange to Frances. Once Alasdair had spoken of the men of the new kirk, who held neither by priests nor by Our Blessed Lady, and whose delight it was to rant of godliness as though none but themselves held the key. But with her, Glencairn had always played the urban, polished gentleman. What did this new manner mean? Frances turned wide, blank eyes upon Glencairn and waited for him to go on.

"It may be deemed treason for one to unlawfully enter and possess a stout castle like Beauly without a title that his majesty recognizes," Glencairn went on at last. "Worse than treason, if the castle be taken by force, and the lady of the castle also. In these troublous times, his majesty desires greatly to civilize you barbarous Highlanders—yes, even though he should extirpate the race."

He gave her a smile that did not reach his eyes. "I have given you every excuse, Lady Frances. I have represented to his majesty that you were the innocent victim of a rape, rather than the partner of Cameron in his villainies. But as you persist in calling the man your husband, in your obdurate rebellion against my loving and paternal care, I can but agree with his majesty. You are as guilty of treason against the king's goodwill and order as

Cameron himself. And, since through your obduracy Cameron cannot be found and brought to trial, you are to be tried in his stead."

Frances summoned up all her courage to defy him once more. "Fine words, Glencairn! But they are not fine enough to cover up the truth. Why not say that since you could not have Beauly by wedding wi' me, you will have it from my corpse instead? And all just to cast a glimmer of lawfulness about your thieving of my lands. Before God, I had rather my 'barbarous' Highlanders, as you call us, than such civilized ways. They, at least, would scorn to attack a defenseless woman."

"I should prefer not to do so myself," Glencairn said in reply, with his bleak smile. "Your death seems a sore waste. Let us hope that it may not be necessary."

Frances stared. "How not? If you think that I will sign my lands over to you on threat of the gallows, you mistake me for my craven brother, Glencairn. And I am not flattered by the comparison."

But in sober truth, she wondered, would she die rather than grant him those words on parchment? Would anybody be so mad? A man, perhaps. Men had queer notions of honor. But she—she had life, and the hope of rejoining Alasdair someday, and the child within her to guard. Who knew what she might not give up to preserve those three things? But there was no need to admit as much to Glencairn now.

Glencairn flicked the heavy jeweled gloves he carried in his right hand. "A woman's signature? Hardly worth the trouble. No. But if Alasdair Cameron will surrender himself to be tried, then you will be free."

"You will wait a long time to hear if that bargain be taken," Frances said with a fine show of indifference. "I doubt not he is out of the country long syne." Or would be soon.

"Indeed?" Glencairn nodded. "A pity, if true. But if he should by any chance still be in Scotland, I make no doubt he will hear of the bargain. I have sent messengers to all the ports. A man on a fresh horse, riding fast, might make better time from Beauly than one who had to keep to the byways, might he not?"

Yes. Glencairn had moved fast. He could see to it that the news would be at Leith long before Alasdair reached there. And then? Frances did not doubt that Alasdair would put himself in Glencairn's power in the hope of saving her.

There was an aching pain in her chest. If Alasdair came back to his death for her sake . . . No. She could not let him do that.

There was only one thing left to do.

Frances kicked her horse with the sharp little heel of her riding boot and yanked the reins out of the grasp of the astonished man-at-arms who had been trailing along beside her. The guard had been paying little heed to the conversation and vaguely resenting the order to guard a pregnant woman in chains, as though Glencairn thought she might do anything.

She had several paces clear lead, crashing through the heather by the side of the drovers' track they had been riding on. Then there was a steep plunge downward into a stone gully where small trees grew. Their branches whipped her face and she could not defend herself, for the chains forced her to keep both hands together on the reins or risk losing her hold entirely. The horse floundered going up out of the gully, its hooves slipping on the round tumbled stones, and she had to heave herself ungracefully forward almost to its shoulder bones to keep her seat.

At the top of the rise the horse collected itself and Frances scrambled back into the saddle. But before they could set off down the close-cropped grazing land, a single horse, ridden hard, came around the brow of the hill and intercepted her.

It was Glencairn. Faster to react than any of his men, he had skirted the gully to come round at the point where he knew she must reach open land again. Following close after him were three of his men. He kept one hand on her bridle until they came up.

"Were you trying to escape, or just to kill yourself?" he asked acidly.

"Either," Frances flashed back, "so long as it foiled your plans, Glencairn."

After that, there was no more conversation. Frances rode between two soldiers, each holding a leading string to her horse's bridle.

There was no proper road south from Beauly, only the drovers' track along which the herds from the north came down to the cattle markets in the Lowlands. Now the pitted track had turned into a series of slippery mud washes and deep, sucking pits with the first rain. The horses had to pick their way carefully, and at Glencairn's speed it was a jolting trip that before long sent shooting pains up Frances' back and into her shoulders. She would have begged him to slow the pace if he had been anywhere within earshot, but since her abortive attempt at escape he had ridden at the head of the cavalcade, with Frances in the middle securely surrounded by his men.

On the second day they had the grace of an early freeze to harden the mud track, but this was offset by the biting wind filled with needles of sleet that assailed them in the open places. Twice they had to ford streams.

At the second ford, recent rains had swelled the stream until it cut away part of the bank, leaving a sharp muddy cliff down which the horses had to scramble as best they might. The clay-yellow waters swirled as high as the horses' thighs in the middle of the stream, and Frances could feel that the streambed was full of shifting rocks that made the animals back and fill. She shut her eyes and clutched at the wet mane in front of her, praying to the Blessed Virgin. If she were swept off her horse, with her arms chained and clumsy with her pregnancy, she would have little chance to save herself.

Did it matter? She was so cold and wet and miserable already. A little while in the water, and then she would not be cold anymore, and Glencairn would not have her to use against Alasdair. It wanted only a little resolution to throw herself from the horse.

But there was the gentle slope, and they were out of the water, and no more streams to ford that day. The edge of Frances' plaid was soaked, and on the windy hills it plastered itself to her legs and left her colder than before.

By nightfall Frances was too cold and miserable to feel anything except relief when they topped the last of a series of barren hills and saw ahead of them the thin clump of trees that meant some human dwelling. It was only a turf-walled peasant house, reeking of peat smoke and of the animals on the other side of the low wall that divided the one room. But Frances was grateful of the opportunity to sit by the peat fire and steam herself dry by its smoky heat.

The bowl of milk curds and oatmeal brought her by a shy child with uncombed hair tasted more delicious than any of the kickshaws and dainties contrived by Glencairn's French cook. At length, with her damp curls untangled and spread out on her shoulders and her skirts spread around the low three-legged stool, Frances felt enough recovered to tax Glencairn with the cruel pace he was setting.

"You have proven you can ride fast enough when you want to," was his only reply.

Frances had felt cramping pains in her stomach since the middle of the day, when they had crossed the second ford. "You will kill the child," she protested, and then wished she had not spoken.

Glencairn favored her with a bleak smile, then wheeled and left the hut. His dignity was somewhat impaired by the fact that he had to stoop to get out the low door, but the cold meaning of his smile was clear. It was nothing to him if she rid herself of the babe she carried, and he could hardly understand why it was so much to her.

In the following days, although he did not speak with Frances again, Glencairn allowed his troop to ride at a slower pace. He even halted two or three times during the day for Frances to rest. But the chains remained on her wrists, and since her attempt at escape they were drawn close to her belt-chain, so that she could scarce raise her hands far enough to feed herself. By the time they reached Edinburgh her wrists were raw and sore from the constant chafing of the iron manacles.

The cold winds of the Highlands had given way to clouds and a penetrating damp as they rode south. A fine rain was falling as they entered the city, and Frances kept her head down to shelter it under her plaid as best she might. So she marked little of their entrance into that ancient city, the new stone walls built in the years after Flodden, the stone-faced houses with their wooden second and even third stories projecting out over the streets, the castle rising like a great stone beast crouching over the city. She rode with her chained hands before her on the saddle, letting her two guards guide them as they would, letting the raindrops splash down from the edge of her plaid.

Suddenly the plaid was thrown back from her head, and a hand at her back forced her to sit upright in the saddle. "You shall not crouch and hide yourself?" Glencairn said. "I will that you show your shame to the city!"

A blow on her cheek finished the speech. Faint with hunger and fatigue, Frances reeled in the saddle. The unexpected blow brought tears to her eyes, but she sat straighter in the saddle and stared at Glencairn.

For the first time since entering the city, Frances became aware of her surroundings. They were riding through a spacious quadrangle of houses, fine buildings of stone and timber with glass windows. A curious crowd had gathered to watch their progress. Burning with shame at being thus paraded through the streets like a common felon, Frances raised her head higher and forced a smile to her lips.

"Lady Frances!"

Her head jerked around involuntarily at this use of her name. A poor woman, her head covered by a ragged shawl, had pushed her way between the guards and now thrust a bundle into Frances' chained hands.

" 'Tis goose grease for yer hands, leddy," she said. "My son had sores from the chains too, before they hanged him over there." She jerked her head toward the east end of the quadrangle, where Frances saw a gaunt silhouette rising from the shadows. A gallows! She stared in fascinated horror.

The slow pace of the little procession had been almost brought to a halt by this interruption and by the curious onlookers pressing closer on every side. Now Glencairn turned back from the head of the procession and struck at the peasant woman with his whip.

"Out of our way! No talking to the prisoner!" he shouted harshly. He roughly took Frances' reins himself. "This way!" He pointed ahead to a dark arch between two houses, little more than a tunnel, sloping steeply upward.

They were followed into the tunnel by the shouts of the gathering crowd, and by a gobbet of mud which some enterprising soul hurled at Glencairn. Two of Glencairn's men, at his orders, stopped at the mouth of the wynd and crossed their swords before it, to keep the crowd from going farther.

Frances did not mind the shouts now; to her they were friendly. But she wondered why Glencairn should lose his temper and treat her with such severity before the mob.

The wynd opened to daylight and the imposing sight of the castle. Frances was hustled through the heavy outer gates, again to the accompaniment of sympathetic calls from a crowd around the walls.

Frances was taken to a small room within the castle. Not a prisoner's cell, but a simply furnished, comfortable room with tapestries hung about the walls, an oaken bench covered with cushions, and a brazier at which she could warm her hands. Here Glencairn left her, without a word of explanation. She supposed his part was done, in delivering her to Edinburgh.

She waited there for some hours, huddling over the brazier as the chill of evening drew in. In late afternoon two men came, one of whom watched while the other struck off her chains. He was not as skillful as Peadir's brother; several times the file rasped her skin, and once the work-heated metal touched her and left a painful scorch.

Neither of the men spoke, nor would they answer any of her questions. Only, when leaving, the one who had stood by watching grinned and opened his mouth to show a hideous scarred cavity where his tongue should have been. Frances felt a wave of queasy dizziness at the sight, and hastily averted her eyes. What if it should mark the child?

But the man seemed to wish her no ill. He patted her on the shoulder, a bit roughly, as though to offer consolation; then grinned again, mercifully with his lips closed, and left with his fellow.

At dusk she was brought candles and a tray with wine and bread and cold meats. But the woman bringing these amenities also would not, or could not, speak.

Somewhere nearby there was a kirk tower with a great bell that boomed out the hours. Frances counted them over and watched the flickering candles on the wall burning lower. They might be her life, or Alasdair's, she thought: bright for a while, and now almost burned out. Where was Alasdair the night? She prayed for him to have gotten safe on a boat for Leith.

How cold it was! The warmth of the brazier was no help; the cold penetrated to her heart, making all her past struggles seem useless. The summer on the island was a dim memory without the power to warm her, the night in the cave was a dream. Nothing was real but these stones, the discarded chains, the power with which men entrapped and surrounded her.

It was near midnight when the door opened again.

This time it was Glencairn. She could not control an involuntary shrinking toward the wall as he approached, remembering his harshness earlier. He put one hand under her chin and turned her face toward the candle, as if to inspect the bruise that was already forming. Frances suffered the handling with a set face.

He stroked the swollen cheek with an unexpectedly gentle hand. "A pity I had to hit you so hard," he observed. "Pray believe, it is not my usual manner. But the crowd found it convincing, did they not? The chains, too, had their effect. But I flatter myself the master stroke was to have put them on when we left Beauly, rather than just before we reached the city. After these days riding in chains, you had very much the air of the defeated prisoner. It quite tugged at my heartstrings, I assure you."

"I find it difficult to believe you have any such organ," Frances retorted, freeing herself from his grasp and retreating to the other side of the room.

"Oh, I have, I assure you," Glencairn returned absently, "and it beats for you, my dear. I found you quite affecting in chains. A woman defeated, persecuted, alone among her cruel enemies. A sad picture, do you not think? Immured in the castle, too. Poor young thing. The mob was most affected."

Now he smiled coldly. "You played your part quite well, by the way. I regret it was not possible to warn you in advance, but I feared lest knowledge might detract from the realism of your bearing."

He unfolded the cloak he had been carrying over one arm and wrapped it, most solicitously, about her shoulders. The warm velvet, lined with fur and smelling of the sweet herbs that had been strewn in its storage chest, was like a breath of luxury from another land. Frances snuggled gratefully into the soft folds even while her mind was racing with unaswered questions.

"There's a black frost outside," Glencairn said, "and we must go on foot. I would not that you should be chilled."

"Your new concern surprises me."

But he ignored her gibe. Instead, he continued his cold explanation. "Alasdair Cameron has been cried at the cross of Edinburgh and at the pier and shore of Leith these three days. But he has not come forward to rescue his ladylove. Perhaps, as you would make me believe, he is already abroad. But perhaps he was but waiting to see if I would carry out my threats. If so, this day's performance should have convinced him. By the time he hears of it, the mob will have increased your sufferings a hundredfold. If the young man is of as rash and chivalrous a spirit as you pretend, he should lose no time in hastening to free his leman and unborn child from my clutches."

Frances clutched the cloak about her, grateful for the deep hood which shaded her face as she spoke. "And why would he be trusting your word? Will he not be thinking that he might give himself into your hands, and I still be kept close? Better one of us should be free, than both be caught by the heels."

Glencairn's bleak smile chilled her inside the heavy furs. "Do you think he will take the risk? Would he want to live free, knowing you paid the price of his freedom?"

It was unanswerable. Frances felt tears prickling her lashes, and cursed herself for a romantic fool. Through her long captivity, she had been at such pains to convince Glencairn that her love for Alasdair was true and that she would never give him up. It seemed she had succeeded just so far that Glencairn had seen how she could be used as a tool to trap Alasdair.

What a fool she had been, to give him any information that he could use against them. "God's curse on my tongue," she cried out, "that ever I was speaking a true word to you."

Glencairn bowed as though accepting a compliment. "I see that you acknowledge the force of my reasoning." He offered her his arm. "Shall we go?"

Frances looked around the barren little room where she had been kept. "Why, I am better here than in a worse place."

"It does not suit your ladyship's condition. You will be more comfortable, I assure you, where I am taking you." Glencairn laughed out loud at the confused mix of expressions on Frances' face. "Why, did you think I meant to keep you immured in a dungeon? Understand, Frances, the threats I have been forced to make against you were only for the public ear. While we remain in Edinburgh, you shall be treated—in private—with all the courtesy due to my future wife. You are going to stay at my house, in the care of my sister. The king himself has graciously agreed that I should have the wardship of you until the trial."

"And when will that be?"

Glencairn's smile deepened. "Ah. That depends on young Cameron, does it not?"

And he bowed low before escorting her from the cell and out of the castle by a little-used door which led directly to a narrow dark wynd. He had hired no linkboys to light their way, and their shoes slipped now and again on the dark sheets of frost that covered the stones. But two of his men went before them and two behind, and the house walls on either side were high and strong as prison walls.

16

Outside the walls of Edinburgh, Alasdair paused a moment beside the North Loch to look at the dark mass of the city before him. The gray waters and the dark clouds scudding overhead would be his last sight of freedom. Staring at them, he could imagine himself beside a Highland loch once again. There had been the summer with Frances; he was rich forever in the memory of those months. But now it was a bleak November, and the reckoning must be paid.

It was hard not to fight, when he reached the town gate and the watch challenged him and bade him give up his sword. The guards had it in mind to make rough sport with him then, being well pleased with themselves to have caught the dangerous criminal who'd been sought so long. One of them made a rush at him, after he was safely unarmed, and planted his dirk in Alasdair's shoulder. It would have been his heart, had he not twisted out of the way.

"Haud yer hand, Jockie," cried the captain of the watch. "He's to be delivered alive." He walked beside Alasdair to the castle, chatting companionably all the way. Alasdair guessed that it might be worth a promotion to the man, to be the one who delivered him up, and so hardly begrudged the man's good humor.

After that, it was the stone walls of the castle and a not unfriendly warder. But it took the sheer gritty effort of his will to keep Alasdair on his feet till the door of his cell closed and he was left alone. He stripped off his shirt in the darkness and felt out the damage the guard's dirk had done in that first rush.

The cut was deep, but had not bled much for all the pain it was giving. He bound it up as best he could with a strip from his shirt, and sat on the wooden plank that was the room's one furnishing, to consider his probable future. There did not seem to be much of it, hardly enough to make it worthwhile binding his wound. He hoped they would let him see Frances once more.

His first visitor came expressly to destroy that hope.

He had been left two days in the stinking cell, and began to wonder whether Glencairn meant to let him die of cold. But it was no part of his intention to give up any sooner than he had to. They had demanded he come to Edinburgh to stand trial; very well, he was here, and he meant to live until his trial if he possibly could.

One bad mistake, he realized in those two empty days, had been to come to the city as he had—alone, at night, with nobody but one friendly watch captain to swear that he'd come at all. What was to prevent Glencairn from leaving him to rot in this cell, and doing as he would with Frances? But at least he would now have no reason to punish Frances. He must, at least, let her go free.

Alasdair clung to this thought, and to his own pride. Those were the only things he had left.

But when the door to his cell finally opened, he gave no sign of the hell he had been going through in his mind. The water supplied for drinking had not been too foul to wash with, and it was a large part of his pride to appear as well as possible. When Glencairn entered the cell, he found Alasdair sitting on the wooden bench, composed as though he had only been waiting for a moment, immaculate in the style of a Highland gentleman. The brownish stains on his linen shirt were covered by the tartan cloak, which he wore partly over one shoulder and wrapped about his arm, his blue bonnet sat jauntily on his brow, and his long legs were clad in trews of a coarser and darker tartan than the cloak.

There was a moment of mutual summing-up. If Glencairn was surprised to find his prisoner apparently still in good health and spirits, Alasdair was himself surprised at the civilized aspect of this man who had pursued him so long and ruthlessly. He could not restrain a short laugh of surprise.

"I am delighted to find that captivity makes you so merry," the earl said. "Might I inquire the cause?"

Alasdair leaned back on the bench and stretched his long legs comfortably out before him, taking up nearly the entire width of the cell.

"It's the incongruity of it struck me," he explained. "Here have I been linking it over yon hills these two months syne for fear of your soldiers, and what do I see now? A douce, quiet, sober gentleman who might well be an elder of the kirk."

"As a matter of fact," Glencairn said pleasantly, "I am an elder of the True Reformed Kirk."

Alasdair drew in his breath. "That's new. When I was a student, the word was that ye were sib and rib with the Cock o' the North."

"The day of the great Catholic lords has passed," Glencairn said. "A wise man observes the prevailing winds."

"And trims his sail accordingly. I am thinking you will no' be the poorer for the change?"

"I lay up treasure in heaven," Glencairn said.

"And lands on earth."

The earl made a dismissing motion. "Enough talk of religion. I can understand that you would be thinking of your latter end, but we have other matters to settle, you and I."

Alasdair spread his hands. "Only one, and I trust in your good word that is soon settled. The lady goes free?"

"Of course," Glencairn agreed. "She has been free to do as she wished for some time now."

"She'll be back in Beauly then, I make no doubt."

"Why, no." Glencairn toyed with the lace at his wrists. "She has chosen to remain in Edinburgh for some time. Women will take these whims."

Alasdair could no more restrain the light that crossed his face than the sun could choose not to rise. "I can see her?"

"If she wishes. You note she could not be troubled to accompany me this morning. Some matter of a visit to a mercer's shop, I believe—or was it the spicer's? My memory for these matters of the womenfolk is so poor. I know she and my sister Anna were mightily set-up about it. Indeed, they were chattering so hard I could scarce get a word in edgewise to tell them of your capture."

Glencairn slapped one glove lightly against another and affected to be concerned only with the play of the light on his jeweled rings. "No doubt, in a day or two, the lady will find time to visit you."

Alasdair laughed as though Glencairn's words

had touched him not at all, but there was a puzzled frown between his brows. "I'd like fine to see the poor lonesome word Glencairn could not slip in where he wished! You're not fooling me, Glencairn. The bargain was that I give myself up, and Frances goes free. How do I know you've not got her locked up somewhere else in this stinking rock, while you spin me your tales of mercers and spicers and your good sister?"

Glencairn drew on one glove, affecting great care to smooth the soft leather over each finger. "Perhaps I can persuade the lady to visit you herself. And then . . . perhaps not." He polished the gold seal ring on his right hand with the fingers of the remaining glove. "I fear she is somewhat ashamed of the trick we played you."

"Trick?" Now Alasdair's brows were knit in earnest.

"Why, yes. There was never any thought of putting the Lady Frances on trial for your crimes. Indeed, I scarce hoped you'd believe such a tale, but she persuaded me otherwise."

"*She* persuaded . . ." Alasdair rose to his feet. "You lie! Whatever you may have planned, Glencairn, you'll never persuade me Frances knew aught of it."

"As you will." Glencairn drew on the other glove with finicking care and stood as though to take his leave, though his eyes flickered with the other man's every move. "You'll not think the lady would choose the barefoot life of a Highland cateran, once she knew what other options were available to her? I had two months with her at Beauly, Cameron. Time enough to woo and win her. We have only the small matter of your trial to arrange, before the wedding banns are called. I'm sure 'twill comfort you in your imprisonment, to know that by coming to surrender yourself you have ensured the lady's future comfortable life . . . with me."

"It's a black lie from the black heart o' ye!" Alasdair launched himself at the other man's throat like a Highland fury. Glencairn went down under the onslaught, calling loudly for help as they fell onto the stone flags.

Suddenly the room was full of men. They hauled Alasdair off Glencairn's prostrate form and fell to beating him with obvious enjoyment. For a few moments he remained upright in the midst of his attackers; then a harsher blow than most felled him, and they went to work with boots and fists.

Glencairn at last stopped the beating, when Alasdair lay all but unconscious on the floor, one eye swollen shut and a great purpling bruise rising on his cheek

"Enough," he said sharply as one of the guards swung back his foot to deliver a punishing kick to the head. "I'll not have him too damaged to stand trial."

And he saw that the guards left the cell ahead of him.

At the cell door he paused and looked down at the prostrate figure. His starched ruff had been torn loose in the affray, and one white glove was stained with Alasdair's blood. But he still looked a very proper gentleman compared to the bruised and bloodied man on the cold stone floor.

"And that, my young friend," he said very softly, "settles any score for the mock you made of me these two months past while my men chased you through the hills. We'll leave it to the king's justice to settle other matters."

Glencairn announced to Frances only that Alasdair had surrendered himself and that arrangements for the trial were to proceed at once. But she heard of the beating he'd suffered in quite another way. It came through a winding chain of gossip, from a castle guard to his auntie at the Westbow and finally to the girl who brought fresh milk to Glencairn's kitchens. On the way the tale had been spiced and magnified, until what Frances heard was that the desperate murderer Cameron was like to die of the beating he'd had at Glencairn's orders.

She wasted half a day crying in the luxurious chamber Glencairn had appointed for her use, then rose, splashed her face with cold water, and berated herself for the loss of time. If she was going to cry, let it be where it would do some good: before Glencairn's sister, Lady Anna, for instance.

Frances had had the measure of Glencairn's elderly maiden sister before she was in the house five minutes. The little lady was soft and rotund, whereas Glencairn was tall and lean; sentimental, whereas he was cold. She was given to fluttering bits of lace about her person and an equal fluttering in whatever she used for a mind. Had it been Lady Anna alone who had the charge of Frances, without those men of Glencairn's at every door and window, Frances would have been free in the first hour that Glencairn had left her there.

Now she turned her considerable histrionic talents to the task of getting in to see Alasdair. It was not difficult. A few tears that came all too easily, a promise that if she could just see Alasdair once before he died then she could accept Glencairn's rule with an easy mind, and Lady Anna was persuaded that her brother would only be grateful when she brought Frances back, meek and mild and courteous as she had not been since he imprisoned her.

Glencairn's men had no instructions to prevent Frances and Lady Anna from going where they would in the city; only to escort them closely. And with Glencairn's very sister to vouch that she was to be allowed in to see the prisoner, Frances had no trouble penetrating the rocky walls of the castle. Lady Anna, with a tact born of her romantic soul, waited in the passage outside Alasdair's cell so that the two poor young things might have their last moments together in privacy.

Frances peeped through the grille of the cell before the guard opened it. She was shocked to find so little change in Alasdair. His face was still bruised, but he had contrived to dress himself almost as neatly as before the fight. He was seated on the bench as was his wont, whistling "Ranald of Islay's Pibroch" through with all the variations.

Alasdair looked up when the keys grated in the cell door. Frances entered and he jumped up, his face alight with joy. "Frances! I'd little hope to see you."

But he was bemused by the appearance of this elegant young lady of fashion. A far cry, this, from the ragged girl that rumor had told him of, chained and beaten through the streets by Glencairn.

Looking at her, he could not but remember Glencairn's tale that Frances had thought of the plan to entice him into the castle, so that she might be the easier rid of an inconvenient husband. All lies, of course, but still . . .

Instead of the homespun dress in which he'd seen her last, she wore a long-trained coat of emerald-green velvet, with short puffed sleeves. The square neckline of the bodice revealed her creamy white skin, set off further by the perky little white starched ruff around her neck. Her hair was looped up and partially concealed under a soft cap of the same velvet as her gown, and her little shoes of soft kid were protected from the slush of the streets by high wooden carved pattens.

In spite of himself he drew back a little. Frances sensed his involuntary movement of withdrawal and stopped short in the very moment of embracing him. She drew back herself, too proud to make the first move.

"It's yourself that's in it, Alasdair Cameron," she cried, "and me plotting how to attend you on your sickbed. Could you no' appear a little weak and wan? Lady Anna will be sore disappointed to've brought me here to view a healthy man." She could not keep her voice from quivering a little while she teased him. But she'd come to help, and was determined not to collapse weeping in his arms like some Lowland lady with no backbone.

Still he stood a few paces apart from her, regarding her with cool, questioning eyes.

"What's the matter, Alasdair?"

"Oh, naught," he mumbled. But he could not restrain the sharp question that followed. "Glencairn has the dressing of you now? Such fine braws never came out of a poor Highland glen."

Frances looked down at her extravagantly slashed and puffed sleeves, and colored. "I am a prisoner in his sister's house," she said quietly, "and must wear what I am told to. It was not easy to get coming here to see you, Alasdair." And now he was treating her like a stranger. "Will you not be giving me one kiss, then?"

Alasdair colored in his turn. "Sorry I am, Frances. Glencairn was saying . . . I thought . . ."

He took her by the shoulders and gave her a chaste, respectful kiss on the forehead. Frances waited, eyes half-closed, for the trail of kisses down her face to her lips that would reawaken the ecstasy they had once shared. But instead he moved back a step and let her go again, as if he could hardly bear to be near her.

Frances clenched her teeth. She would not, she must not break into crying and reproaches! She seated herself on the wooden bench and did not speak until she was certain that she had her voice under control. "What would Glencairn be saying, that you are treating me like a stranger? Alasdair, there is not time. We must plan how to get you out of here."

Alasdair gave a strange, short laugh. "As well plan how to fly from the Rock. Glencairn said you'd maybe not find the time to visit me at all. He was thinking you were too taken up with the sights of the city."

Frances frowned. "I am thinking you have both run clean mad. Where would I be so taken up with the sights, whatever? Have I not told you I am kept strait in his sister's own house?"

"Not so strait that you could not get coming here."

"And none too easy it was." Frances reached out and took his hands. They gripped hers with all his soldiers' strength. But still he would not look at her. "Alasdair, tell me what is running in your mind! I cannot bear this."

He told her all then, the sorry tale Glencairn had spun him. And he told her he couldn't help but wonder, what with the words the soldiers had spoken when they stole Frances from Eilean Duin, and the trap around the cave. And then, to see her dressed so richly . . .

Every word was like a whiplash across her face. Was this what he had been thinking, while she plotted and schemed to get to see him?

Frances sat very straight, and two spots of fire were burning in her pale cheeks. "And you were believing that of me."

"You believed worse of me, once," Alasdair reminded her.

Frances gave a little choking sound, halfway between a sob and a laugh. "So I did. Och, Alasdair, we must never be heeding what other folk will say of us, for it seems their words are a web of lies to trap us. Only look at me, now, and believe this."

She pressed his hand to the white swell of her bosom over the green coat, above her heart, and gazed into his eyes. "You are my true wedded husband and my only love. I will never be leaving you of my own will." He must believe her. She strained to infuse him with her own certainty, and saw the hard set of his mouth softening. "Please, Alasdair . . . if you do not trust me, then you might have spared yourself the trouble to save me."

Alasdair buried his face in the sweetly scented

cleft between her white breasts. "Frances, Frances," he murmured, "you are my only heart and my delight."

His arms went around her and he clutched her to him so strongly that she cried out. She wept then, the tears running down her neck and bosom, and stroked the red head that was so dear to her.

After a time, they broke apart and gazed into one another's eyes, hands clasped. Frances gave a defiant sniff and fumbled for her kerchief. "Well . . . enough of that. Now we'd best plan how to get you free."

"There's no thought of that," said Alasdair more soberly. His hand imprisoned hers and covered it. "It's enough that I should have seen you this one last time. My life is bought and sold, Frances. You canna' save me."

"And how would you be knowing that?" Frances cried indignantly.

"I've had long enough to think on it, here."

"You will have had time enough to think on some other matters, too," she reminded him, "and come to some braw conclusions. You've had things all twisted endways in the time you've been alone, Alasdair Cameron. You're a bonny fighter, but I am thinking you're no' just terrible clever at the reasoning.

"Now, tell me about this trial. It's beyond me how Glencairn can hope to bring you to court for abducting your own wedded wife."

"He'll twist it in court," said Alasdair, "so that it will sound all different."

"And if he does, will I not be speaking for you, and telling the way it was? We must be trusting in the king's justice, Alasdair. The truth will have its day."

"Gin it be the king's justice I get," Alasdair murmured gloomily. "They tell me Argyll is lord chief justice these days, and don't he and Glencairn aye have their hands in one another's pockets?"

"Go on," Frances said. "Give up before you get there—is that the new Cameron style of fighting? It's astonished I am you do not go to Glencairn with the humble offer of your head to season his broth, and maybe a hand or foot too if he'd like."

Alasdair kissed her and forebore to argue. Where was the good, indeed, in convincing her of what was all too clear to him? She had not spent the nights he had, alone and shivering in this bleak cell, feeling the ends of his broken ribs grate against one another. A man could be the bonniest fighter in the world, but it was only in the songs of old days that one man could stand against a hundred. And the law courts of Edinburgh were not where he would choose to stand, in any case. He had studied in the city long enough to know all too much of the crooked ways justice could be bought and sold. Frances might not be in it, but Glencairn's intention was plain: to rid her of an inconvenient husband and put himself in the place.

"Frances, promise me one thing," he said solemnly.

"Anything."

"Do not be taking Glencairn, after I am gone. You'll need a man, Frances. I don't want you to be burying your heart in my grave. But not that one."

But she would not entertain even the possibility that he might not be freed.

"Frances?"

Lady Anna stood at the door. They broke out of their embrace as guiltily as though they had been talking black treason.

"Frances, we must go now."

Unwillingly Frances glided from the bench by slow degrees. Alasdair rose with her. They stood looking into each other's eyes for a long moment, saying all that could not be spoken in words. Then Alasdair put his hands on her shoulders and gave her a gentle push toward the door.

"Go now, my love. Go quickly . . . I canna' bear a long farewell."

"I'll come again," Frances promised.

That word, and the touch of her scented hand on his head, were the last things he took with him into the darkness that settled on his spirit with the closing of the door.

But it was not as easy as Frances had thought to keep her promise. On the way from the castle they were stopped by Glencairn's men, who had grown suspicious while they waited, fearing that Frances' errand would not please their master. Frances was hustled away from Lady Anna without ceremony and rudely searched for messages. Only when they were satisfied that she carried nothing did they let her return to the house.

That evening Glencairn called and spoke a long while with Lady Anna. And after that Lady Anna's eyes were red for a day or so, and there were no more harmless little excursions. Frances was kept strait within the house, and when she complained to Glencairn, he merely told her that she would not wish to walk abroad in the inclement winter weather, nor was it consonant with his concern for her health to allow such risks.

She had little but black thoughts and dark days throughout the rest of that long winter while Glencairn was assembling the depositions of witnesses and buying the judges of his choice. It was almost a relief when, in March, the trial was finally announced. At least now she would see Alasdair again.

17

Glencairn was of two minds about allowing Frances to attend the trial, since she had remained obstinate all winter long about not bearing witness against Alasdair. During one encounter, the foolish girl even expressed an intention of speaking in his defense. Glencairn explained that this would not be permitted.

Frances' chin set in the look of mulish obstinacy which he found one of her least attractive expressions.

"Then I'll cry out against your witnesses."

"That also will not be permitted," Glencairn said. "The most you could achieve would be to have yourself removed bodily from the court."

He took pity on her and deigned to explain further. "Why d'you think it's taken so long for Cameron's case to come to trial? I'd not risk having the wrong opinion handed down. It takes time to arrange these things. Now I've the depositions I wanted, and the judges in my pocket. By the end of this week you will be a legal widow, my dear."

The absolute certainty in his words chilled Frances' blood. She felt crushed by the weight of the silks and furs he would wrap her in, by the great stones of the castle where Alasdair was kept, by her own body grown so unwieldy in these final weeks of her pregnancy. It would almost be easier to give up, to be dulled into acquiescence by Glencairn's words that blended so well with the harsh cry of the March wind outside. She couldn't help but listen as he went on.

"Do not think there is anything you can do to save your lover. His life is bought and sold before he steps into the courtroom."

Alasdair himself had used the phrase when she saw him in the castle. It fell on her like a blow. Frances put up one hand before her face.

Glencairn smiled, well enough pleased at the effect he was having. It was not so very difficult, after all, to break a woman's obstinate mood. One needed only to know what tools to use.

He bent over her and placed one hand on her shoulder. "Consider well, my dear. There is no hope of saving Cameron. That much you may take as settled. But there is yet time to buy my favor. Continue in this spiteful manner, and I shall remember it after we are wed and I have all rights over you. Show me that you can come to me in a spirit of compromise, and I can be an indulgent husband."

"What do you want?" Frances asked dully. It mattered little. Not if he was telling the truth. All her resistance had been set against accepting his power. In a day or so, that would be over. If Alasdair died, it made no difference to her what she did.

"Bear witness yourself against Alasdair. Wipe out your shame in the courtroom."

For a moment Frances could not believe what she had heard. Then she welcomed the anger that coursed through her body. It was something akin to life.

Frances lumbered to her feet, both hands pressed to the small of her back against the ache that had been troubling her for days. Gone were the days when she could have jumped up and run from the room. But when she was on her feet, she laughed in Glencairn's face.

"Still harping on the one note, Glencairn? You're a fool, if you have been talking with me all these months, and still think I would betray my man for the sake of pleasing you for any reason."

Glencairn's face darkened. "As you will. I have enough to hang him three times over in the depositions. It is you who are the fool. You will not have many more chances to earn my favor. Think what you wish to be when you are a widow, Frances—my wife, or my prisoner?"

He left her then, and she turned her attention to cozening Lady Anna in the matter of going to the trial.

But in the end it was Glencairn's own decision that she should attend, although well chaperoned against the possibility that she might make any public display. It would help to break that obstinacy of hers, he reasoned, to see her lover chained and sentenced. He might even force her to attend the execution, if she were not brought to bed by then. To put her through so much suffering would, of course, be distasteful to him, but he had never spared the necessary effort to break hawk, hound, or woman to his will.

But by the end of that first day of the trial, Glencairn considered his decision to allow Frances to attend as one of the very few errors he had made in a long and well-planned life. Nothing had gone according to plan. The mob laughed at the depositions, Argyll himself demanded witnesses, and the crowd's maddening chant for "La-dy Frances! La-dy Fran-ces!" still echoed in his ears.

After the trial had been adjourned, the lord advocate, Sir Walter Kerr, waited on him in his paneled office on the lower floor of the town house. It was an unpleasant meeting. Sir Walter informed

Glencairn bluntly that the case might not succeed without Frances' testimony.

"What in God's name were you about, man?" Glencairn snapped. "With all these months, could you not prepare a case that would hold without the testimony of one girl?"

Sir Walter drew himself to his full, if stubby, height. Even so, it was a choice between tilting his head up to Glencairn like a child or looking him straight in the neckband. Staring at the starched pleats of the ruff, Sir Walter said, "I prepared my case, my lord, according to the evidence and the depositions I was given. There was no suggestion that . . . that . . ."

He floundered for words, unable to explain what had gone wrong with his beautiful case. The depositions had been clear enough. There should have been no difficulty in bringing the cateran to justice. But somehow, when you saw the principals in the case—that tragic girl in her black veils, the lean, tough man who walked chained between guards and could still crack a joke with his questioners—somehow the story was no longer one of murder and rapine. What one saw instead was two lovers separated by the might of Glencairn's arm and the land-greed that was in him. Even the justices were seeing it.

But as Sir Walter stared at Glencairn's starched neck ruff and watched the small folds quiver with the man's outrage, he felt it was better not to tread on such shaky ground.

"Well?" snapped the earl.

Sir Walter cleared his throat and started over. "I can but repeat what I have already told your lordship. The mainspring of the case is Lady Frances. It is said in the streets that she loves her abductor and went with him of her own will. Without her testimony to the contrary—"

"Never mind the streets," Glencairn interrupted him. "What's said in the courtroom?"

Sir Walter spread his hands. "The same, my lord."

A brooding silence settled over the room with the early dusk. Sir Walter shivered and tucked his hands inside his velvet sleeve-bands to warm them, while Glencairn brooded and stared at the paneled walls of the small room. Finally, Sir Walter thought of one last suggestion. "Perhaps the lady's brother could persuade her?"

"Donald? That drunken sot?" Glencairn gave a bark of laughter. Then his eyes narrowed. "Aye, nane so ill a notion, could he be found and sobered—and cleaned up, I've no doubt." Ringing a small bell, he bade an abrupt farewell to Sir Walter.

Glencairn thought the idea worth a try. Donald knew that his allowance depended on pleasing Glencairn. And he was totally convinced of the earl's power. Perhaps he could have some effect on Frances. Not having heard the words that passed between the bench and the advocate, or Sir Walter's blunt and discouraging summary of the case, she might still believe that the outcome of the trial was in the palm of Glencairn's hand.

Telling her that her lover was doomed to die had only increased her sullen obstinacy. But a sharp lesson in the manner of that death might shock her into cooperation.

For once in that disastrous day, Glencairn was lucky. Donald was hardly drunk at all when the servant found him, and the walk back to Glencairn's town house in the bitter March wind, followed by a dip of his head in a cold bucket of water they had standing ready, sobered him enough to receive his instructions from Glencairn.

"Frighten her if you will," Glencairn said, "but no violence. Understand?"

Donald nodded.

"The hard part," Glencairn mused, "will be to get her out of the house. She is so big with child that she will have trouble walking. If she resists, tell her it is my order."

But Frances was willing enough when Donald told her that Glencairn had consented to let him take her out for a walk. She had been sitting in her room, chafing under her enforced inactivity. Her brain was buzzing round and round the words and events of the trial till she was crazed by them.

Over and over she looked for a sign of hope for Alasdair. But without knowing what the justices and the lawyers had said in those murmured consultations, how could she guess? She clasped her hands and tried to pray, but that was as hopeless as trying to think.

When Donald appeared, she was only too ready to huddle into her fur-lined cloak and brave the March evening.

"A braw cloak," Donald said. "Glencairn's gift? You've fallen soft, little sister."

"Half-sister," Frances corrected. "I've no wish to be closer kin to you than God made me." But then she sighed. "Oh, it's sorry I am, Donald. I should not be insulting you, and you kind enough to take me out of that house for a few minutes."

"The habit will be strong with you." Donald chuckled.

Frances flashed him a suspicious look. What had put him in such a good temper? Good moods on Donald's part never boded well for her. But he was fingering the cloak again. He liked being near rich folk—perhaps that was all there was in it.

"A braw cloak," he repeated. "I hope you'll remember me when you're raised to high position in the land."

"Och, havers!" snapped Frances. If she could, she would have stalked ahead of him down the street, but her heavy body forced her to move slowly. "The highest place I wish to be is the hills of the Highlands, Donald, and it's there I will be going as soon as Alasdair will be freed of this tangle." She spoke more stoutly than she felt. But she dared not, she *would* not envisage any other outcome to the trial.

"Ah, never hope for that, Fan," Donald told her. "You'd best forget Alasdair, and set your mind to please Glencairn. It was a lucky day for our family when he set his mind on you. Have you not thought of the riches and power that will come to you as his wife? All the furs and jewels you want, Frances. No more huddling in your threadbare plaid, listening to the wind howl over a bare glen while you count up the black cattle and the scabby sheep."

He went on to paint a glowing picture of the life Frances could expect if only she pleased the earl. She turned her thoughts from him as best she could. With a little concentration she was able to make his voice blend in with the wind that shrieked and howled round their ears.

It was a foul night for an outing, but she found a kind of relief in the fierce concentration needed to battle the gusts of wind and keep her footing on the slippery stones. They were going down from the High Street now, along a narrow alley where the wooden fronts of the houses, leaning overhead, almost met in the upper reaches of the street. Few honest citizens were abroad on this blustery March evening, and those they passed cast curious glances at them, as if wondering what business they could have in the streets at such an hour.

Even the small effort of making her way down the slippery street roused creaks of protest from Frances' unused muscles. She had long ago given up fashionable lacing in favor of a loose, sacklike gown that somewhat concealed her condition. Now even that seemed intolerably constricting. Her face felt hot; she pushed back her wide fur hood and let the cold air on it.

"Why, what ails ye, Fan? Do you want to take an ague, going unhooded on a night like this?" Donald broke off his discourse to readjust her hood, and Frances let him do it. A sudden fit of shivers had succeeded the heat, and she was grateful to huddle within her cloak.

"Where are we going?" she asked. When they set off, she had been so glad to be out she had hardly cared what their destination might be. But since they had been walking she had been troubled by a vague pain in her back that came and went with disquieting irregularity. She tried to stand straighter, thinking that would ease her, but it was hard to balance with this great belly sticking out in front of her. She was beginning to wish they would turn around and go back to the house.

"Not far now," Donald assured her. He shot her a sharp glance. "Wearied, are you? You will never have to walk again if you dinna' wish it, Frances. Glencairn's wife can take her ease—if you find favor with him. I've warned you before, Glencairn is an ill man to cross. Since he's set on having you, best thank your good fortune, and think how to please him. 'Twould make a good beginning if you were to speak against Alasdair tomorrow."

"You and Glencairn will be aye harping on the one note," said Frances wearily. The pain came back again, stronger this time. She leaned against a nearby house pillar to catch her breath. This time it was hurting more in her stomach. Could she have eaten some bad food? Disjointed thoughts of poison and unknown enemies flashed through her mind. Then the cramps eased, and she laughed at her own fears.

"Why should I speak against Alasdair?" she asked Donald. "Nay, do not be telling me. You will aye be saying, 'to please Glencairn,' and I will aye be answering that it is not in my mind to please him. Rather tell me this. Why is it of such matter to Glencairn that I speak against Alasdair? Can he not buy enough witnesses without me?"

"No such matter," said Donald, remembering the detailed instructions he had received from Glencairn. "Alasdair's a dead man, sister. You can take that for granted. Glencairn has won greater matters than this. Do you think he'll let one Highland nobody stand in the way of his getting Beauly and you? You're the only one can save Alasdair now."

His small bright eyes were watching her sharply

to see her reaction. But Frances could not conceal the leap of hope that flooded through her. Save Alasdair? Was there yet a way?

"Tell me—how?" In the middle of her sentence the pains came on her again, and she had to stop to gasp. A new thought struck her. Could it be the child coming before its time? Perhaps they should turn back now.

She slowed her pace again, taking very small, precise steps, as though that would stave off the pain. They were coming to the mouth of the alley; a vaguely familiar wide square opened before them.

"Not his life. Nothing you can do will buy his life. But you may be able to spare him something in the manner of his dying. Glencairn is not a vindictive man. Alasdair's life was forfeit from the day he wed you, for Glencairn means to have you and Beauly. But if you show your willingness to obey the earl in this matter, he will see that Alasdair gets a quick, clean death. That is the most you can buy for him."

The story sounded thin enough. Donald feared to give Frances time to think it over. She might wonder why Glencairn was so eager for her testimony, and that might unravel all.

"Come on," he said, gripping her elbow. "We're almost there."

They had reached the mouth of the alley now, and the wind howled round them with renewed force. A fine sleeting rain filled the air and added a thin layer of black ice to the slippery cobblestones. Frances gazed about her, recognizing this was the square she'd ridden through when she arrived in the city.

Donald grasped her shoulder and spun her roughly around before him. Frances gasped in fear that the sudden movement would waken the pain that lay sleeping within her. She felt her ungainly body slipping on the icy cobblestones, and clutched backward at Donald for balance. He hauled her upright, and his fingers bit into her shoulder.

"Few smiles that's brought to this place," he said. "Do ye no' mind yon machine? It should be familiar to you. Your lover had one built outside my prison window."

It was the gallows, a gaunt shadow in the evening light. Frances had a moment of double vision. She remembered the gallows at Beauly, and how she had begged Alasdair to take it down. Now it had risen here, like a ghastly specter out of the past, to have his life. Frances shrieked aloud and buried her face in her hood. Donald pushed the hood back and held her head back by the hair, forcing her to look.

"Look well!" he rasped. " 'Tis that you'll send your lover to, do you remain obdurate. And not that alone. 'Twill not be an easy dying, Frances. It could be counted treason to take a castle from its rightful owner. Glencairn will see to it that a bill of treason is brought against him. Do you mind what that means?"

She knew. She writhed against his hands, trying to free herself, to bring her own hands over her ears to stop his voice. But the inexorable words went on. Fresh pains stabbed through her body as she listened.

"They will bring him in a cart to this place. You will be seeing everything. Glencairn means to hire one of the windows above, so that you may watch in comfort. It's no' a simple hanging they'll give him, Frances. He'll be let dangle at the rope's end long enough to dance and amuse the crowd. But when his face goes black and his tongue is sticking out he'll be cut down, and the surgeon will aye be giving him a sip of wine to revive him. They want him conscious for the next bit, see. Then they'll tear out his bowels and burn them before his living eyes. D'you think he'll cry out then, your bonny lover? I'm told there's no pain like it. And at the last, when they've had their fun of him, he'll be cut in quarters and the pieces tarred and hung in chains. No Christian burial for him, Frances, no rest in life or death. Is that what you will condemn him to?"

It was unbearable. The pains racking her body and the dreadful images called up by Donald's words blended into a universe of torment. Unable to close her ears, Frances began to scream to drown out all the pain—a thin, high, steady scream that cut like a knife across the unctuous flow of Donald's voice.

He cuffed her lightly. "Shut up! You're to hear it all—that's Glencairn's orders. Will I go over it again?"

Glencairn, always Glencairn! The heat was back upon Frances now, and through the feverish flush that suffused her whole body it seemed to her that she could see his lean, skull-like face dancing and jabbering at her in the wind. The face that spelled death to all she loved.

There was a wrenching pain that felt as if it would tear her back in two, and for a moment she lost sight of everything else. Then it eased, and she came back to consciousness of her surroundings—the dark square, the shadow of the gibbet in one corner, and Donald beside her rolling off the description of Alasdair's torture with such pleasure. And now she could no longer delay the knowledge and the fear that coursed through her. Was her child to be born now, and herself with only Donald near? Donald, who must hate her to take such pleasure in torturing her with his words, and who would kill the child himself if he thought it would please Glencairn.

The thought, once voiced, captured all her mind. Glencairn would kill Alasdair. He would kill her child too. She must get away, get away from Donald this minute, before the pains came so fast and close together that even he must guess what they meant. Afterward, she could think what was to be done to save Alasdair. But now her duty was to the child that kicked out so strong within her.

She turned to Donald and leaned on his arm, feigning weakness even as her decision gave her new strength. In the intervals between pains, she felt as though she could conquer armies. But now she let her head droop. "I'll do whatever you and Glencairn decide is best, Donald," she said. "Only dinna' fright me more with such awful tales."

Donald smiled and patted her arm. "There's a good lass. Glencairn will be pleased. Will we be going back now, then?"

"In . . . a moment." There was no kind of a plan at all in her head, but Glencairn's house was the last place she intended to go.

"I'm faint . . ." There was the dark opening of a wynd in the house wall to their right. Leading where? She hadn't been in this part of the city since she'd arrived. She put one hand to her head, staggered a few steps to her right, and leaned against the house wall. Donald, perforce, followed her, but at least he was not holding her arm any longer. He must have been convinced she could not get away from him.

"Perhaps I could be walking back if you were to get me some spirit to drink," she suggested. "Please, Donald, I feel faint. 'Twill put the heart in me again."

Donald was sorely tempted; she could see that.

He glanced over his shoulder at the tavern on the north side of the Grassmarket, where candles burned within, showing that not all citizens were at home in this night.

"You come with me," Donald said.

"I cannot . . . walk so far." The pain returned in the middle of the sentence, cutting off her breath. She leaned against the house wall and waited for Donald's decision.

The temptation of the warm alehouse was too strong for Donald to argue, and he was all too ready to believe Frances had given in.

"Hurry back," Frances pleaded with him. "Do not be leaving me alone for long and it so dark here!"

That convinced him. He set off at a brisk walk for the other side of the square. She waited until she saw him disappear into the dimly lit doorway under the creaking sign. Then she picked up her skirts and was around the corner, scrambling up the steep malodorous wynd for her life and the child's.

18

Praise be to all the saints, but the wynd was not a dead end into some rich merchant's courtyard. On both sides were passages into other streets. To her right, every thirty or forty steps, was an arched opening that let into the street of the West Bow, where they'd come down. To her left were narrower passages leading God knew where.

She took one at random and found herself in a crooked, narrow street where most of the cobblestones had been prized out and it would be easy enough to break her ankle on those that remained sticking out of the mud.

The pain took her there, sharp, and she leaned against the wall and groaned aloud. The noise in the deathly quiet street startled even her. And not a moment too soon, for next she heard hurrying steps and shouts in the West Bow. Damn Donald! He'd been quicker in and out of that tavern than he had ever been in his life. And from the sound of it, he'd brought out the rest of the scaff and raff in the tavern to turn out and hunt for her.

Frances set her teeth against the pain that threatened to burst her body in two. A fine brother she had, hunting her through the Edinburgh streets with the tavern rabble. And her like an animal diving to its hole. Never, *never* would she forgive him this.

The scalding pains passed and she could move again. The wynd was quiet, the noise came now from up the hill. They had passed by her bolt hole. Frances crossed herself in thankfulness and felt her way through the dark street, heading back downhill toward the Grassmarket. Hinds doubled on their tracks to throw off the hunt, and so would she.

It was a weary walk, and the streets of this poor quarter lacked even the miserly lamp before each house which the city council had forced the well-to-do householders to put out. Indeed they were not houses at all, but stinking hovels where whole families crowded in a single room and threw their slops out into the gutter for pigs to forage on. Here and there about her children played in the dark amid the refuse heaps, or a woman with her plaid pulled tight over her head hurried past with an incurious glance at Frances.

Taking at random one turn after another, she was soon hopelessly lost in the narrow, winding passages. No need to go on, then. Where would she be going to? Weary and cold, she huddled in the angle of a wall that gave some shelter from the sharp wind. Down the street she could hear the shrill cries of some children at their game.

When she had run, she had had no thought but to put the streets between her and Donald. But the black cold would kill her and the baby just as surely as Glencairn. She would have to knock at a door and beg for shelter.

Still she put off the moment when she would have to cast herself on the mercy of strangers, using as an excuse that the pains were coming so hard and close together now that she could scarce walk.

She pushed herself on from the sheltered corner and found herself in the path of the playing children. One of them came full tilt out of a narrow passage between two tall tenements and cannoned into Frances. His skinny hands scrabbled at her cloak for purchase to keep himself upright, and he screamed a malediction at his pursuers. The other children dared not approach too close to the noble lady in her fur-lined mantle, but they formed a half-circle round her and hopped up and down, chanting a rude song. Frances could not make out the words, save that the name "Ailsa" and the word "whore" were coupled time and again, with many variations.

The pain gripped her again and she bent double. A ragged scream echoed through the alley. The children broke off their chant for a moment to listen, then renewed their song with extra force.

Frances heard another scream, that died away on some babbling words, but her own lips were clamped shut and her teeth caught in her lower lip so tight as to draw blood.

"Mistress, can ye walk?" the boy who had run into her asked.

Belatedly Frances realized that she'd been leaning on him in her pain, resting her full weight on the skinny little shoulder. It was a wonder they'd not both gone down in the gutter.

Now he was urging her to move on. "Jist a wee bittie farther, mistress," he said. "Me mother's in-bye with her fourth."

The words made no sense to Frances. But it was easier to follow the tug of his hand than to argue.

The ring of children fell back as they approached, then opened to let them through.

"Is yon the witch-wifie?" piped up a shrill voice from a little mite not three years old.

The boy helping Frances growled in answer and shook his fist at the other children. They took up their hopping dance again as he passed, this time chanting, "Guthrie's daft! Guthrie's daft!"

"Pay no mind, mistress," the boy said in a voice hoarse with the cold. "Jist a bittie more. On ye go, then."

The room he steered her into was lit by the flickering light of a single iron cruisie lamp with a twist of a rag sticking out of the grease for a wick. It was bitterly cold, with no fire, nor a place to light one. But the flicker of light and the relief of being out of the wind made it seem like heaven to Frances.

In the corner farthest from the door a woman was lying on a bed of straw, moaning and tossing her head from side to side. A black-shawled old crone knelt beside her and felt up her skirts.

"Ye've a way to go yet, Ailsa lass," she said at the end of this examination. "So dinna' mak' sic a business out of it. After three times ye should know how to dae it."

An incoherent murmur was the only answer the woman in the straw gave. As Frances watched, she drew up her legs to her belly and gave a series of piercing shrieks. Only then did Frances realize that she, too, was pregnant. Her swollen belly stood out like an obscene bulge against the thinness of her arms and legs. Her hair was matted with sweat and there were sores on her lips and cheeks.

Frances crossed herself against the sight and stumbled backward, but the boy was behind her. "Lay out a bittie mair straw, Mallie," he shouted in his queer hoarse voice. "I've mair customers for ye the nicht."

Another pain seized Frances and she sank to her knees on the dirt floor. Through the haze of fear and pain she was dimly aware of people moving around her. "Just lie you down, lass," the old woman was urging her.

Hard hands under her armpits, helping her stumble to the hastily piled straw where she sank down in exhaustion. The same cracked old hands loosening her clothing. "My, but yon's an awfu' bonny cloak," the voice said. "Raise her up noo, the way I'll slip it off. 'Twould be a pity to be gettin' bluid all over it."

It was a wrenching agony to raise her hips, but Frances knew her only hope now was to do as she was told. She followed the old woman's orders, bracing her legs against the floor, grasping the old woman's dry hands and pulling with all her might.

The pain never let go of her now. Her eyes gazed about wildly now, and she moaned in near-delirium.

"She'll be out of her heid wi' the pain," suggested the woman Ailsa, resting between her own pains. She propped herself up on an elbow and surveyed the pale, girlish face beneath the tangle of black curls. "I mind wi' my first—"

"Aye, you made a great hubble-bubble about it," the old woman, Mallie, told her. "But this yin's lucky. She'll be done ere ye've weel started."

"Likely she'll dee," Ailsa prophesied. "She's too pale now, and when the babe comes fast like that, they'll tear ye to pieces inside. I mind wi' my third—"

"Ach, give ower wi' yer mindings. Better ye should shut yer gob and walk a bit, to bring it on." Mallie gave Ailsa a rough but not unkindly shove, and moved again over her new charge. "She'll no' die," Mallie muttered, bending over Frances and stroking her brow with one worn old hand. "Not while I'm wi' her."

Later Frances was to recall all this conversation, but at the time she seemed to be drifting in and out through a red mist where nothing stayed the same for long, except the pain that squeezed her body. There was the sound of a woman screaming, on and on with a disgusting high note like a pig being stuck. Not herself? But another time she came out of the mist, and her throat was raw and her lips dry, and Mallie wetting them with a rag that she dipped into a cracked earthenware jug.

Then the hands were about her again, pushing and pulling and making her half-squat over the straw. There was a tearing, burning sensation, as if something bigger than herself was pushing its way out of her body, a warm wetness gushing between her thighs, and then the blessed cessation of pain.

She wanted to sleep then, but Mallie's hands were at her, pushing and massaging.

"Aye. That's the afterbirth. Good lass . . . good lass," crooned Mallie. "I tell't ye, Ailsa, she'd be done or ever ye started to work. And a bonny little lass she's made."

Mallie held up something wrinkled and red in her hands, and Frances felt her own arms longing for the burden. "Give me my baby," she whispered.

Mallie wrapped a scrap of cloth around the baby and tucked it into the crook of Frances' arm. Tired though she was, Frances could not keep from smiling as she looked at the child's fuzzy little head. So much she and Alasdair had been through, to get this little baby and keep her safe. "Always . . . you'll always be safe," she vowed in a whisper.

Her eyes closed and she drifted off in a hazy dream while the old woman cleared out the soiled straw from under her. Then, through her broken, feverish half-sleep she was dimly aware of more hustle and bustle in the small room. It was an eerie echo of her own experience. Ailsa walked from wall to door and back again, over and over, and Frances bit her lip in sympathy when she too cried out in the final pains. But Ailsa's birth was easier than her own; a few sharp cries, and then there was the howl of a newborn infant.

"A good healthy bairn," pronounced the old wife, holding the baby up. Frances heard the words and finally fell into a deep, healing sleep with one arm curled protectively around her own small child.

When she woke again, the lamp was out and a dim gray light filtered into the room through the half-open door. She and Ailsa lay side by side, both covered with Frances' fur cloak. Mallie was seated on a three-legged stool by the door, holding something wrapped in a rag.

A lusty cry split the air and Frances realized that there was a baby lying beside Mallie.

"My son—give me my son," Frances whispered through cracked lips.

Mallie chuckled. "Nay, lass, that yin's Ailsa's bairn. You've made a bonny wee lassie." She stooped over and handed Frances the tiny wrinkled morsel she had been rocking. Frances pulled the rag back and looked with awe at the little red face.

"But she's so tiny . . ." she whispered.

Mallie clucked her tongue and shook her head back and forth. "When-abouts were you due? Not till next month, it looks. She's come early. And you had too many troubles while you were carrying her, I'll wager."

Frances looked at the old woman with the beginnings of fear. There'd been talk last night of a witch. Surreptitiously she crossed herself under the fur cloak. Mallie caught sight of the gesture and chuckled.

"Nay, dinna' fear. I'm no' gifted to see the things that arena' there. I know ye, Lady Frances. Ailsa and I saw you ride in through the Grassmarket, these many months syne. I gave you a pot of grease for the sores. It's no chance guess that you've had a hard time since."

Frances fell back on the straw, exhausted. "Why did you let me stay, if you were knowing who I was? Did you no' know there was danger in it? Glencairn will be having the soldiers out to find me."

"Last night?" Mallie cackled. "Nay, they know better than to come sticking their lang noses in here at night. Days, now, that's a different matter. If you've the strength, lass, you'd best be up and moving. Hard it goes against me to ask it of you, but we canna' have the soldiers here. You can leave the bairnie here," Mallie added on an afterthought. "Likely she'll no' live, any road, being so puny. And yon great earl will no' want to be troubled wi' her."

"No!" Frances clasped the babe to her breast so fiercely that she set up a thin, wavering wail of protest. Her cries roused the other baby who joined in so lustily that Ailsa was awakened, and Mallie passed her the boy to put to her breast.

Frances was surprised to see how full Ailsa's breasts were, when the rest of her body was thin from lack of proper nourishment.

"Aye, 'tis always so wi' me—eh, Mallie?" Ailsa said with a gleam of pride. "Seems my body makes milk for the bairns if it has to draw the strength from my ain blood and bone. Ah, but ye should ha' seen me when I was younger. I had the siller then to keep bread on the table and a fine gown on my back."

"An' best not be talkin' about how you got it," muttered Mallie.

Ailsa gave an impudent shrug of her shoulders, and in her expression Frances saw an echo of the perky little boy who had guided her here.

"What's it to you? You take the siller when I have it, don't you?" Ailsa said. She bent over her child with a look of pride. "Aye, he's a fine strong lad," she crooned, and stroked the wisps of reddish hair on his head. "Your father must ha' been that red-heidit captain o' the nicht guard. Mayhap if I tak' you to him, he'll tak' and raise you to be a soldier. Would you like that, my bonny lad? Tae be a braw soldier, with the shining breastplate and the steel helm on you?"

The child pushed with both hands at her breast and began to cry. Ailsa laid him across her lap and patted his back rhythmically. A sharp sigh followed this vision of her son's future. "If that doesna' work, it's the streets for you, my bairn, wi' the rest o' my brood."

She stared at the wall with vacant, sad eyes, then roused herself with a laugh. "Aweel, and what are we sittin' gloomin' here for! Mallie, go and get us a tankard of ale from the public."

"And where's the coin to pay for't?" the old woman grumbled.

"I'll pay you double when I'm well again," Ailsa promised.

Grumbling into her black shawl, Mallie hobbled off to do the errand.

Frances' baby began to wail again. She lifted her up and began to unfasten the loose bodice of her dress as she'd seen Ailsa do.

Ailsa leaned over and inspected the child with professional-seeming interest. "I'd no' bother wi' putting her to the breast if I was you," she said. "You'll no' be let nurse her, gin you go back to the earl. Ladies never nurses their ain bairns. Likely the earl will have her sent out."

Frances clutched her baby protectively. Already she could not bear the thought of being parted from her. "You're all I have left," she whispered. "I'll never let them take you from me."

The baby screwed up her face and began to cry. Ailsa stretched out her arms. "Let me have her a minute." She cradled the child in the bend of her free arm and offered a white breast full to overflowing with milk. The baby quieted as she sucked ecstatically.

"I have plenty of milk," Ailsa declared. "Maybe you'll be needing a wet nurse?" She glanced at Frances with hopeful, hungry eyes. Frances realized that the chance to follow her to Glencairn's household, with plenty of food and warmth, could mean the difference between life and death for Ailsa and her own baby.

But who was to say that she'd be allowed to keep her baby? Obviously, these women of the slums had heard all the gossip and judged the situation accordingly. The Earl of Glencairn would not let Frances keep a living reminder of the husband he had killed.

If only she had borne a boy! A boy who could grow up and take Beauly from Glencairn. The past months had taught Frances how helpless women were when the men were playing their land and power games. One small girl-child was of no account when men were settling affairs of state. But if she had born a boy, then . . .

An idea stirred in Frances' sleepy mind. What if she had borne a son to Alasdair? Their marriage by a priest might not count for much in the new kirk, but in the months of Edinburgh she had learned that even the Reformed Kirk had not been able to change Scots marriage law that much. No marriage was considered invalid if the two parties agreed to it and a child was born of it.

But a son would be more than just a child to prove their marriage. A son of hers, if she declared him legitimate and the true son of herself and Alasdair, would be heir to Beauly on both sides. And more. He would grow up to be a man who could be the chief of the clan, as her girl baby could never be. Would Glencairn get Beauly then? Or would the king appoint her guardian in her son's name, as Donald had wanted to rule as Hugh's guardian?

It all came together for Frances in a dazzling burst of light. If she had borne a son in the privacy of Glencairn's house, the dangerous child would no doubt have been strangled at birth. But if she came back publicly with her son in her arms, they would be safe. A death or disappearance then might raise too many questions for a man like Glencairn who liked to get his lands with a gloss of legality. He'd be seeking some other way.

A son would be the tool she needed to bargain for Alasdair's life. And a boy had been born this very night. If she could keep Ailsa's baby for a day or two, only long enough to convince Glencairn that there was an heir to Beauly . . .

It would never work. Ailsa's child was so strong and big and red-haired, and hers puny, dark, and obviously premature; she could never pass them off as twins.

But she could, maybe, exchange them.

The daring thought startled her and was immediately rejected. Give up her own child? *Never*.

But for a day—only for a day . . . And it would mean so much . . .

Frances felt her breasts aching at the thought of being parted from the fragile little thing. Not yet a full day old, and already she was a part of her life.

But how long would Glencairn let them be together? If she took the cowardly way out, and went meekly back to his house now, she might lose all. If she changed the babies for a day, she might get all back—Alasdair and her baby both.

If her bargain with Glencairn worked, she would have enough power to ensure that the child stayed with her. Then she could bring Ailsa into the house as wet nurse, and they would both have their own babies again.

And if it didn't work? Frances put that thought from her. If it didn't, then there was no hope for her, or Alasdair, or for the child they'd made. It had to work. She had to try it.

There was just one small thing to settle first.

Frances propped herself up on her elbow and watched Ailsa's face as she suckled the girl baby. She seemed to treat her just as she'd treated her own son.

Ailsa was worried about what was to become of the boy; that much had been clear from her murmured words to him.

And he had red hair.

"Ailsa." Frances spoke in a low voice, but with the tone of command that came from being lady of Beauly. "Ailsa, will you help me?"

The two women murmured together for a long time, drawing Frances' fur-lined cloak about them to shield them from the cold.

"It's aye a risk," Frances said. "I'd not be concealing that from you. But what chance will he have here?"

Her gesture encompassed the fireless room, the few broken sticks of furniture, the filthy street outside where pigs rooted in the gutter.

"It's true," Ailsa sighed. "Small chance for any of us. I canna' rear Guthrie proper, and this new one will have less chance even."

"I'll be taking care of Guthrie, too," Frances promised recklessly, with no idea how she would fulfill the promise. "And yourself."

And she repeated over and over again, "Whatever happens to me, your son will be raised among gentlefolk, in a good stone house with plenty of malt and meal."

"A gude stone house," repeated Ailsa wonderingly. "And always enough to eat. Never did I think to see such a fortune for one of mine." She fell silent a moment, cradling the red-haired boy in her arms so tightly that he began to wail. Frances waited, holding her breath, and hoping—she hardly knew what she hoped for. It was a way to save Alasdair. But at the thought of being parted, even for a few days, from her own baby, her heart ached. And yet, her babe might well be safer in this hovel than in Glencairn's house, until she'd made her bargain.

"You'll take care of her as if she were your own?" she implored of Ailsa for the fourth time.

Ailsa looked down at the little black-haired girl sucking at her breast, and her expression softened. "Aye, that I will," she said, almost inaudibly. "Once ye've held them to the breast, seems as if they were your own." Her white face, drained from the rigors of childbirth, lightened with an impish grin. "Aye, my lady. You see to mine, and I'll tak' gude care o' yourn. And I'll bring her back to ye tomorrow."

"Tomorrow," Frances echoed. "Come to the kitchen door. The cook will be expecting you. Just say that you've come to be Lady Frances' wet nurse."

Both women were silent for a moment. Frances reached out one hand to caress the light fuzz of baby hair on her little girl's head. So little she was, and so vulnerable. For a moment her heart failed her. Did she have the right to use the baby as a bargaining counter, even for Alasdair's life? But she knew she had no other choice.

"Aweel," sighed Ailsa, "let's get on wi' it, then." She wrapped her baby tight in a rag and thrust him at Frances with all the grace of a woman handing over a sack of flour. "Tak' him," she said in a roughened voice. "Guthrie will guide you. Gang on, then! Tak' him, afore I think better o't." She turned her head into the straw and lay with her face to the wall, clutching the weakling girl-child, who fretted and wailed continously.

Frances stooped over the two for a moment longer. But it was past time to go. The morning was far advanced, and Glencairn's men might come searching for her at any time. "If . . . if I don't come back, call her Sarah," she said. Her throat was closing up with unshed tears as she left her daughter behind, not knowing if she would ever see her again.

The pale black-haired young woman in her loose velvet gown, carrying a red-haired baby wrapped in linen rags, attracted a number of curious onlookers in the Grassmarket. The boy Guthrie, who guided her, was willing enough to stop and repeat his gossip to anyone who asked. Before they'd turned into the steep passage leading to the High Street, all the fishwives, shopkeepers, and market women of the west side of town knew that Lady Frances—"the lass whae was treated sae foul by the earl," one of them reminded her neighbor—was the lighter of a bonny boy.

By the time she reached the High Street, the crowd that followed at her heels were all willing to swear to the bairn's amazing resemblance to Alasdair Cameron.

He's red hair, at least, thought Frances, and forced a smile to her lips at the shouts of congratulation that surrounded her. Rumor had bade fair to make a popular heroine of Lady Frances during the months she'd been immured in Glencairn's house, and the Edinburgh mob were ready to show their favor.

The crowd was in this boisterous mood when they encountered the first of Glencairn's men.

Searching unsuccessfully for Frances since daybreak, they were drawn to the noisy procession and promptly buffeted about in it.

A soldier with a pike cannot do much good with his weapon if a grinning, cheerful crowd of apprentice boys and sturdy beggars presses him so close that he cannot bring it down to point at anyone. And most of the men remembered the riots of 1595, and had no strong desire to protect Glencairn's interests at the cost of getting their own heads bashed in with a paving stone.

So they were swept along with the mob to the Canongate, where Frances marched into the Tolbooth and demanded that the bailie register her son Alexander Cameron, born to Frances Murray of Beauly and Alasdair Cameron of Beauly.

"Legitimate or not?"

That had to be left undetermined until she could bargain with Glencairn. Frances looked down and blushed.

"Need you be writing that?"

The bailie was no more immune than any other man to the blushes of a pretty sloe-eyed lass with the lilt of the Highlands in her voice. He'd also been following the proceedings against that same Alasdair Cameron with great interest and thought that to be able to say he had registered the birth of his son would be a tidy bit of news to tell the wifie! So he did not insist, nor did he point out that it was, properly speaking, the business of the parish clerk in Giles' Kirk to be writing down births.

He inscribed the details Frances gave him in the ledger used to record the doings of the Privy Council, on a blank half-page under the declaration of outlawry. On the opposite page was recorded the putting to the horn of one Robert Gilham of the Lawnmarket for the murder of his master and subsequent flight from the city. The bailie wiped the quill on the edge of the page, and thought deeply on the irony that the next thing he wrote might be an account of the sentencing of this child's father.

"It would be a pity if anything were to happen to him," Frances said. "You'd no' think the Earl of Glencairn would be taking vengeance on an innocent babe?"

The bailie did not think so. But after Frances had planted the seed of the thought in his mind, he agreed it would be good if a soldier of the city guard were lodged at Glencairn's until the trial was finished.

Before talking with the earl, Frances spent some time arraying herself in the finest of the dresses he had given her. It was a shimmering confection of blue satin over an exaggerated wide-wheel farthingale, with a low, straight neckline that compressed and heightened the white curves of her breasts. The sleeves and undergown were of quilted yellow satin, finished with gold lace at the wrists and hem, and there were rows of gold embroidery along the neckline of the blue satin bodice. The long, pointed bodice could only be worn over one of the new long-bodied corsets. Frances felt as if she were wearing a suit of armor. But that was, after all, entirely appropriate for this type of interview. And with the corset she had the satisfaction of seeing the gown slide smoothly into place, fitting as close and tight as if she had never borne a child.

My lord of Glencairn was waiting for her in the small paneled downstairs room, overlooking the sad winter garden, where he conducted his difficult interviews. Frances sailed in with a dignity only partially compromised by the fact that she was carrying a squalling bundle wrapped, for the moment, in one of Lady Anna's lace-edged table linens. The soldier assigned her by the bailie followed her in.

Glencairn frowned at the sight of this stranger. "Do we really need him?" he demanded.

"Why, no," replied Frances with as much composure as she could muster. "He may wait for me outside the door. His only concern is to see to my safety."

Since the bailie's excuse for sending a guard with Frances had been his concern for the protection of an important state witness, Glencairn could not well have the man thrown into the street as he would have liked. He gave a curt nod and waited before the door had shut before speaking again.

"What is the meaning of this escapade?"

Frances lowered her lashes. "Indeed, my lord, I know not. Breeding women will take strange fancies. I pray you will rejoice with me to see that my son is safe and well."

Glencairn averted his eyes from the squalling bundle she held out to him.

"A fair babe," he said in haste, "so far as I understand these things. But you would be wise not to grow too attached to him. Bairns sicken and die very easily."

A chill ran through Frances. She settled the child in her arms, taking her time about it. When her features were composed, she smiled up at Glencairn. "Oh, I am thinking he will thrive, my lord. The Tolbooth bailie assures me he has never seen such a fine, healthy child. He will be thinking it is very strange if the bairn should be carried off by a sudden . . . illness."

Threat for threat; steel for steel. Frances' bright smile never wavered as she waited for Glencairn's response.

"Enough," he said harshly. "You have displeased me in this. But at least now you wear one of my gowns. Does this mean you are prepared to submit to my will?"

This was the meat of the matter. Frances leaned

forward slightly, the child in her arms all but forgotten. "On certain conditions, my lord."

Glencairn's eyes were colder than the sleeting rain, and held less mercy. "I am not accustomed to bandying about 'conditions' with half-grown girls."

"No?" Without heeding his disapproval, Frances swept on. It was a simple matter as she outlined it. With the birth of a son to her and Alasdair, matters had changed. Alasdair's death would now do Glencairn no good. There was still an heir to Beauly and a head of the clan: the babe in her arms. Granted, a child in swaddling clothes could not rule a clan; a tutor would have to be appointed till he came of age. The tutor would have control of the lands, the income, and the clan until that time. Whom would the king name? It might be Frances; it might be Glencairn. But in any case, Glencairn would not be joining the lands of Beauly with his own. He would at best have the use of them until the baby she called Alexander was grown.

All this, of course, only if the marriage between Frances and Alasdair stood. But if she swore in court that she had been forced before the priest and had not consented—why, then it was not a true marriage. Neither handfasting nor the nuptial Mass would hold if she denied her consent. Alexander would be a bastard who could not in law inherit.

"And this you are prepared to swear to?" Glencairn asked.

Frances returned his look with a level gaze. She kept her hands clasped round the child to still their trembling. "As I said, my lord, on certain conditions. Alasdair's death will do you no good now. Swear that he will go free, and I will testify in court as you wish."

So, she has no idea how close I am to losing the case altogether, he thought with relief. He kept his expression neutral as he spoke. "And join him as soon as he's free? I could not agree to that."

Frances lowered her lashes to conceal the glitter of tears in her eyes. Here was the hardest part of the bargain. But it must be made. "No, my lord. I will remain and do your bidding. I ask only that you spare his life."

Glencairn rose and strode to the window. His back to Frances, he looked out over the desolate winter garden where last autumn's roses still hung, frost-blackened, on their thorny vines. Why repine over a season's frost? Spring would come again, and the garden would bloom. And just as surely, this cold girl would forget her tragic airs and warm his bed. It was not in the nature of women to feel deeply, or long. Why should it trouble him that she so clearly still fancied herself in love with this Cameron?

He swung about and caught Frances in an unguarded moment. The baby was fussing again, and her head was bent over the child as she soothed him. Posed thus, she had just the look of the Madonna he'd saved from Giles' Kirk when the image-smashers were at their work. Yes—he must have her in his house. Not just Beauly. Her.

"I agree to your . . . condition, madam." He said the words with a deep sense of relief that the bargain was sealed, but also underlying that, he felt a cold fear. If she ever learned that he'd tricked her into forswearing her love, when Alasdair might have gone free without . . . Pshaw! Women were to stupid to understand these matters. She'd been fool enough to believe his and Donald's statements that Alasdair was doomed already; she'd not look further.

Frances bowed her head in agreement. "Will I have it in writing, my lord?"

"In writing?" Glencairn was pleased with the fine irony of it. "You gave me your word. Is the word of Glencairn not equal to that of a Cameron?"

Frances made no reply to this. She simply looked at him with that curious shuttered expression on her face, waiting, till at last he threw himself into the carved oaken chair behind the table, took up quill and ink, and scratched away furiously for a few moments. He scattered sand over the paper and threw it at her.

"There you are, madam. Alasdair Cameron to go free after your testimony to the rape, and you to remain in my house after the trial. Does that content you?"

Frances read over the paper, folded it, and tucked it into her bosom. "Yes, my lord. Thank you, my lord."

She rose, somehow managing a curtsy with the child on one arm, and left the room before he could think of an excuse to detain her further.

19

After an adjournment of nearly three weeks, the trial of Alasdair Cameron opened with a surprise for the observers. Lady Frances appeared in court, brazen as you please, wearing a gay-colored satin dress and showing no sign that she'd ever borne a child. The whisper quickly ran through the court that the long adjournment had been for the purpose of allowing Lady Frances to recover her strength after the birth. Was she going to testify, then?

It was common knowledge, of course, that the child was a boy who was the spit of Cameron himself. And the town had been fascinated to hear that Lady Frances had hired a wet-nurse from the

West Bow area, one Ailsa, popularly known as Ailsa the Hoor for her former means of earning her livelihood.

"I aye said thae Highlanders werena' proper leddies and gentlemen," cackled the auld wifie of the Nether Bow who'd been an avid spectator since Alasdair was first marched from the castle.

"Look at the fine gown on her back," sighed another. "Crimson satin, and a great gold chain to her neck. If I had such braws, I'd be out to show them off too."

"D'ye think she's here to show off her braw duds?" demanded her husband. "Weemen! She'll be giving testimony the day. The question is, which way will it go?"

The lords justice and the advocate, Sir Walter, were in no such suspense, having been in conference with the Earl of Glencairn almost daily while they waited for Lady Frances to recover her strength. In fact, they had already agreed on the conclusion of the trial and the sentence to be passed. But in deference to public opinion and the forms of law, the play must be carried out.

Glencairn did not help matters by appearing that day in a magnificent costume of ruby velvet slashed with white taffeta, and bearing a gold chain equal in weight to Frances' own. The intent was clear: they were to appear as a couple. Only a few women among the onlookers, being concerned with trivial matters as usual, whispered that his ruby clashed vilely with her crimson.

Frances had taken leave of Glencairn early that morning, being escorted early to the Tolbooth by the bailie's guard that she might avoid the crush of the crowd. When Glencairn made his entrance she started from her seat, colored, then sank down again with her hands gripped together in her lap.

"See that blush? Nae better than she should be," whispered a man. "I'll warrant she's already been at her tricks wi' Glencairn."

"Haud yer wheesht," his wife whispered back, and elbowed him. "A woman just risen from child-bed doesna' think on such matters. Shouldna' I knaw, and me bearing six of yourn, ye lustful gowk?"

"Aye, if they were all mine—" began the reply. But he was cut off by the heralds' cry for silence and attention in the court.

The prisoner Cameron had made his entrance. He walked with a firmer stride today. They said he'd been let exercise in the courtyard.

His first incurious glance round the crowded room halted, like a bird shot in flight, when it fell on Frances. He gave an involuntary start forward and his hands reached out for her, but the chains around his wrists, fastened to the iron belt, caught him up short. In the next moment he took in all the significance of her rich attire and of Glencairn's almost matching suit, and he retreated even before his guards had to pull him back. Thereafter, lips compressed, he looked only at the lords justice on their high bench, and would not turn his head a fraction of an inch to give Frances another look.

"Against—she will speak against him," the whisper ran through the courtroom. He must have heard, but the only sign he gave was a kind of stiffening of the whole body, as if preparing himself to receive a blow.

The first hours of the trial were taken up with the reading and entering into evidence of yet more depositions, going over the same ground that had been covered on the first day. There were statements about the gallows that Alasdair had erected outside Donald's cell; about the midnight chase through the castle, until poor Lady Frances was cornered in the tower keep, where Alasdair had ripped the clothes from her body and bade his followers hold her while he slit her stays with his dirk; about the bagpipes playing to still her shrieks of protest at the mock marriage.

Sir Walter was determined that all of his painfully gathered evidence should be heard.

Partway through the readings, the prisoner was observed to give several jaw-cracking yawns.

Sir Walter stopped and peered over his papers. The lord chief justice, Argyll, did the same.

"You find the matter boring, Mr. Cameron?" Sir Walter asked. "To be sure, these rapes and robberies may be everyday occurrences in your life, but we simple Lowland folk find them of some interest."

The prisoner smiled and apologized for yawning. "It is only that the matter will be a thought . . . ah . . . repetitive? Forgive me, but I thought we had heard most of these fantastic tales already."

The audience cheered. The substance of the depositions was, as Cameron had said, a touch repetitive. It was Lady Frances' testimony they were all waiting for.

Presently the disorder in the court was settled. Argyll, looking severe over the pile of papers before him, made it clear without actually saying so that the onlookers had two choices: they could sit through the rest of Sir Walter's depositions or they could be cleared from the courtroom.

They sat. Through two more long, weary hours, they sat. Then the moment for which all had been waiting arrived.

Lady Frances was called to the witness stand.

The packed courtroom fell silent as she walked to the front of the room, her satin skirts whispering and rustling against one another.

Then, in a small clear voice with the Highland lilt to it, she answered "aye" and "nay" to the prepared list of questions that Sir Walter led her through.

"Were you at Castle Beauly on the night of June 8 of the year previous?"

"Aye."

"Did Alasdair Cameron taken the castle by force on that night?"

Here she hesitated. "It was no' exactly by force, there being but the three men in it altogether."

The crowd stirred and tittered. Here was matter that was not in the depositions. Three men! They had been picturing a vast Highland army, ready to march on Inverness and Edinburgh next.

Sir Walter rephrased his question, bowing to the mood of laughter in the room. "However it was, he did not exactly come by invitation, did he, Lady Frances?"

"They climbed through an open window," she said.

The packed room broke into open and hilarious laughter. They'd come to hear of a rape, and here was a farce!

Glencairn signed to Sir Walter. A ten-minute adjournment was agreed upon, to quiet down the audience. That was all strictly legal and according to form. But it was not strictly in the form of law that Glencairn and Sir Walter closeted themselves with the Lady Frances for those ten minutes.

In the little room off the courtroom, Glencairn gripped Frances by the shoulders with fingers that dug deep into her white flesh. "What do you mean by this?"

Frances looked back at him with a gaze as clear and innocent as spring water. "By what, my lord? I am but answering Sir Walter's questions as you bade me. Or is it your wish that I will be lying about these matters, too, as well as about the marriage? A fine fool I would seem, and me claiming that three men took the hold of Beauly by force."

Glencairn's hands dropped to his sides. "Very well, mistress. Sir Walter, shorten your list of questions. Ask her only of matters pertaining to the marriage. And you, madam"—he turned his chilling gaze upon her—"see that you answer as we agreed. Do not be having any foolish notions that you will save your lover's life by speaking for him now. It is too late for that. Claim that you're married to Cameron, and you'll be a widow before the month is out—and I'll have you watch his death."

In those cold gray eyes she saw no fires like the dancing lights in Alasdair's gaze. Frances shivered in the tiny overheated room and nodded her acquiescence.

From the time they reentered the courtroom, her eyes were fixed on Alasdair's face, silently pleading with him to read their unspoken message. But he would not look at her as, back straight, she answered the rest of Sir Walter's prepared questions.

Had she gone willing to the bed of Alasdair Cameron?

Nay.

But he forced her?

Aye.

And the next day, did he marry her?

Nay.

It was a mock marriage, and she was prevented by force from speaking?

Aye.

Thereafter, he abducted her and took her into the Highlands?

Aye.

She was rescued by the Earl of Glencairn?

Aye.

She repudiated the form of marriage which Cameron claimed to have gone through?

Aye.

She understood that this meant that her son was a bastard, not able in law to inherit Beauly?

At this last question Alasdair whirled around, unable to contain himself. His face was alight as when she'd first walked in. "We have a son, Fan?"

The guards jerked him back by his chains.

"You will not harass or threaten the witness," Argyll said. "Need I remind you that a gag may be brought?"

"My lord, with permission, we have it ready." One of the guards raised his hand to show the gag—a fearsome metal device, helmet-shaped, with three iron prongs to enter the prisoner's mouth and hold his tongue back. Gagged with this instrument, a man could not speak, hardly dared breathe, for fear of slicing his tongue and mouth open on the sharp prongs.

"Good. Lady Frances, I did not hear your answer to the last question?"

Frances felt sick as she stared at the ugly instrument of torture. Please, God, let Alasdair not bring this on himself. Let him understand—oh, let him understand that what she did was only to save his life.

Sir Walter had to repeat the question twice before Frances was able to answer. Finally she gave the word that made her child a bastard.

"Aye."

That was very nearly the end of the trial. Frances heard little of Sir Walter's summing-up. Presently the three justices went out of the room to confer together. Alasdair stood between his guards, not looking at her. Frances comforted herself with the thought that as soon as he was free, she could explain it all to him. Surely he would forgive her for going with Glencairn, when he knew it was the price of his life?

The waiting was torture for Frances. Was not the conference taking a long while, for a matter that was supposed to have been bargained and settled before ever the trial recommenced this day?

The tight corset with its long flat front oppressed her unbearably. She was held rigid as in stocks, unable even to draw in a deep breath. A black dizziness of fear swept over her. What if her agreement was not enough? What if Glencairn meant to cheat her? She put one hand to her bosom and surreptitiously felt for the reassuring crackle of the paper he had signed. How much power did such a paper hold?

Frances' head was bowed and her eyes were closed in prayer when a rustle throughout the courtroom warned her that the lords justice were returned.

From his high seat Argyll pronounced sentence on the prisoner.

"Alasdair Cameron, we find you guilty of the murder of Hugh Cameron of Beauly and of the abduction and rape of Frances Murray, his widow. These crimes being committed with intent to take the castle of Beauly from the loyal servants of the king, we find you also guilty of treason."

Treason! The black tide swelled up around Frances again, roaring in her ears. She could not breathe. Dear God, not that death for Alasdair. Glencairn had played her false. She would proclaim him forsworn throughout the land. She would . . .

But Argyll was going on. Dimly, through the rushing sound in her ears, Frances heard the sentence pronounced. "By reason of the great and noble gentleman who has entreated the mercy of this court, you are sentenced merely to banishment. Within three days you must leave the country, never to return."

But not dead! Frances was nigh choking on her

relief. What was exile? She would follow Alasdair anywhere . . .

She would follow him nowhere. That, too, was in the bargain. She had sold herself to the Earl of Glencairn for Alasdair's freedom, and Glencairn had taken the surest route to ensuring that Alasdair would trouble him no more.

She would never see him again.

The judge had finished speaking now. It was over. There was no more to be said or done, no more to listen for. But Alasdair must look at her once before he was led away.

"Alasdair . . ."

Those nearest the Lady Frances saw her lips move, but heard no sound come out.

Then the black waters rose above her head, and with a kind of relief, she slipped under them and knew no more.

20

Frances recovered consciousness in her room at Glencairn's house. She was lying on the bed. Her stays had been removed, and she savored the easy breaths she took. There was a smell of something burning in the air. Her right arm hurt, as though she had been pricked or stabbed.

She considered all these things for what seemed like a long time before she could persuade her eyelids to open. All her limbs felt heavy and languorous, as though she had just made some extraordinary effort and from that had sunk into sleep. What had she been doing?

With the suddenness of the tide breaking down a sea wall, the truth rushed in on her. Those last moments in the courtroom . . . Alasdair still not looking at her as the sentence was read out . . . her lips forming his name, unable to speak . . .

Frances put one hand to her head and cried out as all the memories came back to her.

There was a stir in one corner of the unlit room. Ailsa rose from the hard bench where she had been keeping vigil and came to look at her charge in the gathering dusk.

"I thocht you'd no' be so cheerfu' when you cam' round," she remarked. "So I told the auld leddy to keep hersen oot of my road. 'Twas her was burnin' the feathers, tryin' to rouse you. I said, 'Let the puir leddy sleep!' She doesna' know what it is to lose a man, that yin. Me, now, haven't ah seen enough of mine march awa' to the wars?" She gave Frances a rough pat on the shoulder. "The old leddy called the surgeon to bleed you, too. That's why your arm hurts."

Ailsa sat down again after delivering this forthright summary of events. Frances raised herself and stared about the room. "Alasdair, I must see Alasdair." She could think of nothing else but the need to go to him and explain.

Ailsa gave her patient a pitying look. "From what they told me of the courtroom, he'll no' be exactly longing to see yoursel'."

"That doesn't matter. I must go to him." Frances sat up in the bed. How dizzy she felt! It didn't matter. "Bring my clothes." Her voice had the unconscious ring of command in it.

"Hoot! I'm no' your slave." Ailsa lit a candle and brought it near the bed. "You're no' to gang anywhere the nicht," she decreed. "The day was enough for you to do, and you just risen from childbed." She put one hand on Frances' brow and pressed her back down into the bed.

"Bide easy, now. It's near time to feed the bairns. Will I bring them in here to feed them?" She laughed. "Funny, when you think of it. Both mine, both yours, aren't they?"

Frances grabbed the woman's wrist. "Never say that again," she hissed. "Never in this house . . . do you understand? If harm comes to my child from your foolish talk, it's myself will have the bones out of your body."

Ailsa nodded and backed away a step, staring at Frances with wide, frightened eyes. Frances swung her legs over the side of the bed and tested her balance with wobbly knees. "Now," she said with more assurance than she felt. "Bring me my clothes."

Ailsa gave her that pitying look again. "I didna' want to tell you—there's soldiers posted all round the house. There's been orders given. You're not to be allowed out o' the house till the three days are past."

Frances sagged back onto the bed. She felt her body being enveloped by the soft feather bed. It was like Glencairn. Always present, and no way you could fight him.

But she tried, all the same. The first interview was a failure, she decided, because a recurrence of her weakness forced her to receive Glencairn in her bedroom, tucked up under the feather comforter and the velvet coverlet, with the embroidered linen of her night rail showing. One could not make an impression that way.

The next day he was away "on affairs of state" all day. Frances fretted and fumed and tried bribing one of the guards with the Cameron emerald, with no more luck than before.

"Dinna' fret," Ailsa told her that night. "He's three days' grace before he must leave or be outlawed. He'll no' leave till the last day is gone by."

"Why?" Frances demanded, and then, "How do you know?"

"Guthrie." Ailsa's expression softened momentarily as she thought of her oldest boy, the only surviving child before this one. "He's into everything, that yin. I wouldna' be surprised if he couldna' tell you the pattern o' the king's nightshirt."

Frances blessed the day when, with reckless generosity, she had promised to support Guthrie as well as Ailsa and the child. A plea to the cook had found Guthrie a place in Glencairn's kitchens, as scullion, scrubber, and general errand boy. A dozen times a day the black-haired imp was sent for something the cook had forgotten or was too lazy to search out in the stores, and he used every trip to the market to pick up the gossip of the streets.

"As for why . . ." Ailsa gave her mistress an unblinking stare. "That's something you'd maybe better think on yoursel'. I didna' hear as Cameron was makin' sae free o' his reasons for anything he did."

Frances gave an unwilling laugh. "That will be Alasdair, true enough. Alasdair was always one to keep his own counsel."

His dangerous lingering in the country, using up his days of grace, should have frightened her. But she felt irrationally happy. What should he be staying for, but to see her once again? So maybe . . . maybe he understood why she was forced to do as she'd done. Maybe he did not hate her entirely.

But she could not depend on that slender chance. On the day following, the last grace day, the Earl of Glencairn returned to his town house early in the morning and found the way to his private chambers blocked by a pale, determined woman with her black hair falling loose about her shoulders.

When she heard the noise of the earl's return, Frances had not had time to dress herself. She had thrown on a loose overgown of quilted and padded white taffeta, the first thing that came to hand, and hurried forth barefoot to meet him.

"You wear my gifts again." Glencairn smiled and

extended his hand to her. "I take it as a sign of favor."

Frances curtsied low, bowing her head. If Glencairn wished to think that she began to favor him, now was not the time to disillusion him. He might be more disposed to grant the dispensation she sought.

But no pleading could soften him.

"It is not in the bond." Glencairn tapped the much-creased paper that she had cast on the table before him in her anger at his continued refusal to let her meet with Alasdair.

"It is written here that Cameron goes free, and so he does. It is written that you remain in my house, and you do. All as we agreed. I cannot let you walk the shore of Leith crying after your lover, my dear. Quite apart from the scandal you would cause, I do not think it safe for you. There are those who will fall upon Cameron at the end of his grace days, which end, I may remind you, at sunset. I have no intention of allowing my future wife to risk herself in such an imbroglio."

"But Alasdair will be thinking that I have betrayed him." Frances could not believe that Glencairn would be so cold as to force them apart without one word of explanation.

A wintry smile was her only response. "He will be the less likely to trouble us again. If the young spark thought you went to this marriage unwillingly, he might conceive some mad plan to descend on

Scotland again and carry you off. I will have peace in my household."

Frances rose to her feet and gathered the quilted skirts of her overgown about her. The deep green of the ribbons that bound the white taffeta mirrored the green light in the Cameron Emerald on her finger. Strange, how one noticed those little things, when everything that mattered had been destroyed. She felt as if she were standing alone in a wilderness. Glencairn's eyes were cold.

"You are a cruel man," she said quietly. "I meant that Alasdair should go free in Scotland, not be exiled, and that he should understand I was not betraying him. I will not feel bound to be honoring my promise to you, for you have twisted the meaning of our bond for the pleasure of hurting us."

Glencairn's face changed subtly, and the lids dropped down halfway over his eyes, so that she could not read his intent. "No? You are kind to warn me."

Ringing the little bell that stood ever on the table, he presently gave orders that the Lady Frances should for the remainder of the day be escorted everywhere she went, even to the door of her chamber, by two guards. She might have freedom to go where she would within the house, but the guards left her on pain of their own lives.

She conferred with Ailsa in the privacy of her chamber. They whispered lest the guards outside should hear, and between times conversed loudly of refurbishing Frances' wardrobe and swaddling the baby Alexander, lest a prolonged period of whispering should draw suspicion on them.

"The thing is just no' possible," whispered Ailsa. "You'll never get away from here in time. I could maybe get a message to him. They'll no' be watching me."

"No," said Frances. "They won't."

Later the babies were brought in to nurse, and they were able to make further plans under cover of the children, one of whom would be crying at any given time, or could be persuaded to by a surreptitious pinch. Frances mentally apologized to the babies: When you're grown up, you'll forgive me . . . if you grow up.

"Look, Ailsa," she would coo loudly, "your little Sarah is going to have black hair." And in an undertone, "Take the old black velvet, and my plaid. And there's a frieze cloak, worn, but still good . . ."

Later that day Lady Anna was pleased to report to Glencairn that Frances seemed to be settling down at last. She had been going through her wardrobe and had sent the wet nurse Ailsa out with a parcel of old worn clothes to distribute among the poor. "Including most of those pitiful rags she brought with her from the Highlands," Anna said with satisfaction.

More than that, Frances had even taken an interest in cookery, and was just now descended to the kitchens to learn from the cook her way of making a marchpane castle.

"Good." Glencairn nodded and returned to his accounts without more than half-hearing what Lady Anna said. It was no more than he'd expected, the pattern of women's behavior that he'd learned with his first two wives. First they argued, then there were floods of tears, then, after one had shown them who was master, they submitted.

It was no more than an uneasy whisper in the back of his head, that Frances had not yet tried the tears on him. She had shown herself as firm as he was. Well, what matter! She had learned her lesson now, at all events. Anna's report had proved that.

He was still congratulating himself on having broken Frances to the leash when the outcry broke out in the nether portions of the house.

Among the crowds that thronged Leith shore, doing business in a babble of all the tongues known to man, it was not such an easy thing to get word of one attainted Highland man presently taking ship for the Low Countries. Frances and Ailsa, cumbered as they were with the babies, were lost in the crowd.

Burghers in fur-lined gowns rubbed shoulders with half-naked porters, bare to the chill wind and sweating as they staggered ashore with bales swinging from both ends of their yokes. Street traders cried the virtues of their cakes and wine punch, pickled calves' feet and fine herring, while clerks labored to tot up the account of goods going and coming. Hides and wool from the Highlands were loaded aboard ships that had brought building timber from the Baltic; smaller loads of luxuries such as dried figs from Spain and silk from Flemish looms were paid for in good Scots silver, though not without some heated discussion on both sides.

Guthrie wriggled his way in among all this clamorous crowd, creeping under the horses' bellies and jostling a cake seller, picking up news here and there until a word with the seller of Flemish silks got him the information he wanted.

"He'll no' be taking ship here," he reported, returning to where the two women stood with their bundle and the swaddled babies.

One decently hooded and cloaked in unremarkable frieze, the other with a tattered plaid drawn over her head and half-veiling her face, they looked like any poor women who might have come down to the pier to welcome their men home. Frances blessed the forethought that had led her to send Ailsa out early with the decent shabby clothes for them to put on over Glencairn's rich gowns. There was nothing in their dress or demeanor to draw the attention of a casual onlooker.

Nonetheless, Frances had become aware of glances thrown at them that were more than casual, and she was glad when Guthrie urged them away from the crowded pier to walk on down the shore where business was less intense.

"They're no' lookin' at you," Guthrie reassured her when she mentioned the stares that had bothered her. "Or, no' to bring you back to Glencairn, any road. Where have you been, that you'll no' recognize how a man looks at a pretty woman? You're a braw lass to be standin' out on the pier on a raw day. An' me mother's nane sae bad either, gin you fatten her up a bit," he concluded with an appraising glance at Ailsa.

Ailsa giggled, slapped Guthrie on the ear, and allowed there might be some truth in his words.

"He'll be doon the shore." Guthrie returned to his news. "The word's oot as Glencairn wad no' be sair displeased if someone was to tak' a wee crack at Cameron before the grace days are up. It'll no' be safe for him to be boarding openly, you ken. He's to wait at yon tavern till the last moment." He pointed down the shore to a ramshackle construction standing some distance from any other buildings, which the Fleming had pointed out to him.

"But how will he get to the ship?" Frances was almost breathless in her effort to keep up with Guthrie as he trotted down the shore.

"That micht hae been a problem," Guthrie replied over his shoulder. "But you'll mak' grand cover for him!" He gave his hoarse hooting laugh and put on speed. "Naebody wad be looking for the murderer Cameron in a wee bit family party, I reckon."

Alasdair, when at last she stood face to face with him, did not seem to share Guthrie's opinion.

"What are you doing here?"

They were standing just outside the tavern. Alasdair had come charging out before they could enter. Now he was standing before the door as if to shut them out of this one last refuge. His feet were spread and he stood lightly, as if ready to fight, with one hand on his dirk.

Frances felt sick and faint. She had come to be with her love; instead she found an enemy. She tossed back her ragged plaid and confronted him bareheaded.

"I'm coming with you."

"That you are not. What, never be telling me the luxuries of Glencairn's house pall so soon? You canna' be selling a man one day and buying him back the next, Frances. Stick to the bargain you have made."

The words were like knives going through her. Rather would she have been lying in the straw again, enduring all the pangs of childbirth, than to see Alasdair closed to her and turning away with a bitter gibe.

"What do you know of the bargain I made? It was to save your life."

Alasdair laughed. Half the sound was blown away by the wind that whipped across their faces, bearing tiny stinging grains of sand. "Find a better story than that. Without your witness, Glencairn had no case at all. Do you think I did not see you two sitting together, all proud in your satins and velvets? Were you dressed in red for the blood of mine that he should have had, only that Argyll would no' satisfy him? Admit it, Frances. He told me he'd had time enough, in Beauly, to woo and win you. And I . . ." Alasdair laughed again. "Fool that I was, I gave him the lie to his face, and got a drubbing from his men for my pains."

The wind was rising. A man she'd not seen before tugged at Alasdair's sleeve. "Time to be going, *mijnheer*. The captain will not wait to miss such a fair wind."

Frances felt as if her own words were being blown away like the grains of sand that swirled around them. But she could not let Alasdair be leaving her so, and him believing until the end of his days she had betrayed him. "Alasdair, wait! You must be hearing me."

But he was already going. She ran after him, heedless of all else but the need to catch him, and the baby in her arms let out a wail of protest at being jounced about when he had just got off to sleep.

Alasdair turned on his heel at the sound of that cry, and came back to her with something more of gentleness in his face. The little man in the felt hat danced at his heels, jabbered something in a foreign tongue, then threw up his hands and scurried away toward the crowds on the pier.

"Our son, Fan?" He reached out his hands for the baby. Frances realized that she was still carrying Alexander, Ailsa's child. The poor bairns had been so jostled and changed about in their hurried flight that the only way she knew which one she had was by the tuft of red hair sticking out of his hood.

"It's not . . ." She started to say. But Alasdair had already taken the baby, his sinewy hands suddenly gentle. He dandled the child and Alexander opened his eyes, hiccuped in surprise, and left off his roaring. "Our son," Alasdair repeated. "Ah, Fan, I'd forgive all, that you come to me bearing my son in your arms."

Frances felt a wash of anger at the injustice of it. She to be forgiven! She opened her mouth to tell him the truth about the child, but the cutting words would not come. Not when she looked at Alasdair's face, aglow with a pride and untroubled joy such as she'd not seen there but two or three times in her life. So had he looked on the day Lord Gair gave him his first sword; and on the day they lay under the rowan tree making plans to marry. The last day of her girlhood. How could she destroy his newfound joy in his son? Later, when they were all safe in the Low Countries, she could tell him, and perhaps he would not be so very disappointed. Perhaps she would be pregnant again by then. She signed to Ailsa to keep silent.

The noise at the docks had been growing steadily louder as the time came for the big Flemish ship to sail. Porters shouted and cursed as they raced to get their bales aboard before the turn of the tide, whips cracked over patient donkeys plodding with their wagons of grain, and the shore women screeched good-byes to their Flemish sweethearts. Now, suddenly, all the shouting and squealing stopped, as if a wall had come down between them and the ship.

Alasdair was the first to react, with his trained soldier's reflexes. He glanced over his shoulder, cursed, swung the baby over to Frances, and had his dirk out, all seemingly in one quick motion.

It was a wall indeed—a wall of armed men, cutting them off from the ship. As the sun sank toward the harbor wall, they advanced through the crowd, pushing women aside, stopping and pulling the caps off men's heads in search of that betraying Cameron red hair.

"Alasdair, no!" Frances put her hand on his right arm. "There are too many. Is there no place we can be hiding?" As she spoke, she moved between Alasdair and the ship. Guthrie ran to her side, so that if the men looked this way, they would first see only a woman with her two children.

Alasdair sheathed his dirk reluctantly. "You'll maybe have the right of it," he agreed, "but I'd like fine to get fighting Glencairn. . . . Through the tavern, then."

And grasping Frances' free arm, he pulled her with him to the door of the ramshackle building dignified by the name of tavern. Ailsa and Guthrie followed hard on their heels. Frances could spare just one glance back to be sure Ailsa followed with her own baby; then they were scuttling for their lives through the tavern. Shouts went up behind them, in the distance, as they came into the malodorous single room.

"Oh, praise the saints," Frances sighed as she caught sight of the slanted hole between two planks that served as a back exit.

Alasdair took the baby from Frances and pushed her through the crack ahead of him.

The next half-hour was a nightmare of winding alleys, passages through stinking yards piled with refuse, and one or two quick trips right through the houses themselves. In one, Alasdair seemingly was a friend of the owner, who opened the front door to him and pointed out a side exit through a low window. In the other house he bussed a ragged girl who dropped her work and stared in amazement at the trail of fugitives coming through. A word in her ear, and she too was helpful, showing them a way through the coal hole. They came out begrimed but with the pursuit somewhat farther behind than they had been before.

They had a moment to catch their breath; then

it was off again, bending double, running behind fences, twisting to double back on their tracks. Frances could hear Ailsa's breath whistling behind her, and Guthrie cheering his mother on. For herself, she had Alasdair's hand in hers at rough moments, and the memory of the games they'd played over the hills of Beauly.

After an interminable time of these tactics, the sounds of pursuit slackened, grew fainter, then were no longer heard.

They rounded one last corner and Alasdair slowed to a walk. "You can rest in a minute," he promised the women.

They came to the very house they'd passed through at the start of the chase, where the owner seemed to know Alasdair. This time they entered discreetly, through the narrow kailyard at the side of the house. The owner, a stout man in his forties with wisps of black hair that inadequately covered a shining dome, was standing ready to welcome the bedraggled party as they crawled in through a window he had thoughtfully left open.

"Mon, yon was a fine chase you led them," he remarked, mopping his forehead with a crumpled linen rag as he spoke. "Fower o' Glencairn's men I had tearing through the hoose after you, and them checking every wardrobe and bit cupboard in the place. The dame clouted one o' them wi' the griddle, and it hot from the baking. I hanna' laughed sae weel since the day the wee mouse ran up the precentor's breeches in the middle o' the kirk service, and him sae strang against the dancin'. He danced the day, though!" And he laughed at the memory. "But it was naething to the way you shook them off. Wi' a tail o' weemen and bairns following, too! Never did I think to see the day Captain Cameron wad be changin' a bairn's nappy."

Alasdair looked down in some dismay at the child in his arms, by now soaking wet, and thrust the baby at Ailsa.

"And this'll be your good lady?" the black-haired man said, nodding to Ailsa.

"No," Alasdair said. "The other one."

His host slapped his knee and broke into more delighted laughter. "Weel, trust Cameron to have the twa at the one time!" He turned and bowed to Frances. "No offense meant, mistress."

"This gentleman," said Alasdair, "is my good friend Jamie Drummond, late of the king's men in the Low Countries, now a very successful . . . ah, trader here in Leith."

"Forby not all the goods I trade have the king's mark on them," Jamie put in with a smile. "Sae you're safe enough the noo, mistress. I've places the soldiers wouldna' think to look. Else I'd no' be in such a fine way o' business, you see?"

Frances could not refrain from glancing at the shabby room with its one splintered table, the windows with shutters hanging half off the hinges, the plain wooden bowls ranged on the one narrow shelf.

"Ah, you'll be thinking my house is no' sae rich. Weel, you see, a gentleman in my line o' trade can hardly be laying oot his siller in ways that would be seen, and questions asked," Jamie explained with no sign of offense.

Frances spread her ragged skirts and sank to the floor in the stiff-backed court curtsy she had learned from Aunt Grizel so many years ago. "I meant no offense, sir. We are all grateful for your hospitality."

Jamie cackled inordinately at this speech. "Ah, she's a well spoken one, your lady!" He clapped Alasdair on the back. "Does she go on making such pretty speeches, you'll have me believing there was some truth to your tales o' being a great laird in your ain country!"

He slapped Alasdair on the back again, winked, grinned, nudged him with his elbow, and took up a greasy tallow candle-end that stood on the half of a broken plate. "Come along doon, now, I'll show you where you're to stay the nicht."

21

The room where they were to spend the next several days was an underground chamber whose entrance was through a trapdoor in the flagstoned kitchen. To the uninitiated eye the trapdoor looked like any other of the broad, somewhat irregular stones that paved the kitchen floor. It was only when Jamie Drummond pressed a brick in the chimney that one of the stones rose a quarter-inch and allowed him to pry it up with a lever.

"Whiles, I've goods comes through here there's no need the provost should trouble himself about," he explained, "and sometimes the buyers canna' just take them off the day. Then they can lie snug in this wee bit chamber beneath."

"Snug" was hardly the word for it. The narrow room was little more than a sloping passageway leading down to the water. At the high end it was lined with stone; at the low end it trailed off into mud, and Frances could hear the sucking sounds of the tide in the distance. She could not restrain a shiver as she looked down the rickety ladder that Jamie pointed out. "Ye can have a lantern," Jamie promised, "and I'll have the wife throw down a few covers for ye."

Frances was thankful that at least the babies were to be spared this place. Alasdair and Jamie had decided that Ailsa and Guthrie, together with the infants, would arouse no suspicion if they stayed abovestairs.

"What's anither passel o' brats in a place like this?" Jamie had said expansively. "If any asks, they're my wife's cousins frae Glasgow, come to stay when her man left her and the bairns to fend for themselves. The two bairns are near enough an age to pass for twins. They'll maybe both be yourn?"

Alasdair denied this explosively. "The woman's a wet nurse my wife hired, and the sickly girl is hers. They're none of mine."

Guthrie, listening under the table, spluttered in explosive laughter, was discovered, and was hauled out by the ear and delivered to his mother.

So they settled that only Alasdair, for whom the hunt was up now that his grace days were ended, and Frances, whose face was known to half Edinburgh, would have to hide until they could get another boat.

"Though when that will be," their host warned as they waited for his wife to search out furs and coverlets for the hiding place, "I couldna' precisely say. Ye'll ken I'll need be careful these next few days, if I'm to be inquirin' after passage to the Low Countries."

Alasdair clasped Jamie's hand briefly. "I know, and I am not asking it of you. You've risked your neck enough, giving us this place to hide."

Jamie sighed. "Man, the traveling will have addled yer brains, seemingly. How would I rather be riskin' my neck . . . findin' you a boat, or feedin' you the next three years, till it's safe for you to pit that red heid o' yourn out o' doors? I remember how you ate at the camp in Flanders."

He turned to Frances. "Mistress, be warned. He's a monstrous appetite for a thin man. Now me, I've but to think o' taking a glass o' wine, and the weasand on me grows another ell." He slapped his rounded paunch. "Do you want to be takin' on such a fellow? You'll be cooking all your life."

Jamie's wife, a harassed middle-aged woman with her hair strained back into a tight knot, bustled into the kitchen with her arms full of furs. Jamie took them from her and pitched them down without caring where they landed. He handed Alasdair the lantern and clapped him on the shoulder. "I'll let you know when it's safe to come out."

Frances picked her way carefully down the rickety ladder by the light of Alasdair's lantern. While he was coming down himself, she spread out the covers Jamie had given them, noticing that many were so fine the Earl of Glencairn might not have scorned them for his house in Edinburgh.

Then the flagstone trap closed, and they were left entirely alone. Alasdair threw himself down on the furs with a sigh of relief.

"How can you just . . . just sit there!" Frances snapped. Her nerves were thoroughly on edge from being shut into this dark hole. For want of better employment, she paced up and down the small section of stone flooring with restless energy. It would not have been so bad if she had the baby with her. Since that first day when she'd been forced to leave Sarah at Ailsa's lodging for a few hours, the child had scarcely been out of her sight. She was haunted by the fear of losing her.

"There will be nothing else to do," Alasdair said. "And I am not sitting, I am lying. One thing I learned in the wars was not to waste my energy unnecessarily. You can never know when you will be having to march again. And neither do we. Come, sweetheart." He stretched out his hand again. "Rest while you can."

What he said made good sense. Frances stretched out on the furs beside him, wondering what was the matter with her that she could not take his advice. Always before, when she was with Alasdair, nothing else had mattered. His love and the joy of being close to him drove all else from her mind. But did he love her anymore? Or was he simply making the best of it, shouldering her as one more burden that he had to bear?

"Alasdair," she said suddenly.

"Mm?" he answered lazily.

"You didna' want me coming with you."

He raised himself on one elbow and looked down at her. "It's a hard life, Fan, being a soldier's wife."

"Would you rather I wed wi' Glencairn?" she shot back.

"I don't know, Fan," said Alasdair, and her heart turned over at his sober tones. "For a while I thought . . . You testified against me. What was I to think?"

Here it was, the thing she'd feared. And even though she'd half-anticipated it all along, the cold reality of it took her like a stone on her chest, pressing it down, pressing out her breath. No! She would not stammer and look guilty before him. How dared he, how *dared* he judge her this way!

"That was the price of your life. Or did ye not know? I'm surprised the great earl didna' trouble himself to explain it to you. If I would swear you were no true husband to me, and wed wi' him after, then he would let you go free. Else . . ." Her voice broke over the words. "It was a traitor's death he meant for you, Alasdair. Donald showed me the gibbet, told me how it would be." And that memory broke her. She could feel her face crumbling before him. Donald's words still haunted her in dreams. And it might still come to be—they might still hear Glencairn's soldiers come to get them like rats in this trap.

Alasdair stroked her face and felt the tears running down her cheeks. He put one arm about her and hugged her close to him while she buried her face in his shoulder and shook with suppressed sobs. "It's all right, sweeting. It's all right now," he repeated mechanically, over and over, while with his free hand he stroked her hair and the long sweet line of her back.

"You canna' blame me too much, Fan," he said when her shuddering ceased. "Alone in that cell . . . You said you would come back, but I never saw you again until that day in court. And then it seemed you were blithe to swear my life away."

"You should have known better," she cried indignantly, half-rising in his arms.

"How the devil could I know?" he snapped back.

But a moment later he recanted. Frances could not know—must never know—of his belief that the trial would have gone his way had it not been for her damming testimony. She believed that her bargain had been made to free him. And thinking that, how could he doubt her? Or ask how it came that she broke the bargain at the last? Glencairn did not strike him as the kind of man to let a prize like Frances go so easily.

Again that niggling doubt in his mind. He pushed it back and set himself to the business of soothing Frances.

"Yes," he agreed. "I should never have doubted you."

Frances relaxed against him, her black curls falling across his neck and shoulder in a sweet-scented cloud.

There was a small sound above them, and Frances jerked upright again. But Alasdair laughed as the flagstone was lifted to reveal Jamie's rotund face.

"Dinner," Jamie said, handing down an iron hot-pot of mutton stew and dropping the trapdoor again without waste of words.

"And all untimely! Ah, well. We may as well be eating while it is hot," Alasdair said with a shrug.

So Frances ate her dinner sitting cross-legged on a pile of velvets and furs worth a king's ransom, and washed down the stew with a bottle of what Alasdair said was the finest French claret that never passed the excise.

These signs of Jamie Drummond's success reassured her somewhat. Seemingly the little man knew how to arrange his own trade. Surely he could also figure out a way to get them out of the country, if only for his own safety.

After they had cleaned out the stew pot, Alasdair

gave a contented sigh and stretched out full-length on the soft pile of fur coverlets and velvet cloaks. He turned the lantern so that its light was cast against a crevice in the rough wall, leaving the cave shadowy. "Now I feel more the thing. Lie down beside me, Fan. It's long since we've had the leisure."

Frances sat beside him, hands folded in her lap. His arms gently urged her down into his embrace.

"That's better." His hand stroked her forehead and cheek with long, rhythmic caresses that gradually continued down to the curve of her neck and shoulder, then farther, to her swelling breast, until he could feel her relaxing under his hand. Poor girl, what a time of it she'd been having. He could almost imagine how Glencairn and Donald between them would have bullied and berated her into thinking that his life was indeed in the palm of Glencairn's hand. Why not? He'd thought that himself for months, till the trial actually started and he could see what way it was going. And even then, who was to say that Glencairn's gold might not have weighted the scales of justice at the last moment? No, Frances might have done him no ill turn by testifying as she had, though her witness had brought him some bitter, black moments between the trial and now.

She gave a soft, incoherent murmur in the darkness and half-turned toward him. He held her there and stroked the springy curls, ran his hand down her spine, and felt her relax against him with a shudder of delight. That had aye been one of the sweetest things about Frances, he thought, the way she responded so fully and naturally to his touch. He caressed the curve of her hips through the coarse fabric of her worn dress, then raised the skirts to touch her more fully.

Frances let go her worries under Alasdair's soothing caresses. Her mind wandered back to the summer they had shared on the island. In the dark, her memories became as vivid as if she were living those days again. Alasdair's hand stroking her thighs and sending shivers of pleasure through her became part of the dream. She sighed and shifted on the furs as he bent his head to kiss her.

His tongue invaded her mouth and she tasted the sweetness of his kiss while his hand moved smoothly upward from her hips to the soft undercurves of her breast. His fingers fumbled with the bodice of her dress and pushed the fabric away so that he could touch the soft skin beneath. The cool air struck her skin and she drew him closer, for warmth, for love.

With a groan he buried his face between her breasts and clasped her to him. She gasped and arched her body toward him as he trailed kisses up the curve of her breast until he came to the summit. His tongue teased her nipple into a hard quivering peak. His lips closed over his prize and with one hand he reached up to touch her face. The feather-light caresses of his fingertips, combined with the insistent pressure at her nipple, sent her into an agony of anticipation in which nothing mattered but reaching the fulfillment toward which they both strained. She felt his hand tugging at her dress and she raised her hips to help him. The soft furs beneath her caressed her as Alasdair freed himself from his clothing. And then she was in his arms again where she belonged and there was nothing between them—not Glencairn, not prison walls, not suspicions or misunderstandings.

"So good to hold you again," he murmured. Frances gasped again as he buried his face in her neck, kissing her throat and shoulders. When she thought she could stand the aching anticipation no longer, she felt him gently entering her body.

He paused and she bit back a cry of protest. "I won't hurt you, it's not too soon?"

"No." Frances clasped her legs about him to keep him there. She was beyond caring if he hurt her or not.

Then he was moving inside her, igniting the flames of her passion until she cried out and felt the warm sweetness rushing through her veins. He groaned aloud and clasped her to him so tightly that she thought her ribs would crack. Then he collapsed by her side, his face buried in her shoulder and one arm flung out over her as if to guard his prize.

He could hear her heartbeat gradually slowing,

her ragged breathing calming. Or was it his own? For a few moments of ecstasy they had been not two, but one.

But now they were drawing apart into their separate selves again. His arm tightened over her. At least he could hold her close again. That was wealth, after the long, lonely winter.

Still, it was a strange thing, the way that whenever Frances came to him, the soldiers were not far behind. First that time in the cave, and now on Leith shore. In the cave she had seemed so innocently unaware of any danger, he would have sworn she'd been tricked by Glencairn. But a second time? Strange it was indeed, that she'd not come to him until the last minute, when meeting her might delay him beyond the end of the third day and cause him to miss the ship.

"Frances?"

She raised her head a fraction of an inch from his shoulder.

He spoke as casually as he could. "How did you get free from Glencairn's house? Never tell me he let you go free to come and meet me?"

She sat up and the one beam of the lantern fell across her disheveled curls and her pretty breasts bare under the loosened bodice.

"Are you thinking he sent me out as bait to catch you, Alasdair Cameron? And if so, it's the fool you are, to think he'd need go to such a risk. Half the town knew you were lying low here in

Leith until the end of the three days. I had it from Guthrie, the wet nurse's boy. All he'd to do was set his soldiers ready to come at the pier when that Flemish ship sailed. He had no need to be employing me in the matter at all."

Alasdair sighed. What she said was true enough, and he was a fool to be suspecting her. But . . . she hadna' answered his question.

"I'm thinking it will have been difficult to get yourself out of Glencairn's hands, let alone trooping off with a wet nurse, two babies, and a boy. How did you manage the thing?"

Frances smoothed her disordered curls and fastened the bodice about her with quick, irritated movements. "If you must know," she snapped, "I set fire to the kitchens. And I hope that's enough of your questioning and wondering, Alasdair Cameron."

Alasdair gave a crack of delighted laughter and gathered her into his arms, muffling her cries of protest with kisses and rolling her over on the furs until she returned his embrace. "Did ye now? I'd have liked fine to be seeing that. And the great earl himself louping to fetch the water buckets?" He went off into spasms of laughter at the thought.

They had time enough, the next few days in their hiding place, to go over that and many other questions.

Once Frances reproached him for not believing in her. "Were we not promising one another not to believe other folks' words? And yet you were deciding that I would betray you."

"Ah, Frances." Alasdair felt for her in the dim light. "But these were your own words out of your own mouth. It's not rational to be blaming me for feeling a moment of doubt."

"A moment!" She was aghast, thinking how she' given him her story in the blowing wind, with his face hard and blank as any stone. "Very well. I'm not rational. And I do blame you."

But he kissed her back into charity with him.

Another time she questioned him as to how he knew Leith so well as to have a bolt hole ready for them to hide in.

"Planning," Alasdair told her with a touch of smugness in his voice. "A good soldier always plans ahead. Ye'll mind I was three weeks in Edinburgh before I came north to get you at Beauly last summer? I didna' spend all that time roistering in the stews. Your suspicions were clean unworthy." He rumpled her hair with teasing familiarity.

"Indeed." Frances had to laugh at his superior tone. The urge to take him down a peg was irresistible. She injected a note of awe into her voice. "So you had it all planned out aforehand, this place ready and all?"

Alasdair nodded.

"That's awfu' impressive," Frances said. She imitated the lilting tones of a naive Highland crofter. "I'm thinking himself will be the clever man indeed, to be seeing so well all that was coming. To plan to get himself locked up in the castle and near beaten to death, arraigned for treason and exiled from the country, all so he could get hiding in Jamie Drummond's cellar."

Alasdair laughed. "Very well . . . I may not have planned precisely all that's come to us. But you'll not deny it came in useful, this place?"

"Ach, by-ordinar' useful," Frances agreed. "Haven't I always wanted to make love at the bottom of a well?"

Alasdair rolled over and seized her wrists. "Indeed? A thought more of the sarcastic tongue, my fine lady, and it's in the tide mud I'll have you! Or do you beg my pardon, you'll get staying on the furs."

But even with such diversions, they had many a weary hour to pass in the darkness of the cellar, wondering how Jamie fared in the search for a boat to take them off. Once only did Jamie deem it safe for them to come above, late at night. Frances spent the time hanging over the wall bed where Ailsa was sleeping with a bairn on either side of her, while Alasdair and Jamie talked over their plans in low voices. She saw with a quiver of joy mixed with fear that little Sarah's hair was indeed coming in black and curly, like her own. And when she moved in her sleep, thrusting out one little fist and nuzzling against Ailsa's side, didn't the expression of innocent greed on her tiny face remind her of Donald?

"Here now, that's the wrong one." Alasdair had come up softly behind her. "Ours is the red-headed brat on the other side, remember?" He raised the candle over the bed to get a better view of Alexander.

Now, if ever, was the time to tell him. "Alasdair . . ." Frances started to say.

"Hmm?" He had put a finger to Alexander's cheek, and the baby, waving his hands aimlessly, had clutched at it. "Look. He's a strong grip, our son. He'll hold Beauly. Yes, he will. I'll come back and win it for him. It's the thought of that gives me the courage to go on."

After that, how could she tell him that he had no son? "Hush now," she said. "You'll wake them."

The ship's captain came the day after that. He was Lewie Gib, onetime master of the packet on which Alasdair had been transported to Leith on Donald's orders.

He was a tall, broad-shouldered man with a fine set of whiskers on him and hands as big as the tuns of Bordeaux he brought Jamie. He seemed to fill the small kitchen. Frances, coming up through the flagstone trap, felt as if she were rising through the floor at the feet of one of the giants of the old tales.

"Do ye no' mind me, man?" he bellowed before Alasdair was fairly out of the cramped space.

"I do that," Alasdair replied. "You were taking me out of Scotland once before, I mind, and I was maybe not just exactly grateful to you for it."

They stood one each side of the scrubbed table, taking the measure of one another. Alasdair was balanced lightly on the balls of his feet and there was a half-smile on his face, but no answering light in his eyes. The ship's captain was planted solidly on his spread feet and his hands rested on the edge of the table, lifting it lightly up and down as if it were a featherweight.

Suddenly he gave a roaring laugh and dropped the lifted table square on the flagstones. "Ye'll do, man," he cried over the echoing bang. "Aye, I'll tak' ye off, for the goodwill I bear our friend Jamie here."

"And the good price I made ye on the Bordeaux," Jamie added with a sour look.

"Wheesht, never mention it, man. 'Tis all between friends." He extended his hand to Alasdair. "You'll maybe no' credit it, but whiles I've wondered how ye were getting on. A rare bit o' spirit ye showed as a lad. I'm no' forgetting how ye cursed me an' the first mate when ye cam' round. And your friends too."

"You've word of them?" Alasdair asked. He turned to Frances. "Duncan and Sandy were on the boat we were to have taken."

"That they were not," the captain corrected him. "They cam' aff as soon as it was seen ye'd no' be joining them. It was yon big Hielandman—Duncan, did you say?—wha recognized my packet."

"My lady," Alasdair said, nodding at Frances. "There will also be her maidservant and three children, two infants and a boy of . . . oh, twelve or so."

Frances noted Ailsa's promotion with amusement. Seemingly Alasdair was embarrassed to mention wet-nursing in this company of men.

"Three childer!" The captain gave a low whistle of astonishment. "Ye'll have been a busy man. And the boy twelve—weel, I've aye heard you Hielanders were a lusty crew, but this beats all. Ye'll no' be above five-and-twenty yoursel', I'm thinking. It'll no' be easy, getting all yon crew aboard. Ye'd not consider leaving a bit o' the family here the while? Aweel, 'tis your own business. I've contracted tae bring yer party aff safe, and what Lewie Gib contracts to, that he does, even if there are a wheen too many bairns in it." And he brought his great fist crashing down on the table to signify his determination to hold by the contract.

Alasdair, Jamie, and the captain settled around the table then to discuss how the escape might best be arranged. Frances left them to it and went to play with the babies, though her ears pricked up at the low-voiced words coming from the table now and then. "Leith sands . . . the signal . . . moonrise or after . . ."

Infuriating, to be relegated to a woman's place

while those great gowks made the plans that all their lives depended on. But she could see Alasdair was a tried man, with the captain's incessant gibes about family life and bairns' nappies. Frances smothered a smile. No, this was not the time to insist on being admitted to their counsels.

She regretted that decision that evening when they crept out into the half-light of dusk with their bundles, and she still knew nothing of the plan but the few words Alasdair had given her.

"It's simple enough," he'd said. "We've but to get down to the shore unobserved, to a place I know of. He's to send a boat for us there."

In practice it turned out less than simple. There were men watching all around the borders of the town, taking no particular care to conceal themselves. They simply stood here and there, leaning on their long pikes and stopping all who went on the roads.

Alasdair swore when he saw the long shadow of the pikeman on the bridge.

"Glencairn's gold," he said bitterly.

Then Frances was grateful he'd told her so little of the plan, and that they'd been together in the cellar ever since the captain came. At least, this time, he could not be suspecting her of having given him away.

"Do you bide here," Alasdair instructed her in a whisper. "Cross the bridge when he leaves."

"What . . .?" But before she could question him,

he was gone, slipping through the twilight as silently as the shadows of the long reeds.

A moment later there was a dog that barked from under the bridge, and a stone that came from the same direction hit the pikeman on his steel-plated jack. He cursed and bent over the side of the bridge. Two more stones decided the matter. He scrambled down the embankment, shouting, "Halt ye!"

The sound of footsteps across the bridge alerted him just too late. He came back to see no more than Ailsa's petticoat tail as she and Frances and Guthrie, laden with the two babies and their basket, vanished in the dusk.

Alasdair rejoined them half a mile down on the far side of the bridge. He was breathing hard, and there was a smear of dried blood along his cheek, but Frances thought he was enjoying himself more than usual.

"Not far now," he promised Ailsa, who was leaning on Guthrie. He took the basket and one of the babies from her.

In truth it was only a few steps to the point of the shore where Alasdair had agreed to make rendezvous.

"We wait till moonrise?" Frances asked.

Alasdair shook his head. "Nay. The boat should be here before moonrise. Else he'll lose the tide." He looked out to sea, then back toward the land, whistling a jigging tune under his breath. "I'd as soon lose no more time here. Glencairn—or someone—has spilt a load of siller to keep us in the country."

"Who else but Glencairn?"

Alasdair shrugged and began playing with his dirk. "That's what I'd like fine to ken. But the pikemen arena' the only danger. 'Twas another fellow gave me this." He touched the long scratch on his cheek where the blood had dried. "One of our own, Frances, for he cried out in Gaelic to me from the ditch. A friend, think I, and run toward him, when the cateran meets me with steel out."

A Highlander! Frances drew a long, troubled breath. "And he did not say who was his master?"

"I could not exactly be questioning the man," Alasdair replied. "He's wearing his long knife between two ribs now. But the question I'd like answered now is: was he alone?" He stood up. "Is that the boat?"

Soon the splash of oars was plain to all of them. Frances shifted herself on the rocks, kilted up her skirt, and tucked the baby Sarah into her bodice. She was so little and frail to be out in this cold night! "Never mind, sweeting," she crooned to the child. "Soon we'll be all warm and safe."

Alasdair stood in the shallows and reached his hand to Frances to help her balance in the perilous leap from rock to boat. Strong, familiar hands caught her around the waist and lifted her aboard. "Mind the babe," she cautioned, and then, "Duncan?"

"The same. It's yourself that's looking well, Lady Frances."

At that moment the muffled sound in the distance became clear. There were horsemen bearing down on them around the curve of the shore.

"Awa'," cried the man in the front of the boat, "this is no part of my contract."

There was a frantic struggle to ship oars and row out into the safety of the deep water, while Alasdair held the gunwale of the boat and cursed them. "Stay, you fools! They canna' ride through the rocks."

And it was true. All but one of the riders had paused where the rocks thrust through the sand and broke up the clean shore land. That one, more daring than the rest, urged his horse out fetlock-deep into the water and was coming at them around the outcropping of rocks.

"I'll no' stay," repeated the captain.

Duncan grasped Alasdair's hand on the gunwale and hauled him aboard by main force. He knelt on the wet planks and reached his arms to Ailsa. "Come awa' now!"

Ailsa, teetering perilously on the wet rocks, held the baby Alexander out for Duncan to take.

The horseman came riding down between them. He knocked Ailsa backward with a backhanded blow, caught the baby under his arm, and rode on in an unbroken semicircle. Before he reached the shore again, the oarsmen had their oars in the water and were pulling away, leaving a groaning Ailsa on the rocks and her son Guthrie trying to raise her.

"Damn you," Alasdair cursed the captain. "Put back—put back, I say!"

They were already some yards out, with salt water lapping between them and the shore point. Alasdair scrambled for the side of the boat. "That's my son back there!"

The wooden bailing bucket descended on his head with a hollow thud that sent Alasdair, limp as a bundle of rags, into the bottom of the boat again.

"I doubt ye'll just have to get another one," observed Lewie Gib, looking down at his handiwork with satisfaction. " 'Tis nae part o' my contract to lose my boat for a wean."

22

By the time Alasdair came to himself, Lewie Gib's boat was well on the way to Flanders, heeled over before a fair wind and scudding along with nothing to be seen but the white-capped waves behind them.

"This business of leaving Scotland is growing fair monotonous." Alasdair gave a rueful grin and raised one hand to feel the lump on his head. "Just once I'd like to be taking a proper farewell of my native land."

Frances, who had been hovering over him since he was laid in the roundhouse to recover, gave a sigh of relief. She had expected him to awaken in the same thrashing, violent mood he'd been in when Gib hit him. Seemingly, he had forgotten all that had passed on the shore.

Her relief was too soon. Scarcely had Alasdair finished his sentence when a strange look passed over his face.

"My son!" He was up and peering through the roundhouse windows before she could stop him.

The land was a dark line behind them, barely visible in the moonlight that shone on the white-capped waves. The ship wallowed through the trough of a wave and Alasdair's hands tightened about the bars of the window till the knuckles were white. But he spoke calmly.

"Tell Lewie Gib to be turning back."

Frances shook her head. "Alasdair, he will not be returning. We barely got off with our lives. Do you not remember?"

Alasdair's hand dropped to his dirk in a gesture of menace. "He'll do as I say. Did you think I would be leaving my son there?"

In two steps he would be at the roundhouse door, and then out on deck to menace the captain. Frances reached the door just ahead of him and placed her back to it. Now it had to be said. There was no more time for temporizing. "Alasdair, listen to me first. I'll not be seeing you throw your life away on a bairn that's no more yours than it is Lewie Gib's."

The urgency and certainty in her voice communicated themselves to Alasdair. He stopped a pace from the door and his hands dropped to his sides. "Frances . . . this is true?"

Her heart broke for the grieving note in his voice. But she dared not stop now. "It is true. Alasdair, you never asked me why Glencairn was willing to bargain with me at all. It was because he thought I had a son by you. That way, even though he killed you, there was still an heir to Beauly. He needed me to repudiate the marriage, say the boy was illegitimate."

Alasdair's face was as cold and hard as Glencairn's. Frances felt as if she were being crushed between these two gray-granite men. She stretched out her hands and made one last plea. "I was trading Beauly for your life, Alasdair."

"Never mind Beauly." Alasdair was staring into her face as though he could read more written there than the bare facts she had told him. "Why did you not speak of this before? Was it so amusing to watch me cosseting a bairn that was none of mine?"

Frances felt her throat tightening with the beginnings of a sob. She would not give way now, not till Alasdair understood. "You . . . you were so proud to have a son. I could not bring myself to tell you. Not when we were in such fear and danger, and might all be dead before we got away. I was going to tell you later, when we were all safe."

"Were you now?" Alasdair said. "I wonder."

With a sinking heart she saw that he was no longer looking at her, but out the window where there was nothing to be seen but the moonlight glancing on the roiling sea. Three times his gaze swept the roundhouse, and each time he looked on her, he winced and looked away as though he could not bear the sight of her.

"But it is yours," he said at last. "You were surely pregnant when you came to me in the castle—so much I know for sure. Your child, but you left him to be stolen by strangers. You must not feel overmuch fondness for the child, though you were willing enough to pass him off to me as my son." His voice softened, but he still would not look directly at her. "Whose bairn is it, Fan? Glencairn's? Did the bastard force you—is that why he was so sure of wedding you? You can tell me. I won't hold it against you."

Burning anger crackled in Frances like the sparks of a fire that sweeps through the heather, leaving nothing behind but a black desolation on the hills. "I have never known a man with your talent for adding two and two to make five, Alasdair Cameron." Had that crack on the head so addled his wits that he could not be counting the months since they parted? Very well! If he was so ready to accuse her of deceiving him with Glencairn, he didn't deserve to hear the true story at all. She would just leave him to come to his wits by himself. When he grew calm enough to think that there was another baby in it, she would tell him that he had a daughter if not a son. For now, she was too burning angry to stoop to explanations.

She swept out of the roundhouse to look for Sarah, whom she had left in the care of Duncan Dhu while she worried about that blockhead she was, unfortunately, married to. More fool she! she snorted. It would take more than a crack on his wooden head to ail that one. Where, pray tell, did he think Sarah came from—under a kale leaf?

"He doesna' deserve a lovely daughter like you, my precious," she crooned to Sarah later, rocking her in her arms. The baby opened her bright black eyes with a knowing look that startled Frances. "Black eyes, black hair," Frances crooned. "You're all my own, aren't you, my sweet? We won't be troubling ourselves about any men in it at all."

In the crowded quarters of the ship, Frances and Alasdair had no more privacy for further explanations, in any case. She had a hard enough time finding a secluded corner to nurse the baby. But that was a delight she'd not expected. At first she was just relieved to find that the trials she'd been through since giving birth had not been enough to stop the course of nature. The first time she put Sarah to the breast, neither of them got much satisfaction out of it. But by the third attempt her milk was flowing as copiously as though she'd nursed since childbirth. She spent the days on shipboard as much as possible wrapped in her own private world with the baby.

Once Alasdair came in search of her, but he recoiled when he saw her nursing Sarah.

"You are as tender of that whore's get as you were of your own child," he remarked, dropping the corner of sailcloth which Duncan Dhu had rigged up to screen Frances from the curious eyes of the crew.

Frances' anger flared. "Get out! I've no need of you and your tongue flapping in the wind. I've a good mind to leave as soon as we've made port. I'll not wander around Europe at the shirttail of a man who does naught but jeer at me."

Alasdair ducked out of the way of her wrath, and Frances tried to still the anger within her so that it should not disturb Sarah as she nursed. When, oh when would Alasdair come to his senses? Calling Sarah a whore's get! She compressed her lips and covered the baby's head with a corner of her plaid. Not for worlds would she have told Alasdair the true story now. It would be just asking him to call her a liar.

She could not know that Alasdair had regretted his bitter words before they were half out of his mouth. He did not need Duncan Dhu's glowering look to tell him he'd spoken ill. But Duncan took the freedom of an old friend, and the privacy of the Gaelic, to give Alasdair a rare tongue-lashing all the same.

"The lass will be grieving sore for the loss of her own bairn," he told Alasdair. "And you will be making it harder for her. Will you be wanting her to wail and weep aloud before strangers? It is proud you should be to have a lady that will follow you through all, and glad you should be she has a bairn to comfort her in her grief. But instead you will be doing all you can to drive her away from you, it seems. Ach, it is sorry I am that ever we were at the trouble to be bringing you safe away from Scotland. Yon lady will be worth ten of you, whatever, and her beggaring herself to follow you barefoot across Europe."

And Duncan Dhu stalked off to sit outside Frances' screened corner and glare at any possible interlopers. His loyalty had shifted, and he did not care who knew it.

Sandy Ruadh heard the end of this speech and sought to raise the black cloud from Alasdair's brow.

"Do not you be thinking of what Duncan was saying. Are you not knowing by now that lasses will have their fancies? You'll can talk her round fine when we come to Flanders."

Alasdair flung off Sandy's hand on his arm with an oath. "You know nothing of it. I deserve everything that Duncan was saying to me—aye, and more, too."

He stalked off to stand at the stern of the ship and brood over all he was leaving behind—the glen of Beauly that might have been his, the son that he believed was his for a short while. And what was there ahead? What could he offer Frances, but the life of a mercenary captain's lady, to follow the camp and march at the tail of the troops? Well served he'd be if she left him in Flushing.

"I'll make a better life than that for you," he promised Frances when they were landing. "You shall not follow the army. I will find lodgings for you here in Flushing to begin. And soon I'll make my name and fortune, and you shall live like a fine lady again."

He had not mentioned Sarah, Frances noticed. Likely he thought she'd be ready enough to put the "whore's get" out to nurse, now that they were landed. "You need not be troubling yourself for me, Alasdair," she said coldly, wrapping the plaid around herself and Sarah to shelter both of them. "I shall be doing very well by myself."

A porter pushed between them, staggering with the weight of the box on his back. Frances stepped out of his way and two men on horseback pulled back, shouting angrily at her in a strange tongue as their horses fretted and stamped. She clutched the baby closer to her and looked around. So many people, as many as in Edinburgh, and the strange flat land and the strange talk she could not understand. For a moment her heart failed her.

"The devil you will," Alasdair shouted at her, and Frances felt a shaming relief that she would not be left alone in this strange place. "I'll provide for my wife as fits her station."

"Very well," Frances said, wrapping the plaid more tightly around her against the wind. "If I must go with you, I must."

She had thought that Alasdair meant to remain with her and Sarah. But as soon as they were installed in lodgings in the town, he informed her that he would be reporting to his old regiment at once and that he might not be able to return for some time. He would have to stay in camp most of the time, he told her.

"Oh." Frances felt horribly naked and alone. "You'll . . . not be back the night?"

Alasdair took a tentative step toward her. "Would I be welcome?"

Sarah chose that moment to wake with an ear-splitting squall of outrage at the change in her surroundings. Alasdair frowned and stepped back.

"Go to the camp," Frances skirled after him. "Stay there, for all I care! We will be doing very well by ourselves."

Alasdair took his leave and rode out to the army camp to find out whether he could still have a place in the regiment.

This matter was settled a few seconds after he had his name sent in to the colonel.

"Cameron!" Colonel Murray roared, erupting from his tent. "Dod, man, but I'm fain to see ye! What brings you back? Could ye no' bide the endless rain of those forsaken glens, once you claimed your inheritance?" Then, after a glance at Alasdair's face, he asked, "Or maybe the inheritance was not so certain after all, eh? There was some matter of a cousin, no? Well, never mind. A commission? Man, your old commission's still waiting for ye. D'you think it's easy to find a man to take on your wild company of Highlanders? I've Logie o' Buchan overseeing them, and the troubles he brings to me have me fair deaved."

"Logie'll maybe no' be wanting to return to a lieutenant under me," Alasdair suggested.

Murray laughed. "Show me the man would rather do a captain's duties for a lieutenant's pay! Logie's Lowland tongue can't wrap itself around the Gaelic at all, forby he can handle the arquebusiers with signs and all. But the pikemen are clean beyond him. I canna' understand that. The arquebus is no gentleman's weapon. He's halfway to becoming a grimy engineer like those fellows in the artillery. No, Logie'll be fidgin' fain to see ye."

And with as little ceremony as that, Alasdair was able to return and report that he held his captain's commission again.

"And you'll stay with us?" Frances asked. She heard the anxious tone in her voice, and despised herself for it. But Sarah was ailing, so fretful and feverish that Frances was continually walking the floor with her. And she couldna' understand these folk at all. English was bad enough, but this! They were no' civilized, these folk with their fast flat speech that sounded like rocks clattering on each other.

Alasdair's eyes slid away from Frances when she picked up Sarah again. "I'll be wanted in the camp. Seemingly Logie's had a wee bit trouble with the men since I've been gone."

Already he was half gone, Frances saw. In his mind he was already back in the muddy masculine atmosphere of the camp. Well, let him go, then, and be damned to him! She was Lady Frances of Beauly, not a beggar.

But she was ready to cry with relief, for all that, when Duncan Dhu proclaimed his intention of staying with her. "I'm no' so eager to run my head into the army's yoke again," he told Alasdair, "but I'll see ye on your road."

Outside he was more explicit. "You'll leave your lady here alone," he demanded incredulously, "and her with the wean to care for, and not having a word o' the Flemish?"

Alasdair's face hardened at the mention of the child. "Frances is very competent," he replied. "She'll be managing fine. But if it's your fancy to stay and watch her nursing a whore's bairn, I'll not be stopping you."

Only the ingrained habit of years kept Duncan from hitting Alasdair on the spot. He watched his departure with a black look. "Man, if I were a gentleman," he muttered, "it's myself would be courting your lady, for you are not deserving her at all."

For all Duncan's disapproval, he was unable to change the course that Alasdair took. He spent most of his time at the camp, drilling his Highland pikemen and trying to get the sadly depleted company into shape.

"Twenty pikemen, and but sixty-five arquebusiers! Logie, what were you thinking of, to let the company fall so below strength?"

Logie shrugged. "You werena' at Turnhout in January. We lost some good men there while you were taking your ease in Scotland."

"Taking my . . ." Alasdair bit off the words and shrugged. "Someday I'll tell you about my visit home. It wasna' precisely easeful."

Logie's soft brown eyes gleamed. "No? Weel, maybe I'd be tired too, did I spend my nights wi' yon black-haired darling you brought back. They werena' growing them like that when I left Scotland."

Alasdair knocked Logie down for referring to his wife, which relieved both their tense feelings, and they went off to see what the colonel would say to giving them a draft of the next recruits from Scotland.

In the following days Logie understood that his reference to the black-haired beauty had maybe been a wee bit ill-timed. Alasdair was spending most of his nights at the camp. He went into the town only on business, to check stores and the like, and he always took Logie with him. His occasional visits to Lady Frances were as short as common courtesy allowed—mayhap shorter. It seemed he allowed himself only time to greet the lady and ask if she needed anything.

Logie understood his captain's reasoning well enough, but it seemed a pity. Lady Frances was not only bonny, but a sweet friendly lady such as could even smile on a poor younger son the likes o' himself. Well, if Alasdair kept his distance, there was no need for Logie to do the same. He fell in the habit of treating Lady Frances' comfortable lodging as an extension of his own, where he could drop in on the excuse of carrying Alasdair's messages and stay for a good dinner and a comfortable gossip.

Frances was glad of his company. Though she was developing a routine that left her feeling less lost in this strange country, Alasdair's absence hurt her sore. She could not even ask him about it, for he never visited her except in Logie's company.

As for telling him about Sarah—the thing was just not possible. One could hardly say to a man, in the presence of his Scots lieutenant: "By the way, the baby you have sent to the kitchens every time you visit is your own daughter, whom I traded with Ailsa so that I could claim you'd gotten a boy and an heir on me."

No. He would very likely give her the lie to her

face. There was nothing for it but to keep her back stiff and the smile pasted on her face, and hope that the day would come when Alasdair could bear to see her alone.

But in the meantime, Logie was a welcome companion in her loneliness. Her days in Glencairn's house at Edinburgh had given her an appetite for conversation of a sort that Duncan could not supply—for talk of the policies of state and the New Learning that came from Italy, for news and gossip and all the wide world at her doorstep. This Logie supplied, and in full measure. Frances saw with some concealed amusement that the young man was a worse gossip than any Leith fishwife.

"Young man—why, I'm a year older than yourself," Logie exclaimed indignantly when she told him this to his face one day when he had brought an excellent story about Prince Maurice and Colonel Murray to pay for his supper. He rose to his feet and stroked the soft brown beard that never would grow in as fully as he would like.

"I've led a troop of my own, too," he went on, "and taken prisoners. Let's have less of this 'young-man' nonsense. D'you think I'm no' old enough to notice a pretty woman before me?" And he clasped Frances around the waist and forced an awkward, nose-bumping kiss upon her before she could get away.

Frances' moment of panic gave way to amusement. Why, it was only a boy, after all. But the touch of a man's hand upon her aroused uninvited memories. She thought of Alasdair's strong fingers, the warmth of him beside her, and blushed even while she was pushing Logie away. She was relieved to see that he was almost as embarrassed as herself.

"Really, Logie," Frances scolded when she disentangled herself, "are you bringing the rude soldiers' manners into my house, then? Will I have to ask you to be leaving? Sore I would miss your company and the good talk we have been having," she added, "but you will force it upon me, if you behave so."

Logie gave her a sullen look, but he backed away and mumbled some fashion of apology. "Though I dinna' know why you should be sae carefu' of Cameron's honor," he ended with a flash of spirit, "when the man never comes near you at all."

Frances felt as though she had been publicly slapped in the face. Was the whole camp speculating on the details of her marriage? "I will be thanking you to keep your tongue to yourself," she told Logie. "It is not for strangers to be speaking of my husband and myself."

Logie moved nearer and patted her hand. "Strangers? I thought I was your friend."

At this small display of gentleness Frances felt herself undone entirely. "Oh, do not be kind to me, for I cannot bear it," she cried. "Only . . ."

She dropped onto the bench in the chimney corner and sat staring at the fire. "Why does he avoid me?" she murmured. "Logie, you call yourself our friend—you must have some notion of the reason why. I know he does not like my keeping Sarah, but it's not in Alasdair to hold a grudge for so long. There must be something keeping him away."

Logie looked away. "The captain isna' confiding in me."

Frances watched the small blue flames licking around the base of the glowing sea-coal fire. The warm light of the fire danced off the copper cooking pots that the Flemish girl scoured daily with sand, off the tiny diamond-shaped windowpanes that showed the bleak world outside, off the string of shining beads that Logie had hung up one day on Sarah's cradle. The tiny room was warm, cozy, domestic—and cramped beyond bearing. Did she not grieve sore herself for the freedom of the glen? How much worse it must be for Alasdair, who'd been used to a soldier's life, out and about in all weathers. Perhaps it was simply that he could not abide this tiny lodging with its inescapable smells of cooking food and drying baby clothes.

"I will be going into the camp to see him myself," she decided. "Logie, you'll escort me?"

At this simple request the young man started and backed off a few paces. "I . . . I dinna' think that would be suitable, Lady Frances," he babbled, plucking at his beard with nervous fingers. "The camp . . . rough men . . . bad language—not at all the sort of place you would be used to."

Frances dismissed these objections with a wave of her hand. "I have been in worse places."

Logie searched frantically for some other excuse that would keep Frances from the camp. He knew well enough why Alasdair did not wish her visiting there, but it was hardly a matter for a lady. Indeed, he had been most strictly charged to keep it from her ears.

Frances listened to his evasions for a while with growing disbelief. Finally she shrugged into her old frieze cloak and called the Flemish girl to watch over Sarah. "Duncan will be taking me, if you will not," she said. "There is something else you are not telling me, and I will find out what it is."

Logie's expression of intense embarrassment brought one other thought to her mind. "Logie!" she exclaimed. "Is it . . . has he . . . will he have a woman there with him?"

Relieved at this solution to his problem, Logie gulped and nodded. "It's nothing serious," he hastened to assure her. "Men will have these times—means nothing . . . best to ignore it, Lady Frances."

"Ignore it!" Frances took off her cloak and tossed it across the bench. "Indeed not. What, after all Alasdair and I have dared to be together, will I be sitting here and patiently waiting for him to be tired of his Flemish whore? I'll have her from his tent before I'm an hour older, or it's the first packet back to Leith for me. I didna' come all this way to hang on the tail of a man who doesna' want me. But first," she added with a meditative smile, "I will be killing her, and him too. Or they'll wish I had, before I'm through with them."

When the maid appeared, Frances snapped out rapid orders to lay out and brush her black velvet dress, stitch the lace she'd bought yesterday to the best linen petticoat, and heat water over the fire for a bath with sweet herbs in it. Logie she banished to the antechamber to wait for her.

A little over an hour later, she sallied forth, dressed in her own way for battle. Nothing could repair the worn patches on her black velvet dress or take away the rusty hue of the material, but the braw show of lace below and fresh-starched ruff above did much to draw the eye from it. Her curls were braided and pinned back under a starched lace bonnet such as the local women wore, and she was laced so tight into her stays that she could feel them pressing into her back. But it was worth it, to have the comforting consciousness of a waist as narrow as when she'd been a girl.

"Forby the stays will maybe give you some backbone," she whispered to herself, acknowledging ruefully that she felt sorely lacking in that commodity for all the brave show she put on for Logie's benefit. At the mere thought of confronting Alasdair with his Flemish whore, her knees felt wobbly and her brain seemed turned to jelly. What if he truly did not want her anymore, and was only too kind to say so after she'd given up everything to follow him?

I could not bear it, she thought, and then: Havers, I can bear what I must. Folk do. Besides, there's Sarah.

The thought of her daughter gave her the internal stiffening that the stays had failed to supply. Alasdair might not fancy her any longer, their marriage might not hold in the law, but she still considered herself his wedded wife and Sarah was still his child. Come what may, he should hear that story at last, and recognize his child. She would not be creeping back to Scotland to rear Sarah as a bastard on Glencairn's charity.

"Duncan," she commanded, "you'll watch over the lodgings till I return. You're the only one I can trust to see that Sarah is safe, besides myself."

The ride out to camp was short and silent. The day was clear and cold, and the mud churned up by the horses' hooves earlier had frozen solid, turning the roadway into a devastated landscape of miniature mountains and crevasses. Logie had to watch his horse carefully as they picked their way along the treacherous, slippery ground. Frances, sitting behind him, had enough to think on without trying to make conversation.

So wrapped up was she in her thoughts, the

babble of the camp passed unnoticed. Only when Logie set her down at Alasdair's tent did she return to the present. She almost turned to him and asked to be taken back, now that it came to the point. But the lady of Beauly did not show fear. Frances lifted the tent flap and marched in with a quaking heart.

It took her a moment to adjust to the dim light after the sun outside sparkling on all the frozen puddles. What she did make out was not like the scene of drunken orgies that she had been imagining. There was barely room in the tent for a writing table covered with papers and a single narrow cot where Alasdair was stretched out, asleep. The ground between table and cot was strewn with pieces of armor and tools whose use Frances could only guess at.

The sound of her steps roused Alasdair. In a single motion he was up from the cot. "Logie? I told you to call me . . . Oh, hell." This last as he saw and recognized Frances. "What are you doing here? I told Logie to keep you away."

It was confirmation of her worst suspicions. Frances kicked a steel helm out of her way and advanced on Alasdair. "Where is she?"

"Who?" Alasdair scrubbed one hand over his face and through his hair. "Frances, this is no place for you. Let me take you back to the lodgings."

"Oh, no. It is tired I am of being 'protected' while you whore in the camp." Frances stumbled over a heap of polishing rags and kicked them away. "Logie told me about you and your women. No wonder you never find the time to come in and see us."

She could not keep up the anger. Not when the thought of Alasdair with some other woman was hurting her so. She held out her hands to him. "Och, Alasdair, what is coming to us? Have we dared so much to be together, that you should be forgetting me for some camp follower? Are you truly not wanting me anymore?"

Alasdair's look of confusion gave way to a dawning amusement. "Frances, my sweet. Of course I am wanting you."

"Then why do you never come into town?"

Alasdair looked away into the corner of the tent. Frances knew that look. It was the way his eyes would shift when they were children and he was looking for some excuse not to take her along on some exciting expedition. "The pressure of work . . ." he began.

Lies again! Lies and pretense! And no words of hers could break through to him. Her hands shaking with frustration, Frances picked up the silver-mounted ink pot on the writing table and threw it at him. Alasdair ducked and a splash of ink soaked into the back wall of the tent. "Pressure of work? My torture! Can you not at least be truthful with me?"

Alasdair began to laugh. That was the last straw.

Frances grabbed a piece of iron at her feet and swung it with vicious intent. He moved a half-step forward and with neat economy of motion caught her wrist and forced her hand downward. Frances launched herself at him, her other hand clawing for his eyes. "You laugh at me! You and your whore!"

They went down in a heap on the littered floor, and Alasdair gave a yelp of surprise as he landed on the winding mechanism for a crossbow. Frances sought to get her wrist free and instead found herself with both hands hauled over her head and her skirts about her knees. Somewhere in the background, someone was laughing. Not Alasdair; he was panting between gritted teeth.

"Forcing yourself in here . . . brawling like a soldier's drab . . . it's skelp you I will!" he yelled.

Frances wriggled about and fastened her teeth on the first portion of his anatomy that became available. He jumped and slapped her away, then hauled her upright again, his arms pinioning her close.

"*Now*, my lady!" With slow deliberation he bent his head and kissed her. She turned her head this way and that, but was forced to his lips for all her struggling. Warm and firm, they closed over her mouth like a seal.

After a moment she succumbed to the taunting pressure and her mouth half-opened. She leaned against him. As his grip slackened, she put her arms around his neck.

An unbridled bray of laughter behind them startled both out of the embrace. Hand in hand, they turned to face Logie Buchan. He had followed Frances into the tent and was now half-sitting, half-lying on the ground, grasping the leg of the writing table for support in the paroxysms of laughter that bent him double.

"I think I understand . . . the reports . . . of the rape trial," he gasped before being overtaken again by laughter.

Alasdair's hand descended on Logie's shoulder and pushed him toward the tent flap. "Then go and practice your new understanding on some of the camp lasses," he advised Logie, not unkindly.

Logie scrambled out of the tent before his captain's mood should change for the worse, and Alasdair turned back to Frances. "Come, then," he said in a low voice that sent delicious shivers of desire up and down her spine. "I know one way to convince you how much I have been missing you, whatever."

He drew her toward the narrow cot.

23

"I'll no'—" Frances began, but her protest was silenced by a demanding kiss. She pushed in vain against his chest as he prolonged and deepened the kiss, backing her toward the cot.

"Struggle as you will, sweeting," Alasdair advised her, "but never fear that I'll let you away." He laughed as he pinned her body down on the hard narrow cot with his own weight. His kisses grew rough and greedy, his tongue flicking in and out of her mouth even as his lips bruised hers against her teeth. Frances felt the world spinning. She could not breathe. A feeling almost of panic came over her and she struck out at Alasdair wildly. He loosened his hold upon her and sat up, stroking her face with one hand.

"Och, Frances, I was not meaning to frighten you. Only I have been needing you so."

"Have you? You have not been acting like it." Her fury was draining away. She felt a drowsy lassitude stealing through her limbs with Alasdair's caresses.

"There were . . . reasons." His kiss this time began as no more than a gentle touch of his lips to hers, then grew warm and demanding. This time Frances was able to respond with all the love she'd not expressed since they came to Flanders.

Alasdair drew away and looked at her somberly. "Trust me, Fan. Never have I wanted to be rid of you." He sighed and unfastened his leather jack. "I think they are determined to keep us apart."

"Alasdair, who?" Frances sat up and turned her back on him so that he could unlace the stays that were crushing her into a rigid mold. He whistled between his teeth and played tunes on her back with his fingers as he slowly unfastened the tight laces, but not another word out of him could she get. Only the light, maddening touch that roamed over her body as more and more of her was exposed to his view.

Her breasts sprang free of the whalebone constriction and Alasdair bent her back over his knees, lowering his mouth to the tip of one breast and flicking his tongue over the nipple until she moaned and clasped his head to her. When he raised his head at last, she tugged at his open shirt, drawing it off his shoulders and down his back. He winced as the rough material dragged across his right arm.

"You're wounded!" Frances' stomach lurched sickeningly as she caught sight of the deep, ugly red gash on his upper arm. How had that happened? The Scots Brigade had seen no action since she and Alasdair returned from Scotland.

Alasdair looked into a corner of the tent, avoiding her eyes. "An accident. Some fool seemingly moved the crossbow practice range, and I missed the notice."

"And this?" Frances ran her hand along a long row of dark bruises on his side.

"A . . . fall. From my horse," he added after a second.

Frances faced him, arms akimbo, with her discarded bodice trailing about her waist. "Alasdair Cameron! Will you cease these havers and tell me the truth? You're a rude, overbearing, captious man, but never yet have I seen you stupid enough to cross a shooting range or clumsy enough to lose your seat on a horse."

His only response was to gather her into his arms again. "You'll be cold, sitting there half-naked," he murmured into her cheek. "Let me warm you."

Sinking into the intoxication of his embrace, Frances retained strength of mind for one last protest. "You could at least have made up a better lie."

And then she forgot everything but his touch, as they helped one another to struggle out of the last of their clothing until they lay together naked under his cloak, until his kisses and his roving hand grew wild and urgent and demanding again. Her thighs parted under his practiced caress and she felt him trembling within her until it seemed they were only one person crying out in mutual ecstasy under the sheltering cloak.

Then they were again two bodies, with digging elbows and ill-placed legs and a certain amount of mutual adjustment and accommodation to be done before they could both find space on the cot. Frances lay with her head pillowed on Alasdair's shoulder, pressed close against him.

"You're so sweet," Alasdair murmured in sleepy satisfaction. "I wish you could stay a little longer. But you'd best be on your way back to town before it grows dark."

"Go back? I will not be going back to the town at all." Frances sat up and reached for her shift. "I will be staying here with you."

"No." Alasdair's hand gripped her with the force of a soldier used to being obeyed. "Put your dress on. You are going back to the lodgings. The camp is no fit place for you to stay."

Frances regarded him through narrowed eyes. "I am thinking you will have used that excuse once too often, Alasdair Cameron. Any more argument, and I will be thinking Logie was telling me the truth when he said you had a woman in camp already." She halted, struck by a new thought. "And why would Logie be telling such a story, whatever?"

Alasdair's eyes shifted again. "Because I told him to keep you away from the camp, whatever excuse he had to use. Forby I'd thought him a bit more inventive. It doesna' matter. What matters is what I say. And I am telling you to dress yourself and go back to the lodgings to tend our daughter, woman." He gave Frances a hearty smack on the bottom to emphasize his order.

She yelped in surprise and jumped out of the cot, dragging the fur bed robe with her. "Our . . . daughter?"

Alasdair lay back, lacing his hands behind his head and regarding her with a lazy smile. "Did ye think I couldna' count the months?" His smile deepened. "Frances, I think my wits must have been addled indeed when I accused you of playing me false with Glencairn. When I came to my senses, I saw you could never have done such a thing."

"And you maybe pulled out your ten fingers and counted the months." Frances could not resist the tart comment. Alasdair's suspicions still rankled.

Alasdair shrugged. "You'll admit your statements to me were maybe a touch ambiguous. You told me Alexander was not my son. But never a word as to where you got him. A bit more explanation would have helped."

Frances shrugged. The fur robe slipped a few inches, exposing her bare shoulders to the cold air. How could Alasdair be lying there so unconcerned, and him without a stitch on his body? She snuggled down onto the cot and threw the robe over them both. "I was maybe a wee bit irritated with you at the time," she confessed. "It seemed you should have figured it out for yourself, that Sarah was yours, instead of being so sure that I'd been with Glencairn. You were aye too suspicious of me and Glencairn, whatever."

Alasdair slipped one arm around her and pulled her head down to rest on his shoulder. "I may have been a trifle overwrought myself," he admitted. "It was not hard to reason out, Frances, when I took the time to think instead of ranting at you. You didna' seem overconcerned about the loss of the boy. And I knew you had some feeling in you, for I've seen you crooning over the wee girl. You'd maybe care to tell me how it all came about?"

So then, lying huddled close against him on the narrow cot, Frances finally told Alasdair the full story of those hours when she'd thought him condemned to a traitor's death in the Grassmarket, and herself lost in the narrow streets of the West Bow at night with her pains coming on.

"Poor lass." Alasdair stroked her tangled hair. "And I'm thinking I made it no easier when you came to me. Surprised I am you did not stick my own dirk in me."

"It will maybe have crossed my mind a time or two," Frances admitted. She stretched luxuriously and pulled the fur robe higher around them. "But where would I be getting such a braw man again as Captain Cameron, and him always ready to pleasure the ladies when they come to his tent?"

Alasdair chuckled and hugged her close. "We're made for each other, Frances. Forby I'm sore ashamed of ye. After all my training in the art of fence, you should ha' known better than to come at me swinging that pike like the kitchen spit! Ah, well. I'm maybe not exactly so clever myself. I should have guessed sooner about Sarah, seeing she has your eyes exactly, and your smile."

"More like Donald's smile," corrected Frances. "And a shock to see it on an innocent face. But she's a greedy wee thing, for all she was so puny to start with."

Alasdair stroked her under the furs. She shivered with pleasure and ran her hands down his body, seeking and finding the hardness that proved her effect on him. "Your smile too, love. I'd no' call you exactly greedy. But insatiable . . ."

So suddenly that she was surprised, he sat up and swung his feet over the edge of the cot. "No, love. Not now. I've orders to write, and men to drill. The new recruits arrive today, hopeless clumsy crofters that they'll be, and Logie and I are for the port to take our pick of them before the other captains come swooping down like so many vultures to the feast. We can set you down at your lodgings on our way through the town."

"Aye," Frances agreed. "That would maybe be for the best."

Alasdair, already half-dressed, had his back to her and did not catch the glint in her eye. "I'm glad you've seen reason at last."

"Oh, yes," Frances affirmed. "I know where my proper place is."

He swung around at that, but she was expecting it and had schooled her features into proper meekness before he shot a suspicious glance at her.

Her place, she had already decided, was here. She did not believe for one instant Alasdair's vague story about some accidents during training. Her red-headed soldier, the best stalker in the glen and the best horseman of the clan, to have grown suddenly clumsy? To take a fall from his horse for no reason, and wander in the path of a crossbowman at target practice?

No, there was something going on here, and until she sorted it out, her place was with Alasdair. Duncan Dhu and the maidservant could care for Sarah for a time.

But it would be a good idea for her to go back to the lodgings. She needed to hire a nurse for Sarah, and pack her things. With luck, she would be back in the camp before Alasdair returned from inspecting the new drafts. An hour alone with Sandy Ruadh was just what she needed to get to the bottom of this mystery.

And so it proved. Frances swept in and out of her lodgings in a whirlwind of activity that left the servant girl amazed, the baby crying lustily, and Duncan Dhu thoroughly bewildered. In record time she had hired a wet nurse, packed the few necessities she required for life in the camp, and sent Duncan for a horse and cart to transport her and her things.

"You're to be going straight back, mind," she instructed him when he had helped her unload at the camp. "I cannot be leaving my little girl with no one but these foreigners to look after her. I must have someone of the glen there."

The last service Duncan did for her was to drag Sandy Ruadh out of the chaos of the camp and deposit him at her feet. Frances questioned him in Gaelic, leaning on all the authority of her three years as mistress of Beauly, and before long had enough out of him to confirm her suspicions.

There was even time, before Alasdair and Logie returned, to unpack the things she had brought and arrange them to her satisfaction.

They came back in the chill half-light of dusk, laughing and splashing through the muddy ground that an untimely thaw in the afternoon had turned from a frost forest to a slushy sea. Frances judged from the sound of their voices that they had been drinking, but not enough to preclude her having a sensible talk with Alasdair.

Logie was the first to put his head through the

tent flap. He recoiled with exaggerated surprise. "Losh, man, we've come to the wrong tent and all."

Alasdair pushed him aside. "Havers. I'm no' so drunk that I'll not be knowing my own tent."

He staggered through the flap and stopped just inside.

"*What are you doing here?*"

"That's aye your greeting to me these days," said Frances. "It is becoming fair monotonous. Could you not be trying something different for the variety of it? Perhaps you could begin by sitting down so that we could talk this over like civilized people."

She was rather proud of this speech, which she had been composing ever since she guessed exactly what Alasdair would say in response to her uninvited presence. But it failed to achieve its intended effect. Alasdair shook his head as if to clear the lingering wine fumes from his brain and stumbled across the glowing carpet she had laid down, leaving a trail of mud behind him, until he fell into one of her cushioned chairs. He gazed around him and shook his head again.

"It's fair bewildering to a simple man like myself," he said. He counted off the changes in the tent on his fingers. "Lamps . . . carpets . . . cushions . . . a proper bed? You will have been working most of the afternoon to accomplish this."

"Oh, no," Frances said. "I had time for a very interesting conversation with Sandy Ruadh."

Once again Alasdair ignored her lead. "And it will not work!" he bellowed in his parade-ground voice, well developed after a month of drilling troops in Prince Maurice's new theories of field evolutions. "You can just be taking your cushions and your carpets and your feather beds and silk coverlets, I make no doubt—you can just be packing all these things up and removing yourself to town by the same way you came."

Frances moved to a chest opposite Alasdair's chair and settled herself comfortably on its broad wooden top, spreading her black velvet skirts around her. "I have sent Duncan Dhu back to town with the cart," she said. "I doubt you'll just have to put up with me the night, Alasdair. Now we will be talking. Will Logie stay or go?"

Alasdair jerked his head at the tent flap, and Logie vanished.

Frances watched the swaying wall of the tent until all movement ceased. She was conscious of Alasdair's eyes on her face, watching as one measures an enemy who may strike at any moment.

"Who is trying to kill you?" she demanded when the tent was entirely still again.

Alasdair raised his eyebrows. "Are you thinking that the whole world shares your tastes? It may surprise you, but most of my men find it possible to deal with me without throwing things or swinging the haft of a pike at my head."

"That is not an answer," Frances pointed out.

She clasped her hands and sighed. "I have been talking with Sandy Ruadh, Alasdair."

His face changed only by becoming frozen in its expression of courteous inquiry. "And?"

Frances tilted her hand in the lamplight and watched the flash of the great flawed emerald in the Cameron ring. "There have been too many accidents. Your saddle girths cut nearly through before you lead a troop in practicing the cavalry charge."

"That is not usual work for my company," Alasdair said quickly. "My men are infantry. No one could have predicted I would take Captain Haartje's place that day."

"Someone did," Frances said. "And someone misdirected a group of crossbowmen so that their arrows flew across the path you were walking. And loosened a piece of the city walls when you were coming to visit me."

Alasdair sighed and crossed his legs. "All right. Whiles, I wish I had married a stupid woman. Yes, there have been a few accidents. Naught that could be proved, you understand. And it willna' make my life easier to have you to watch out for. Why d'you think I stay in the camp when all the other officers sleep soft in their town lodgings? Why do you think I tried to stay away from you and Sarah? Why do you think Logie had orders to keep you out of the camp? Frances, I didna' want you involved."

"Very chivalrous," Frances snapped. "And could you not have given me a wee word of explanation? Your notion of protecting the women and children has had me half-deaved with worry. Not that it matters now," she added. "My place is with you, and here I intend to stay."

"That," Alasdair said, "is why I didna' explain." He laughed like a loon and Frances scowled at him. She could not see what was so funny.

She won a limited compromise that night, seeing that it was late, and freezing again, and Duncan well away with the cart. The next day Alasdair was called out before dawn to oversee the arrival of the new draft, and Frances occupied herself with procuring meat and potatoes and cooking a stew for his dinner. When he came back that night, wet and muddy, she stripped his armor and handed him clean, dry clothes and a bowl of hot food, and no more was said about sending her away that night.

By midmorning of the next day, they had news to think about that drove the earlier quarrel out of both their heads entirely.

It started in the morning, when Alasdair was shouting at Frances that this day she would return to her lodgings in town if he had to throw her over his saddlebow and carry her there himself. Frances retorted that at least, since she'd been there, no more "accidents" had occurred.

"Are you thinking that your very presence is a magic shield?" Alasdair shouted.

At that point Logie stuck his head and shoulders in through the tent flap.

"Are ye quarreling or making love?" he inquired in mock-respectful tones. "From outside, it's no' so easy to tell the difference."

"We're no' quarreling," Alasdair said. "I am just explaining to Frances that she will be going back to town the day."

"We're wasting our breath," Frances said promptly. "I will be going nowhere."

"Ah, well," Logie said, "while you decide what you are doing, I've a new recruit here comes from your own part of the country, Alasdair. Or so he claims. I found him sneaking round the back of your tent and took this off him." Logie opened his hand and a bright streak of silver dropped toward the carpet, twisting and flashing in the morning light as it fell.

"A sgian-dhu." Frances picked up the blade and balanced it on her finger. "A fine piece, too. Too fine for a poor man."

"I would have put him to the question for his story," Logie said with grim humor, "but his ignorance saved him. He has no speech but the Gaelic, and I did not just want to call in any man to interpret for me. From the few words I could get, he's some tale to tell of Beauly, but I couldna' well make it out, his English being worse than my Gaelic."

"That itself is hardly believable, for a beginning,"

Alasdair commented. He took one glance at the shivering specimen that Logie hauled in by the scruff of his neck and dismissed him out of hand. "Beauly? That's no Cameron man. Or, wait . . ." He turned to Frances. "Would you be knowing him? Had you been settling new people up the glen while I was away?"

Frances studied the bearded man whose eyes glittered with a strange feral light as he looked back and forth, trying to follow the talk in this strange tongue that would decide his fate. "I think . . . I cannot just be sure," she said slowly, "but he will have a look of my brother Donald's man Seumas Murray. But Seumas was a much older man."

"Seumas!" The Highlandman clung to the one word he understood and fell at Frances' knees, babbling his story so rapidly that she was hard put to follow it.

"What is it? What does he say?" Logie was fairly dancing up and down with impatience.

Frances held up her hand for silence.

The tale was easy enough in itself, but several points in it made her frown and question the man sharply.

"*Donald?*" Alasdair exclaimed as the story unfolded. He leaned forward to hear better.

"Who's Donald?" Logie demanded.

It was several more minutes before he got an answer at all.

The man was the younger brother of Seumas Murray, and had come into Donald's service since Frances was taken away to Edinburgh. He had been sent by the great lord of Beauly to kill a man known as Alasdair Cameron, whom he would find in the camp by his high rank and his red hair. It was a matter of clan feud, he had been given to understand, but he did not think much of a lord who could not do his own killing. No, the lord of Beauly was Donald Murray, not Glencairn—would he go to kill on the bidding of a foreigner? He served his own clan, little honor though there might be in it. Donald was not even rightful lord of Beauly; he held the castle by right of his infant nephew. Nobody knew where the baby's mother was. Some said she had been taken away south and killed by a great lord of the Southrons. Yes, the great lord might be the Earl of Glencairn. He would not be knowing the deeds of the great ones. And now, since he had failed in his mission, would the great Captain Cameron be merciful and kill him quickly?

"I think that can be arranged," said Logie. He drew his sword and gestured at the man to rise and precede him.

Alasdair shook his head. "No. There will be another in his place, and another. Make a soldier of him, and let him tell the next man who comes how he failed." He leaned forward and spoke for a minute to the crouching man in Gaelic. "There.

He understands now. We'll make a pikeman of him, Logie."

"Better to let his heid on a pike be the message to the next fellow," Logie said. But he sheathed his sword and led his captive away peacefully enough.

There was a long silence within the tent. Frances stared at Alasdair and wondered what he was thinking. Finally he laughed and shrugged. "Well, this alters little, after all."

She stared incredulously. "Little? But now that you know who is wishing to kill you, will you not be going home to kill Donald yourself?"

"And me with a price on my head?" Alasdair's laugh was less pleasant this time. "You've little head for political realities, Fan. This isna' a matter of some hill feud any longer. The king's so-called justice has entered in. I'm a tainted traitor. Killing Donald willna' remedy that. But I wonder . . ." He looked through the walls of the tent, as though he could see some fair vista beyond the camp. "I do very much wonder, what is Glencairn's part in all this?"

They were to learn before the day was out.

The same packet that brought the new recruits had brought a letter to Logie from his brother in Edinburgh. He'd carried the oiled package in his doublet for a night and a day before the settling of the new men left him with leisure to spell it out by candlelight. And then, rather than ride back to his own bare lodging in the town, he invited himself to sit in Alasdair's tent and share their evening meal while he puzzled out the close-written lines.

"Ach, I'm no hand at all as a scholar." Logie gave up in disgust and tossed the letter over the table at Alasdair. "But I'm thinking there's something in there you'd maybe care to read, could you make it out. He's some tale of the Earl of Glencairn, at all events. Is that no' the man had ye hunted out of Scotland?"

Alasdair nodded. He held the paper close under the circle of light from the lamp and turned it this way and that, frowning over the narrow, spiky writing. His brows went up and he gave a low whistle.

"What will he say?" Frances demanded.

"Glencairn has not been granted Beauly."

"Well, we knew that! Would Donald be holding the castle if Glencairn had art and part in it? I was hoping the letter would bring you news that Glencairn was down entirely." *Then*, she thought but did not say, *then they might be able to go back to Scotland. Home to Beauly*. Her whole being sang at the thought. Away from this monotonous flat land of dikes and fields bordered with their little pollarded willows, back to the wild free glens.

"Not entirely," said Alasdair. He smoothed the paper and handed it back to Logie with a calmness she found maddening. But one finger was tapping on his thigh, and the dancing lights were alive in his eyes. "But it seems that King Jamie himself, God rest his royal soul, is asking after you, Frances. He finds it suspicious that the lady of Beauly should have disappeared from Glencairn's very house three days after the lord of Beauly is gotten rid of in a trial based on her evidence. He suspects Glencairn of having nasty habits where the heirs to land are concerned. In short, Frances, Glencairn's not down, but the king willna' confirm his grant to Beauly unless he can produce you alive."

He broke into delighted laughter. "I'd like fine to have seen the interview. Glencairn's overreached himself at last."

Frances jumped up and paced about the narrow confines of the carpeted space. Her whole body was trembling with the need for action. "Then we can go home."

Alasdair shook his head. "No, Fan. Will you walk into Glencairn's hand a second time?"

"But it need not be like that," she cried. "Will you not see, Alasdair? If Glencairn is already in trouble with the king, there may be questions raised about your trial. There must be! I will simply go and explain how I was forced to bear witness against you. We can get the trial reversed."

Alasdair raised one eyebrow. "You're going to walk into Holyroodhouse, curtsy nicely to the king, and say, 'Please, sir, everything I said at Alasdair Cameron's trial was a black lie, and I'd like my castle back, if you please.' I'd like fine to see that."

Both he and Logie burst into raucous laughter. Frances felt a blush rising to her cheeks. It did sound stupid when he put it that way. But surely there must be some way to put things right.

"Seriously, Frances," Alasdair said when he had calmed down, "we'll not think of it. I've work to do here. There's a price on my head in Scotland. And do you set foot on Leith shore, Glencairn will whisk you up and have you married to him, lawfu' or no, before you've time to cast your eyes once round the port. So let me hear no more talk of this."

Frances bowed her head. "Very well, Alasdair," she murmured. "You'll hear no more talk."

That much, at least, was a promise she could safely make.

24

Frances drew rein at the head of the glen and gazed down the green way before her. It was not her own dear glen of Beauly, but any part of the hills of Scotland was a balm to her after the months in flat fen-lands and the weary journey of the past days.

Spring came earlier to this southernmost border of the Highlands than it did to Beauly. Though there was still a damp, penetrating chill in the thin mist that wrapped about her, the sky was a pale blue and hints of new green life dotted the furze bushes on the hills. A handful of thin black cattle, emaciated and wobbly-legged from their hard winter, grazed the green buds off the bushes and whatever else they could find to nibble on. A hard life it was for them, and harder yet for the people that cared for them.

She remembered Glencairn then, and the rich house his sister had furnished in Edinburgh. How he had mocked her for preferring these barren hills to the luxury that he could buy for her.

The memory gave her fresh strength to go on. She straightened her back and pushed back the fold of the plaid that covered her head. Ach, but it was good to breathe the free wind again. That was one thing that Glencairn would never understand. All his gold chains and silken cushions could not pay for her freedom.

Yes, and Beauly need not be so poor. Were there not salmon in the stream and deer in the hills, grazing for sheep and cattle, patches of rich land for barley and poorer land for oats?

Just such a place could Beauly be, with good management and without Donald to suck the place dry of what little siller she managed to lay by. Let the king give her and Alasdair back Beauly, let them have just five years without clan war or disastrous harvests, and she would show him that Highlanders were not all maurauding cattle lifters. By God, she would keep the Beauly crofters too busy to think of making trouble on the fat lands of the South.

But before she could accomplish all that, two major battles lay before her. First she must plead and win her case before King James himself, having laboriously followed his northward progress out of Edinburgh to this remote Highland castle. And then . . .

Frances felt a breath of cold fear pass through her. Then there was Alasdair. She could well imagine the fury he'd have been in when he discovered that she had packed up herself and the baby and set out on the Leith packet, with only Duncan Dhu for protector. Her one hope was that if she won her case with the king, the pardon and the grant of Beauly that she took back to Flushing would ease his wrath.

One more deep breath of the cold, fresh hill air, and then she was guiding her shaggy little pony down the glen to the castle of Dumbarton, where King James had come to rest as he made his progress through the Highlands.

There'd been those in Edinburgh who snickered that the king would likely make it no farther north than Dumbarton, but Frances cared not, so long as she caught up with him there.

The gossip in Edinburgh had conveniently furnished her with the pretext she required to demand an audience. Men said that this progress through the North was but the beginnings of the king's intention to establish his rule in the Highlands. Soon he intended to require that all the chiefs, chieftains, and landlords appear before him and show title to their holdings. So he should be willing to hear her case.

The castle was many times greater than Beauly. Frances was awed despite herself as she passed through the echoing halls and up the spiral stone staircase that led to the public rooms on the second floor.

The hum of conversation came from the grand audience chamber. To Frances' surprise, she was not shown there, but instead to a small room richly furnished with tapestries and carved wooden paneling. The gentleman who had escorted her bowed, promised that she would have only a few minutes to wait for her audience, and shut the only door behind him as he left.

Frances sighed and fell to examining the figures on the tapestries for amusement. She was not wise in the ways of courts, but already she had learned that a courtier's promise often meant the exact opposite of what his words stated; she might have some hours to while away in this small chamber.

When the door clicked behind her, she whirled and was halfway into her curtsy before a gasp of surprise froze her where she stood. The man before her was not the king, but her old nemesis, the Earl of Glencairn.

As always, he was richly attired and seemed entirely at ease. As always, the mask of his face gave no clue as to whether he was as surprised as she by this encounter. He crossed the parquet floor with unhurried steps and gave Frances his hand to lift her from her interrupted curtsy.

"I understand I am to felicitate you on a miraculous transformation," he began. "My gentleman tells me that the puling girl-brat downstairs is yours. Such rapidity in breeding is truly amazing. Tell me, is she the twin of the boy? Or was there a substitution?"

Frances' brain seemed as frozen as her body. All she could think of was her terror for Sarah. She had thought it best to leave her with Duncan and her maidservant for this interview. "If you hurt her . . ." she managed, and got no further. What could she threaten? She gazed helplessly around the tapestried room for some means of escape. Might there be another door behind one of the hangings?

Glencairn watched the panicky darting of her eyes with amusement. "You may spare yourself that trouble," he remarked. "There is no other door. I had you shown in here so that our interview would not be interrupted." His tolerant smile was infuriating. "You were naive indeed, my dear, to think you could announce yourself at the door of Dumbarton Castle and be shown directly into James's presence. But then, your innocence was one of the things I found most attractive in you."

"Folk know I am here," Frances threatened. "If I do not come out—"

"Your devoted Highland servitor will, no doubt,

storm the king's audience hall," Glencairn finished for her. "Pray curb your barbarian imaginings, my dear, and try to believe that I mean you no harm—or your children, either, for all that your facility in producing them may become something of an embarrassment. For the moment, both you and the girl-child are a help rather than a hindrance to my plans. I wish only to have an informal chat with you before you speak with the king."

Frances leaned her back against the wall and crossed her arms. How much could she trust Glencairn? He had not said that he would not harm her—only that she should believe so. He had reason enough to take revenge on her for the way she had run away from him.

With an internal sigh she accepted that whether or not she trusted him was beside the point. He was between her and the door. And she made no doubt that the antechamber was full of his men.

"Talk," she said at last. "I will be listening."

Glencairn sighed in his turn. "I do hope we can achieve a more amicable relationship before your audience with the king. It distresses him to think that any of his subjects are enemies."

"I am sure you will be very concerned with the king's feelings," Frances snapped.

Glencairn smiled. "Oh, but I am, indeed I am. Especially those feelings that concern me. To put it bluntly, my dear, the king's feelings toward me at this moment are not of the warmest. It will improve my position greatly if I can produce you, alive and well. But only if . . ." He paused.

"Only if we appear to be on good terms," Frances filled in for him. "You do not wish me to be complaining to the king of the way you lied to me and coerced me and kept me prisoner. Tell me," she asked, curiosity momentarily overcoming her fear, "how were you meaning to explain that you had me brought to Edinburgh in chains?"

Glencairn made a dismissing gesture. "A *ruse de guerre*. You can testify that you were gently treated at my house."

"And if I do not choose to say so?"

Glencairn gently stroked the white lace that lay in folds around his wrists. "Then your life would be of little use to me."

The threat hung between them for a long moment, like a bright glittering blade poised in the air. Then Frances gave a sharp sigh and dropped her arms to her sides. "You will be helping me to see the king if I speak as you desire. Very well. I will not speak against you. But you must help me get a pardon for Alasdair, and I want my title to Beauly confirmed."

"How well we understand one another," Glencairn mocked gently. "You see? You have nothing to fear from me. The plain fact is that I am now the last man the king would grant Beauly to. With your help I intend to regain his trust, but I am willing to pay the price. Besides, you will have heard of your brother's actions?"

"Half-brother," Frances corrected. "Yes. He thought to rule Beauly in the name of my son. I am surprised you did not crush him like a bug. What were you at to let him play you such a trick?"

Glencairn studied his immaculate nails and once more smoothed the lace at his wrists. "We do not all have your perspicacity," he murmured. "I thought Donald a malleable tool. By the time I learned otherwise, his accusations about your death had stirred up enough of a hornet's nest that I was busy defending my position—which may have been just his intention. At any rate, I believe I would prefer even to see Beauly in the hands of you and your mad Highland husband than left with Donald."

"We will never be your friends," Frances said. Somehow she felt obliged to make that much clear. Friendship could be no part of the bargain.

There was a hint of irony in Glencairn's twisted smile. "No. It was never your friendship I wanted." He bowed and offered her his arm. "I think we are well enough agreed. One word of advice. Best let me manage the interview. His majesty has never quite believed that women have the wit to hold their own lands. Do not be offended if I must imply that you are as foolish as the rest of your sex. Only remember that I will assuredly not play you false—and if I do, the remedy is in your own hands."

Frances curtsied low and took the proffered arm. She found that her knees were trembling and her whole body was damp with perspiration, as though she had just been through some prodigious trial of strength. Perhaps, in a way, she had.

After that, the promised interview with King James was only an anticlimax. Frances curtsied to the ground when they entered the audience chamber and kept her eyes modestly lowered to the floor while Glencairn explained, in his smooth way, that the testimony she had given against Alasdair at his trial was all a mistake; Lady Frances had spent most of her life in the Highlands and, not understanding English well, had not fully comprehended that her description of a momentary marital quarrel might cause her husband to be exiled. She and her husband were now reconciled and the lady pleaded that the king would see fit to confirm her in her title to the lands of Beauly.

"And you plead her case?" James's small, hard eyes darted between Glencairn and Frances as if seeking the truth they had combined to conceal from him.

"My lord, it was never any part of my object to gain the castle and lands of Beauly for myself," Glencairn responded smoothly. "My one concern was, as your majesty's loyal subject, to maintain order in those sections of the Highlands which your majesty has been pleased to entrust to my guardianship. In my zeal to maintain the peace, I may have erred in supporting the cause of Donald Murray, whom I then believed to be your majesty's faithful servant. But after having talked again with Lady Frances, I am satisfied as to the justice of her claims."

James mulled over the statement. "There has been overmuch rule by the strong hand in the Highlands. It pleases me little to give over Beauly to one who would seize it by force."

Frances raised her head at this statement. "He has no right to it."

"What, woman!" James's fist came down on the broad arm of his chair. "You say your own—"

"Your majesty . . ." Glencairn interrupted his king and moved closer to the chair. He bent his head and whispered into the king's ear.

"What?" James queried him aloud. "She doesn't know?"

Glencairn shook his head. A smile played about the corners of his thin lips. "The lady has been traveling in search of your majesty since she landed at Leith."

"Well, well." James was silent for a moment. "Then she is innocent of . . ."

"Entirely, my lord."

The muttered exchange was incomprehensible to Frances. What was it she did not know, and what could she be presumed innocent of? She could only guess that Donald had been up to some new devilry. She straightened her back and addressed the king.

"Your majesty will be known for your justice and learning. I am sure that you will not be permitting a lawless man to be taking Beauly by the strong hand. I beg you to honor my claim and I promise that my husband and I will keep the peace in Beauly and bring our clansmen to live in peace and make your Highlands as prosperous as the rest of your country."

James guffawed and slapped his knee. "By God, Glencairn, you're right! She doesna' know." He bent forward and fixed Frances with his unwavering stare. "Very well, my lady. You shall have your title confirmed, on one condition. I would see you dispossess the lawless rogue who now holds the castle and reconcile yourself with him." He laughed again, most inappropriately it seemed to Frances.

"My lord . . . your majesty!" she gasped at this ironic reversal of her hopes. How could she, alone and without gold to raise men, force Donald out of Beauly? She grasped at one straw of hope. "Your majesty will be sending men with me to explain your will?"

"No men," James said. "If you cannot carry the matter with the master of Beauly by your personal charm, you must e'en whistle for your castle."

Frances would have argued the matter, but

Glencairn's warning pressure on her elbow stopped her. "Withdraw now," he whispered. "It does no good to argue with him."

She had backed almost to the door when James called out to her one last time. "Ah, Lady Frances?"

She stopped. "My lord?"

"Don't look so worried. I think you may find your task is not so difficult." James laughed again, bending almost double in his chair at some private joke. When the door closed behind her, the last sound Frances heard was that hiccuping laugh.

Glencairn took her elbow and steered her swiftly through the crowd of courtiers who parted on either side to make way for the Earl of Glencairn and the Highland beauty they'd heard so much about. A train of curious whispers followed them, but Frances was oblivious of the interest of the crowd. She could think of nothing but the cruel joke the king had played upon her. And there'd been no word said of a pardon for Alasdair, or was that supposed to rest upon her first impossible task? Lord, but she was weary! When Glencairn ushered her again into the little waiting room, Frances was too confused to feel any fear of him.

In their absence chairs had been brought. She sank into one and pushed the stiff linen coif back from her head, running her fingers through the masses of black hair just released. "My temples ache so," she explained to Glencairn. "I've no head for these ways of courts."

"And many who use the ways of courts end by having no head." Glencairn seemed out of reason pleased with his epigram. "You should wear your hair uncovered more often. It suits you."

"And me a decent married woman with a child in my arms," Frances cried. "A fine thing that would be seeming."

"It is all the fashion at the English court." Glencairn leaned over and took her hand. Unresisting, she allowed him to carry it to his lips. "Frances, I could show you the ways of courts. You are a beautiful woman, and clever too. I will admit I underestimated you last year. Else you'd never have escaped my house."

His wry smile had a certain charm. "I should hold that against you, you know. You embarrassed me before the town and left a fair disaster in my kitchens. I doubt the broth still tastes of smoke. Not to mention the difficulties I have encountered with good Jamie—I mean, his majesty."

He sighed and let her hand fall. "But when I look at you, I can't see the rebel who angered me, but only the beautiful woman who would be an ornament to any court. No"—he held up his hand against her quick movement of fear—"I hold by the bargain. You shall come to no harm at my hands. Only think a little, Frances. You have seen the temper of the king. I may tell you that once he makes his edicts, there is no going back on them. The only way you can dispossess Donald from

Beauly is with my help. Will you join with me now? We can get your ancestral home back, and I can see to it that your outlaw goes free where he will. You can even deed over the drafty castle to him, if that satisfies your primitive sense of justice. Only do not waste your life, Frances. Which will it be? Will you go back to follow the army through the dikes and fens of the Low Countries? Or will you be my lady of Glencairn, and let me show you the great places of the world? Together, Frances—with your will, and my power, your beauty, my wit—together we could rule this little kingdom."

Frances had hardly listened to the torrent of words pouring from Glencairn's lips since it became evident that he meant her no ill. Only when his speech at last came to an end did she move rather stiffly in the chair, feeling all the weariness of her long journey and ultimate failure. What was there to say that would not anger him? "I will be thanking you for your kind words, my lord," she said at last. "But I will be going back to my husband now."

Glencairn turned half away from her, so that all she could see were his hands clenched on the tabletop and his averted face. After a moment he turned back to her, as pleasant and imperturbable as ever, so that she almost thought she had imagined that moment. "So be it," he said. "I have never spoken so to a woman before. I was right. Women are all fools, incapable of seeing their own advantage. And I . . ." He gave a short, bitter laugh. "I, too, am a fool. Else I'd take you by the strong hand, vows notwithstanding, and make you mine as the Highland chiefs did in the days of old. But being a politic man, and a fool, I will stand by my word. You shall even have my help to get back to this firebrand of yours."

Frances half-rose from her chair. "When will we be leaving?"

"And I thought you so travel-weary," Glencairn mocked. "Stay and eat first. And have the child brought to you. Babes must rest, even if mad Highland girls will be riding day and night. Meanwhile, I will give orders for the horses to be saddled. You shall have an escort of my men for the journey, and what comforts are to be obtained. It will be a matter of several days' riding; you will at least allow me to see that you are safe and comfortable on the way?"

Frances put one hand to her head. So much happening in so short a time, it addled her wits. "It is but a day's ride to Edinburgh. I will take ship at Leith. You will not be needing to escort me, Glencairn." Could this be another trap?

Glencairn gave his short, dry laugh again. His next words confirmed all her fears.

"Not Edinburgh, my dear. Did you not hear the king's instructions? You are for Beauly, there to make your peace with the master of the castle—if you can." He looked at the black curls spilling out over her sadly crumpled and unstarched ruff, and his voice softened. "You are well matched. A mad Highland girl who takes ship alone, rides day and night to beg a pardon for her husband; and a firebrand who leaves his good safe post in the army and comes dashing after his wife, for all there's a price on his head here."

For a moment his words made no kind of sense to Frances. Then she gasped and felt their meaning like light pouring over her. "Alasdair is in Scotland!"

"Yes," Glencairn mocked her, "Alasdair is in Scotland. Alasdair is, in fact, at Beauly. Your mad husband, my dear, landed two days behind you with a picked troop of men fresh from the wars in the Low Countries. Finding you no longer in the city, he assumed you had gone north to Beauly—why, I do not know. That cold glen seems to hold some almighty attraction for those of your blood. While you were stravaigling over half of Scotland in search of our monarch, he rode directly to Beauly and demanded of Donald to give you up. Your fat brother was, of course, unable to satisfy this request. So young Cameron threatened to pull the castle down about his ears. In fact he took it without doing quite so much damage, and finding you not there, sent a message next to me—whom he conceived to be your chief persecutor after Donald—offering to trade the castle for your person. I had the news only this morning."

"And I walked in here like a bird to your snare," Frances finished. She leaned back against the hard wooden back of the chair and sighed. "And are you going to make the trade?"

"The thought did just cross my mind," Glencairn admitted. "But I'd a greater need of showing you to Jamie, alive and seemingly in harmony with me. My good influence with Jamie is worth a wheen of scraggy Highland glens to me. And since the king has taken it in his good humor to send you back to Beauly to keep it for him, I shall just have to let you go."

"Then why could you no' tell me straight out that Alasdair had Beauly?" Frances asked. "You let me think it was Donald. You let me think I'd failed in my mission."

Glencairn shrugged and pretended to be examining a figure in one of the tapestries with great interest. "D'you need to ask? I thought to test your devotion. If you could be weaned away from your Highlander when you thought all had failed, I thought you might yet turn to me."

His laugh was as dry as last winter's leaves rustling in the wind. "There was a time when I meant to take you so as to get Beauly. Today I found myself thinking to take Beauly so as to get you. It turns out I shall have neither."

"You still hold a good third of the Highlands," Frances pointed out. "I make no doubt you'll console yourself nicely."

This time Glencairn's laugh was unforced. "Ah, Frances, what a good enemy you are! No quarter even to the last blow. You are in the right of it. Power's a great consolation. The more pity you'd not share it with me. Well, go and make peace with your husband, if you can. Make his peace with Jamie. Make peace with the wolves on the hill and the bare-legged Highland caterans in your glen! I don't put it past you. But it will be a dull life compared to what I could have given you."

"I will be remembering that," Frances said, "when I will be sitting before a peat fire with a bowl of kale and crowdie between my two knees." She held out her hand to him with a slight smile. "And I will be remembering that in the end you helped to put me there, and I will be thanking you for it."

Glencairn bowed and brushed his lips across the back of her hand once more.

25

The man posted at the southwest tower of Beauly saw the body of horsemen riding down the glen and squinted to make sure he saw aright. Eight, no, ten riders, and the foremost were wearing the red-and-green tartan that Glencairn favored for his men. He waited no longer, but fairly tumbled down the narrow stone spiral that led to the bailey, shouting out a warning as he went.

Alasdair had been prepared against this moment since he took Beauly. Already the crofters had driven their thin black cattle within the bailey for shelter. The women and children were camped along the inner wall of the keep, while the men sharpened their rusty weapons, not ill-pleased at the prospect of some excitement after the dull, peaceful years under the lady of Beauly. Alasdair's own men from the Low Countries were ready to swing to the gates and soak them with water against an attack by fire. A few crisp orders, and Alasdair paused only to see that the seeming flurry of activity in the bailey was actually in good order as men ran to their posts or snatched up their weapons. Then he was mounting the narrow spiral stairs, two at a time, with the guard panting at his heels.

Beauly was as well prepared as it had ever been to stand a siege. If only Frances had been there . . . Alasdair felt his stomach tighten into a knot of anxiety. Where was she, and what was happening to her? Had his desperate gamble to bargain Beauly for her safety worked, or was he a fool to sit here in his great stone castle while his lady was God knew where? Reason told him he'd done the best thing possible in staying at Beauly and using it as a base of power. But reason was of little help now, when the men coming might bring news of Frances. Alasdair gripped the parapet and squinted against the light at the advancing riders, willing the cold fear in his breast to dissolve away.

As they came closer, he could make out the glint of steel helms and the alternating broad stripes of red and green in their tartans.

"It will be Glencairn, right enough." Alasdair slapped the guard on the back. "You've keen eyes,

Dougal. But what will the man be at?" He leaned over the parapet and squinted into the setting sun. "Eight men only?"

Dougal coughed. "I make it ten, sir."

"Your eyes are better than mine," Alasdair conceded. Why ten? Too many for a message; too few for a siege. His best hope had been that Glencairn would send a man to parley. What did this group mean to do? They rode so bunched together that he could not see into their midst. Perhaps they were trying to conceal something, one of the new cannon from Italy, for instance. Glencairn might well be gambling on the chance of getting a gun in place under cover of a parley.

That was how Alasdair would have attacked the castle himself. The Scots still scoffed at artillery, but Alasdair had seen it used to devastating effect in the Low Countries. One culverin dragged up the glen on a cart could be mounted at a safe distance from his archers and hackbutters and still blast the wooden gates to shreds.

"If they're bringing guns," he said half-aloud, "they will turn now and go up to the high ground commanding the castle. That's where I would place it."

Dougal coughed again. "With respect, captain," he ventured, "it will no' be a cannon. They couldna' bring the cart so fast—it would be needing oxen to pull it."

And as if in confirmation of his words, the little

party turned onto the low path leading directly to the castle gates. Alasdair looked a bit surprised. "You will be right. They will be coming to parley only."

The exhilaration of planning for action left him, and once again he felt fear for Frances settling in a cold lump on his breastbone.

A few minutes later the riders had drawn close enough that Alasdair could make out what had been concealed by the central group. "By God, it's a woman!" His hand clenched the stones of the parapet until his knuckles were white. "Frances. If they harm her . . ." He snapped out two more orders, and Dougal raced to obey.

By the time the riders were in shouting distance, Donald had been brought from his cell to stand beside Alasdair, hands bound, a rope around his neck. His ashen face seemed already to have taken on the pallor of death. Alasdair had to borrow two sturdy clansmen from the defenses of the curtain wall to prop him up.

"You can halt there," he shouted as the riders drew up level with the gate. "Send Lady Frances forward. If you've harmed her, I'll hang this Murray bastard from the castle walls." He gave a jerk to the rope around Donald's neck to emphasize his words.

Frances rode forward from the group of riders. Alasdair strained to make out her expression. Her hair was crackling loose from the coif in the way it always did when she was out of temper. But her hands were unbound, and she could not have been hurt, the way she was sitting so straight in the saddle.

"That will be perfectly all right with me, Alasdair Cameron," she shouted back up. "I've no need for the useless scum. Now will you open the gates and let your wife in, or will we shout here all night like the Red Etin and the banshee?"

Alasdair broke into delighted laughter. "If I'm red, you will be screeching like the banshee, right enough. Bid those Glencairn men ride back."

Frances dismounted and tapped her foot while the escort Glencairn had provided her backed their horses off to what Alasdair considered a safe distance. When they were positioned several hundred yards away, he ordered the gate opened a bare crack, just enough for Frances to squeeze through.

By the time he had clattered down the spiral staircase once again, she was standing in the middle of the bailey, stripping off her leather riding gauntlets and looking about her with her nose wrinkled against the smells of a hundred and more people and their animals crowded into the courtyard to live.

Alasdair devoured the sight of her with hungry eyes. Her dress was limp and travel-stained, but there was a sparkle in her black eyes that boded no good. Before she could open her mouth, he had crossed the courtyard in a few strides and was squeezing her in his arms. And good it was to have her there again, after the sleepless nights he'd spent imagining her Glencairn's prisoner or worse.

"*Never* serve me such a trick again," he murmured in her ear, "or I'll give ye such a skelping you'll be eating your porridge standing up for weeks." He could almost be truly angry with her, in his relief from the fear that had haunted him since he had discovered she'd stolen away from the camp in the Lowlands.

Frances widened her eyes in feigned terror. "Losh, man, maybe I should have been staying with the great earl after all. He promised me silks and satins and all, and here I come home to the bowl of crowdie porridge and the husband who beats me." She raised up on tiptoe to kiss him before drawing back to look around the courtyard.

"Not but that a bowl of porridge would likely strain the resources. What are you at, man, to be bringing all these folk into the castle, and the spring plowing to be done? Will you be increasing your consequence with a tail of followers in your hall, like the great chieftains of the old days?"

"You know perfectly well why they are in here," Alasdair growled. "For protection against Glencairn's armies. I'd no mind to be taken by surprise and forced out a second time. Do you know what his plans are?"

Frances moved a few paces away from Alasdair, daintily dusted off a mounting block with her gauntlets and sat down, spreading her skirts around her. "I left his lordship in good health at Dumbarton Castle, where he attended on his majesty King James," she replied at length. "He was not telling me where he planned to go from there, but he was good enough to provide me with an escort when the king ordered me to ride for Beauly and retrieve the castle from a certain outlaw who had occupied it by force. The arrangement was that if I would do the king this small service, he would confirm my title to Beauly and also pardon my husband."

Alasdair exhaled a long, shaky breath. "It seems while I thought myself to be rescuing you, you were rescuing me and Beauly."

Frances' heart sank at his tone. Men! Was she ever to be explaining and apologizing? Her fingers trembled with frustration. It would have been all right if he'd rated her for causing him anxiety. But no. To him it was just moving pieces on a chessboard, and he was peeved because she'd made the final move.

She felt so frustrated and helpless, she wanted to throw something at him. But there was nothing handy to throw. Maybe, just this once, they could both try to act like reasonable adults.

"If you want to be thinking of it in that way, you

can," she replied at last. "Myself, I was thinking that we work well together."

"We might be doing better at it if we shared our plans before running off to Scotland to put our heads in the king's noose," Alasdair growled.

Frances felt a smile twitching at the corners of her lips. This was more like Alasdair. "Might be," she conceded. "And now, husband, will you be so good as to invite my escort within? If they are half so tired and hungry as I am, it is glad indeed they will be of the rest. I would not have it said that the Cameron of Beauly failed in hospitality."

"You . . . you . . . Words fail me," Alasdair said. He edged Frances to one side of the mounting block so that he could sit down beside her.

Frances succumbed to temptation. She could only be polite for just so long. "There will be a first time for everything. Och, Alasdair! You willna' be tickling me before all the folk. Oh!" She collapsed into helpless giggles and fell off the mounting block as she tried to evade Alasdair's fingers. He stood over her and pulled her to her feet with one hand.

"I'll see a little respect from you in future," he said with mock sternness.

Frances lowered her head. "Aye, Alasdair."

"And no more taking it into your head to run off and settle my affairs after you promised not to do anything."

Frances peeped up through her eyelashes.

"Please, Alasdair, I did not promise not to come to Scotland. I only promised not to talk about it."

"And no arguing back," Alasdair roared.

"No, Alasdair."

Alasdair waved his hand at the men guarding the gates. "All right, let them in."

He turned back to Frances. "I suppose you left our daughter in Dumbarton?"

"No, Alasdair. She is outside with Duncan Dhu and Glencairn's men."

Alasdair snorted in disgust and strode over to where two of his soldiers were slowly swinging the ponderous outer gates open. "Hurry it up, you!" He put his shoulder to the gate himself and heaved.

It took some time to find stabling for Glencairn's horses and places in the hall for the men, especially since all the while Frances was trying to get them settled the baby was wailing for her attention, Ailsa was trying to tell her all that had happened since Donald kidnapped her and Alexander, and the Beauly crofters were picking up their belongings and driving their kine out of the bailey. Finally, when a modicum of peace was restored, Frances was able to collapse at the end of one of the long benches in the hall with a mug of ale and a platter of meat scraps from the kitchens. She looked up after a few bites to find Alasdair sitting on the end of the trestle table, swinging one leg and regarding her with a quizzical expression.

"I take it you will be through with stirring up my castle?" he inquired. "You'd maybe not wish to turn out the bedding in the upper chambers and have the rushes changed on the floor?"

Frances kicked a half-gnawed bone out from under the table and let Alasdair look at it. "I'd maybe wish to turn the river through *our* castle to cleanse it," she mocked back, "but that I'm a wee thing tired. We'll finish setting all to rights in the morn. Unless you'd be wanting to take our clansmen on a cattle raid?" she inquired with a delicate sarcasm to match his own.

Alasdair regarded her with a wariness bordering on respect. "No doubt we'll come to some accommodation."

Frances sighed. Since that first embrace in the courtyard, Alasdair had not touched her again. Perhaps, after all, he could not forgive her for taking such an active part in settling their affairs. Perhaps she should have stayed in Flanders. At least there they were together. Here, two feet of air and a thousand unspoken words separated them.

The noise of revelry in the great hall swirled about their island of silence. Glencairn's men, rested and fed, were unlacing their stiff leather jacks and making friends with the kitchen girls. Steel helmets were turned upside down to serve for ale mugs, Gaelic innuendo competed with broad Lowland jests. Only the lord and lady of Beauly remained silent and apart.

The baby had fallen asleep in Frances' lap, one leg trailing drunkenly off the edge of the bench. Alasdair leaned forward and brushed her fluff of black hair with his forefinger. "She's a bonny wee lass," he said.

Frances felt a leap of hope in this gesture of his. She longed to reach out and touch the tanned fingers that were brushing across Sarah's head, but she dared not.

She lowered her eyes. "You'll not hold it against me, that I lied to you about Alexander?"

Alasdair's eyes shifted to where Ailsa sat beside the fire, nursing her own baby and waiting to take Sarah from Frances. "No, love. This one's a bonny lass," he repeated. "I think I'll keep her."

"You wanted a son," Frances half-whispered, still looking down at the boards of the table. She was afraid to look up and see what might be in his eyes.

Alasdair lifted her chin in one hand so that she was forced to look up at him. He was smiling. Her own lips curved in a tentative answering smile.

"There's ways to achieve that." His fingers caressed the soft curve of her neck. "But then, you've been traveling around the country so long, belike you'll have forgotten how it's done. Come away upstairs and I'll remind you."

Frances leaned her cheek into the warm curve of Alasdair's callused palm and looked around the crowded, noisy, disorderly hall with contentment.

She was home again. Tomorrow she'd have a task before her, setting all to rights, and no doubt quarreling with Alasdair in the process. But for tonight, they were together again, and nothing else mattered.

Passionate Historical Romances from SIGNET

(0451)

- ☐ JOURNEY TO DESIRE by Helene Thornton. (130480—$2.95)*
- ☐ PASSIONATE EXILE by Helene Thornton. (127560—$2.95)*
- ☐ CHEYENNE STAR by Susannah Lehigh. (128591—$2.95)*
- ☐ WINTER MASQUERADE by Kathleen Maxwell. (129547—$2.95)*
- ☐ THE DEVIL'S HEART by Kathleen Maxwell. (124723—$2.95)*
- ☐ DRAGON FLOWER by Alyssa Welks. (128044—$2.95)*
- ☐ CHANDRA by Catherine Coulter. (126726—$2.95)*
- ☐ RAGE TO LOVE by Maggie Osborne. (126033—$2.95)*
- ☐ ENCHANTED NIGHTS by Julia Grice. (128974—$2.95)*
- ☐ SEASON OF DESIRE by Julia Grice. (125495—$2.95)*
- ☐ KIMBERLEY FLAME by Julia Grice. (124375—$3.50)*
- ☐ PASSION'S REBEL by Kay Cameron. (125037—$2.95)*

*Prices slightly higher in Canada

Buy them at your local bookstore or use this convenient coupon for ordering.

NEW AMERICAN LIBRARY,
P.O. Box 999, Bergenfield, New Jersey 07621

Please send me the books I have checked above. I am enclosing $________ (please add $1.00 to this order to cover postage and handling). Send check or money order—no cash or C.O.D.'s. Prices and numbers are subject to change without notice.

Name ________________________

Address ________________________

City __________ State __________ Zip Code __________

Allow 4-6 weeks for delivery.
This offer is subject to withdrawal without notice.